THE PASTOR

THE PASTOR

Philip Trewinnard

VICTOR GOLLANCZ

LONDON

First published in Great Britain 1997
by Victor Gollancz
An imprint of the Cassell Group
Wellington House, 125 Strand, London WC2R 0BB

© Philip Trewinnard 1997

A catalogue record for this book is
available from the British Library.

ISBN 0 575 06396 3

Typeset by CentraCet, Cambridge
Printed in Great Britain by
St Edmundsbury Press Ltd, Bury St Edmunds, Suffolk

97 98 99   5 4 3 2 1

For Salita, with love.

PROLOGUE

PROLOGUE

TWINS

The first week of September. A still, hot day. The sun blazes down on the Land's End peninsula.

Nudists are scattered across the beach at Treveene Cove.

Women, bronzed and shaved and pierced, lie flat out at attention, like dead sentries.

Middle-aged men with sagging bellies, bald and lonely, paddle in their flip-flops at the water's edge.

Young jocks with muscular physiques massage oil into each other's backs.

And by her rock – her special rock – Briony lies naked on the hot sand and sleeps and dreams.

Briony dreams that she is lying on the beach – exactly where she is – and a shadow falls across her face. She opens her eyes and sees her twin sister, Tamara, looking down at her.

Tamara smiles – the crinkly-eyed, toothy smile of hers that Briony loves so much – and says, 'Hey, Sis.' She always says Hey, Sis.

In her dream, Briony props herself up on one elbow, shields the sun from her eyes with one hand and says, 'Hi, Tam. What are you doing here? You're supposed to be in London.'

'Tell Nan I'm sorry,' Tamara replies.

'Sorry why?' says Briony. 'For what?'

'I won't be able to make it,' says Tamara. 'Just tell her I'm sorry.'

With that, she turns and walks towards the sea.

Briony watches her, wondering what she means. Tamara walks into the water and keeps on walking . . . Through the glassy shallows, through the splintering surf, and deeper . . .

Up to her knees and deeper ... Not floating, just walking, and her body slowly disappearing beneath the flat, blue sea ... Deeper, deeper, until her head appears to sit like a fishing float upon the ocean. Then that too sinks inch by inch until she has disappeared completely beneath the surface of the water.

Briony wakes up from her dream, sits upright and looks around her, around this tiny secluded cove. She sees the usual scattering of glistening, nut-brown flesh, roasting in the sun. There is nothing strange or different about the cove today and yet she feels uneasy.

A line of small footprints in the sand leads away from the spot where she has been lying. It tracks all the way down to the sea.

She remembers Tamara walking towards the water. She feels increasingly unsettled by the dream. She gets up and follows the footprints, all the way down to the water's edge. She stands in the shallows, her arms folded across her bare chest, the incoming tide lapping across her feet. She peers out, as though willing her sister's body to come bobbing up to the surface, to see that crinkly-eyed, toothy smile again.

Instead, she sees an object floating on the ocean, quite far out.

Something goes cold and dark inside her, as if the shadow that fell across her face in the dream has just fallen across her heart.

She recalls an incident from her childhood.

When she was six years old, she had an acute attack of asthma and almost died. She was in hospital in Penzance – the hospital where she and Tam were born. The paediatrician didn't think she could survive the night. Tamara overheard her father talking to her grandma on the telephone, trying to explain that Briony could not take air into her lungs. She heard him say that Briony was sinking fast.

He was a Newlyn trawlerman, their father, and Tamara thought and dreamed a lot about the sea. That night she lay awake in bed, imagining her sister's body floating on the ocean and deflating like a punctured Lilo. Afraid that Briony would die if she let that air-bed disappear beneath the waves, Tamara focused her mind intently on the image and thought of herself as a pump, pushing the air from her own lungs into her sister's.

She kept on and on, keeping that picture in her mind, pumping the air into Briony's body until she could see her floating safely on the ocean once again.

Briony survived the night; no one knew how. The nurses said it was a miracle.

That same morning Tamara was found unconscious in her bedroom. She was taken to hospital. Her blood pressure, her heart rate and her temperature were dangerously low. She was put in the bed beside her sister. They were both fully recovered by the morning. They never did discover what had been wrong with Tam. The paediatrician told their parents that twins could do strange things like that. There was no rational explanation. It was a symbiotic phenomenon, she said, a mystery to medical science.

Twenty-odd years on, Briony stands here at Treveene Cove, staring out to sea, like an anxious daughter awaiting first sight of the homebound fishing boats. Something is lying on the surface of the swell, some way out, not quite afloat but not yet submerged; brightly coloured and easy to see. Viewed from this distance it could be almost anything, but she knows exactly what it is: an air-bed, somebody's Lilo, drifted out to sea, punctured and sinking.

The surf is breaking around her knees. She has not noticed it until now. She turns and walks back up the beach. Her arms are prickly with goosebumps. It feels to Briony as if the sun has suddenly gone cold.

She cycles home to the cottage near Newlyn where she lives with a friend called Julie. She looks after Julie's child in the mornings and works around the house and garden, in return for board and lodging.

There is a message waiting on Julie's answering machine. Briony plays it back. She hears Tamara's voice:

'Hey, Sis . . .'

A pause. She can hear Tam breathing, as if she has a heavy cold.

'I think you'd better . . .' Tamara hesitates again. 'Better call me. I've kind of . . .' She seems to be laughing but it's all so breathy that Briony finds it hard to tell if Tam is laughing or wincing or crying or what. 'Kind of screwed things up. Like, ah . . . bigly.' And now she does laugh. But it sounds as though she's in pain as well. 'Not so good, Bri . . . Think I need you. Gotta help me, Sis.' A tremor in her voice now. 'Been a bit silly. Thought I could handle it but . . . Sort of all gone too far.' Another pause. 'So bad I can't believe it's happening. All gone crazy on me. Can you come up? So scared, Bri. Christ's sake, please come . . . While there's still time.' Another pause. 'If I'm not here, ask for Gloria. Get her to let you in. Stay here and wait for me, okay? Don't let me down, Bri . . .'

There is a long hesitation. And then the sound of Tamara putting down the telephone.

Tamara is a staff nurse: unflappable, phlegmatic, and reliable in a crisis. Briony has never heard her break down in this way. Briony is not like her sister. She is temperamental and emotional. Seized by a kind of panic, wondering what on earth might have happened, she runs upstairs to her room to fetch the diary in which she lists her phone numbers. She goes into Julie's room, sits on the bed, picks up the telephone and taps out Tamara's number in north London.

It begins to ring.

THE HERMITAGE

A young woman vanished in this house today – this large, shabby house at the end of Styles Lane.

Vanished: literally.

It is not anywhere in particular, this little backwater. It is past Upper Clapton but not yet South Tottenham. And it leads nowhere, this quiet, tree-lined side street of terraced Victorian houses. Styles Lane ends abruptly and, from there, a broad footpath leads down to the River Lea which flows through the East End of London and out into the Thames at Docklands.

At the point where the road ends, there is one house that stands quite alone, the only detached house in the street, made conspicuous by its size and its large, uncared-for garden. This house is called The Hermitage. Older than the other houses in Styles Lane, it must have looked imposing in Victorian times, displaying wealth and status in an area that was still open countryside in those days.

It has been converted long since into small flats and bedsitting rooms. It looks a shy building now, almost ashamed of itself. It seems wary of visitors and gives the impression of wanting to retreat, unnoticed, inch by inch, into the seclusion of its own tangled garden, which has been left to run wild.

The house is on four floors and of unusual design, with a number of steeply pitched roofs at different levels, a small, turret-like protrusion at one corner, and stained glass in the window of the stairway landing. At the very top there are attic rooms, where servants once slept. And this is where she disappeared, right here, in this attic room that looks east across the marshes.

Charlie Stillman, a friend and one-time lover of the young nurse who rents this room, stands at one of three dormer windows, wondering what happened here today. He is gazing beyond the Lea, across the broad green swathe of Waltham-stow Marshes towards the redbrick streets of Leyton, a mile distant. His focus shifts to the railway tracks that cross the marshes, where a four-car train trundles down the line to Liverpool Street. Beyond it, boys are playing football – even in this heat; the last week of their summer holidays. And beyond them, traffic speeds along Lea Bridge Road, small and safe as Dinky toys, and two ponies emerge from the Lea Bridge Riding School.

Today is such an ordinary day, an ordinary September afternoon. Kids are playing in the recreation ground across the marshes, like scraps of coloured litter at this distance, blowing in the breeze. Men sit fishing down below; a mother pushes her toddler in his buggy along the towpath.

His father used to take him for walks along that river bank and tell him stories about the London Blitz, the fire-red sky above the London docklands. A doodlebug landed there somewhere – beyond the railway marshalling yards, the other side of Hackney Marshes. His father heard it coming, one summer's afternoon, a young lad's eyes turned in wonder to the sky; then heard the awful silence that seemed to last for ever. And then a crash, like thunder, somewhere among the old Dickensian slums of Bow. An ordinary summer's day like this.

Charlie looks upstream towards the reservoir near Totten-ham Hale and watches two youngsters with small backpacks approach along the towpath. It was a couple much like this who looked up and saw smoke drifting through the open dormer window a few hours ago and called the fire brigade.

A firefighter put his shoulder to the door and broke into the room at about two o'clock this afternoon.

The room was full of smoke. The firefighter saw a woman lying just there, on the bed – a young woman, lying on her side, with one arm laid out as if she were reaching across the duvet to a lover. A second firefighter saw her too. They thought, at first, she was asleep or unconscious. They looked away for just a moment – looked around to see what was burning. There was no fire: a cigarette end, carelessly dropped into a wastebin, had set light to paper and had filled the room with smoke, but had burned itself out. They turned back to attend to the woman on the bed . . .

But she had disappeared.

She was nowhere in the flat – if it could be called a flat, this long studio room – and she could not have left the top floor without passing a third firefighter waiting on the stairs. And he didn't see a soul.

Charlie Stillman finds it hard to believe, the way the firefighters tell the story. Women do not vanish into thin air. And yet . . . Why would they lie?

So who was she? And what happened to her?

The nurse who rents this room is called Tamara. Tamara Carkeat. Charlie has not seen her for some time, although she telephoned him recently – telephoned him several times – and left messages on his answering machine. She sounded desperate. But he has no idea why.

And now this.

Tamara's family live in Cornwall, but Charlie does not know where exactly. Her father is a fisherman. She calls him Dennis. And there is a twin sister, Briony, who was once a little wild and rode with bikers, but now plays guitar and sings folk songs.

He is wondering if there are many Carkeats in Newlyn, if he could obtain a number from Directory Enquiries. He is standing at the dormer window, wondering this, when – as if triggered by some telepathic response – the telephone begins to ring.

Charlie turns from the window, crosses to the bedside cabinet and picks up the phone. He says hello. A woman enquires if Tamara is there.

'I'm afraid she isn't,' Charlie replies. 'Who's speaking?'

'Her sister,' says Briony.

SECRETS

CHARLIE

Briony had not been here before, not to this present flat in Styles Lane; she had visited Tamara a number of times at the house where she used to live, in Clapham, but she was a stranger to the east side of London. Charlie Stillman had given her instructions: Circle Line from Paddington to Liverpool Street, Central Line to Bethnal Green, then a bus to Upper Clapton. It was a twenty-minute walk from there, he'd said on the phone, but she got lost in the backstreets and had to ask the way.

Charlie was waiting for her outside the house. He was smiling as she approached.

'Briony . . .?'

'Charlie?'

They shook hands.

'She told me you looked alike,' he said, 'but she never told me *how* alike.'

Tam had mentioned Charlie Stillman on several occasions, but not for a long time. She had never said very much about him. He was a physiotherapist or something of the kind, she couldn't quite remember. They had been out together a few times and she had been quite fond of him, but the passion had sounded rather one-sided, the way Tam had reported it. Briony was not even sure whether they had been lovers or just friends. He was a good-looking man. Sand-coloured chinos and a yellow polo shirt. Fair-haired. Not tall but quite broad, muscular-looking. Mid-to-late thirties, she guessed.

The house was much larger and scruffier than she had imagined from the way Tamara had described it. The garden had been allowed to run wild and part of the brick boundary wall had fallen down. An old wooden gate lay among the weeds and brambles. She could make out 'The Hermitage' painted on it in white letters, though little more than a flaky ghost of it remained.

'Still no luck?' she said.

Charlie shook his head. 'Been phoning everywhere, calling everyone I can think of.'

They walked up a narrow path to a brick porch. Dark green paint was flaking off the front door. Bellpushes were scattered down each side; several of them had no name or number beside them, and one or two looked as if nothing was holding them to the woodwork but the wiring itself. Charlie had a key. She wondered why but didn't ask. Perhaps he had lived here with Tamara for a while. He opened the door and went in. Briony followed.

They were inside a large gloomy hall. On the far side of the staircase the hall narrowed into a long passage that ran to the back of the house. Every door was closed.

'Like a mausoleum, this place,' said Charlie.

They started up the staircase. The treads were carpeted, but the fabric was so worn that it was impossible to make out the original colour, let alone the pattern. They climbed up and up. The stairs were lit by mullioned windows at each mid-floor landing. Some of the lights contained coloured glass. The air was cool and smelled stale.

It was as quiet as a church.

They climbed one final, narrower, flight of stairs that led to the attic rooms. At the top was a smaller landing, covered with blue linoleum. The only natural light came from a small skylight window.

'The old servants' quarters,' said Charlie.

He led Briony round a corner and along a short, narrow passage to a door that was ajar. He rapped on the door and called out, 'Tamara . . .?'

Silence.

'Doesn't look like she's been back,' he said, referring to the broken lock. He pushed the door open and went on in. Briony followed.

'The firemen had to break in,' he explained. 'They split the wood on the inside. I tried pushing it back in place but it won't hold.'

They were in a long, wide room, with a steeply pitched ceiling of white-painted hardboard – the slope of the roof immediately above – and three dormer windows symmetrically placed along one side.

'There's a little kitchen through there.' Charlie pointed towards an opening in the nearest side wall, where three steps led up into a small dark space. 'Bathroom and toilet's on the floor below.'

It was not as gloomy up here as it was on the other floors. The three dormer windows let in sufficient light, and the walls and ceiling were painted white ... All except the long back wall behind Tamara's bed, where someone had painted a mural: a pastoral scene, with meadows and trees, a church, a shepherd and a flock of scattered sheep.

'When she called you yesterday,' said Charlie, 'what exactly did the message say?'

'I wish I could remember.' Briony sat down on the bed. 'I've been going over and over it – five hours on the train. I should've written it down.'

'Well, just the gist of it,' said Charlie.

'She sounded hysterical. Said she'd messed up – or screwed up – bigly ... That's a sort of jokey word she uses but there was nothing jokey about the message.'

'Screwed up how?' said Charlie. 'Screwed up what?'

'She didn't say. Said she'd thought she could handle it but it had all gone crazy on her.'

'What had?'

'I've no idea. She said it was really bad, whatever it was. Said please come ... to London, she meant. As soon as I could. Said she was scared. Very scared.'

'Of what?'

'I've no idea.'

'She didn't even give you a hint?'

Briony shook her head. 'I can't imagine what it could be. I've never known her get in a state like that. She's not the kind of person who gets hysterical about things. The first thing I did was phone here. And that's when I got through to you.'

'What about her pals down there? Or the family? They know anything?'

The word 'pals' made her smile. He sounded like an East End boy made good; a Cockney accent was still there, somewhere, in the background.

'She hasn't got many friends left in Newlyn,' said Briony. 'Not now. She's been in London too long.'

'Haven't we all,' said Charlie.

'I did call my mother but I didn't want to worry her. She's been ringing Tam, these past few weeks, because our grand-mother's dying. She's left messages but Tam hasn't called back.'

Charlie moved across to an oval, dropleaf table with four shabby dining chairs set around it. He pulled one out and sat down.

'I can't understand where she's disappeared to,' he said. 'She called me about two weeks ago and left a message on my machine – a bit like the message she left for you – saying something terrible had happened and could I come and see her. I was away at the time, working in Birmingham; I didn't get back to London till the day before yesterday. By which time there were about six more messages from her. So I phoned her straight away, but I got no answer. The machine wasn't on either. I tried again yesterday morning, but no joy. So I drove over here in my lunch break, and there was a fire engine outside, all whirly blue lights, and blokes in yellow helmets clumping around. I asked the sub-officer what was going on, told him who I was, and he told me someone dialled 999 because smoke was coming out of the attic windows. I went upstairs to have a look. What they think happened is, Tam – or someone – emptied an ashtray into this wastebin.' He indicated a small metal bin with a horse's head motif on the side. 'But her cigarette wasn't properly stubbed out, they think. There was some paper in the bin – just rubbish – and it was a hot day, so all the windows were wide open and a breeze was blowing through. The rubbish began to smoulder, making lots of smoke. Someone saw it drifting out of the open windows and called the fire brigade. A couple of firemen broke in and saw a woman lying on the bed.'

'And it was definitely Tam?' said Briony.

'We don't know *who* it was,' said Charlie. 'But it can't have been Tamara, can it? Or she'd have come back.'

'Then who was it? What did she look like?'

'The firemen didn't get a close look. They came over to the bin, gave it a burst with the extinguisher . . . Turned round to see if the woman was okay . . . And she'd gone.'

'Gone where?' said Briony.

'That's what they couldn't work out. If she'd gone downstairs she would have passed another fireman at the top of the stairs, but he didn't see anyone. The only other place she could've gone is the room next door . . . But that's just a store room: the door's locked and the housekeeper's got the only key.'

'Then . . .' Briony was confused. She wondered if she had missed something. 'Where did she go?'

'There's nowhere she *could've* gone,' said Charlie.

'I could understand someone waking up, seeing smoke and firemen, and dashing out in a panic,' said Briony. 'But Tam wouldn't panic like that. She's used to emergencies, she's used to pressure.'

'So who was it?' asked Charlie.

Briony thought about it.

'Maybe she's been working out of town?' she suggested. 'And she's had a friend staying here, minding the flat.'

'Well, if she did,' said Charlie, 'and even if this friend got past the fireman without being noticed, why didn't she come back?'

Briony couldn't come up with an answer. It made no sense to her either.

'Another thing,' said Charlie. 'The woman had nothing on. She was naked. That was about the one thing the firemen were sure of.'

'Well, if she was in bed,' Briony reasoned, 'maybe she was a nurse on night duty and—'

'That's not the point,' said Charlie. 'Where did she find clothes so quickly? The most she could have done in half a minute would've been to grab a bathrobe.'

'I suppose so,' agreed Briony.

'Has she *said* anything about a friend staying here?'

'I haven't spoken to her recently.'

'How recently?'

'Oh . . . A few months ago. June, maybe.'

'And when did you last see her?'

Briony had to pause a moment to recollect. 'Well . . . She didn't come down last Christmas so . . . It must have been in the summer.'

'Not this summer just gone?' said Charlie. 'You mean the summer of last year?'

'Yes, but that's not unusual,' said Briony.

'I'm not suggesting it is.'

'Nurses don't get that much holiday. Christmas and New Year she's usually working. And I can't afford to come up here very often.'

'No, sure, I wasn't trying to make a point of it,' said Charlie. 'But the strange thing is, I can't find anyone who *has* seen her. Not since Christmas last year. And that's nine months ago.'

'Since Christmas? Oh, that's ridiculous,' said Briony. 'Come on . . . Lots of people must have seen her.'

'Well, I can't trace a single one,' said Charlie.

'When did *you* last see her?'

'About the same time you did. Summer last year.'

'I thought you both worked at the Hackney Hospital?' said Briony.

'At one time,' said Charlie. 'But not any longer.'

'You're a physiotherapist, did she say?'

'*Psycho*therapist,' said Charlie. 'I deal with stress-related problems at work. It's mainly counselling.'

'But what do you mean, nobody's seen her since Christmas?' said Briony. 'How can you possibly know?'

'I've been phoning around. None of her old mates at the Hackney have seen her. They say she stopped getting in touch ages ago. And when they tried calling her, she didn't want to come out, go to parties, do anything. Seems to have turned her back on everyone. Become sort of reclusive.'

'*Reclusive*?' said Briony, incredulously. 'She can't bear being on her own, she's party-mad. I can't think of anyone less likely to be reclusive. And, anyway, phoning a few old mates at the Hackney Hospital doesn't prove much ... She hasn't worked there for the past eighteen months.'

'That's true,' Charlie agreed. 'But nobody knows where she's been working for the past year. Do *you* know?'

'Sure,' said Briony, 'that's no mystery. She's agency nursing – has been ever since she left the Hackney. That's why she quit the NHS: to go private.'

'Do you know which agency she's working for now?' asked Charlie.

'No. But it wouldn't mean anything to me even if Tam told me.'

'When she left the Hackney Hospital in March last year, she started working for the Egerton Nursing Bureau in South Kensington. She stuck it for six months. She gave it up at the end of August because there wasn't enough work for her. She couldn't make ends meet.'

'That doesn't tally with what *I* remember,' said Briony. 'When she came down to Cornwall last summer, she told me everything was going really well. She was glad she'd left the NHS and everything was hunky-dory.'

'Is that so?' said Charlie. And looked as if he didn't believe her. 'That's what she told you?'

'Why?' said Briony. 'She told you something different?'

'She told me something *very* different,' said Charlie. 'She told me she was barely earning enough to pay the rent.'

'The summer of last year?'

'The summer of last year.'

'Well, maybe she was going through a quiet spell,' said Briony.

'And when I spoke to her on the phone a few months later,' Charlie continued, 'about this time last year, she told me she was packing it in.'

'Packing what in? *Nursing?*'

Charlie nodded. 'Said she thought it was a mug's game. It had all been taken over by accountants and business managers and efficiency consultants. The Armani suits and BMW brigade.'

'A mug's game? Tamara told you that?' Briony smiled in disbelief. 'No way. Absolutely no way in a million years.'

Charlie gestured, casually, a please-yourself shrug.

'She would never say a thing like that. She's worked so hard to get where she is. She's a staff nurse. She wouldn't throw away her whole career like that.'

'She threw it away when she quit the NHS. She swapped her staff's job for the odd week or two of geriatric care, here and there. That's the only work the agency could put her way.'

'I can't believe she told you she was quitting. Nursing was everything to her.'

'Well, that's what she said.'

'When?' said Briony. 'When did she say that?'

'About this time last year. About September time.'

'On the phone?'

'What difference does it make?'

'I've talked to Tam on the phone dozens of times since then,' said Briony. 'She'd have said if she'd given up nursing. She'd have told me if things had got that bad.'

'Are you sure she'd tell you?'

'Of course I'm sure. I'm her sister, for Christ's sake, she tells me everything.'

'Maybe she was too embarrassed,' said Charlie.

'Or maybe there was nothing to tell,' said Briony, getting irritated now. 'Perhaps she was getting along just fine.'

'She left the Egerton Nursing Bureau in September,' said Charlie, 'twelve months ago. Where has she been working since then?'

'How should I know?' said Briony. 'She's probably changed agencies. There must be dozens of them.'

'There probably are,' Charlie agreed. 'But why haven't any of her friends seen her? Why hasn't she answered your mother's calls? Why did she phone you in such a panic? Why has she gone missing?'

'She's not *missing*,' said Briony, scoffing at the notion. 'I had a phone call from her only yesterday. She's not missing, she just doesn't happen to be here right now.'

'Okay, she's not missing,' said Charlie. 'It's just that nobody knows where she is. Nobody knows where she works. And nobody's seen her since last year.'

TAMARA (1)

Briony?
  Look at me.
  Please . . .
  Can't you sense me? Feel my presence?
  No?

Oh, God, it's good to see you. You don't know how glad I am you've come. I'm so glad to see you I could cry. Except . . . we can't cry where I am now. None of us can. I want to hug you. I can't bear not hugging you. Just a touch . . . Touch fingers . . . But I can't touch either. I can't feel anything much at all.

Can't you feel a thing? Try. Concentrate.

I don't know where you think I am but I'm so close, sweet sister. So very close.

Just turn and smile at me or something, just give me a sign that you can sense I'm here.

Sis . . . ?

I'm right here in front of you. I've not gone anywhere. I can't go anywhere. I'm trapped here in this place, just watching, listening, waiting.

Can't you sense me at all . . . not even a very little?

THE MURAL

Briony was hungry; she had had nothing since breakfast at the crack of dawn, except coffee and a sandwich on the train. She walked up the three narrow steps that led into the kitchen. She had never seen a kitchen so small . . . she'd seen bigger galleys on a trawler. It was equipped with a miniature everything: sink and drainer, electric water heater, Baby Belling cooker, microwave oven, electric kettle, and a compact fridge, about two feet square.

She looked in the fridge: eggs, milk, Flora, tomatoes, mixed salad in a plastic bowl. On top of the fridge sat a white plastic bread bin. Inside, she found a small, sliced Hovis loaf. She opened a cupboard and found rice, pasta, dehydrated soups, cans of salmon, tuna and kidney beans. And on an open shelf: tea bags, instant coffee and sugar.

She made herself a sandwich with tuna and tomato, and a mug of coffee. She took them into the main studio room and sat down at the oval table where Charlie Stillman had been sitting.

She and Charlie were not going to get along, she decided.

Okay, she's not missing . . . It's just that nobody knows where she is. Sarky bugger. And that patronizing smirk.

In the middle of the table sat a stump of purple candle that had burned down almost to the candle holder itself, leaving gnarled encrustations of spilled wax around it, like the lip of a volcano.

Beside the candle holder lay a large slab of fruit and nut chocolate – Tam's favourite. She had opened it but had eaten only one row of pieces so far.

Next to the chocolate lay a bank statement and an electricity bill.

She unfolded the bank statement. The balance brought forward from 30 July was twenty-two pounds and eighteen pence. The balance at 30 August was twenty-two pounds and eighteen pence. Tam had paid in nothing, had drawn nothing out, for the whole month of August.

That seemed strange.

The envelopes were still on the table. Briony looked at the postmarks: the third of September. So Tam must have been here as recently as the fourth – the day before yesterday – to have opened them . . . And possibly as recently as yesterday, the fifth.

Briony turned and stared at the bed. *Could* it have been Tamara who was lying there when the firemen broke in? If it was, then where on earth had she disappeared to? And why hadn't she come back?

And now she noticed something on the bedside cabinet . . . She was amazed she hadn't seen it before, it was so obvious: Tamara's handbag.

Why hadn't Tam taken her handbag?

She got up, crossed to the cabinet, picked up the bag and tipped the contents on to the bed. Apart from all the usual junk, there was her purse, with about ten pounds' worth of cash in it; her wallet – containing her driving licence, three ten-pound notes, a credit card and a NatWest service card; a cheque book, and a bunch of keys – door keys.

Where would Tam have gone without her house keys?

She looked around the room. There had to be something here that would tell her what Tam was doing these days, where she was working. She wondered where Tam kept her salary chits. She was obsessively tidy – everything had to be put away somewhere, in its own special place and out of sight. Along the side wall, next to the steps that led up to the kitchen, stood something that was designed like a sideboard, with two wide drawers and a full-width cupboard beneath. But it was no work of art; it had been painted a glossy, poppy red and looked like a toy cupboard from a child's playroom. Tamara had laid out her sound system on top of it, with her tapes and compact discs ranged on either side.

Briony opened the drawers. One of them contained stationery, the other contained some document files in bright colours. She lifted the topmost folder out of the drawer and flipped it open. It was full of old bank statements.

The statement on top was dated 30 July. The balance brought forward from 30 June was twenty-two pounds and eighteen pence. The same balance that was on her August statement.

She looked back at the preceding month: still twenty-two pounds and eighteen pence.

She continued flipping back through the months. Incredible: Tam's bank balance had not moved throughout the whole of the past twelve months. It had been twenty-two pounds and eighteen pence in September 1994 and precisely that amount on the August statement that was lying on the table. Tam had not paid anything into her account for an entire year. Not one penny. Nor had she withdrawn any cash or written any cheques.

Briony looked back to the statements for the early months of '94. She could see when Tamara had left the Hackney Hospital: her final NHS salary credit had been paid into her account in March.

Throughout the following six months, when (according to Charlie) she was working for the Egerton Nursing Bureau, sporadic payments had been made into her account. But they didn't amount to very much ... A few hundred here, a few hundred there.

She looked in the other document files. She found electricity bills, phone bills, council tax bills, water rates, correspondence from Guy's Hospital, correspondence from Hackney Council, tax returns, tax demands ... And, lastly, a folder full of old salary chits, bunched and paper-clipped together in date order.

During the six-month period from March until August '94 Tam had filed only five receipts – all from the Egerton Bureau, Harrington Gardens, SW7. And those five payments accounted for all the credits on her bank statements during those six months.

But there were no salary receipts at all – from the Egerton Bureau or from anybody else – from 27 August 1994 onwards.

What had she been doing for the past year? How had she been paying her rent?

Briony wondered how much the rent was. The furniture was old and tatty for the most part. There was not much of it. It was such a motley collection of junk it was hard to believe a landlord could get away with calling this a furnished flat.

Next to the 'toy cupboard' was the dining area, with the oval table and the four rickety upright chairs, no two of them alike.

Near the centre of the room, two heavy armchairs, draped

with faded loose covers, were angled towards each other and facing the middle of the three dormer windows. In the window bay itself sat a television and a video recorder – both very new, by the look of them – side by side on a low table.

Against the gabled wall at the far end of the room stood a dressing table, a large chest of drawers and a free-standing clothes rail, hung with Tamara's coats and skirts and dresses. Her shoes were ranged along the floor beneath the rail.

Not much sign of poverty there.

The bed dominated the centre of the room, dividing it in two. It looked almost new: a king-size double on a pine base fitted with drawers beneath. It was so out-of-keeping with everything else in the room that Briony wondered whether Tam had bought it with her own money.

She looked at the mural behind the bed. The whole wall was one enormous painting, from floor to ceiling, from one end to the other . . . Thirty feet long, at a guess.

It was primitive in style, childlike. The figures were not properly formed, nothing was in proportion and there was no perspective.

A woman was standing on a country road, at a point where the road divided, forking sharply left and sharply right.

One path led over undulating countryside to a little village, like something out of toytown, with cosy little houses in fondant colours, and happy families, pushing prams and licking ice creams. A rainbow arced across the sky and ended above the village, bathing it in beautiful colours.

The other path led to a church. A very dark church built of black stone blocks, separated by cream-coloured mortar. There were bars on the windows: vertical bars. They looked like prison cells. Faces were peering out. All the faces had eyes, but no mouth.

The church had a tower: the largest object in the mural – about five feet high. There was a clock on the tower. The hands of the clock were gold. There were twelve numerals around the face of the clock, but every numeral was the same: the figure zero.

Above the church the sky was thunder-dark. Almost purple. Cracked by lightning.

The woman who was standing at the point where the road forked to the left and the right was being drawn two ways: her feet were pointing towards the black church, whilst her face was turned towards the kitsch village where the rainbow ended.

Close to the church, a shepherd kept watch over a flock of sheep. The faces of the sheep were flesh-coloured. They had a human quality. There were hundreds of them, scattered over hills and valleys. All of them – no matter where they were – were looking towards the shepherd. And none of them had legs; they were woolly blobs with pink near-human faces, trapped where they were, unable to move.

The shepherd was out of all proportion to everything else in the mural. He was as tall as the church tower. He looked ancient. His face was shrivelled like an old potato. He was holding a shepherd's crook. He looked more like a priest than a shepherd – a Victorian country priest, in a long black coat that buttoned to the neck, and a black hat with a broad, flat brim and a rounded crown.

There was something cruel and malevolent about that wizened face: fierce black-brown eyes, a turned-down mouth, no perceptible lips.

His crook was a strange-looking thing ... More like the ornate ceremonial crook carried by a bishop.

Beside the church tower lay a graveyard. Headstones protruded from the dark earth in cluttered profusion. All the stones bore an inscription along the bottom, the same inscription on every one: *For ever with us*. But only one gravestone bore a name: *Petra Pascali*. In clear white letters on dark slate. Beneath the name, the date: *20. vi. 91*.

The letter P in both Petra and Pascali were in the Gothic

33

style. It imitated the shape of the ornate, knobbly crook that the priestly shepherd was holding.

She looked at the church again and noticed something even more macabre: through one of the barred windows could be glimpsed a masked man removing something from the heart of a brazier of red-hot coals. And, behind him, a naked woman stood, legs and arms akimbo, chained to the high altar.

TAMARA (2)

Creepy, isn't it?

What the hell's it all about? she's thinking.

Oh, sweet sister . . . The hell indeed.

It hints at secrets, doesn't it? So many dark and horrible secrets. And no one there can ever tell what happens . . . for no one has a mouth to speak.

Look at him, the shepherd. Look at that face. Thousands of years old. God knows how long he's been on earth. Did you ever see such evil in a pair of eyes?

I'm attracted to evil.

You never knew that, did you?

I have always been attracted to evil.

I'm not evil myself, I'm simply attracted to it. It turns me on.

Not every kind of evil . . . I don't know what kind exactly. Evil is not a thing I can define, it's something I sense. I pick it up like a radio signal that other people don't seem to tune into. Or sometimes I feel it: touching me, like fingers. Its touch can be so soft, light as a feather, but I always sense it. Evil touches some nervous sensor inside me. It excites me, switches me on, makes my heart twitch, break rhythm, beat a little faster. I give off some kind of response in the presence of evil – without even knowing it, like some musk or secretion, or some pulse that flickers through the electromagnetic field . . . I don't know what it is, I don't have to do a thing, it just seems to happen. I attract evil. And evil arouses me.

There is evil in this house, Briony. Once you have given yourself to this house she will never let you go.

I sensed evil the very first day I came here.

It was a cold November afternoon. I walked slowly down the path and looked at that wild garden.

It is full of souls, that garden, forgotten souls, lost and waiting among the tangled weeds. But feel no sorrow, waste no pity on them. They feel nothing – no pleasure, no pain. They have no sense of time. None of us has any sense of time where I am now. We are in a dimension where there is no time and so there is no ageing. There is no hunger, no thirst, no illness, no feeling of any kind. They look sad, these long-forgotten souls but they feel nothing very much.

I suppose that's why nobody bothers with the garden. It has grown as much as it ever will. It gets no worse, it gets no better. No one notices. In a big city no one notices anything very much.

I came to the porch, that November afternoon, and the front door was standing wide open. I don't know why. I peered inside that dark hallway. I could feel my pulse quicken. A kind of dryness crept into my mouth. I sensed the evil. I sensed it just standing at the open door, peering in. And it sensed me, this house. It was waiting for me. It seduced me.

I could have walked away. I should have walked away. You have a choice with evil. It lures you, it tempts you, but you always have a choice. You choose to walk through that door. It's so easy. It's only later that you realize there's no turning round and walking back.

I walked inside. I walked as far as the staircase. A voice spoke from the back of the hallway. She was standing, watching me. I hadn't seen her until now, it was so dark in there.

'My name's Tamara,' I said.

'I know,' she said. 'I've been expecting you.'

That was when I should have walked away.

She brought me upstairs. Every door was shut. The whole place reeked of lonely isolated souls banged up in their little cells; it echoed with their silences.

She brought me to this musty attic. I looked around. There wasn't much to see, just this junk-shop furniture, and an awful saggy bed – a sort of tubular steel thing, like they used to have in hospitals in the bad old days . . . And Petra's mural.

I looked at the painting and saw the eyes of the shepherd, the despair on those mouthless faces barred up inside the church, and I felt a little tremor quiver through my insides, felt that tingling sensation in my flesh. I knew then that I should walk away.

I had a choice, Bri. But in a sense I had no choice . . . I'm drawn towards evil. Like a moth to a candle.

GLORIA

Briony went down to the second floor in search of the bathroom. She found an old, unpanelled, cast-iron tub on claw feet. Limescale had encrusted itself, thick and yellow, on the chipped enamel beneath the taps and around the plughole. Past generations of bathwater had left their tidemarks. A large, old-fashioned Ascot water heater overhung the bath and beside the door, at floor level, was a gas meter with two slots for coins: one marked 1/- and the other 2/6d.

The walls were flecked with a black fungus of some kind.

She wondered how many people had to share this.

As she stepped back out of the bathroom she found someone standing at the end of the landing, watching her: a woman of middle age, to judge from her face, and yet she stood with the stooping posture of a woman in her seventies. She was wearing a floral-print robe, tied at the waist, and reaching almost to her ankles. A pair of slippers on her feet, trodden down at the heels. Her blonde-grey hair was a tangled mess. She looked as if she had only just got out of bed.

A door stood partly open behind her.

'Hi,' said Briony. 'I'm Tamara's sister.'

The woman did not respond.

'Tamara Carkeat?' said Briony. 'The attic flat?'

The woman had a sallow complexion. Her face was inexpressive. She stared at Briony as if someone had switched off her brain.

'I wondered if you'd seen her lately?' Briony asked.

Still no response.

Briony wondered if she was subnormal in some way.

'Could you tell me where I can find the housekeeper?' she asked.

Silence.

Briony was on the point of giving up, when the woman spoke. 'You must see Gloria,' she said. 'Mrs Packerman. This is necessary. She is looking after things.'

She had a European accent – German perhaps? – and such a hollow, deadpan tone she sounded as if she was under hypnosis.

'And where do I find Mrs Packerman?' Briony enquired.

'On the ground floor,' the woman replied. 'Her door is brown.'

'Okay, thanks,' said Briony.

The woman turned and went back into her room, shuffling like an invalid, and closed the door.

Briony went downstairs. Every door, she noticed, was brown. The skirting boards and dado rails were brown. Everything that was made of wood was brown. A dull, depressing brown.

On the ground floor there was a front hallway which led

from the front door to the stairwell. And, behind that, a rear hall passage that extended to the back of the building.

There was a room on each side of the front hallway, and four rooms on either side of the rear hall passage. She walked slowly along the rear hallway, listening at each door. It was so deathly quiet everywhere . . . Didn't anybody else live in this house? At last she heard some sign of life . . . A radio or a television. She knocked at the door. She heard someone approaching.

The door opened and a woman said, 'Yes, dear?'

'I'm sorry to bother you,' said Briony. 'I'm looking for Mrs Packerman.'

'Are you indeed?' The woman looked pleasantly surprised. 'You must be Tamara's sister?' She sounded Australian.

'That's right.'

'Bridey, isn't it?'

'Briony.'

'Jeez . . . You are so like her. A tad taller, I'd guess, and a bit more flesh on your bones but . . . Can see you're from the same egg, all right.'

She was a broad, busty woman, with a plump face. Her hair was golden blonde – absurdly blonde for someone who must have been sixty, at the very least – and hung loose to her shoulders. She looked like the madam of some tacky bordello. Her lipstick was too thickly applied and too sugary a pink for her age and complexion; her eye-shadow was too vivid a blue. She wore a satin kaftan: black, with silver and bronze leaves.

'Well, come along in, dear, don't be shy,' she said.

Her wrists jangled with bracelets.

Briony walked into what must once have been the sitting room in the days when this was a family home. It was a large room with a deep bay window and a pair of French windows that opened on to the rear garden.

The air was blue-grey with cigarette smoke.

'Call me Gloria,' she said. 'I don't like all that Mrs Packerman business . . . Makes me sound like an old dame.'

She pointed to an armchair. 'Sit yourself down, sweetheart, take a load off.'

Briony sank into the chair. The springs were exhausted and the loose covers had been washed too many times – though not recently, to judge from all the cat hairs.

'I take it Tamara's not back yet?' said Gloria.

'No. She phoned me yesterday and left a message, asking me to come up to London. Said she had a problem. I suppose she's had to go somewhere but I don't know where. Has she said anything to you?'

'Haven't spoken to her for yonks,' Gloria replied. 'Didn't even know she'd gone anywhere till all these firemen started thumping up and down the stairs. You've just arrived from Cornwall, have you?'

'Just this afternoon.'

'A friend of hers called Charlie was here yesterday. He told me you'd phoned. He said you were coming up but he didn't say when. Have you eaten?' She looked concerned.

'Yes, thanks,' said Briony. 'I had something upstairs.'

'Well, have a drink, anyway.' Gloria started towards an open doorway. 'I've got beer or gin or Vermouth. And some very nasty Greek brandy that my fellow, Jack, brought me back from holiday.'

'A beer would be fine, thanks,' said Briony.

'Coming right up,' said Gloria, and disappeared into her kitchen.

Briony looked around her. The room felt like something out of the 1940s. The striped wallpaper was old and dis-coloured; the flowery-patterned curtains at the two bay win-dows were dirty and faded. The sofa and armchairs were bulky and had that postwar 'utility' look to them. There was a bed behind her, along one wall; draped with a green candlewick cover.

Gloria reappeared a few minutes later, holding a can of lager and a tumbler, half full.

'So tell me, dear,' she said, handing the can and the glass to

Briony, 'what's been going on upstairs? Firemen walking in and out ... A mystery woman asleep on the bed ... Now you see her, now you don't. What's that sister of yours been getting up to?'

'I wish I knew,' said Briony. 'Does she have a flatmate?'

'Search me, dear, I haven't asked. But I think she should have mentioned it, if she has.'

Gloria ensconced herself in the other armchair and picked up a packet of cigarettes. Senior Service. Briony had not seen those for donkey's years.

'I mean, I don't particularly *mind*, but I do like to know who's got keys to this place, who's coming and going.' She put a cigarette between her lips and lit it with a chunky Zippo.

'That's another strange thing,' said Briony, 'Tam's keys are still in the flat. And not just her keys: her handbag with her purse, her wallet, money, everything in it.'

'You don't say?' Gloria's face crumpled a little. 'Well, that doesn't quite add up, does it?'

'The obvious thing is to find out if she's been in to work,' said Briony. 'But I don't know where she's working these days. Do you?'

'I don't, dear, no. I haven't seen hair nor hide of her, this last couple of months. I think she was on nights for a while, but my fellow, Jack, bumped into her the other week and she told him she'd packed that in. I don't think she's been doing much the last few months. I think agency nurses are having a hard time these days.'

'It's a mystery to me how she's been managing,' said Briony. 'I just had a nosey through her things to see if I could find some salary chits and she hasn't used her bank account for a whole year.'

'Ahh ...' Gloria shook her head, knowingly. 'Cash, sweetie, cash.' She snapped her fingers a few times. 'No cheques, none of that rubbish. I've had a few 'stralian girls here, down the years, agency nursing ... They work all hours,

40

out-of-the-way places, and it's always cash, darling. Used and folding – grubby readies – that's the colour of wages. The bloody tax man, the social security, the agency, they've all got their hands in your piggy bank ... They leave a girl with bugger all by the time they've had their whack. Cash, darling, cash, it's the only way to keep your head above water.'

'Is there anyone here who might know where she could be?' said Briony. 'Is she friendly with anyone?'

'You could try Dee,' said Gloria. 'She's got the second-floor room that's right under Tam's. But she's not very often here. She's shacked up with a moody Russian called Misha. Knock on the door on your way back up, but I doubt if she's there. I don't know about the rest. They're a funny crowd, this lot. All women. I don't like male tenants – they have such unattractive habits, men on their own, especially as they get older. Have you noticed? The younger girls here come and go, they don't seem to stay very long and no one's very neighbourly. It's very English, that, in my experience. But it's worse in London. You get used to it. And as for the older ones ...' She pulled a face. 'Oh, 'struth, some dreary bloody drizzes here, dear, I can tell you. One or two of them have a few slates missing, I think.' She touched her temple a few times. 'It's like zombies' night out up there sometimes.' She glanced up at the floor above.

'I met someone earlier on,' said Briony. 'She didn't seem very friendly. A woman on the second floor. Sort of grey-blonde? German maybe?'

'That'll be Lotte, I expect,' said Gloria. 'Take no notice, dear, she's from the far North, Lapland or some God-forsaken place. I'll be charitable and say she's not quite eight pints to the gallon, that one. They don't get much sun, where she comes from, it depresses the brain. Look what it did for Hamlet, poor bastard.'

SHEILA

Briony walked back upstairs. When she reached the second floor she stopped to work out which was Dee's room. The room beneath Tam's, Gloria had said, but it could have been either one of two doors. She knocked on the one nearest the staircase; there was no reply.

She knocked on the other door. It opened a few inches – just enough for Briony to make out the face of a very young woman; no more than a teenager by the look of her. She had spots around her mouth. Her skin was the colour of putty and the hollows of her eyes were a grey-brown colour.

'Hi,' said Briony. 'My sister, Tamara, lives upstairs. I wondered if you'd seen her at all? Or if you know where she's working?'

The girl shook her head ... as if she hadn't really understood what Briony was saying. She looked as if she'd been on intimate terms with a glue pot all evening.

The door closed before Briony could even say thank you.

She tried the rooms that lay behind the stairwell along the rear landing. There was no answer from any of them.

She went down to the first floor.

She knocked on every door. She spoke to a woman of about her own age, dark and slender, with green eyes and a twitchy smile, who said in halting English that she was sorry but she was from France and had seen her sister one or two times, but not since several months.

She spoke to a middle-aged woman with a tired expression, who shook her head and said that it was nothing to do with her, and promptly closed her door again.

Briony spoke to a black woman in one of the rooms off the rear landing and got a similar response.

Next door to the black woman – above Gloria's room – an owlish-looking girl in shorts, a denim shirt and granny glasses said they'd been on vac, she and Amanda, and hadn't seen Tam since June. She indicated her flatmate who was sitting on a cushion on the floor, with her back against an armchair, watching television.

'Been *where*?' said Briony.

Vac, said the girl. University vac. They had only just come back.

'Actually,' she confessed, 'I thought you *were* Tamara.'

Briony knocked on the room next door but there was no reply. The owlish-looking girl opened her door again and said, 'I'm Francesca, by the way. If you need anything any time.' And added, as Briony waited at the neighbouring door: 'She's a bit odd, that one. She never talks. Hardly ever goes out.'

'Seems to be the fashion around here,' said Briony.

She went down to the ground floor. As she reached the foot of the staircase, a door opened off the rear hallway, almost opposite Gloria's room, and a young woman emerged. She looked about twenty. She was beefy, with a broad frame, wearing a white miniskirt that paid her no compliments, and what looked like a leotard in electric-blue Lycra.

She walked past Briony without a glance, as if she was not even there, and rapped on the door of one of the two rooms at the front of the house.

'D'reen?' she called out. ''S Tracey.'

Briony walked towards her and said, 'Excuse me?'

Tracey looked round. Her hair was a deep copper colour. She wore violet eye-shadow and coral pink lipstick.

'Do you know my sister, Tamara? She lives in the attic flat.'

Tracey's mouth was hanging open, in rather a stupid way.

'Nah, not really,' she said. 'Nuffin to do wiv me. D'reen might.'

The door opened. Doreen was an older woman with a raddled-looking face and a beaky nose. She was wearing a red nylon négligé, which she held closed at her throat with one hand. She looked enquiringly at Briony.

'I was just asking about my sister,' said Briony. 'She lives in the top-floor flat. Do you know her at all?'

'I know who you mean, pet,' Doreen replied. Her hair was cut in a bob and dyed jet black. Her face was deeply lined and wrinkled and heavily made up. The hand that clasped the neck of her négligé was dotted with liver spots. It looked knobbly and arthritic. She had put on too much perfume or eau-de-Cologne; the smell was overpowering. 'We say hello, like, if we're passing,' she added. She sounded Geordie. Her breath smelt of cigarettes.

'Have you seen her recently?' Briony asked.

Tracey was shaking her head.

'I thought she'd moved out,' said Doreen. 'Haven't seen her for months.'

'You don't know where she was working, the last time you saw her?'

'I didn't even know her name till you just said,' Doreen replied.

'Okay,' said Briony. 'Thanks anyway.'

'Welcome, pet.' Doreen smiled, revealing some large gaps between tar-browned teeth. Tracey entered the room and Doreen shut the door.

Briony turned to go back upstairs and noticed someone hanging back in the shadows of the rear hallway.

'Is it Briony?' she said, as Briony approached the stairs.

'Yes . . .?'

The woman came towards her. She was wearing a belted raincoat, with a scarf tied over her greying hair – which seemed strange to Briony, for it was such a warm September evening and there had been no threat of rain all week. It was difficult to guess her age – forties, fifties perhaps. She looked tired and careworn.

'My name's Sheila,' she said. 'I'm a friend of Tamara's.' She was Irish and spoke very softly, as if she didn't want to be overheard. 'I heard you talking to those two . . .' She nodded towards Doreen's room. 'I think I know where Tamara might be. She's been to see me several times. Brought me something for translation. Did she mention?'

Briony shook her head. She wondered if she'd heard correctly; Sheila was speaking so softly she was almost whispering.

'For *translation*?' said Briony.

'From Italian,' said Sheila. 'Petra's book. She didn't say?'

'I'm sorry, I don't know what you're talking about.'

Sheila glanced behind her as though she was afraid that someone might be listening. 'This is very complicated. Did she never talk to you about the house at Leysholme? Or the Pastor?'

'The house *where*?' said Briony, wondering if everybody in this house was slightly barmy.

'She never did then,' Sheila concluded. 'Are you staying here?'

'In Tam's flat ... Well, for a day or two, anyway. She phoned me in Cornwall and asked me to come up. Said she was in some kind of trouble. Do you know what it's about?'

Sheila hesitated. Briony could tell from the look on her face that she knew something.

'I'll come and see you tomorrow,' said Sheila. 'Will you be home?'

'Can't we talk now?' said Briony.

'I have to go out, I'm late,' said Sheila. 'And this is not the place to talk. I'll come up and knock on your door tomorrow.'

'Can't you just tell me where she is?' Briony pressed gently.

'It's not that simple,' she said. 'I wish to God it was. I'll see you tomorrow.' She walked past Briony towards the front door and then stopped and turned: 'And tell absolutely no one that we've talked,' she whispered. 'Not a word.' She put a raised forefinger to her lips, to emphasize it.

'No, all right,' said Briony.

Sheila walked quickly out of the house and pulled the door closed very quietly, as if she was afraid that someone might hear that as well.

SECRETS

Briony went back upstairs to the flat.

What *was* that strange woman talking about? The pastor
. . . Something for translation . . . Petra's book . . .

Petra was the name on the grave in the mural.

Briony went to the far corner of the room and looked at
the wall, at the graveyard beside the church tower.

For ever with us, inscribed on every headstone. White
letters on dark slate. But only one stone bore a name: *Petra
Pascali. 20. vi. 91.*

Curious, the way she had styled the letter P in both names
– in old German script – so that it looked exactly like the
ornate shepherd's crook that the hideous old priest was
holding. Was that who Sheila meant by the pastor?

Her attention shifted to the church, to the mouthless faces
behind the barred windows, to the masked man beside the
brazier, the naked woman chained to the high altar.

There was something odd about the tower. The church
walls were not straight – in fact, there was scarcely a straight
line in the entire mural . . . With the sole exception of the
church tower. The walls of the tower were so meticulously
straight, they looked as if they had been painted with the aid
of a rule of some kind.

She ran her fingers down the vertical lines. She could feel a
tiny gap, all the way down. The tower had been painted over
a door – a cupboard door perhaps, about five feet high and
half as wide, and flush with the wall. As the tower was the
exact size of the door, and painted with black stones and
putty-coloured mortar, it was almost impossible to detect it
with a casual glance. It was clever, the way it had been
disguised. Only the slight protrusion of the hinges down one
side gave it away.

Briony pushed at the door. It didn't move. She ran the flat

of her hand across the surface and found a small hook screwed into the door at about waist height. She pulled it and the door swung open.

It was a walk-in closet, about six feet deep.

The lintel was so low, she had to duck to step inside. She wondered if there was a light in here. Her hands fumbled across the wall. She felt a thin cord dangling from the ceiling. She pulled it and a light came on – a bare bulb, dangling from old braided flex, hooked over a long nail that protruded from the side wall.

A brass rail ran the length of the closet, packed tight with clothes. Everything was black. Conspicuously black.

Briony couldn't quite believe what she was seeing ... Clothes was not really the appropriate term – this was a fetishist's dream. Everything was made of rubber, or leather, or some kind of shiny PVC fabric.

She reached up and unhooked the nearest item. It looked as if it might have had something to do with Scuba diving. It was made of glossy latex and styled like a leotard ... but it covered the neck and head as well. There were holes for the eyes, the nostrils and the mouth, and two larger openings where the bust would be.

She looked through everything that was hanging from the rail. There were dresses and skirts; whole bodysuits; long lace-up corsets; and contraptions that looked as if they belonged in the tackroom of a riding stable – complex tangles of dangling leather strapping and steel buckles.

On the floor, beneath the rail, lay a row of spiky-heeled shoes – some of them looked like six-inch stilettos – and boots, knee-length, thigh-length and practically hip-length, in hide and patent leather.

Tamara . . .?

Briony stood staring at it all in bemusement. She went back into the other room and began to open the drawers of the dressing table.

She found a couple of wigs, on polystyrene heads. One was

styled in a bob with a low fringe; the other was long and parted in the centre. Both were raven black.

She found a drawer full of make-up. Tamara hardly ever wore the stuff and, even when she did, it seldom varied: always the same billiard-ball red for her nails and lips, the same smoky-blue eye shadow. But all this ... Briony was amazed by the sheer quantity of it. Nail lacquers, lip glosses, eye shadow ... And the colours ... Lip colours that Tamara always said she would never be seen dead wearing: aubergine, damson, purple, viridian, midnight, ebony ...

She found a drawer stuffed with hardcore underwear; nothing delicate, no soft silks or satins, no frills or lace, this was all studded leather, coarse fishnet and shiny rubber, glinting with buckles and hoops and zips.

Briony made some coffee and sat in an armchair, eating the fruit and nut chocolate that was on the table and watching the twilight creeping in from the east, across the marshes.

Could all that stuff really be Tam's?

Where would she have found the money for it? And why would she want so *much* of it?

Tam, of all people ... Tam had always been the angel of the family. She was the prettier and the cleverer. Tam had done everything right, ever since they were babies. Tam had never cried when she was teething. Tam was never ill. Tam was never fretful. Tam had been the first to walk, the first to talk, the first to read. Tam had always kept her room tidy, had always done as she was told, had been a good Brownie, had sung up at Sunday school, had collected money for good causes, had worked hard at school, had not hung out with yobs and oiks, had got good grades in her GCSEs, had taken herself off to London to do something worthwhile with her life, had passed all her nursing exams, had been commended and awarded and medalled and praised. Everyone in Newlyn thought highly of Tamara. Her father could feel proud of her.

Whereas Briony had always been the black sheep, had done

48

everything wrong; had been the fractious infant, the difficult child and the wilful teenager. Briony had played around at school, had hung out with riff-raff – first with bikers and then with New-Age travellers. Briony had messed around with drugs and had got herself into trouble with the law. She had scraped together enough GCSE passes to get into Cornwall College to study art and design. Dennis had dismissed it with contempt; a waste of taxpayers' money. 'Damn'ee, that edden goan to get'ee work,' he used to tell her with scorn. 'That edden goan to put bread en your mouth, girl. You need a trade behind'ee, a skill. Art edden any use to anywan.'

Time had proved him right, as well. All Briony had ever done since leaving college was work in pubs and cafés . . . And even that was only seasonal.

He had never approved of her friends, either – the students, the painters, the potters, the arts-and-crafts fraternity . . . Most of whom lived in rundown cottages and scraped a living, or got by on State handouts. 'Beatniks' he called them, with quaint disgust.

Briony had been a bitter disappointment to her father. 'Why can't 'ee be more like Tammie?' Dennis used to say, resentfully, as if everything she had ever done had been designed to spite him.

So was this the other side of the family angel? Was it possible? Nurse Carkeat, in her starched white cap, with her scrubbed-clean hands . . . Bustling round the wards, busy-busy, so efficient . . . Scuttling home to her attic hideaway . . . Unclipping her tight, white belt, fingers trembling with anticipation . . . Unbuttoning her cotton tunic and slipping off her sensible blue tights with quickening pulse . . . Stepping naked into her secret closet and emerging . . . Queen of the Night, a lady of leather, a vision in plastic . . .

Was this the *real* Tamara? Was this Daddy's girl?

Whatever would Florence Nightingale have said?

TAMARA (3)

Soon it will be night. I love the night.

Have some more chocolate, why don't you?

No, don't chew it . . . Hold it in your mouth a while and let it melt. Taste it. Savour it.

I can't taste a thing, you see . . . I have no sense of anything. I feel no pain, no pleasure.

None of us does, none of the souls here.

There are a lot of souls here, Sis. This house is full of souls. You may sense them. But you won't see them. Not yet. In time, maybe.

We have no sense of time, did I explain? We are in a place where there is no time. And no ageing. And no hunger, no thirst, no illness, no feeling of any kind.

Gets lonely though.

I suppose that's a feeling. Or is it simply absence of feeling?

It's so good to see you, so good to know you're here. So I guess we must feel some pleasure.

What are you thinking, Bri?

Has it upset you, what you've seen?

You look kind of shell-shocked.

What can I say? I am what I am.

I wish I could have explained it in my own way instead of you finding out like this.

But we all have our secrets.

There are secrets in these houses, Bri . . . Oh, nothing to set the world aflame, but secrets just the same. Secret goings-on behind the dark doors, the secret scurryings of hermit crabs, the fantasies, the solitary lusts and human longings. And there are horrid secrets here, sweet sister.

I love secrets. You know how I love secrets. We had so many secrets, didn't we? That's why I love these attic rooms, with their little dark recesses – hidden, cupboardy sort of places, tucked away under the rafters.

Do you like this strange and silent house?

I love these kind of places; where no one knows anybody else's name, or where they go, or what they do. I'm secretive. Always have been. That's what I love about the night: it's so full of secrets.

I've always loved night. I have this secret darkness deep in my soul, that I have always felt myself drawn into. I've always been drawn to the night, always felt I belonged to the night, that I came from the night and would go back to the night, and the other me that exists through the days is merely a shadow, a cipher, a pretend.

Something deep at the core of my being has always come alive in the night. It makes me feel anonymous, invulnerable, immortal. It frees my spirit, it makes my pulse quicken. Something breaks loose inside me, something gets off the leash, gets out of control. Something I secretly want to get out of control, something that's drawn to the black depths, something that's excited by fear, fear of the unknown, excited by danger, and the fear turns me on, makes my adrenalin flow, makes my heart trip and kick up a beat.

I have always longed for the night, and now I am trapped in the edge of night. Now that's all I have: approaching night.

Sit there and watch the light die. Eat the chocolate and think your thinkings, ponder your ponderings.

Has it upset you, what you've seen? Are you shocked, poor lamb?

I'm afraid a lot more things may shock you before too long.

Welcome to the world, sweet sister ... To my world ... The other world.

NEWLYN

Their grandmother passed away. Briony returned to Newlyn.

Her parents lived in a 1950s council house, high above the village and the harbour. She entered the kitchen by the back door. It was late afternoon. Her father's terrier, Jack, scampered in from the hall, barking and jumping up at her. She walked through the kitchen, into the hallway.

'Mum . . .?'

She pushed open the living room door. It was a poky little room. Her mother, Kathleen, was sitting in 'her' chair – the one that faced the television. Dennis did not approve of television; he refused to watch. 'His' chair was next to the wireless.

Kathleen's face was angled towards the fireplace; she was gazing at the empty hearth. A little heap of knitting sat beside her feet on the patterned carpet, and an empty cup and saucer rested on the vinyl-covered pouffe to one side of her.

The house seemed strangely silent. No more groans and gasps and soft moaning from that back bedroom, where Dennis's mother had lain these past six months, bedridden and half-demented. No more up-and-down, up-and-down for Kathleen.

Her gaze shifted from the hearth to the doorway, where Briony was standing.

'Tamara?' she asked, with just a trace of hope.

'I'm sorry,' said Briony. 'I don't know where she is.'

'Ah.' A little sigh. Kathleen's gaze returned to the empty hearth. An unexpressed thought settled on her face. An unhappy one.

Briony knelt down beside her and took her hand.

'I didn't know what to tell her,' Kathleen said. "She'll be here djreckly, Ma," I kept saying. "Be here djreckly." All she wanted was to see Tamara.'

'I'm sure she'll make it for the funeral,' said Briony. But did not really believe it.

Kathleen was upstairs, clearing up in the back bedroom where her mother-in-law had lived these past six months. Briony was in the kitchen, preparing her father's evening meal.

He would show very little grief over his mother. He was deeply religious, Dennis, but in a dour and introverted way. He seldom showed emotion or affection.

Shortly before six she heard the familiar exhaust note of his Reliant three-wheeler outside on the road; and then his plodding seaman's walk, approaching along the side path in no great hurry. He never did anything in a hurry, Dennis. 'Haste don't get'ee anywhear,' he preached. 'Slow and steady, that's the key.'

He walked into the kitchen, stooped to make a fuss of Jack, and then crossed to the Formica-top table without a glance at Briony.

'Right 'en, father?' she said, buttering slices of bread.

'Iss.'

'Purdy day.'

'Iss, 'andsum, he es.' He unhitched a small army-style webbing bag from his shoulder, put it on the table and took out an empty sandwich box and Thermos flask.

She lit a burner on the stove to boil water for his tea.

'Still hedging, out Botallack?'

'Iss.'

He was repairing drystone walls for a farmer up the coast. A trawlerman all his working life, he had seen Tory ministers and the bureaucrats of Brussels sign away his livelihood to foreign fleets; like so many Newlyn fishermen, he now did casual labouring jobs, anything he could find to make ends meet.

He took off his blue denim cap – stained with sweat and oil and fish guts. His close-cropped hair looked surf-white against the tan of his wind-bitten face. Of slim build and no great height, he had acquired a scrawny look in middle age. But he was muscular: strong in the back and arms. He wore baggy workman's jeans and a pale blue short-sleeved shirt – one of a pair that Kathleen had given him for Christmas, so long ago that Briony was too young to recall.

'I'm sorry about Nan,' she said.

'She's at peace now,' he said. 'That's all that matters.'

He picked up some mail that was waiting for him on the table and looked at each envelope in turn. The kettle came to the boil. She made a pot of tea. He sat down, put on his reading glasses and began to open the letters.

'Whear's your sister to, 'en?' he said.

'I don't know,' said Briony.

'Nan was asken for her.'

'Mum said.'

'Asken over and over.'

'I think she must be working out of town somewhere.'

He looked up at her, pushing his glasses lower down his nose so that he could see over the top. 'Whad'ee go to London for, 'en?'

'I went to see Tam. She asked me to.'

'So why didn't she come back weth'ee?'

'She doesn't know Nan died – because I didn't see her, she's not at the flat. Must be away somewhere.'

He had fierce little eyes, Dennis, so deep a brown they were almost black. He was glaring at her with an accusing look. It was a look she had become so accustomed to through the years it no longer unsettled her in the way it had when she was a child.

'Why 'ould Tam ask'ee to go all that way if she edden thear?' he demanded.

'I don't know, do I?' said Briony, pouring out his tea.

His eyes were still fixed on her, hard as drill bits; could have bored through granite with that look.

'Somethen wrong, edden thear?' he said.

54

'I haven't seen her, Dad,' Briony protested, 'so how would I know?'

'She'll be here for the funeral, I hope.'

'I'm sure she will if she can,' said Briony. 'I left a note for her about Nan. What else could I do?'

It was dark by the time she left her parents' house. She walked to Julie's cottage, on the outskirts of Paul village; she had not taken very much with her to London and it was all in one backpack.

A table lamp was burning in the sitting room and the light was on in Julie's bedroom, above. Perhaps she was reading; she would do that more and more as the autumn days became shorter and the weather turned colder. The rest of the house was in darkness and almost completely silent; just the ticking of the grandfather clock and the mewing of Julie's ginger cat, padding into the kitchen to say hello as Briony switched on the light.

She slipped the backpack off her shoulders and put it down. A large, old-fashioned kettle filled with water stood on the side of the oil-burning range. Briony shifted it on to the hotter of the two hobs and unhooked a mug from the dresser. She reached for a jar of coffee but it slipped through her fingers and smashed on the slate floor. Briony swore softly. The cat fled.

About thirty seconds later, a door opened upstairs, floorboards creaked and Julie's voice enquired nervously, 'Hello?'

(A hundred-and-one ways to address the burglar.)

'Only me,' Briony called back. And went to find the dustpan and brush to sweep up.

More creaking of floorboards and then the sound of Julie's bare feet coming down the uncarpeted stairs.

'What was it?'

'The Nescafé.'

Julie appeared in the doorway, wearing an unbelted robe of many colours, with baggy, batwing sleeves. It came from

Africa. An ex-dancer and topless showgirl, Julie had 'divorced well', as her cattier friends chose to put it. She had opened a shop in Penzance, selling arty-crafty and 'ethnic' things; doing her bit for the Third World.

'Gave me a fright,' she said.

'You thought I was a sex-fiend breaking in.'

'You might have been,' said Julie.

'Which is why you came downstairs in a supermini wrap, wide open, with nothing on underneath.'

'A girl can hope,' said Julie, 'even at my age.'

Briony sank on to her haunches and began to sweep up the spilt coffee powder and the broken glass.

'When did you get back?' said Julie.

'The train got in at half-three,' said Briony, 'but I went straight to Mum's. Nan died last night.'

'Oh,' said Julie, without expression. 'For the best, I suppose.'

'For sure.'

'How's Tam?' Julie crossed to the pantry and brought out a fresh jar of coffee. 'What was all the trouble about?'

'I've no idea,' said Briony. 'She wasn't there.'

'Kidding?' said Julie. 'You haven't *seen* her?'

'Nobody has,' said Briony, 'if one of her ex-fellas is to be believed. Not since before Christmas.'

'Well, there's a letter for you ... I don't know if it's from your sister. It arrived the same day you went to London.'

'Where is it?'

'I left it on your bed.'

Briony went upstairs.

It *was* from Tam ... Posted on the twenty-ninth of August, a whole week before she'd phoned. She had put the wrong address on the envelope – St Buryan, where Briony *used* to live; it was a miracle it had arrived at all.

She tore open the envelope. It was a thick letter, eight pages long, and written in a hurry, judging from the messy handwriting.

THE BEACH

This was their special beach when they were kids: this little patch of sand tucked away beneath the high cliffs – hidden from the view of the coast-path walkers and submerged at high tide. This was their secret beach, this was the forbidden beach. This was the weirdos' beach, as Tamara used to call them. It was such a climb – a hundred and fifty feet – and such an effort, getting up and down by the rough rocky steps that had been hewn into the cliff face, that there were never any holidaymakers here, no emmets; only dedicated sun worshippers, Tam's weirdos.

When they were children, they were fascinated by the weirdos: adults with no clothes on, grown women with no hair between their legs, men shadow boxing, making strange balletic movements with their arms and bodies, women paddling at the water's edge hand in hand with men sporting grotesque erections.

Strictly forbidden, this beach. That was why it used to be their secret beach. They came here on their bikes, any warm day, from spring till autumn. Lied to Mum and Dad. Kathleen was easy to tell fibs to but Dennis was the canny type . . . Fixed you with those hard brown eyes, looking for lies. Preacher's eyes, he had, always looking for deceit. He saw through you, Dennis. X-ray eyes. 'If you'm lyen I'll know, girl,' he used to say, 'and I'll give'ee some git poamen.' (Good hiding.)

They were the only ones at the cove who ever sunbathed with their bikinis on. Nobody ever spoke to them, nobody seemed to notice them . . . Maybe just a glance of curiosity as they walked across the sand, two giggly girls, obviously twins, with their backpacks full of fizzy drinks and chocolate bars and the precious tranny – with tapes of Van Morrison, the Eagles, Queen and Peter Gabriel.

This was their spot: just here, in front of this rock. This was *their* rock, their special sunbathing spot. No other spot was quite the same, no other rock, no other patch of sand.

Tamara was the first to take off everything ... She was always the first at everything. She dared Briony. Tam was always daring Briony. 'Come on, rabbit,' she used to say, calling back over her shoulder, as she ran naked towards the water's edge. 'Come on, rabbit,' she taunted her. 'What have you got to hide?'

Briony crept reluctantly towards the sea that first time: fifteen years old, her arms folded nervously across her chest, so self-conscious ... While Tamara was horsing around, up to her knees in surf, squealing and yelping, like a five-year-old in a paddling pool, and yelling, 'Come on, rabbit, come on!'

Briony sat on the rock – *their* rock, their special rock – this overcast September morning, took Tam's letter from her pocket and read it through – again – for what must have been at least the twentieth time.

Bri,

I don't know where to begin this or how to put it without you thinking I'm out of my tree. Things have got really bad. A terrific lot has happened since I last saw you – stuff I haven't been able to tell you and I can't really say in a letter. Not properly, explain it, I mean.

It all went really really wrong after I packed it in at the Hackney and tried agency work. I got in with this bunch of women who are ... I mean, there's a lot of things about me I don't understand – will never understand – but these people are just like not on this planet. Things have gone so wrong. I screwed up so badly and – I don't know how to start. Because there's so much we've never talked about.

There's this woman I met called Drusilla who works at a place called the Casa Negra. And these women she's involved with are all involved in this thing they call the Foundation. And through that lot I met this – I don't know what ... They

58

call him the Pastor. I can't describe him because I've never actually seen him – although I've been <u>with</u> him, or so they say. But I don't know what's really gone on. I didn't mean to get in so deep – it just started out as being silly one weekend but one thing led to another and I was a bit depressed at the time, things weren't going the way I wanted, so it was just kind of one stupid weekend, and Drusilla said do you want to go, and I said yes, so she took me along, and it all started out from that.

I got hooked on this whole experience, you see. You know the old stuff they used to tell us about drugs to scare us off – how someone smokes a bit of dope to see what it's like, and ends up a crack addict or on heroin or something? Well, that's sort of how it feels, being with him – this Pastor. It's like a junkie's fix. Starts out you think you can handle it but all the time it's taking you over. You think you're controlling it but he's really controlling you. It's just like that. It hooks you and you don't know it, so addictive, slowly getting inside you, taking you over till you can't say no, you want it so much.

It's the feeling after, that's the thing. Not during. It's afterwards that's the high. I can't describe the sensation. Gets to a stage you want it so much you can't stop yourself. And nothing awful happens at first. That's why it's so insidious. It makes you feel fantastic, out of this world. The ultimate make-over. You're no longer you. And I needed something at that time. They got me when I was down, I had no resistance. But it wears off – this fantastic feeling – and leaves you drained, really tired. Then you start to notice it's not just making you tired, your body isn't recovering like it should. The energy's going out of you but the body's not replacing it. It gets worse very quickly and by then it's too late, there doesn't seem any way of stopping it . . . Like a retrovirus that keeps on replicating, spreading from cell to cell, right through your body.

I can't explain, Bri, because I don't understand what's

59

happening myself. And I'm so scared. There doesn't seem anything I can do. Feels like my whole metabolism's slowing down. Like it does with animals hibernating. All the energy goes out of my body and I kind of black out. And I'm in a kind of dream-life where it's like I'm seeing everything through sunglasses and I don't have the strength to move, but the rest of the world's going on around me, ignoring me. It feels like someone's turned down the voltage in my body. And then suddenly I wake up out of it and everything's normal again. But they keep happening more and more often, these kind of blackouts and seem to go on for longer. It's like he's taking all the energy out of me, draining the life out of me. I don't know how.

There's this woman, Petra, I think must have been on to him for some time, because she wrote stuff about it – exactly what I'm saying – so it's not me who's cracking up or anything. But being in Italian I had to give it to this friend who can speak it because of some Catholic thing she was involved with in Rome once and she's going to try and make sense of it all. Once you read some of it you'll realize I'm not so crazy.

I went to this private doctor because I thought I might have something really wrong – like MND – 'cos of these blackouts. But I couldn't tell her everything . . . There's stuff I don't know how I'm going to tell <u>you</u>, let alone her. She's referred me to a consultant who wants me to have tests, but obviously they all think I'm bloody bananas. And anyway the waiting list's miles long – I don't even have a date yet. I was going to go private somewhere but these attacks are coming so often now I'm scared to leave the house. It's scaring me to death but no one believes me, I think they think I'm going out of my mind. I'm terrified they'll say I'm schizo or psychotic or something and section me, bang me up, fill me with drugs and stuff.

It's getting desperate, Bri, and I can't be alone, I've got to have someone here with me, and I don't know who else to turn to because that Foundation lot it's like I feel I've got enemies everywhere, there's no one I can trust. Can you come up and stay for a while, Bri – I don't know what's happening but I have to talk. I'm not working now so any time, day or night, just turn up. I'm so scared of these blackouts, I don't dare go out hardly, just essential things. Ring if you want but I can't always get the phone so probably better if you just come up here as quickly as you can manage. If I'm not here get Gloria to let you in and you just wait here at the flat. Something so bloody horrible is going on, but is it all in my head? Am I mad? Do come up, for Christ's sake, Bri, I've no one left I can turn to. Help me, please.

Love, T.

That night she said to Julie, 'I'll have to go back to London.'

Julie, she knew, would not be very pleased. Briony looked after little Beatrice most mornings, that was the deal.

'How long for?' said Julie.

'I don't know.'

'What's the matter with her?' Julie was referring to the letter. Briony had not told her anything about its contents.

'Oh, just . . . man problems,' said Briony.

Alluding to the thickness of the letter, Julie said, 'Must be a lot of man.'

'To be honest, it sounds as if she's having some kind of a breakdown. She sounds desperate.'

'But you've been up to London once already, and she wasn't there.'

'That's what worries me,' said Briony.

Julie said nothing.

'I've got to go,' said Briony. 'She needs me. She says she's got no one left she can turn to. I can't ignore her.'

Julie looked unconvinced.

KATHLEEN

The morning of Nan's funeral came. They sat waiting for the car: Dennis, scowling in his Sunday best, tight-jawed and righteous; Kathleen pale – wisht as a winnard, as they say in those parts; and Briony, holding her mother's hand.

Tamara had not appeared, had not even telephoned.

After the burial, the family gathered at Dennis and Kathleen's house. The Carkeats were an extended family, divided by money and religion. One side were north coast Anglicans, drapers and bakers by trade. The other side were old Newlyn stock, chapel folk, devout Wesleyans, descended from mariners and fishermen. The drapers and bakers were a pushy and outgoing lot. The Newlyners were quiet and clannish. The men shifted uncomfortably in ill-fitting Sunday suits, chatting in low rumbles. The women fussed with plates and teapots, warbling like pigeons. There was no alcohol; Dennis wouldn't have it in the house.

Everyone wanted to know where Tam was. Everyone pestered Briony. Tam was working upcountry, Briony told them, away from home, had not heard the news. But no one seemed to believe her. *Hmm*, they murmured to each other – little groups of women confiding, tutting, suspicion all over their chilly smiles – *Hmm*, they murmured, didn't even send flowers ... Granny's favourite too. Probably a little something for her in the will ... Won't be too busy to get her hands on that, no doubt.

Dennis sat in his armchair, wound up inside, tight as a bow string, supping strong tea and glowering at the hearth in baleful silence, with Jack the faithful terrier at his side ... Probably the only living creature that had never let him down. And then someone must have said something about Tamara just once too many times in his hearing, and he exploded like a stick of dynamite.

'Hush your gossep!' he bellowed, thumping the arm of his chair. 'Mother's passed, and my cheeld wadden here and thear's an end of un!' He sprang to his feet. 'I won't hear another word said about un! So hold your meddlen tongues, the lot of 'ee!'

He pushed his way across the crowded little room and out through the kitchen, into the garden. Jack followed at his heels.

An atmosphere hung in the room like gun smoke. Soft murmurs slowly returned to the gathering.

Briony went upstairs to get away from them all. She sat in the back bedroom. It had been *her* room once. Her grandmother's clothes had been laid out, neatly folded, in little piles on the bed.

She heard the door opening. She glanced round. It was her mother. Kathleen came and sat beside her on the bed. She touched a woollen coat that Nan had only ever worn on Sundays; smoothed her hand across the lavender-scented cloth.

'Don't know what to do with it all,' she said. 'Nearly new, some of these things. Hardly worn.'

Briony said nothing.

Kathleen took her hand. 'Don't take on so, my love,' she said, soothingly. 'He's a difficult man, Lord knows he's difficult. But he's had so many trials in his life. You know how he feels about Tamara.'

'Oh, yes,' said Briony, with feeling. 'He's never made any secret of that.'

'He has expectations, that's his problem,' said Kathleen. 'He expects too much . . . of all of us, himself included. So it feels to him as if everyone has let him down.'

'It's not my fault if I can't find Tamara, is it?' Briony reasoned.

'It's not just that,' said Kathleen. 'He expected more of her. When Mum had her big stroke and came here to live, Dennis thought that Tam would come home for a while and help

63

look after her. He expected that. More or less took it for granted. She is a nurse, after all. And she's freelance now, she's not working for a hospital any more. But she never even came to visit. That hurt him. That cut him deep.'

'I met an ex-boyfriend of hers in London,' said Briony. 'He thinks she's given up nursing.'

'Given up?' said Kathleen with disbelief.

'That's what Tamara told him.'

'When was this?'

'Last year, he says.'

'Then what's she doing now?'

'He doesn't know. He's been trying to find out, but none of her old friends from Guy's or the Hackney have seen her since Christmas.'

'But I've talked to her on the phone, must be a dozen times this past year,' said Kathleen. 'She would have told me if she was giving up nursing. Did she tell *you*?'

'No, she didn't.'

'Where's she to, then?' Kathleen looked directly into Briony's eyes. 'Is there anything you're not telling me? If she's had an accident or she's ill or—'

'No, no, she's not had an accident,' said Briony, 'not as far as I know, anyway. But she wrote me a letter. I didn't get it till I got back to Julie's last week. She says she's in some kind of trouble but I don't know what's happened. Something to do with a man she's got herself involved with.'

'She's not pregnant?' said Kathleen.

Briony shook her head. 'She'd have told me if she was. Her letter doesn't make much sense. But it sounds as if she's been mixing with some very strange people. The way she described it, it almost sounded as if she had a drug problem. She's been to a doctor, she said, and a private consultant, but she says they think it's all in her head. I don't know whether she's cracking up or what. I can't make sense of it. I'm going back to London to see if I can find her.'

'I never wanted her to go away,' Kathleen reflected. 'Not to

London. I could understand why she went when she was a student, in training, but I don't know why she stayed on after. It changed her, London.'

'But she's always been happier up there, Mum,' said Briony. 'She loves it, city life.'

'Does she?' Kathleen sounded as if she didn't believe that. 'Does she really and truly?' Kathleen shook her head. 'I think she's a runaway, at heart, in her secret heart. But what it is she's running from, and what it is she's running to, I just don't know. There's something wrong somewhere. I've never understood. Always was a queer side to that child. You, my love, you were always straightforward. Naughty but uncomplicated. There was never any side to you. Tamara, she's always had two sides. She's like the moon, I've always thought: there's a dark side and a light side, but we only ever see the light.'

Briony waited for her to continue, to explain what she meant. They had never talked about Tamara in this way. It was a family failing: no one ever talked about their feelings.

'She was so devoted to your father when she was a child,' said Kathleen. 'There was something unhealthy about it. He never showed you much affection, either of you. You didn't seem to mind. But Tamara, she craved for something more. She was always there, doing things for him – just silly little things, fetching his slippers, fetching his paper, bringing his tea – trying to please him. And it did please him. But it was the kind of devotion he gets from little Jack. A dog's love, he always says, comes without strings. It's honest. It's pure. And that's what he saw in Tam. It never seemed right to me. A child should love her father but . . . This was something else. She was desperate for affection. She'd do almost anything if he would only give her a hug or a squeeze. Even when she was such a little child, it all seemed wrong somehow.

'I found her one night – literally the middle of the night – wrapped up in his old oilskin storm coat – the one he used to wear to sea. She couldn't have been more than six or seven years old. She'd lifted it off the peg – Lord only knows how she reached. She'd laid it on the carpet, outside in. Taken off her nightdress . . . And rolled herself up in it, all snug and tight, like a Swiss roll. I found her lying on the floor downstairs like that. About four o'clock in the morning. I told Dennis about it but it didn't seem to worry him. He took it as . . . more proof of her devotion, I suppose. In some ways I think he encouraged it, even if he didn't mean to. Or maybe he did mean to . . . I'll never know quite what went on there.'

'How do you mean?' said Briony.

Kathleen's expression changed – as if she had suddenly realized what it was she had just said and looked frightened of its implications.

'What I mean is . . .' she began. 'I'm not suggesting for a moment . . .'

She didn't finish. She didn't even try to finish. And Briony could see in her mother's eyes that she'd let something slip, some innermost suspicion, however faint, that she had never dared put voice to. They stared at each other, mother and daughter, Briony sensing there was some truth that was being hidden from her somewhere, that had been kept hidden for a long time.

'Nobody ever says anything in this family, do they?' said Briony. 'Secrets and silences and atmospheres. That's all this family amounts to.'

Kathleen's eyes began to water. 'He's a good man, your father,' she whispered, with a kind of religious intensity. 'A good, *good* man. You know that.'

This happened all the time in their family . . . Whenever there was an emotional problem of any kind they brushed it away, like the crumbs from yesterday's breakfast.

'I used to think there was nothing I didn't know about Tam,' said Briony. 'Two halves, one egg, we used to say. I used to think we didn't have a secret in the world. But I keep finding out new things. I'm beginning to realize, in some ways, I hardly knew her at all.'

They sat there for a while, hand in hand, saying nothing. Mother and daughter. Two generations. So much hinted at, yet so much left unsaid.

DENNIS

Kathleen sat in 'her' chair. Dennis sat in 'his' chair. The television stood dark and silent, as it did most nights. His newspaper rustled. Her knitting needles clicked and clacked. Jack made soft whining noises in his dreams.

Shortly, she would go upstairs and get herself ready for bed. Dennis would follow later. Neither would say a word till morning.

Kathleen didn't mind the silences. She was used to them. It was his way. He was a complicated man, Dennis; full of resentments, bursting with them, grievances squirrelled away like acorns down the years, buried inside him, higgledy-piggledy, like odds and ends stuffed into a cupboard and never tidied up, never sorted out. He had stored up so many grudges and animosities that he probably no longer knew what most of them were about. He felt let down by life; felt he had done all the right things, had fulfilled his side of the bargain, but Fate had tricked him in return. His soul was weighed down with disappointment.

He was a good man, Dennis, an upright man, with decent values, with strength of character. But he inhabited a world of ghosts. His body was in one place, while his soul was somewhere else, and the two could not live comfortably together. He belonged to the old Cornwall: a land of fishermen and miners, of farmers and hard-working, self-sufficient folk. He lived by principles that were not fashionable any more. He neither drank nor smoked; he never blasphemed.

He believed a man should provide, that was his duty, his purpose in life, to provide for his family. But he could no longer provide. There were no jobs and never would be, not now, not on the scale there had been in the past. That made him angry and ashamed.

He felt defeated: both as a working man and as a father. And Tamara was the defeat he felt most bitterly. He had put all his love and hope into Tamara. Through her he had found comfort and consolation. Tamara had made it all worthwhile, the struggles and the disappointments. She had been the vindication of it all. Tamara had been his one small victory against a hostile world.

But she, too, had let him down in the end. She had deserted him, had turned her back on her family. She never came home for Christmas any more; she never even came for holidays. She had never visited her grandmother, who doted on her, had not offered to look after her – not even for a week or two, to give her parents a short break. She had not been here for the funeral, had not even sent flowers.

Dennis was grieving. But it was for *himself* he grieved. Of all his many defeats in life, Tamara was his very own, his most personal; his and no one else's.

THE CASA NEGRA

LONDON

Someone had broken in.

It would not have been difficult: the lock and the door frame had not been repaired. Briony had simply pushed the split timber and the lock housing back into position and re-tightened the screws. But it was not secure; one hefty shove would have dislodged it. And someone had done precisely that, by the look of it: the door was ajar and the lock housing was lying on the floor.

Briony entered cautiously. 'Tam . . .?'

There was no one there. She put her backpack on the bed and looked around. The note she had left for Tamara was still sitting on the table, propped against the candlestick. There was no sign that Tamara had been here. Her bag was still sitting on the bedside cabinet.

There was a note lying on the floor, just inside the door. Briony picked it up. It was a sheet of paper from a spiral-bound notebook, folded in half. She read:

Sorry about yesterday. Will try later. Sheila.

. . . That strange Irish woman who lived on the ground floor.

She had not come up to the flat the following day, as she'd promised. Briony had stayed in all day, waiting for her. The day after that, Nan had died and she had had to return home to Cornwall.

Briony looked at the door. Could Sheila have pushed it open? But why would she have wanted to?

She looked around the room, to see if anything had been stolen. The obvious things were still in place: the television, the video recorder, the sound system, CDs and cassettes . . .

She looked inside Tam's bag. Her purse and wallet were still there – the cash, the plastic cards, driving licence.

What kind of burglar broke in and didn't take cash or credit cards?

She opened the door of the secret closet and switched on the light. Everything looked exactly as she had left it.

TAMARA (4)

Hey, Sis.

Where've you been? What's been happening?

Did you go home? You look like you went home.

Did Nan die? I heard you on the phone the morning you left. Talking to Mum. I think it was about Nan.

What did they say when you got home? Wondering where I was, I suppose. What did you tell them?

Have you been gone long? I've no way of knowing, you see. I can't tell . . . We have no sense of time here where I am, in this other world. We don't feel time passing, not in the way you do. We don't feel anything much. We get no older, we get no hungrier, we get no wiser.

I've been burgled. You've sussed that, I can see.

Not that it matters now, I suppose.

No use looking . . . I don't think you'll ever discover what it was she took.

It was Dee. She was only in here a few moments . . . Knew precisely what she wanted.

I had to sit and watch her take it. There was nothing I could do about it. And she guessed I was watching, though she couldn't see me. She looked around the room, not sure exactly where I was and said, 'Sorry, Tam. But it's the way it works. It's a bitch, ain't it?'

And sort of laughed. But the thing with Dee – perhaps you'll notice, being the arty, observant type – she never really laughs. In fact, whenever she smiles, there's hardly ever any humour in it.

(Have you met Dee yet? You will . . . if you stick around long enough.)

Sheila came. She looked inside the room and left that note. I don't know what it says, Bri, I don't have the strength to move from here to read it. But ignore it, whatever it says. Sheila and I were victims together. She was helping me and I was helping her. But we left it too late.

Don't hang around, beloved sister. Don't stay too long. This is an evil house. It trapped me and it will trap you too. You won't feel them closing in around you. But they will. Please don't stay. I never meant for you to be involved. I needed you to help me, but it's too late now, there's nothing you can do to help me.

FOXY

Briony sat down on the bed and read through Tam's letter again.

Towards the end she had written: *I'm so scared of these blackouts, I don't dare go out hardly . . .*

So where was she now? And where had she been for the past three weeks?

Briony looked back to the previous page, where Tam had written:

There's this woman, Petra, I think must have been on to him for some time, because she wrote stuff about it . . . But being in Italian I had to give it to this friend who can

73

speak it because of some Catholic thing she was involved with in Rome once and she's going to try and make sense of it all.

This 'friend' she referred to must have been Sheila downstairs.

Sheila had said something about Tamara bringing something to her for translation. From Italian. Petra's book, she had said.

Briony went downstairs to the ground floor to see if Sheila was at home. She was not sure which was Sheila's room. She knocked on all the doors in the rear hallway, except Gloria's, but there was no reply from any of them.

Gloria opened her door and peered out.

'Oh, it's you, Bridey, dear,' she said. 'I wondered who was doing all the knocking. You just got back from Cornwall?'

'About an hour ago,' said Briony.

'Have you heard from Tamara?'

'No,' said Briony. 'She hasn't even phoned.'

'I don't think she's been back here,' said Gloria. 'She hasn't been collecting her post. I brought her letters in here for safe-keeping. Come in a minute. You can take them back upstairs with you.'

Briony walked into the room and closed the door behind her.

'Sit yourself down, dear,' said Gloria, crossing towards the kitchen, 'I'll get you a glass of something . . . Or would you rather have tea?'

'I think I would,' said Briony. 'Thanks.'

Gloria came back into the room, a minute or so later, saying, 'It won't be long. I still use the old gas stove, it takes a minute or two for the kettle to boil.'

She kicked off a pair of silvery slip-ons that looked like ballet shoes and put her feet up on a little, three-legged stool.

'So she didn't make it to your poor old gran's funeral,

then?' she said. 'You don't think there's a man behind it all, do you?'

'Is that what you think?' said Briony.

'Whenever a pretty lass goes swanning off without an explanation, there's usually a man somewhere in the background, in my experience.'

'Has she ever talked to you about her love life?' asked Briony.

'Do you know,' said Gloria, frowning and staring at some distant point beyond the window, 'I think the only fellow she's ever mentioned was that Charlie Stillman who turned up a few weeks ago – the day the firemen were here. She's got a slightly secretive streak, your sister. And I don't like to pry.'

'Slightly?' Briony echoed with irony.

'There's no sign she's been back, is there? Didn't leave a note for you or anything?'

'No. But *some*one's been in,' said Briony.

'In where, dear? In Tam's room?'

'Broke in while I was away,' said Briony. 'The thing the lock clicks into, that was on the floor when I arrived . . . And some bits of wood which split off the door jamb when the firemen broke in.'

'Ah, jeez,' Gloria sighed, 'anything stolen?'

'Nothing I can see,' said Briony. 'None of the obvious things, anyway. They didn't even take Tam's handbag.'

Gloria looked mystified. 'Are you *sure* someone broke in?'

'Well, I can't see how the lock fell off without a good shove,' said Briony. 'But whether they did or they didn't, that door needs to be repaired. Anyone can walk in there, the way it is.'

'I'll get my fellow, Jack, on to it,' said Gloria. 'He does odd jobs around the house for me. I don't think that anybody here would break in, though. Most of them are too bloody wet. There's a French girl on the first floor, Diane. But she wouldn't say boo to a goose. There's a couple of students right above me, Francesca and Amanda, but they wouldn't do a thing like that, they're very nice girls. They're at Queen Mary College down at Mile End ... doing something like zoology and Chinese. But they sit there in front of that bloody telly, nights, glued to *Neighbours*, would you believe? I mean, even *I* don't watch *Neighbours* and my own dear mother came from Melbourne.'

Gloria took a Senior Service from a fresh packet and lit it with her chunky Zippo.

'Then there's Dee,' she continued, 'but she's no problem. She's got the room right under Tamara's but she's hardly ever here. She lives with Misha, her partner ... I think that's what we're supposed to call them these days. Misha's Russian – or so Dee says. Tall, icy-blue eyes and Rudolf Nureyev cheekbones, she says ... she's a touch romantic, Dee, I think she exaggerates. But they've got a nice apartment by the sound of it.'

'Who's the girl in the room next to Dee's?' said Briony, remembering the waif-like creature who looked as if she'd been sniffing glue all day long.

'That's Miriam,' said Gloria. 'She's on benefits – every kind of benefit there is. I don't interfere but I suspect there's a little bit of a drug habit there. I wouldn't trust her much, but if *she'd* broken in I can't believe she'd have left cash in the handbag.'

'That's what I was thinking,' said Briony.

'Then there's big Tracey across the hall,' Gloria pointed disapprovingly, 'I wouldn't trust her any further than I could throw her – and she's no bantamweight. But if it was her, she'd have pinched the handbag, the telly and every damn thing bar the kitchen sink.'

'I met Tracey the last time I was here,' said Briony. 'With the woman who lives at the front. Is it Doreen?'

'Doreen, yes,' said Gloria. 'They're a bit of a double act, those two. Pinky and Porky, I call them. I don't know where they go, nights, and I don't want to know, but I suspect they've been acquainted with the back seats of more than a few cars in the Finsbury Park area.'

'There's another woman I met just before I went back for the funeral,' said Briony, 'I think she's Irish. Is she called Sheila?'

'Sheila Matthews? The room next to me?' Gloria pulled a face. 'She's gone a wee bit peculiar, dear. I think she's a lapsed Catholic and found God again, if you know what I mean. No offence – I was brought up a Catholic myself – but she sort of prays all the time. I hear her in there. I don't know what's going on. Always walking around with a Bible. And every time I see her she looks as if she's been crying her eyes out.'

'She told me she thinks she knows where Tam might be,' said Briony.

'Did she now?' Gloria looked slightly taken aback. 'Whatever did she mean by that, I wonder?'

'I don't know. Said it was a bit complicated. Said she was going to come and see me, but she didn't.'

'Well, first I've heard about this,' said Gloria. 'She's not the most reliable person in the world, it has to be said ... Told me last month she was moving out, but I haven't seen much sign of it these past few weeks.'

'She didn't look very well,' said Briony. 'Has she been ill?'

'I don't know, dear, but this house is full of people who don't look very well, if you ask me. Let's face it, it's no palace. The rent's dirt cheap by London standards and I only take women. So youngsters only stop here until they can afford better. And the oldies ... well, I don't mean to be uncharitable, but if you're living in a dump like this at forty-five, and all alone, then you're a no-hoper, and that's a plain fact.' She smiled and frowned at the same time – not unsympathetically. 'That sounds brutal, dear, I know, but it's true.'

Briony wondered what Gloria classed herself as.

'The other person I wanted to ask about,' said Briony, 'was Petra.'

Gloria looked lost. 'Petra ...?'

'Petra Pascali. Her name's on that strange mural on the wall in Tam's room.'

'Oh, my giddy aunt, *that*!' exclaimed Gloria. 'Now that's a funny thing to put on your bedroom wall, isn't it? Jeez. That ought to give you something to think about. What a thing to wake up to, eh? Is that still there? I told Tamara, I said: "What a horrible sight that is, darling. Get some paint and cover it up." But you say she hasn't?'

'No. So I suppose she must like it . . . If she's lived with it this long.'

'There's no accounting for taste, I guess,' Gloria sighed.

'So who was Petra?' said Briony.

'She had the flat before Tamara.' Gloria hesitated, frowning. 'Or was she the one *before* the one before? I forget, dear, they come and go, these girls, I can't keep track. She came from Milan. She was an art student – can't remember where she was studying. She was a very strange girl. A night owl, Petra, always out, nights. Always looked ill. Anorexic, I suppose they'd call it. Looked like a bag of bones. All she ate was rice. I used to say, you can't live on rice, darling. You'll end up a Chinaman. You need protein, you need a good steak, you need beefing up.' Gloria shook her head. 'But you've got to be strange to paint a thing like that on your bedroom wall, don't you think? Artists are funny buggers, in my experience. Too busy peering up their own fundaments, if you ask me. I had a husband who was arty and he was a temperamental old cuss.'

'What's it supposed to represent, that mural?' said Briony.

'Don't ask me, dear.' Gloria chuckled and coughed, loosening some bronchial congestion, by the sound of it. 'I suppose she had a grudge against the poor old Church or something. The look on that parson's face . . . He's a miserable old bugger, isn't he?'

'Did Tam ever talk about religion?'

'I don't think so, dear, no. Not her cup of tea, I don't think. Why?'

78

'She didn't ever mention a man she called the Pastor?'

'The bastard?'

Briony smiled. 'No, the *Pastor*.'

'Oh . . .' Gloria chuckled again and then frowned, thinking back. 'Well, not that I recall, no. Why?'

'It's just somebody that she mentioned once. She didn't tell me anything about him. I wondered if she might have got herself involved with some kind of religious crowd. I was thinking about Petra's mural, that's all . . . Wondering if there was any connection.'

'Oh. I don't know . . .' Gloria pondered the possibility but seemed amused by it. 'I can't see Tamara going all religious on us, dear, can you? She never struck me as the Holy Jo type. But I could be wrong, of course.'

'Maybe not the conventional kind of religion,' said Briony. 'Possibly – I don't know – a cult of some kind.'

'What, like the Moonies or something? Or that Bagwash bunch?' Gloria looked even more doubtful. 'I don't know much about cults, darling, but it seems to me you always have to follow the leader, do as you're told, become one of the proles. I don't pretend to know your sister all that well but I really can't see her getting involved in anything like that, can you?'

'I guess not,' Briony conceded. On the other hand, nor could she ever have conceived of Tam being a fetish freak. But it was true, most cults seemed to have no room for individuality. They all involved a kind of clone culture; getting integrated. Whereas Tam was her own woman, very independent-minded.

'What happened to Petra?' she asked.

'How do you mean, what happened to her?' said Gloria.

'I mean . . . She didn't die or anything?'

'Die? Lord, no. Not to my knowledge. What makes you say a thing like that?'

'Her name . . . It's on a gravestone in the mural. With a date.'

'Oh. Well, I expect that's the date she finished painting the infernal thing.' She gazed thoughtfully at the ceiling. 'Blowed if I can remember where Petra moved to. They don't stay long, the young ones. A year or so, then they all disappear.'

A soft whistling noise became audible from the kitchen.

'That's the kettle boiling,' said Gloria and pushed herself out of the chair. 'You'll find Tam's letters on the mantelpiece. Help yourself.'

Briony walked over to a large, cast-iron fireplace, inlaid with coloured tiles. The hearth had been covered over with the side of an old grocery box. Gloria had tucked the mail behind a clock that had stopped at ten past three.

'Half of it looks like rubbish, anyhow,' she called from the kitchen.

Briony glanced quickly through the letters: seven in all. Two looked like junk mail; one was a telephone bill; and one was from the Driver Vehicle Licensing Centre, Swansea.

Gloria came back into the room, saying, 'The garbage they push through your door, these days. I think about all the poor bloody trees they chop down for paper, and it makes my blood boil. Do you take sugar, sweetheart?'

Briony was puzzled by the envelope from the DVLC.

'Do I what?' she said. 'Oh, just one. Thanks.'

'To tell the truth,' said Gloria, going back into the kitchen, 'I prefer trees to people in a lot of ways. You don't get much conversation out of a tree, it's true, but trees don't get drunk, and trees don't go around mugging old ladies like me, and trees don't fuck up the poor old planet ... If you'll pardon my scientific turn of phrase.'

'Tamara doesn't have a car, does she?' said Briony, moving into the kitchen doorway.

'Yes, but it hasn't moved for about two months,' said Gloria. 'It needs a damn good wash, poor old thing.'

'I didn't realize,' said Briony. 'She couldn't afford one when she was at the Hackney.'

'I suppose she needed it once she started agency nursing,'

said Gloria. 'They have to travel all over the place. And they work nights, as well.'

'Where is it? Parked outside?'

'No, it's about halfway up the road,' said Gloria. 'On the other side. A white Mini . . . "Foxy" or something like that.'

Briony found it: F 68 OXY. Parked about fifty yards up the street. It was peppered with city grime. The windscreen was so dirty it looked as if the car had not been used in months.

She had Tam's bunch of keys with her. She opened the door and climbed into the driving seat. She tried the starter. The engine moved sluggishly but fired after a few turns, and started at the third attempt. The petrol tank was half full.

She sat with her foot on the throttle, letting the engine warm up, and looked inside the map pockets of each door. There was an A–Z street finder in the driver's side pocket. On the passenger side she found a plastic wallet containing the owner's manual and maintenance booklet.

The ashtray was full of crushed cigarette ends. There was a packet of Silk Cut on the shelf beneath the fascia. Briony gave it a shake: it was empty. Beside it, on the shelf, lay a book of matches. On the cover, printed in Gothic script – silver on a black background – were two words: *Casa Negra*.

COAL STREET

When she got back to the flat she looked at Tamara's letter:

There's this woman I met called Drusilla who works at a place called the Casa Negra. And these women she's involved with are all involved in this thing they call the

Foundation. And through that lot I met this – I don't know what . . . They call him the Pastor.

She put the letter aside and picked up the book of matches. *Casa Negra*, in Gothic script. And on the back, in plain Roman type: *Coal Street, London, E1*.

She looked it up in Tamara's *A–Z*. Coal Street was in Stepney; not so very far away. It was almost a straight line from Upper Clapton, due south through Hackney and Bethnal Green, towards the old docks.

She took a bus to Whitechapel that evening and walked to Coal Street from the Underground station. Coal Street lay between Mile End Road and Commercial Road, tucked away in a warren of cobbled alleys with names like Fowler's Yard, Ricket's Buildings and Dray Passage. It felt like something out of Dickens, all these poky back streets and decrepit old buildings, bunched together, hugger-mugger. Apart from a couple of pubs everything was closed and dark, and there was almost no one about.

Coal Street was deserted and poorly lit, a conduit of shadows, connecting Trinidad Way and Shadwell Road that ran down to the Thames at Wapping. It was about ten buildings in length, surfaced with cobblestones and just wide enough to take a small truck.

She walked up and down it several times. There was no pavement and barely enough light from the streetlamps to read the names that were painted on the boards in the doorways – company names, names that mentioned textiles, fashion, and fancy-wear. She saw job vacancy boards asking for machinists, Hoffman pressers and overlock something-or-other. But no board anywhere mentioned Casa Negra.

She walked into Shadwell Road. A black cab pulled over and stopped. Two people climbed out, a woman and a man. The man paid the cab driver, then he and the woman walked on down the road, passing Briony without a glance. The taxi was still stationery, the driver sat with his interior light on, transferring bank notes to a locked box at his side. Briony spoke through his open window.

'Excuse me,' she said. And when he turned to look at her: 'Could you tell me if there's a place around here called Casa Negra?'

He seemed to find that amusing. He pointed back down the road, the way she had just come, and said, 'Follow them two . . . Coal Street.'

'Are you sure?' said Briony. 'I was told it was Coal Street, but I've just walked along it and all the buildings look closed.'

'You'd better arst them two, love,' he said, nodding towards the man and woman he had just dropped off. 'It's not my kind of club.'

'Okay, thanks,' said Briony and turned to walk back towards Coal Street.

'You won't get in looking like that, though,' the cabbie called out, with a smirk on his face.

The man and woman were turning into Coal Street. She hurried after them and reached the corner just as they came to a stop halfway along and began to descend a flight of steps. They disappeared from view, below street-level.

By the time she reached the spot, there was no one there. A narrow iron staircase led down to a basement entrance. A painted notice on the wall read FIRE EXIT. DO NOT BLOCK. At the bottom of the iron steps was a large door. It looked like access to a boiler room.

She looked around to see if anyone was approaching from either Trinidad Way or Shadwell Road, and began to descend the iron steps. Not a glimmer of light showed around the edges of the door.

She stood and listened. She could just hear the dull throb of music inside the building, but it was barely audible. She could make out the white button of a bellpush beside the door and, in the middle, at eye-level, what looked like a security peephole.

She thought of pressing the bell and asking if there was

anyone there called Drusilla, but what was she going to say to her? She could ask her if she knew Tamara, that would be a start, but what if Drusilla said no?

She dithered. And in the moment of dithering she heard footsteps behind her. Turning, she saw a tall silhouette pause at the top of the staircase and then begin to descend. Steel-tipped heels clattered on the iron treads. It was too dark to make her out clearly but the woman was in black from neck to toe. It looked as if she was wearing leggings and riding boots and a tight-fitting jacket with a high military collar buckled at the chin. Briony couldn't see whether it was made of leather or latex, but it glistened and squeaked as she moved.

Feeling somewhat underdressed in her jeans and BHS zipper-top, Briony said, 'Excuse me, do you know anyone here called Tamara?'

The woman hesitated. Her face looked almost white in the darkness, but her lips and eyes looked black. She shook her head.

'Or Drusilla?' said Briony.

The woman shook her head again. 'Everyone's a Drusilla in here, darling,' she said, with a silly, skittish laugh. 'Who knows? And who cares?'

It was a curious voice. She sounded stoned. And American. And male.

Briony walked back up the steps and along the cobblestones to Trinidad Way.

JACK

She overslept.

Gloria's fellow, Hackney Jack, came knocking on the door at half past ten, lugging a big steel box of tools. The place looked a tip.

Jack said perkily, 'Don't mind me, gi'l. You go ahead and get dressed. Pretend I'm not here.'

He was about sixty, with a full head of silvery hair. A local lad, born and raised a hundred yards from the 'Ackney Empire, he told her, while she was sitting at the table, sipping tea, trying to wake up. Should've been a comedian, he told her, as he spliced new wood into the door jamb. Arthur Askey, Tommy Trinder, Monsewer Eddie Gray . . . he knew them all. His mother, God bless her, was on the stage. A Gaiety Girl. It was in his blood, the stage. But instead, he went to sea. They thought he was a comical chap there, as well . . . A regular comedian, this one, the Chief Petty Officer used to say.

She noticed the rope and anchor tattooed on his forearm.

Funny old life, he said. He said that about a dozen times.

He made a good job of the lock, anyway.

As he was sweeping up, he said, 'Any word from your sister?'

'No,' said Briony. 'Not yet.' She presumed that Gloria had told him all about it.

'Queer old business, eh?' he remarked.

'Gloria said you spoke to her a few weeks ago.'

'Yeah . . . Just in passing, like. I was walking out the front door as she was coming downstairs. She asked me if I'd post a letter for her, seeing as I was on me way out, save her the bother. It was a letter to you, matter of fact. I remember that.'

'When was this exactly?' said Briony.

'August Bank Holiday weekend.' Jack frowned. 'Can't remember which day for sure.'

'You're the only person I've met who's actually seen her in the past three months. Did she look all right? She wasn't ill or anything?'

'She did look a bit pale,' said Jack. 'But she always does. Working nights does it, I suppose. I said to her, you could use a bit of sun, gi'l, I said. All this night-shift caper don't suitcher. She said she'd packed all that in. Said she'd been out of work the last two months.'

'She told you she was working nights?' said Briony.

'She didn't need to tell me,' said Jack, 'I *saw* her . . . Well, I saw the car, leastways. Used to see it nearly every night. Parked down off Commercial Road . . . It's on my way home, you see, I live on the Isle of Dogs. I used to see old Foxy parked there, nights. I saw your sister one day, I said: "I keep seeing your Foxy parked down near the Royal London." She said, "Yeah," she said, "I'm on nights." But then last time I saw her, August Bank Holiday, she said she'd packed it in.'

'And she told you she wasn't doing anything at all?' said Briony.

'Well, I did wonder,' said Jack, 'because she likes to give her car a wash of a Sunday. I said to her, "Poor old Foxy," I said, "he's looking in need of a shampoo and rub-down – he hasn't moved for the last two months." She says, "I'm not working now, so I don't go nowhere."'

'And what is the Royal London?' asked Briony.

'Royal London?' said Jack, and looked slightly taken aback. 'It's a hospital. You haven't heard of the Royal London, Whitechapel? It's all done up now, enormous place.'

'And that's where she was working until very recently?' said Briony.

'Well, I *assume* she was,' said Jack. 'She's a nurse, after all, and that's the only hospital in that part of town. Where else is she going to be working nights?'

'Where exactly did she park her car, then?' said Briony.

'Nowhere you'd know,' said Jack. 'A street called Trinidad Way.'

MAKE-OVER

Briony was sitting at the dressing table. She was wearing Tam's bathrobe. The letter was lying open in front of her. She pulled a brush through her hair and looked at her face in the mirror.

She looked down at the paragraph about the Casa Negra.

> There's this woman I met called Drusilla who works at a
> place called the Casa Negra. And these women she's
> involved with are all involved in this thing they call the
> Foundation. And through that lot I met this – I don't
> know what . . . They call him the Pastor.

It sounded as if he was not a genuine pastor but . . . But what? Some kind of cult figure?

> I can't describe him because I've never actually seen him
> – although I've been <u>with</u> him, or so they say. But I don't
> know what's really gone on. I didn't mean to get in so
> deep – it just started out as being silly one weekend . . .
> Drusilla said do you want to go, and I said yes . . . and it
> all started out from that.

Briony opened the centre drawer and surveyed the choice of lip colours. She chose a shade that was vaguely aubergine. She pushed her face towards the mirror, stretched her mouth wide and smoothed on the lipstick.

What did that mean? Never *seen* him . . . but she's been *with* him.

With him in spirit, did she mean? In a religious sense?

Briony ran her tongue tip over her lips and studied her reflection.

And why didn't Tam know what had really gone on? Was it drugs?

. . . that's sort of how it feels, being with him – this
Pastor. It's like a junkie's fix. Starts out you think you
can handle it but all the time it's taking you over. You
think you're controlling it but he's really controlling you.

Was that why she had never seen this man, although she
was with him? Because she was bombed out of her brain on
something?

It hooks you and you don't know it, so addictive, slowly
getting inside you, taking you over till you can't say no,
you want it so much.

Briony ferreted among the different eye-shadows.

So addictive . . . Getting inside you, taking you over . . .
You want it so much. What else could she be talking about if
it wasn't heroin or crack cocaine or something of that kind?

Hard to believe that Tam would ever let herself get into
that state . . . She was a nurse, she had seen too many victims
and the damage done.

But then Briony would never have believed that Tamara
was a fetish freak.

But then she wrote:

I got hooked on this whole experience . . . that's sort of
how it feels, being with him – this Pastor . . . like a
junkie's fix.

She wasn't saying it *was* a drug, she was saying it was *like*
a drug.

It's the feeling after, that's the thing. Not during. It's
afterwards that's the high. I can't describe the sensation.
Gets to a stage you want it so much you can't stop
yourself. And nothing awful happens at first. That's why
it's so insidious. It makes you feel fantastic, out of this
world. The ultimate make-over. You're no longer you.

Briony brushed on some eye-shadow and thickened her
lashes with mascara.

She contemplated her reflection again. Her eyes were greyer than Tamara's; not much she could do about that. Her eyebrows were thicker too, but she wasn't going to pluck them down, just for a visit to the Casa Negra.

Tamara's hair was longer and a shade darker. She opened the bottom drawer and took out the two wigs. They were black as coal. One was long and straight and parted in the centre. The other was a shoulder-length bob with a fierce fringe that touched her eyebrows.

Briony took the long wig off its polystyrene head and tried it on. She ran a soft brush through it. She didn't like it: the hair was too long, it came right down to the small of her back, it looked too much like a wig. She took it off and tried on the shoulder-length one instead. It was not so very different from the way Tamara wore her own hair. Briony rather liked it; it quite suited her.

So, what could it be, this thing that was like a junkie's fix, the ultimate make-over, no longer you?

Some sort of spiritual experience, perhaps?

But that didn't sound like Tam. She was too down-to-earth. And then she had written:

It wears off – this fantastic feeling – and leaves you
drained, really tired. Then you start to notice it's not just
making you tired, your body isn't recovering like it
should. The energy's going out of you but the body's not
replacing it . . . It's like he's taking all the energy out of
me, draining the life out of me. I don't know how.

So it was not just spiritual, there had to be something physical going on as well.

Briony got up from the dressing table, opened the closet door and switched on the light. She looked up at the rail.

Something uncomplicated, without all those chains and buckles . . .

She tried on a short leather skirt. It was a squeeze – she was about half a stone heavier than Tam – but a manageable squeeze. She looked at her reflection in the full-length mirror on the wall.

She unhooked a zip-front jacket from the rail – a bomber jacket in black hide. That was a better fit.

She tried on a pair of boots – the ones with the lowest heels. She took the same size as Tam; boots were the easy part.

She looked at herself again in the full-length mirror.

What *was* this thing, this ultimate make-over?

Or was Tam imagining the whole thing? Was she having some kind of a breakdown?

She looked at the last page of the letter.

No one believes me, I think they think I'm going out of my mind. I'm terrified they'll say I'm schizo or psychotic or something and section me, bang me up, fill me with drugs and stuff . . . I feel I've got enemies everywhere, there's no one I can trust . . . Something so bloody horrible is going on, but is it all in my head? Am I mad?

TAMARA (5)

Still here, Bri. Still watching, waiting. What else can I do? I haven't gone away. I'll never go away.

I can guess what's going on.

You've found the Casa Negra, haven't you? Listening to you and Jack, I realized . . . Why did you ask where my car was parked? You don't know the East End of London. But you do know Trinidad Way, don't you? You've discovered it.

I did wonder where you were going the other night and what you were so busy looking up in my A–Z.

I know what's in your mind right now. You're tempted, aren't you? Thinking how alike we look. Thinking you could get away with it. Thinking you could fool them at the Casa Negra.

Well, maybe you could. But I don't want you to.

But I think you want to, don't you?

I'm watching you: you're like a woman who's looking at a box of chocolates and feeling guilty, fighting with her conscience, and wondering if she really ought to . . . While all the time she knows she's definitely going to; she's simply dilly-dallying, looking for the most appetizing one, the one that takes her fancy.

What is it, Bri? Why are you going there? What are you looking for? You don't have to do all this to go to the Casa Negra. What's the attraction? Are you trying to understand me, by trying to be me?

I don't want you to go to the Casa Negra, Bri. I don't want you to meet Drusilla. You'll like Drusilla. And Drusilla will be – oh – ever so pleased to see you. She's got a lot of notches on her gun, she's ensnared a lot of weak and unsuspecting women down the years, but I bet she's never hooked a pair of twins before.

The Pastor will be very pleased. Another me.

You'll like Drusilla, Bri. Drusilla will be oh so warm and friendly, just like she was to me. Drusilla will help you. Drusilla will take care of you. Believe me, my sweet, she will take really good care of you. Drusilla will help you. Drusilla will guide you gently down the same path she guided me. Drusilla will show you the way, will lead you through the darkness, will bring you to the edge of eternal twilight . . . And leave you there.

Don't go there, Sis. I beg you.

CASA NEGRA

She took Tam's car; she was too conscious of the way she looked to go by bus tonight, and it was raining, anyway.

She parked the car in Trinidad Way and sat listening to the rain drubbing on the roof, trying to psych herself up for this. She kept telling herself it was just a nightclub: the worst they could do was throw her out. In her student days, this was the kind of thing they would have done for a laugh – getting chucked out would have been half the fun of it.

It stopped raining.

She took off the flat shoes she had been wearing for driving, put on the boots she had brought and switched on the interior light to check her make-up in the rear-view mirror.

She got out of the car and walked down Trinidad Way into Coal Street, unsteady on the heels and the wet cobblestones. Her footsteps echoed off the dingy buildings on either side. It sounded as if she was walking down the aisle of an empty cathedral.

She came to the iron staircase. Hesitated. Now or never. Go down or go home.

She began to descend.

She stood in front of the black door and pressed the bellpush.

Nobody came.

She pressed again, keeping her finger on it a little longer this time.

After half a minute or so the door opened and a tall, heavily-built man peered down at Briony. He was standing in dim red light, not much brighter than a photographer's dark room. He looked like an all-in wrestler. He had dark, curly hair and a dense black beard. He wore a leather waistcoat over a bare torso and loose-fitting leather trousers.

'Tam?' he said. He looked puzzled, a little suspicious.

'What are you doing here?' He was Scots. 'They said you weren't coming back.'

She had come here intending to try to bluff it but her nerve failed.

'I'm not Tam,' she said. 'I'm her sister. But it's Tam I've come looking for.'

'Her sister?' the big man echoed. 'You're kidding me?' He grinned in disbelief.

'I was wondering if there was someone here called Drusilla.'

'You wanna see Dru?' he replied. 'Better come away in then, out the rain.'

She stepped into a bare, empty passageway. The floor was laid with flagstones. The walls were unplastered and the exposed brickwork was painted black. She could hear music in the distance. He made a little gesture with his hand, as if he was offering her the building.

'Go ahead . . .'

He couldn't take his eyes off her, couldn't stop grinning; seemed fascinated with the likeness.

She walked through a pair of fire doors and into a reception area, where a man in fisherman's waders and a rubber raincoat was signing a credit card slip, and a receptionist was retrieving an umbrella from a small room behind her desk. She was a slight, fragile-looking woman, dressed in long, clinging black ciré that covered her head like a nun's wimple. A jet of blonde hair spouted from a hole in the top of the hood like the plume on a guardsman's helmet.

When she had finished dealing with the man in waders, the big, bearded Scot said to her, 'Would you sign this lady in, Lisha?'

'Who, *Tam*?' said Lisha, as if she thought he was pulling her leg.

'Her sister,' said the big fellow.

Lisha gave Briony a funny look, half-smiling and offered Briony a book to sign, like a hotel register. Briony printed her name and Tam's address in Styles Lane. She wondered if they were going to charge her . . . She had glimpsed the credit card slip that the man in waders had just signed and it totalled sixty-eight pounds.

She pushed the register back across the table and gave Lisha back her pen. The big Scot said, 'Go on through, Tam. I'll let Drusilla know.'

He held one of the swing doors open for her. He had a big smile on his heavily bearded face. He didn't seem to believe her.

She walked through into another passage, about thirty feet long, with a stone floor and exposed-brick walls, like the entrance and reception area. The roof was low and arched. There was a door on the left-hand side of the passage with a symbol painted on it: the black silhouette of a leggy dominatrix with spiky heels and a bullwhip.

Briony pushed the door open, stepped inside and found herself in a women's changing room. There were half a dozen washbasins, a row of cubicles and a changing area with benches and shabby steel lockers. The light was better in here. Two women in black were standing in front of the mirrors at the washbasins, adjusting their make-up. One of them glanced at Briony and murmured, 'Hi, Tam,' her gaze returning again to the mirror.

This was going to keep happening all night long, Briony was thinking. This was going to get awkward eventually. She said 'Hi' in reply and walked out again, to avoid a conversation.

She walked the length of the passage to the next set of fire doors and into a very large cellar room, with a vaulted ceiling, like the crypt of a cathedral or the undercroft of a mediaeval building. It was packed with people. She wondered what she was supposed to do now. The lighting was so subdued down here and the atmosphere so smoky she couldn't see how the big fellow was going to find her again.

She wandered among the tables. No one took any notice of her. She was underdressed, if anything. Some of these people were wearing full-body outfits, with hoods and belts and restraints. Some looked like frogmen who had lost their breathing apparatus. Others were barely dressed at all – harnessed would have been a better word for it, criss-crossed with straps and buckles. To judge from the shapes that were squeezed into glove-tight bodices and high-waisted shorts, not all the women here were women, and not all the men were men. But it was so dark it was difficult to see *any*thing very clearly.

It was hot in here, too.

Slow, bluesy jazz was playing.

A lot of people were wearing dark glasses. She was amazed they could see anything at all. Some of the scantier-clad women wore little eye masks, like bandits. Others were covered by hoods that encased the head completely, like the ones in story-book pictures of executioners in the Middle Ages, with holes to see and breathe through.

Must have been so hot under there, Briony was thinking; must have been sweating buckets.

Some couples were dancing, although there didn't appear to be a dance floor. Others were just wandering among the throng, towing their partners behind them, on reins, like Nubian captives being paraded behind the victor in ancient Egypt.

She tried to imagine Tam in this place. What would she actually *do* here? How would she get a kick out of this – Tam who was so down-to-earth, so uncomplicated? No one seemed to be having fun at all, no one was smiling or enjoying themselves. How could they take it all so seriously?

There was a wide drinks bar at one end of this huge cellar room. Briony made her way towards it, easing through the crowd. Maybe this *was* the kick for Tamara ... simply being here, packed in among kindred spirits, wandering around, being both voyeur and exhibitionist. Briony approached the bar. There were several waitresses there, loading drinks on to trays. They wore very little – just a few fetishistic scraps; and small wonder, working in this heat.

Someone touched her on the shoulder. She thought for one moment it was another person mistaking her for Tam but it was a waitress with an empty tray. She had to speak with her mouth close to Briony's ear to make herself heard.

'You can't buy drinks at the bar,' she said. 'You want something?'

'I'm looking for Drusilla,' Briony replied.

'Right behind you,' said the waitress.

Briony turned around. The big fellow had reappeared. He was with a dark-skinned woman, minute beside him, but striking in appearance. She had a long cascade of tightly-curled black hair that could only have been a wig, and studded bands around her upper arms. She was wearing a leather basque and fishnet stockings attached to long suspenders. Her head was cocked a little to one side and she was studying Briony through large round sunglasses, an ambiguous smile on her face.

'Tam told me she had a sister,' she said. 'But she didn't say you were twins. You're the very image, isn't she, Con?'

'Spooky,' the big Scot agreed.

'Are you Drusilla?' said Briony.

'That's right,' said Drusilla. 'Why hasn't she brought you here before? Where have you been hiding all our lives?'

'Cornwall,' said Briony.

'Ahhh . . .' Drusilla nodded. 'Mackerelville. Tam's told us all about Mackerelville. Cornish cream and pasties. That explains this . . .' (Playfully patting Briony's hips.) 'What do you say, Con?'

'The image,' said the big fellow, 'but sassier.'

'Sassier,' Drusilla agreed, 'that's the word I'd use. A sassy lassie.' She held out her hand to Briony, like a teacher to a little child. 'Come down to the vaults, petal, away from all the hoi-polloi.'

She took hold of Briony's hand and led her, through yet

another pair of fire doors and down a curving flight of shallow stone stairs into a lower basement: a smaller cellar. The uneven floor was laid with irregular stone slabs. The bricks of the walls and the very low, vaulted ceiling were exposed, as they were upstairs. It felt like a mediaeval dungeon, something in the dank depths of a castle, but instead of cells there were dark alcoves.

Big Con had not come with them.

They passed several cave-like alcoves occupied by shadowy shapes. Briony caught glimpses of glossy latex shining in the candlelight. She saw figures sheathed in black from head to toe – not a glimpse of flesh, not even eye-holes; like bodies that had been dipped in black lacquer.

Drusilla found an alcove that was unoccupied. It was furnished with a table and backless chairs that had once been beer kegs. They sat down. There was a candle on the table but it was not lit.

The music was quieter down here.

Drusilla snapped her fingers and called out to someone who was not in Briony's line of vision: 'Crystal . . .!'

A woman came up to the table. She was about Briony's age; wearing a transparent body stocking and leather briefs, with heavy boots that laced to the knee and clacked noisily on the stone floor. Her head was shaved – even her eyebrows. There were rings through each nostril and tattoos on both arms.

'Look what just came in out the rain,' said Drusilla to Crystal.

Crystal looked at Briony. 'Hey . . . How are yer, babe? Where yer been?' She took a book of matches from a leather belly pouch belted to her waist, tore off a match, struck it and lit the candle. A soft yellow glow filled the alcove. 'Yer look'n great,' she said. She had a Liverpool accent. 'Yer pudd'n on weight. Whatcher been doing?'

'It's not Tam,' said Drusilla. 'It's her sister.'

'Yer what?' said Crystal. She turned to Briony. 'She on about?'

'I'm not Tam,' said Briony. 'I'm her sister.'

'Geddaway?' Crystal looked more closely at Briony's face, as if Drusilla had just said it was a wax copy. 'How can yer tell?'

'The arse on her,' said Drusilla.

'I'm Briony,' said Briony.

Crystal looked fascinated. 'Say again . . .?'

'I'm Briony.'

'Hey . . .' Crystal turned to Drusilla. 'That's frigg'n amaz'n. Even sounds like her.'

'Twins,' said Drusilla.

'She never told *me*,' said Crystal, 'the sly tart.'

'They say, when we were baptized,' said Briony, 'I was meant to be Tamara and Tam was supposed to me. But we were so alike, the minister christened us the wrong way round.'

'They do that where I come from,' said Crystal. 'But that's 'cause the priest's always pissed.'

'Wesleyans don't drink,' said Briony. 'They take the pledge.'

'So do our lot,' said Crystal. 'But they keep their fingers crossed, the lying bloody getts.'

'Hey, be a doll and bring us a beer,' said Drusilla to Crystal.

'Say yer name was again?' said Crystal to Briony.

'Briony.'

'Frigg'n amaz'n,' said Crystal again, and clumped away into the darkness, her steel heels clacking and scraping on the flagstones.

DRUSILLA

'Why did you come?' said Drusilla.

'I'm trying to find Tamara,' said Briony. 'I thought you might know where she is.'

Drusilla smiled. She had beautifully straight, white teeth.

'Why?'

'Because we've been trying to contact her.'

'We?'

'My mother and me.'

'Ah.'

'My grandmother died recently.'

'My condolences.'

'Tam hasn't been returning our calls. No one seems to have seen her for ages.'

'I meant,' said Drusilla, 'what makes you think I might know where she is?'

She had a dusky complexion – Eurasian possibly, or Middle Eastern; it was difficult to tell in this light. She had no noticeable accent.

'Tam mentioned you,' said Briony. She was not going to say anything about the letter. 'Said you were a friend of hers.'

'How did you know where to find me?' said Drusilla.

'When she mentioned you, she said you hung out at this nightclub called the Casa Negra.'

'Ah.' Drusilla was still smiling. 'Then that explains it.' Her tone of voice suggested she didn't completely believe it.

Crystal came back, carrying two bottles of lager and two glasses. She put them down on the table.

'But she didn't tell me you worked here,' Briony added.

'Work?' Crystal echoed, sarcastically. 'She couldn't even spell the word, her.' And to Briony, hands on hips: 'Person-ally, I think you're Tamara. But if you're not, where is she?'

'That's what I'm trying to find out,' said Briony. 'She seems

99

to have disappeared. None of her friends have seen her since Christmas.'

'Since Christmas?' said Crystal. 'Oh, that's bollocks. Who's her friends? She didn't leave *here* till the end of June.' And turning to Drusilla: 'Or was it July?'

'What are you saying?' said Briony. 'She used to work here?'

'You didn't know?' said Drusilla.

Briony was completely thrown. 'Doing what?'

'Same as Crystal,' said Drusilla.

'Waitressing?' said Briony. And couldn't keep the surprise out of her voice.

'What's wrong with waitressing?' Crystal demanded.

'Well, nothing,' said Briony, 'I'm a waitress myself. It's just a bit of a shock, that's all. One of her friends did tell me she'd given up nursing but we didn't have any idea she was doing this.'

'The money they pay nurses these days, you blame her?' said Crystal.

'How long was she working here?' said Briony.

'About a year,' said Drusilla.

Briony was lost for words. Someone called out to Crystal. She turned and clunked away into the darkness.

Drusilla seemed amused. 'You didn't know your sister very well, did you?'

'Well . . . I thought I did,' said Briony. 'But the last time I talked to her was in June, and she didn't say anything about having packed up nursing to come and work here.'

'It's really no big deal,' said Drusilla. 'She used to come here, anyway. This is her scene. She likes it here. It's the only club like it in the country.'

'Hanging out here is one thing,' said Briony, 'but what made her want to *work* here?'

'Money. What else?'

'You're telling me a waitress in a rubber bikini gets more than a staff nurse?'

'Don't blame me,' said Drusilla. 'I didn't vote the bastards into power.' She took a pull on her bottle of lager.

'She stopped working here in the summer, you said?'

Drusilla nodded.

'Did she say why?'

'It was only a casual job in the first place,' said Drusilla. 'I don't think she ever meant to stay for long. All the girls get fed up here after a while. It's hot, it's smoky, you're on the go all night long, it never lets up. Weekends we don't get home till dawn. A lot of girls only last a few months. So, any time you want a job . . .' Drusilla smiled. She smiled a lot, Briony noticed, but there was never any warmth in it.

'Thanks but no thanks,' said Briony.

'We could always use another Tam.'

'I'm not my sister,' said Briony.

She picked up the bottle and took another drink.

'Do you know where she's working now? Did she say?'

Drusilla shook her head. 'Just said she'd had enough.'

'She isn't in any kind of trouble, is she?'

'What kind of trouble?'

'A man perhaps? Has she been going out with anyone special, do you know?'

'Well, if she has, she never told *me* about him.' Drusilla took another pull from the bottle and added as an after-thought: 'She wasn't really the confiding sort, your sister.'

'You're telling me,' Briony agreed with irony.

Drusilla got up from the table. 'Look, I'm sorry I can't help. I've got to mingle, strut my stuff. But you hang around if you like, feel free. Enjoy. But don't be too surprised if people call you Tam and ask for a vodka-Martini.' She put her fingers to her lips, blew a little kiss and walked away.

Briony sat and finished her beer. After she had been alone for a little while, she became aware of someone watching her: a very tall woman, a few yards away, standing, staring. There was not enough light to see her clearly. Briony wondered if she was a friend of Tamara's and had mistaken her for Tam.

She was about to say something to her, but then the woman turned and walked away.

Briony saw her again as she was leaving: in the reception area, speaking briefly to Con, the big bearded Scot. She was a woman of striking looks: about six feet tall, with a long, slender neck, blonde hair, short and stylishly cut, high cheek-bones, a prominent jawline and a wide mouth. It was difficult to guess her age, for she was standing sideways-on to the light and her face was in partial shadow ... early forties perhaps.

She wore a plain leather skirt and jacket over a black silk blouse. Large silver hoops hung from her ears. She looked almost too elegant for a club of this kind.

Con held open the door for her as she left the club. He did not hold open the door when Briony left, but he gave her a funny look, as if he still believed that she was really Tam, playing games.

Briony walked back up the iron stairs to street level. A stretch limousine – black, with darkened windows – was parked about thirty feet away. The tall woman was bending almost double to step inside it. The driver was not visible. The woman pulled the door shut and the car crept away towards Shadwell Road with scarcely a sound, as if it was afraid of being heard.

Briony walked back along Coal Street in the opposite direction, thinking about Tamara working in that hot, dark, smoky basement, night after night. And not so much as a hint that she had given up nursing. It seemed such a terrible waste ... All that effort, all that studying, all those years of training.

She emerged from the dark narrows of Coal Street into Trinidad Way. It was a wide street but one-way only, north-bound. She walked up towards Mile End Road. That black limousine passed her, on the other side of the road. It slowed suddenly, almost to a stop, until it was crawling along at Briony's walking speed. She looked across the road. The offside rear window began to slide down, until it was fully open. No face appeared. Briony could see nothing at all in the dark interior.

The limousine kept pace with her for about twenty yards, on the far side of the road. She could feel herself being scrutinized. She was sure now that the tall woman had mistaken her for Tamara. Why didn't she stop? Why didn't she say something? Perhaps she was a friend; she might have had some helpful information.

As the car approached the top of the street, the window slid shut again. The limousine turned left into Mile End Road and accelerated away out of sight.

MIDAS

It was pouring with rain again by the time she got back to Styles Lane. There was no space close to the house; she had to park near the top of the street and walk down. She was drenched by the time she reached the front door.

She trudged up the stairs, wet and miserable after her evening at the Casa Negra. What was it that could have made Tam give up her nursing career to work in such an awful place? Drusilla had said it was money, but no one got rich out of waitressing. And it was such a horrible atmosphere down there, so dark and smoky.

She walked into the flat and stripped out of her wet clothes. As she did so, something slipped out of one of the pockets of the bomber jacket and fell to the floor . . .

A plastic card.

She picked it up and looked at it: *City Gate Cashcard*.

She picked up the jacket and felt inside each of the four pockets. She found some money – two twenty-pound notes –

and a receipt from a Link autoteller machine. On the receipt was printed:

11.36 22/08/95.
High Road Tottenham N17.
Withdrawal: £40.
Account balance: £40,373.95

She stared incredulously at that final figure.

Account balance: forty *how much* ...? Must have been someone else's receipt, a previous ATM user who hadn't taken the slip out of the machine.

She looked again at the plastic card: City Gate Building Society. 08–90–90. Ms Tamara F. Carkeat. Expires end 10/97.

Forty *thousand* ...? Tamara? That was ridiculous.

If it was a building society account there would have to be a passbook somewhere ...

She tried the 'toy cupboard'. The left-hand drawer was full of stationery and odds and ends. She rummaged quickly through them: rechargeable batteries, a small sewing box, pliers, screwdrivers, dressmaking scissors, a 13 amp plug, a couple of fob watches ...

She opened the other drawer. Behind the document files she had looked at before, she found Tamara's passport, medical card, trade union card, an almost-new cheque book for her NatWest account, several old cheque books and paying-in books, two passbooks for Woolwich Building Society accounts, and a long, white envelope with the City Gate logo in the upper left corner.

Inside the envelope she found a leaflet about the terms and conditions of the 'Midas' account; and some account statements. But no passbook.

The statements were quarterly. There were three of them: dated 9 January, this current year, 9 April and 9 July.

The very first entry on the first statement was:

10 OCT 94	CHEQUE / OPENING RECEIPT:	3,492.12

The final entry on that statement was:

09 JAN 95	BALANCE C/F:	17,126.47

This made no sense at all . . . In just three months, this past winter, Tamara had paid in almost fourteen thousand pounds. But this was the very time that Charlie Stillman had said Tam was having trouble making ends meet.

She checked the name at the top of the statement: Ms Tamara F. Carkeat, 88 Styles Lane.

The final entry on statement number two was:

09 APR 95	BALANCE C/F:	29,358.78

This was like something out of *Alice in Wonderland*. From January until April this year, Tamara had been paying in almost a thousand pounds a week.

The third statement covered the three months to 9 July. The closing entry on that sheet was:

09 JUL 95	BALANCE C/F:	40,905.87

A further eleven and a half thousand . . . in just thirteen weeks.

Had she stolen it?

Was she involved in some kind of racket at the Casa Negra? Was that why she'd left?

Was she dealing in drugs? Was that why she was in so much trouble?

Briony leafed through the two Woolwich Building Society passbooks. Tam had opened her Woolwich account back in 1986, when she first came to London. She had switched her savings to a different type of Woolwich account in 1988 and had closed it on 9 October 1994.

She had saved three thousand, four hundred and ninety-two pounds over a period of eight years. But in the nine

months that followed, she had put away thirty-seven thousand
. . . All of it while she was working at the Casa Negra.

Briony read through the terms and conditions of this City
Gate 'Midas' account. It required a minimum deposit of two
thousand pounds. Account holders received a quarterly statement in lieu of a passbook, were given a cashcard and a
cheque book, and cash withdrawals could only be made by
autoteller machine.

She sat and studied the statements in more detail.

Tamara had been paying in money almost every week:
never less than five hundred, and sometimes well over a
thousand, but always a round sum, and always in cash.

Interest of five hundred and eighty-odd pounds had been
credited on 31 March.

The deposits had reached a peak around April of this year
and had then begun to tail off. There had been none at all in
July.

Tam had taken very little money out, but three hundred
and fifty pounds was paid by standing order every month to
'Blackwall Properties'.

The rent?

These account statements only went up to 9 July. The next
statement would be due after 9 October – in a week or so's
time. But she could see from the autoteller receipt she had
found in Tam's jacket pocket that the account balance had
not grown between 9 July and 22 August. In fact, it had fallen
by nearly six hundred pounds.

July was when Tamara had packed in her job at the Casa
Negra, according to Drusilla.

Briony went to bed. But she couldn't sleep. She kept
thinking about the Casa Negra, and what Drusilla had said,
and all this money. Why would Tam have wanted to carry on
living in this shabby bedsit, having to share a bath and loo,
when she had over forty grand stashed away?

Another thing: why would Tam have left that cashcard in
her jacket pocket, with the forty pounds, completely

untouched since the day she withdrew it, 22 August? How had she been managing for cash since then? There was her NatWest account, but she hadn't used that in over a year.

She wondered when Tam had last used her credit card. She got out of bed, switched on the light and went to the 'toy cupboard'. She took out the document file in which Tamara kept her credit card statements.

The most recent statement was dated 1 September. The October one was sitting, unopened, on the table – it was amongst the mail that Gloria had kept aside while Briony was in Cornwall. Tamara would kill her for doing this, but still . . . She opened the envelope and unfolded the statement: the balance was zero. The card had not been used during September.

She went back over the statements in the folder. The card had not been used in August either. The last time the card had been used was 4 July: at Bethnal Green Service Station.

The card had been used only once in June: at Woodhurst Service Station.

DEE

Sheila had still not come to see her. Briony went downstairs and knocked on her door, several times a day, several days in succession but there was never any reply.

Perhaps she had assumed that Briony wasn't interested; perhaps she had taken offence.

Briony wrote a note, explaining that she was back from Cornwall and asking if they could meet, and pushed the note under Sheila's door.

The following morning, just before noon, someone rapped loudly on the door. Briony opened it, expecting to see Sheila standing there, but finding instead a diminutive figure with a perky, elfin face.

'You must be Briony,' she said.

'Right.'

'I'm Dee.'

'Dee who?'

'Dee downstairs. The floor below.'

'Oh, right,' said Briony, remembering now – Gloria had mentioned her. 'Hi. Come on in.'

'Gloria tells me you can't find Tam?' said Dee.

'That's right, yeah. Sorry . . . I didn't twig. I thought you were somebody else.'

'Like, ah, Tam?' said Dee.

'Well, that would solve a problem,' Briony agreed. 'Want a coffee?'

'Dunno.' Dee glanced at a big, chunky black watch on her skinny wrist. 'I'm supposed to be on the other side of London about ten minutes ago. Oh, to hell with it, go mad, why not? Just a quickie.'

She followed Briony up the steps into the little kitchen.

'Who did you think I was? Anyone interesting? More interesting than me?'

'Sheila from downstairs,' said Briony, filling the electric kettle. 'Do you know who I mean? Next door to Gloria's room.'

'Uhh . . . She the slaggy, thuggy one with the fat legs?'

'No, I think that's Tracey. Sheila's Irish.'

'Oh, no, right, yeah . . . I know who you mean. Looks like a lush, except she isn't. Gloria said she wants to be a nun or something.'

'Does she?'

'Is she trying to convert you too?'

'She was going to talk to me about Tam. Said she thought she knew where Tam might be.'

'Oh,' said Dee. 'Well, not in a nunnery, I'll bet.'

She was small and dark and boyish-looking, a little older

than Briony. Her skin was a mid-brown tone, possibly Anglo-Indian. She had deep brown eyes and her black hair was cut very short in an urchin crop. She was wearing dusty pink sweatpants, a matching zip top and white Reeboks.

'Sorry I didn't come up sooner,' she said. 'I haven't been back here for a while. I don't know why I bother keeping this place on, really. Waste of money. It's just for when I have a bust-up with Misha. Gives me somewhere to go.'

'Why? Do you fight a lot?' said Briony.

'Do we ever. I always walk out and come back here for a week. Then we make up and start all over again.'

The water came to the boil. Briony spooned instant coffee into two mugs.

'Misha doesn't like me working,' Dee went on. 'I don't know why not – Russian women work. Misha would rather I stayed home and did the Hoovering and cooked beautiful dinners and all that crap.'

She watched as Briony added milk to the coffee, then took the mug and went back down the three steps into the big room. Briony followed.

'What do you do?' Briony asked.

Dee sat in one of the armchairs. 'I'm a sort of assistant manager for a property and leisure group. Basically I just stand around trying to look demure – do I mean demure? – sort of cool and efficient and sexy, anyhow. And make sure the customers are happy. How about you?'

'Anything I can get. There's not much choice where I live. I mind a child three mornings a week. I keep a house clean. Do some waitressing in season. Barmaid. Whatever. Nothing very demure, anyway.'

'Stay in London,' said Dee. 'Plenty of bar work up here. Come here for the winter, go back there for the summer. Best of both worlds. Soon as Tam gets back, you could use my place if you want. It's practically empty – most of my clothes are at Misha's. You don't have to take it over . . . Just hang out there till you get fixed up with something better. We could split the rent fifty-fifty. How about that?'

'Don't hold your breath,' said Briony. 'Tam doesn't show much sign of coming back.'

'She can't have just vanished,' said Dee. 'When did you last see her?'

'She called me and left a message,' said Briony, 'about four weeks ago. Haven't heard a word since. I wondered if you'd heard her.'

'Heard her . . .?' Dee looked puzzled.

'Aren't you just underneath?'

'Oh, I see . . . Yeah, right. Well, I don't usually hear her. She's very quiet.'

'You don't know where she could possibly be, do you? Did she say anything about going away anywhere? Working out of town perhaps?'

'Not to me, she didn't,' said Dee. 'But I haven't seen her in ages. Maybe she's gone abroad. Agency nurses get around.'

'According to a friend of hers, she gave that up. Last year.'

'What, nursing? Who told you she gave it up?'

'Do you know Charlie Stillman?'

'I haven't met him, but Tam's mentioned him a few times.'

'He told me she left the agency she was working for ages ago. August of last year. None of her old nursing crowd have seen anything of her since before Christmas. And I've just discovered that she's been waitressing.'

'That so?' said Dee. 'Well, I'm not really surprised. She went through a bad patch last summer, when she was so fed up with it all. She hasn't been very happy in herself for a long time now, I don't think.'

'This is what I don't understand,' said Briony. 'Last time I talked to her, a few months ago, she sounded fine. I know she was pissed off with her job when she was at the Hackney, but that was last year.'

'She was more than pissed off,' said Dee. 'That was why

she went to see Charlie Stillman. She had a sort of nervous breakdown.'

'A breakdown?' Briony immediately thought of that last paragraph in Tam's letter, wondering whether she was going mad.

'Well, that's how *she* described it,' said Dee.

'When was this?'

'When she was at the Hackney. That was why they sent her to Charlie Stillman.'

'What do you mean, "sent" her? He was her boyfriend.'

Dee looked surprised. 'Is that what she told you?'

'You mean he wasn't?'

'He did fancy her,' said Dee. 'And they dated a couple of times, I think. But he's a shrink. That's how come he knows her. She was his patient. They sent her to see him because she cracked up.'

'His patient?' Briony said indignantly. 'He never told me that.'

'She had a sort of personal crisis, maybe that's a better way of putting it.'

'He didn't even hint at anything like that. Nor did Tam – ever, not at any time.'

'Well, what can I say?' said Dee. 'She's your sister. I don't want to upset you. But from what I've seen, she likes to give the impression she's in control, okay. She's a real control freak . . . But to be honest, she was a mess at the time we're talking about.'

'Which was when?'

'Say, uh . . .' Dee casting her gaze towards the ceiling. 'Christmas before last, maybe.'

'When you say she was a mess . . .?'

'Her words, not mine,' said Dee. 'She used to lie here some nights on her bed, crying her eyes out. And I'd just sit here and listen. Try and say helpful things.'

'But *why*?' said Briony. 'Why was she in such a state? What had gone wrong?'

'Everything – so Tam said. She had a crisis of confidence. Didn't think she was cut out to be a nurse. Didn't think she was a very nice person. She was on a real downer about herself.'

Briony was pole-axed. Where had all this suddenly sprung from? Why had Tam never even given her a hint that all this had gone on?

'How come Charlie Stillman didn't tell me this when I saw him?' she said.

'Don't ask me,' said Dee. 'He was pretty keen on her – or so Tam made out. So maybe he's got his own agenda.'

'I didn't like him when I met him,' said Briony. 'He was a patronizing sod. And sarcastic. But I thought he was being frank and honest, at least.'

'If he was so frank and honest,' said Dee, 'why didn't he tell you he was her shrink?'

'I specifically asked him if he had any idea what was wrong, what sort of trouble she might be in, why she'd left this hysterical message for me,' said Briony, 'and he said he had no idea.'

Dee glanced across to the oval dining table, where Tamara's mail sat propped up against the candleholder.

'Is that post? For Tam?'

Briony nodded.

'Why don't you open it?'

'I don't think she'd like that,' said Briony. 'She's a bit fussy about things like that. Likes her privacy.'

'But there might be something there that'll give you an idea where she is,' said Dee, 'or where she's been. Credit card statements tell you loads of things.'

'I've already opened her credit card statement,' Briony confessed.

'And?'

'She didn't use it once in September. Which is not too surprising, I guess, because her credit card has been sitting over there in her handbag for the past five weeks – along with her wallet, her bank card, her cheque book and her house keys.'

'Her *keys?*' said Dee, and looked puzzled. 'Well, that is kind of weird.'

After Dee had left, Briony opened Tam's mail. It was not very interesting: something from a charity called Child Action in India; some information from the London Borough of Hackney on housing and council tax benefit; a mail-shot from Littlewoods, promoting their winter catalogue; a telephone bill; and a letter in a crisp white envelope from Proctor and Harding, estate agents. The letter read:

Dear Ms Carkeat,
I am writing to confirm that the super-compact, one-bedroom properties at Frye's Wharf have now been reduced to £84,500. Further to our telephone conversation last month, there should be no difficulty in arranging a mortgage facility of £40,000 for you, subject to status, if the City Gate Building Society are unable to assist. I look forward to hearing from you soon.
Yours sincerely.

It was signed, Marcus Hayman.
Enclosed with the letter was a leaflet, displaying an artist's impression of the new Frye's Wharf development on the Thames, and a sketched groundplan of the 'super-compact, City Single' one-bedroom flats.
Eighty-four and a half thousand . . .
So this was what she was planning to do with the forty thousand she had stashed away.
Even so, a forty-thousand-pound mortgage was going to take some paying off. Tam had obviously expected to go on making big money for the foreseeable future.
Briony looked at the telephone bill. Three long-distance calls were listed on the itemized account. One was to her

parents in Newlyn, dated 18 June – her mother's birthday. The other calls were both to the same number, both in July. The number was described on the itemized account as 'Woodhurst'.

She had seen that name just recently – on Tam's credit card statement for June. Woodhurst Service Station.

She went to the 'toy cupboard' and took Tamara's address book from the right-hand drawer. She sat down at the table and worked her way through the entire book. But the number wasn't there. And there was no address in Woodhurst.

She remembered a pocket diary in Tam's bag. She got up, walked over to where the bag was sitting on the bedside cabinet, took out the diary and flipped through it to several pages of telephone numbers at the very back. She sat down on the bed and ran her fingertip down the numbers from the top of each page to the bottom.

She found it: the Woodhurst number that was on the itemized account. And beside it, in Tam's tidy writing: *Leysholme*. That was all.

Leysholme . . . Sounded very like the name that Sheila had mentioned.

But where was Woodhurst?

There was a small bookcase along the wall beneath the middle dormer window. The upper shelf was packed with titles like *Go Softly, My Heart*, and *So Tender, So Cruel*, the kind of fat paperback romances that Tamara often devoured in late-night sittings. On the lower shelf, she found a mail-order catalogue of fetish wear, some glossy German magazines for *aficionados* of the slaves-and-masters scene, and a large, floppy road atlas of Britain.

She searched for Woodhurst in the index. It was in Kent.

She turned to the map. Woodhurst was nowhere in particular: in the middle of a green blot marked Ashdown Forest near the Sussex/Kent border, about thirty-five miles south of London.

WOODHURST

Woodhurst looked like a toy village. It was built around a crossroads, with a green, a pond and a war memorial. It had a church with a spire; one main street lined with terraces of small shops on each side, shops with bulging, half-timbered walls and bow-fronted windows; a coaching inn with an ostler's yard; and a lot of cross-country vehicles, heavily armoured with bull bars.

Briony braked to a halt at the crossroads and studied a four-way signpost. One of the arms pointed to Chelbrook Cross, eight miles, and Upper Leysholme, five miles.

She had no clear idea where she was going. Tamara had listed that Woodhurst phone number simply as 'Leysholme'. She could not remember exactly what Sheila had said. It had stuck in her memory that Leysholme was a house, but whether it was the name of the house or the place where the house was located, she had no idea.

She took the road that was signposted 'Upper Leysholme'. Beyond the village bounds, the road narrowed and wound its way through farming country, past orchards and paddocks, stud farms and large, redbrick country houses.

Upper Leysholme was a hamlet so small and scattered that she had no idea she was passing through it until she saw a sign by the road, reading: UPPER LEYSHOLME FARM STABLES. She slowed down and turned on to an unsurfaced track which snaked left and right for about half a mile and broadened out into the stable yard. A group of children were dismounting from ponies. Briony walked over to a buxom woman in tight breeches and an old army sweater and asked her if she knew of a house called Leysholme.

The woman said she could tell her precisely where the house was, but it was not visible from the road and there was nothing at the entrance to say that it was Leysholme, so she might have the devil's own job finding it. She gave Briony directions. They involved a sequence of lefts and rights, a burned-out barn and a hand-chalked sign offering potatoes at ten pence a pound.

'It's about a mile away,' she said. 'It's a bit of a monstrosity. I've only seen it once and that was from the other side of the woods ... There's a bridle path from Halfpenny Down that goes round the back of the place.'

'What is it?' asked Briony. 'A private house?'

'Used to be,' said the woman in breeches. 'Belonged to Lord someone-or-other, a long time ago. Then it became a public school. Then it was an orphanage. I don't know who lives there now, but I wouldn't want their heating bills in winter.'

Briony thanked her, got back in the car and bounced back up the winding track to the lane.

She found the burned-out barn and the sign offering spuds at ten pence a pound. The entrance to Leysholme looked like the entrance to a field. There was a gap in the hedgerow where there had once been a gate – the gateposts were still in place. Beyond it, a cart track descended a short hill, crossed a stream and disappeared into woods.

Briony left the Mini parked on a strip of grass verge and walked down the track. There was no bridge but the stream was so shallow that she could walk through it and scarcely get her shoes wet.

The track curved uphill through beech woods. The woman in breeches was right: it looked as if it went nowhere very much, this path. But where the wood ended she came to two tall, stone pillars, supporting wrought-iron gates that were open wide. Beyond the gates, the track became a gravel driveway. A sign reading 'private property' had fallen down and lay almost hidden from sight in long grass.

She was now entering the walled grounds of a very large house. The driveway curved around the side and straight across the front of the house, with open pasture to the left.

The house looked late Georgian; it had those elegant, neoclassical lines. It was built of red brick, on five floors, and almost of stately home proportions.

The grounds looked badly neglected. She could see no gardens to speak of ... Just rough pasture on one side and a dense-looking shrubbery to the rear. It looked like a plantation that had been left to run wild.

She came to a portico, with four Grecian-style columns and a flight of shallow stone steps leading up to the double doors of the main entrance. It was in a poor state of repair. Weeds and grass were growing in profusion out of cracks in the steps, and the front doors were badly in need of a coat of paint.

Interior shutters had been closed over some of the windows on the ground floor, as if certain rooms had been closed up. There were no curtains visible at any of the windows.

There were no parked cars, nobody in sight. The whole place looked deserted.

Perhaps she had got the wrong house. There was nothing to say that this was Leysholme ... There was nothing to say *what* it was.

She turned around and walked back the way she had come.

She got back into the car and drove in the direction that she thought would take her back to Woodhurst. But she got lost. She seemed to be turning back on herself in a wide arc. After a mile or so, she came to a crossroads. Woodhurst was not even mentioned ... But Halfpenny Down was.

The woman at the stables had said something about a bridle path from Halfpenny Down that went through woods at the back of Leysholme. Briony followed the sign towards Halfpenny Down but she had no idea what she was looking for – there were woods everywhere, all around her; it was that kind of countryside.

She stopped and studied Tamara's road atlas but the map was too small a scale. She drove on until she saw a tractor parked in a field entrance, where two men were hefting large rolls of fencing wire from the back of a trailer. She stopped, got out of the car and asked them if they knew Halfpenny Down and the woods behind Leysholme.

They pointed to some trees in the distance. She was not very far away.

'You don't know who lives there, do you?' said Briony.

'I don't think anyone does except the housekeeper,' one of the men replied. 'Some say it belongs to a property company and they're keeping it empty till the market picks up and they can find a buyer.'

'Everyone round here says something different,' said the other man. 'I've heard it's going to be a hotel ... a health farm ... a country club ... all bloody sorts. Take your pick.'

'Why are you asking?' said the first man, adding facetiously: 'You want to buy the place?'

Briony smiled. 'No thanks. I don't fancy mowing that front lawn every few weeks.'

She got back into the car and drove on towards the woods. She came to the bridle path, at the point where it crossed the road from Halfpenny Down on one side, into the woods on the other.

There was a pull-in area at the side of the road, partly occupied by a pile of winter grit. There was just room enough to park the Mini. She got out of the car and walked along the bridle path. It kept close to the edge of the woods, where there were fewer trees and it was lighter. The darker, denser side was private property, fenced off with wire. Every now and again she came across the rotten remains of a notice, reading: 'Private – Keep Out'.

There was a point where the fencing posts had rotted away and fallen down, and the wire was no longer visible. She walked across dry undergrowth into the private part of the woods and towards the clearing, where several trees had been felled and the ground was scattered with logs.

She could see the house from this clearing, but only the upper storeys, for she was climbing a slight incline at this point towards a woodland ridge, and the house was at a lower level, in the distance.

She walked on towards the ridge. It was very quiet just here; the occasional snatch of birdsong, that was all. The trees were so close together and so tall that almost no sunlight filtered through the canopy above and there was very little green on the forest floor; only lichens and small ferns. The ground was matted with dry twigs and the husks of beech nuts. The air smelt pleasantly of leaf mould.

She came to the crest of the ridge. On the other side the wood began to thin out and undulate gently down towards a large area of overgrown lawn at the rear of the house and a semi-cultivated area that looked as if it might once have been a kitchen garden.

She saw someone through the trees: a woman, walking up into the woods from the direction of the house . . . A tall woman with a dog . . . Two dogs . . .

Briony stepped behind a tree and watched.

The woman was still some way away but Briony recognized her from the Casa Negra club: it was the woman with short blonde hair who had stared at her in that sub-basement cellar – the woman she had seen driven away in the back of a stretch limousine.

She was not walking with any purpose. She was almost idling. She was dressed in what looked like ski pants and a belted leather jacket with a fur collar and a matching pillbox cap. She looked too chic to be English. Scandinavian perhaps.

The dogs were large, strange-looking animals; crossbreeds by the look of them.

They were still some distance away but she did not want to have a confrontation: the woman would recognize her at once and Briony could hardly say she had strayed here by accident. She turned and walked back towards the ridge, as quickly and quietly as she could. Once she was out of sight of the dogs, she worried less about the twigs cracking beneath her feet and broke into a gentle jog down the more thickly wooded slopes towards the clearing.

But then she saw someone else . . .

Another woman – in the middle of the clearing, sitting on a pile of logs, observing her. A woman in a tweed jacket, pink jumper and brown slacks, with a headscarf knotted beneath her chin.

Briony skidded to a halt on the wet, slippery path. She was astonished: it was Sheila. Sheila from Styles Lane.

She was staring at Briony with a hint of panic in her eyes.

'Sheila . . .?' said Briony.

If anything, the panic in Sheila's expression intensified.

'Sheila?' Briony said again, baffled now as to why Sheila was looking at her in this extraordinary way. 'Sheila, don't you recognize me? It's Briony – Tamara's sister. Whatever's wrong?'

'What are you doing here?' said Sheila, her face creased with anxiety. 'For God's sake, go . . . Don't let them see you, in heaven's name.' And when Briony simply stood there, bewildered, Sheila continued: 'Get out of here! There's nothing you can do!'

She sounded demented.

'Sheila . . .?' said Briony, approaching her cautiously. 'What's the matter? You were going to come and see me. I had to go back to Cornwall for a couple of weeks – my grandma died. You were going to talk to me about Tam. You were going to tell me about this place, about Leysholme, you said. And the Pastor.'

At that moment the dogs began to bark. Briony turned and looked back towards the ridge. She couldn't see the dogs but the barking was heading in her direction.

'You must go, you've got to go,' Sheila pleaded. 'Don't let her see you here . . . I promised I wouldn't say any more, I promised! I did a deal. They said they'd help me . . . help me control it. That's why I'm here. But if they see me talking to you – if they even *see* you here – God knows what they'll do.'

The dogs were growing louder, getting closer.

'Sheila, what *is* the matter?' said Briony. 'What are you talking about? What deal? They'll help you control what?'

'Just go! Run, get out of here, in God's holy name!' Sheila bleated. 'Never, never come near this place again!'

The barking was getting closer and closer. Briony was worried about Sheila and didn't want to leave her here in such a distressed state, but she was clearly making everything worse simply by her presence.

'Okay, I'm going, I'm going,' said Briony. 'I don't understand what's wrong but it's okay, I'll go.'

She ran towards the gap in the wire fencing, where she had crossed over from the bridle path. When she got there she looked back. She could see the clearing but she could no longer see Sheila.

The dogs had stopped barking. They were nowhere in sight. Nor was the tall, blonde woman.

Briony stood watching the clearing for several minutes. She looked through the trees towards the ridge. Not a glimpse of anyone, not a sound.

She still felt bad about running away and abandoning Sheila.

She stood watching and waiting for a few more minutes, and then she crossed the boundary fence again and walked back towards the clearing.

Sheila was nowhere to be seen. She had completely vanished. Briony looked around in bewilderment. She had been watching. Where could Sheila have gone?

She must have been so frightened that she ran away as well, while Briony's back was turned.

But then she noticed . . .

She couldn't quite believe it: Sheila's clothes. They were lying on the ground in an untidy muddle. They were definitely the clothes that Sheila was wearing . . . The tweed jacket, the pink jumper, brown slacks, her headscarf . . . Even her muddy brown shoes and socks.

Now the dogs started barking again. This time Briony saw them – at the peak of the ridge and coming towards her. She ran back to the gap in the boundary wire and along the bridle path until she came to the road.

She sat in the car for a while, getting her breath back.

What a weird woman ... What was she blathering on about: doing deals, making promises not to say any more?

They'd help her control *what*?

Gloria had said she was peculiar ...

Peculiar was the understatement of the year. The poor creature was stark, staring mad.

THE RENT

A week passed by. Sheila did not come up to see her or leave a note. And she was never there when Briony knocked on her door, day or evening. Briony wondered if she was simply avoiding her, refusing to come to the door, after that incident in the woods at Leysholme.

One evening, just as it was getting dark, Briony went downstairs and walked around the side of the house to see if there was a light on in Sheila's room. The garden had become so overgrown that the only way through was by keeping close to the walls.

She passed the window of Tracey's room. Tracey was sitting half-naked in front of a mirror, making up her eyes. Briony could hear her radio – some sort of jangling disco music.

She pushed on, past another dark window, and came to the back of the house. She was not sure which was Sheila's room ... It was such an odd shape, this building, there were so many protruding bays and diagonal windows at the corners. She came to another window, where the room was almost in darkness. The only light was coming from a small television. The curtains were partly drawn. She peered through the window. She could make out a woman in an armchair, watching the television. But it was not Sheila. And, anyway, Sheila's room was next to Gloria's.

She walked around to the side of the house that faced east, towards the marshes, until she came to Gloria's flat. The lights were on in there. She could see Gloria and her fellow, Jack, the odd-job man. He was wearing a suit but the jacket was lying over the back of a chair. His tie was loose and the collar of his white shirt unbuttoned. He was standing in the middle of the room, opening a bottle of wine. He must have been telling one of his funny stories because Gloria was sitting forwards on the edge of her armchair, cigarette in hand, laughing and coughing – that phlegmy smoker's cough she had.

Briony retraced her steps to the window that belonged to the neighbouring room. This was Sheila's room. She looked in through the window. It looked like an empty hotel room: just a few pieces of furniture but no personal belongings anywhere, no clothes, no books . . . And the bed was stripped; just a bare mattress.

Had she moved out? Surely she wouldn't have left without leaving a note or saying something?

Briony went back upstairs.

Gloria had said something about Sheila 'finding God again'. Briony wondered if that had anything to do with the Pastor and the Foundation that Tamara wrote about in her letter. Perhaps she had got herself involved in some kind of wacky religious sect or cult. Perhaps that was who owned Leysholme. Perhaps that was what Petra Pascali's mural was all about.

Briony went down to see Gloria the following day.

It was after ten in the morning but she was still wearing her nightgown. Her absurdly blonde hair was pinned up in a heap on top of her head; a few small ringlets hung down at the side. She was holding a small plate on the palm of one hand and a triangle of toast between finger and thumb of the other hand.

'Bridey, dear . . .' she said, pleasantly surprised. 'An uncanny sense of timing, if I may say so.' And, ushering her into the smoke-filled room: 'You've come to tell me that young Tamara's back, I hope?'

'I wish I had,' said Briony. 'I've come to ask you about Sheila, actually.'

'Sheila who, dear?'

'Sheila here.' Briony pointed next door.

'Oh, her,' said Gloria disparagingly. 'She's in my bad books, dear. She's cleared off. Gone . . . And not so much as by-your-leave. No notice, nothing. Didn't even say goodbye. How d'you like that?'

'But when?'

'A few days ago.' Gloria nodded towards one of the armchairs. 'Sit yourself down, dear, there's tea in the pot.' She turned away towards the kitchen. 'I mean, it wasn't a total surprise . . . She did tell me last month she was looking for somewhere else to live. But I didn't take that as four weeks' notice – which is what they're supposed to give me.'

She disappeared into the kitchen. Briony missed what she said next. It was drowned out by the clunk and clack of carelessly-handled crockery.

The television was on. The picture was black and white and not very clear. An American woman was explaining how seahorses raise their young.

'Fascinating little programme, that,' said Gloria reappearing in the kitchen doorway, wiping her hands on a dishcloth. 'Mum seahorse gives Dad seahorse her eggs, and he not only fertilizes them, he actually *gives birth* to them, would you believe? Goes through labour, the lot. How about that? That ought to give you something to think about. And they mate for life. Did you know?'

'I didn't,' said Briony. 'I didn't know the male gave birth in any animal.'

'Ah . . .' Gloria sighed, moving back inside the kitchen again. 'If only the world was full of seahorses.'

'Or trees.'

'Or trees.' Gloria laughed. 'Isn't that the truth?'

She came back into the room a few minutes later and handed Briony a large, blue-striped breakfast cup with a saucer that didn't match.

'I've given you three lumps of sugar,' said Gloria, 'just say if you want more.'

'No, this is fine, thanks,' said Briony, and took a sip. It was dark and strong, the way her father liked it. Fisherman's tea, Dennis called it.

'You don't have kids, dear, do you?' said Gloria, sitting down with her toast. 'You don't look the type. You've got the fancy-free look about you. Someone special?'

'Not any more,' said Briony. 'There was for a while. But he was more in love with his surf board.'

'Oh, they're obsessed, dear, aren't they?' Gloria sympathized. 'We've got those Surfer Joe types back home. Just seem to live for the bloody waves.'

'Love me, love my board, that was his attitude.'

'Men are selfish bastards,' said Gloria, 'there's no getting away from it. It's in their nature.'

'You were married, weren't you?' said Briony. 'Did you say he was an artist?'

'I've been married five times and widowed five times,' said Gloria. 'How d'you like that? Every flamin' bugger conked out on me. Couldn't stay the course, dear. I'm too much for 'em all. I run the poor bastards into the ground.' She cackled with laughter.

She finished her toast and her cup of tea and lit a cigarette.

'So where's this naughty sister of yours?' she enquired, a more serious note creeping into her voice.

'Wish to God I knew,' said Briony.

'I had a call from the estate office this morning, and they are not best pleased. Tamara's rent is overdue.'

'Really? But I thought she paid by standing order?' Briony was remembering those payments to Blackwall Properties that appeared each month on Tam's building society account statements.

'She does usually,' said Gloria. 'But now the payments have stopped. And the estate office wants to know why.'

'Do you mean she's cancelled it?' said Briony, wondering why Tam would have done that.

'Either that or there isn't any money left in her account to pay the damn thing,' said Gloria.

Briony knew that couldn't be true ... There was over forty thousand on the account.

'How much is owing?' she said.

'She pays three-fifty a month, in advance. It was due on the fifth.'

'But it's only the sixteenth today,' said Briony. 'It's only a little bit overdue.'

'Tenants pay one month in advance, dear,' said Gloria, 'that's the deal.'

'So ...' Briony wasn't clear what this was leading to. 'What do they want me to do about it?'

'That's up to you, sweetheart. Either you get in touch with Tam's bank and find out what's going on. Or you arrange to pay the rent in cash on her behalf. The office don't mind how it comes ... Just so long as it comes.'

'But you did explain to them,' said Briony, 'that we don't know where Tam is?'

'I haven't put them in the picture yet,' said Gloria, 'because I wanted to hear from you what the latest situation is. But obviously there's no change. So I'll call the office and explain that you're in a difficult position. Maybe they'll cut you some slack. Meantime, you could try talking to her bank ... It could just be a mistake on their part.'

THE FOUNDATION

As soon as she got back upstairs to the flat she checked the City Gate account statements that she had looked at before. It was exactly as she remembered: three hundred and fifty pounds was being paid to Blackwall Properties on the fifth of every month.

Then why would Tam have cancelled the order?

Alternatively, why would the building society have cancelled it? It made no sense.

The answer arrived in the post, the following morning: the latest quarterly statement for Tam's Midas account, together with a pro-forma letter that read:

Dear Ms Carkeat,

    The current balance on your Midas account has fallen below £2,000. We should like to take this opportunity to remind you that under the terms and conditions of the Midas account, a minimum balance of £2,000 is required at all times. For as long as the balance remains below £2,000 the interest on this account will be paid at a rate of ½% gross. We regret that any standing order or direct debit instruction will remain suspended until the minimum balance has been restored.

Briony unfolded the statement and glanced at the closing balance: twenty-three pounds, ninety-five pence. She looked down the statement in shock. It read:

09 JUL 95	BALANCE BF		40,905.87
12 JUL 95	ATM HIGH RD N17	50.00	40,855.87
14 JUL 95	CHQ 000106	31.92	40,823.95
21 JUL 95	ATM HIGH RD N17	60.00	40,763.95
05 AUG 95	S/O BLACKWALL PROPERTIES	350.00	40,413.95
22 AUG 95	ATM HIGH RD N17	40.00	40,373.95

05 SEP 95	S/O BLACKWALL PROPERTIES		350.00	40,023.95
19 SEP 95	CHQ 000107		40,000.00	23.95
08 OCT 95	BALANCE CF			23.95

A cheque for forty thousand . . . But where was the cheque book?

Briony remembered seeing two cheque books. One was in Tam's handbag and the other was in the right-hand drawer of the 'toy cupboard' . . . But that was for Tam's NatWest account; she hadn't used that account for over a year.

She looked in Tam's handbag. There was no cheque book in there now. But there *had* been . . . She clearly remembered seeing it when she tipped out the contents of the bag on the very first day she arrived here. Now the cheque book was missing. Someone had taken it.

Had Tamara been back?

She picked up the phone and called the City Gate helpline number that was printed at the top of the letter. A woman answered and said she was Wendy. Briony said she was Tamara Carkeat and her cheque book had been stolen. She asked for the details of the last cheque that had gone through.

Wendy asked for her date of birth to confirm her identity.

Briony could hear her tapping into a keyboard.

'The last cheque was on the nineteenth of September,' said Wendy, 'forty thousand pounds, to the Pastoral Foundation.'

Briony was trying to remember where she was on the nineteenth of September. That was the week after her grandmother's funeral. She was in Cornwall from the tenth to the twenty-seventh.

Someone had broken into Tam's room during that period and taken the cheque book.

Could it have been Tam herself? . . . But then, she would have taken her handbag, keys, plastic cards, everything.

The Pastoral Foundation . . .

She took Tam's letter out of the drawer of the bedside

cabinet and glanced through it again. Tamara had made two references to it:

> There's this woman I met called Drusilla who works at a place called the Casa Negra. And these women she's involved with are all involved in this thing they call the Foundation. And through that lot I met this – I don't know what . . . They call him the Pastor.

And, almost at the end of the letter:

> It's getting desperate, Bri, and I can't be alone, I've got to have someone here with me, and I don't know who else to turn to because that Foundation lot it's like I feel I've got enemies everywhere, there's no one I can trust.

She put the letter back in the drawer.

The Pastoral Foundation . . . It sounded like a charity of some kind.

She looked it up in the phone book. There was nothing under that name, but it only covered the London business area.

She looked it up in the Yellow Pages, under religious organizations, charities and places of worship. There was no entry for The Pastoral Foundation or any other kind of foundation, but this book covered East London only.

She picked up the phone and called Directory Enquiries. BT had no number listed anywhere in the UK for anything called the Pastoral Foundation.

She would have loved to have seen the signature on that cheque. She wondered if the building society would send a photocopy. But that would open up a whole can of worms if it was forged . . . The police would want to know how Tamara came by all that money in the first place.

But suppose the signature was genuine? Why would Tam have given away so much money, almost everything she had?

If the Foundation *was* some kind of religious sect, she might have been coerced or brainwashed into it.

Briony went to the 'toy cupboard' and examined the stubs of the cheque books – past and present – from Tam's NatWest account, to see if she had given anything else to this Pastoral Foundation in recent years. She searched through all the drawers and cupboards in the room to see if she could find any literature about the Pastoral Foundation – anything at all, even a pamphlet or a newsletter – but she found nothing. She looked carefully through Tam's diary and address book: there was no mention of this Pastoral Foundation anywhere – no address, no telephone number.

She drove down to Hackney and went into the central library. A man in the reference department showed her where the directories of religious organizations were shelved. She looked through the *International Register of Charities*; the *World Directory of Religious Institutions*; the *UK Christian Handbook*; the *Catholic Directory*; the *Church of England Year Book*; and *Religions in the UK, A Multifaith Directory*; she even looked through *The Good Retreat Guide*.

But there was no reference anywhere to The Pastoral Foundation.

THE LANDLORD

Briony went down to see Gloria that evening.

'I hope you don't drink vodka, dear,' she said, coming back from the kitchen, holding two chunky glasses. 'I don't trust a woman who drinks vodka ... Unless she's Polish. Or Russian.' She handed a glass to Briony. 'A woman should drink gin ... and a little Guinness occasionally for iron – but not in the same glass, of course. Vodka is the drink for flighty women. Sherry is for drizzes. Gin is a woman's drink.'

She sat down and reached for her cigarettes. She was

wearing her black kaftan again, with the bronze and silver leaves on it.

'I was thinking about that mural today,' said Briony.

'Oh, not that bloody thing again,' said Gloria. 'I'm going to send Jack up there one of these fine days with a big can of paint.'

'I was wondering if Petra was involved in any kind of a cult.'

'A *cult?*' said Gloria, and smiled, bemused. 'Like the secret society of rice eaters, you mean?'

'I'm serious,' said Briony. 'Some sort of religious sect. It might explain the mural. That nasty-looking priest-shepherd character: he's minding a flock of sheep. The sheep have no legs. And there are people barred up in his church. They've got eyes but no mouths. The clock on the church has no numerals: so the time is always zero.'

'Well, I'm not saying you're wrong, dear,' said Gloria, 'but I wouldn't read too much into it, if I were you. She was very down on men, Petra, she had a problem there. I don't mean she was of the Sapphic persuasion, just that she didn't like the male sex in general. But she couldn't leave them alone. To be candid, she was a masochist. And I think it was pretty compulsive.'

'How do you know that?' said Briony.

'Because I had the police here one day. She'd been having trouble with some lover or – client, I think, was the word they used – who'd got a bit heavy-handed with her one night. They wanted to prosecute him for bodily harm but she wouldn't give evidence.'

'But she never talked about religion?' said Briony. 'Or getting involved with any kind of group?'

'I hardly ever saw her, to be honest, dear,' said Gloria. 'She was a night owl, Petra – a bit like your sister, in that respect. And her English wasn't too brilliant.' Gloria raised her glass and murmured, 'God bless, sweetheart. Mud in your eye.'

Briony said, 'Cheers.'

'She was another one who wasn't very reliable with her rent payments,' Gloria added. '*And* she drank vodka.'

'Have you heard anything more from the estate office?' asked Briony.

'I have, dear, yes,' said Gloria. 'And they're a wee bit pissed off about this standing order business.'

'Did you explain about Tamara?'

'I did. I put them in the picture. And they say they'll give you until the fifth of November to find the three-fifty that's outstanding for this month. And on that day, when the next month's rent comes due, they want the month in advance as usual. Cheque, cash or standing order, they don't mind.'

'In other words they want seven hundred pounds in the next two weeks?'

'That about sums it up, dear, yes,' said Gloria. 'But you are getting a month's free credit, in fact. You should look at it that way.'

'And what happens if Tam's not back by the fifth of November?' said Briony.

'That's up to you,' said Gloria. 'You can pay on her behalf. Or you can clear out her belongings and take them with you.'

'But I don't *have* seven hundred pounds,' said Briony. 'I don't even have half that.'

'Well, don't get yourself in a paddy about it,' said Gloria. 'You've got a week or two to think about it. But if I was you, dear, I'd seriously ask myself if I really want to take on the responsibility. It's not *your* rent, after all.'

'Perhaps I could call the estate office and talk to them myself,' said Briony. 'Are they in London?'

'No, dear, they're out in the sticks,' said Gloria. 'I can give you the number if you like, but you'll probably only get the answering machine. And they're devils for not calling back.'

Gloria wrote down the number for her. Briony had a feeling she had seen it before somewhere.

When she got back up to the flat, she looked through the telephone numbers in the back of Tam's diary.

132

She found it: it was the Woodhurst number that Tam had listed in her diary as 'Leysholme'.

Briony called the number, listened to a woman's voice reciting a bland message on the answering machine, and hung up without speaking.

The voice sounded very like Drusilla's.

MIRROR IMAGES

I

I'm watching, Sis, I'm watching.

I watch you make up. I watch you dress.

I watch you poking through my jewellery box and trying different rings on your fingers to see which you like most.

I watch you choose from among my little bottles of perfume; spray each wrist and sniff and think about it.

I watch you unhook each outfit from the rail and drape it across the bed and peel off the previous outfit and try the next one on.

I watch you looking at yourself in the long mirror. I watch you pat your belly, check your profile . . . Then try something new.

I sit here on the bed, watching. And you don't sense a thing.

I can guess exactly where you're going, exactly what you're going to do. You're nervous. You keep dropping things: the tweezers, the mascara brush, my earrings . . .

I was nervous too, my first time. But with me it was excitement, it was anticipation, a kind of knowing that there

133

was something bad out there somewhere in the night, the darkness, that sense of the wild creature inside me straining to break loose, threatening to get out of control, wanting to let go. That fear of the dark spirit that dwells in my soul . . . The fear that makes my adrenalin flow, makes my heart trip and flip and kick up a few beats.

Yes, I was nervous, like you, the first time.

I stood and stared at the mirror, too, thinking: Do I look as good as this outfit makes me feel? Or do I simply look ridiculous?

Do you like the feel of rubber on your torso? Slide your fingertips across it, feel that smoothness. Feel that cold, tight latex squeezing tight into your waistline.

Do you like it, the way you look? Those luscious dark lips, those fruity dark fingernails.

Do you like those long, high boots? They suit you.

You always wanted to be me, didn't you?

And I wanted to be you.

Not so strange. We're two halves, one egg. We have a dark side and a light side. We are both night and day. The night inside me is part of you. And the day inside you is part of me. You are in me and I'm in you. Two halves, one egg.

How will we exist without each other?

I can't come to you, sweet sister. Please God, don't try to come to me. Don't destroy your life the way I destroyed mine.

The Pastor always needs new lambs for his flock. His appetite is insatiable. She'll want you, Sis, oh yes, Drusilla will want you for the Pastor too.

She won't rush it, though. Nothing happens in a hurry, nothing happens until she thinks you're ready, until you really want it. That's the cruellest irony of it all: you end up wanting to give yourself to the Pastor. You'll do anything, you want it so very much.

2

Briony stared at herself in the long mirror.

Tamara meet Briony . . . Briony, Tamara.

Perhaps, she was thinking, there is no such person as Tamara. Perhaps there never was. Perhaps I have no twin sister. Perhaps it's me that's sick, it's me that's schizo, not Tamara. Can't be Tam because there is no Tam. There is only me . . . Only *two* mes: a good me and a bad me. The bad me I call Tamara, the good me I call Briony.

Or is it the other way around?

She picked up the telephone.

She could feel her stomach churning, her hand trembling as she tapped out the number.

She asked for Drusilla.

The waiting seemed endless.

Two voices were competing inside her. One was saying: Hang up. The other was saying: Hold on.

Two halves, one egg.

She was gazing at her reflection in the long glass:

You look silly, one voice said. Another voice said: I look terrific.

It feels ridiculous, the first voice said. It feels fantastic, said the other.

A woman said, 'Hullo . . .?'

Hang up, the first voice said.

Say something, the other voice insisted.

'Drusilla?' said Briony.

'Uh-huh?'

Absorbed in her own reflection in the mirror, she said, 'It's Tam.'

There was a silence.

'Hi, Briony,' said Drusilla. 'I wondered when you'd call.'

WAITRESS

I

'Why?' asked Drusilla.

'I need the money.'

And when Drusilla made no comment: 'Tam's rent's overdue. They want seven hundred quid by the fifth of next month.'

And, because Drusilla continued to stare at her, pokerfaced, from behind those large round sunglasses, she asked, 'Is there a problem?'

They were sitting in a poky little office.

'I've worked in pubs before,' she went on. 'I've done a lot of waitressing.'

'We're not some cosy village pub in sleepy Cornwall,' said Drusilla. 'This is not a beach café selling cream teas to coach parties from Stoke-on-Trent.'

'Fetching drinks is fetching drinks, surely?' said Briony.

She felt defensive. She had not expected this. When they met before, Drusilla had virtually *asked* her if she wanted a job.

'It's not your scene though, is it?' Drusilla murmured, angling her head a little and taking in the latex waspie and crop-top, and the spiky-heeled boots.

Briony shrugged. 'It feels okay. A bit strange, that's all.'

'I don't want to know it feels okay,' Drusilla replied. 'A lot of things feel okay . . . Eating cornflakes feels okay, filing your nails feels okay.'

Briony didn't understand what she was getting at.

'You know why we wear this gear?' Drusilla continued. And, without waiting for Briony to reply: 'Because we like it. It's our scene. It's not a gimmick. I don't need people to make up the numbers.'

'Look, I'm not Tamara,' Briony conceded, 'I'm new to it all, but I'm not shy. Just takes a little getting used to, that's all.'

It looked as if Drusilla was actually going to turn her down and send her away. She couldn't believe it.

'I don't think you're into this scene,' Drusilla replied. 'But you do kind of look like her. Not as raunchy as Tam but . . .' She nodded, giving Briony another look over. 'You sort of carry it off okay.'

She still seemed undecided.

And then she said, as if it was against her better judgement, 'I'll give you a week's try-out.'

'Okay,' Briony agreed. 'A week.'

'And lose weight.'

Briony wondered if she'd misheard.

'. . . If you want to keep your job, that is,' Drusilla added.

Briony said nothing.

'You come in at eight and you go home when I say – which means about five or six in the morning at weekends. We're closed Sundays and Mondays.'

'Okay,' said Briony.

'I'll start you on sixty a night, cash in hand,' said Drusilla. 'Our top girls earn more. If anyone offers you a drink, you take it in cash at the bar and all tips are pooled. You'll make about four hundred in a good week. If you keep back any tips, we'll find out, we always do. And Crystal will break your arms.'

Briony smiled.

'I'm not kidding,' said Drusilla.

2

Is she giving you the tour? Is she taking you round, showing you how it's done, telling you all the dos and don'ts?

Is she explaining that the punters mustn't touch? Look,

Mum, no hands. So much as a pat on the bum and big Con will chuck 'em out.

And is she showing you how to walk that slow, lazy way with the drinks? ... Because it's so dark and they don't want accidents, don't want anybody hurt.

(Don't want anybody hurt ... Excuse me for laughing. Who'd have thought they had so much heart?)

Are you looking around and wondering why anybody bothers going there? Because nothing seems to happen, does it? People just sit there all night long in the thick smoke and gloom, watching, like peeping Toms. They're guys, mostly, the voyeurs; and always lonely. They just want to put on the gear – whatever lights their wick – and drink the night away, and get off on the atmosphere. It stokes their fantasies. And they sit there, like tramps round a brazier, warming their libidos. If they've got the dosh, they pay for a hostess to sit with them for the evening ... There's money there, Sis.

But you get the couples too. The extroverts, the subs and doms parading themselves, the masters and mistresses strutting their stuff, while their slaves crawl like shiny black beetles through the dust and dog-ends. And the introverts – the uptight couples who have wives or husbands or parents or flatmates back home who wouldn't understand their needs, and the Casa Negra is the only place they can meet, furtive, like thieves, and shift around in the darkness, playing out their little fantasies. They feel like freaks, so it's the place they go to be freaks, so there's a guilt trip somewhere, so they never relax.

But most of those are fetishists, just playing on the fringes of the scene. Role-play, that's all. Games.

Weekends, it gets more fun. Fridays and Saturdays, you get the DSSM crowd in – they're hardcore fans, Deadly Serious Slaves and Masters. They get scary, the things they do. They give crucifixion a whole new meaning. But don't worry, Sis ... You won't see anything that'll put you off your

Weetabix. Not on club premises. The real action goes on elsewhere. Strictly invitation only.

Is anybody recognizing you? Is anybody calling you Tamara? Some will, some won't. Hard to be sure who's who, down there, it's all so dark and secretive. It's an underworld of masks and make-up, wigs and shadows. That's how girls can simply fade away down there: no one knows they've disappeared, no one ever discovers what happened.

The heroine returns.

God knows what hour it is.

She looks shagged out, poor lamb. And it's only her first night.

Chucks her boots (my boots) aside, sinks on to the edge of my bed and eases her aching trotters.

Really gets you in the arches, Sis, huh? Heels are a bitch.

Well, just wait till the weekend, driving home with dawn breaking. Ten bloody hours on your feet, without a break.

So tired she can hardly get undressed, poor sausage ...

Rolls that sweaty waspie off, over those meaty hips and Ahhhh ... Feels her waist spread back into its normal shape, like runny blancmange that's sagged out of its mould.

Can hardly keep her eyes open ...

The amount of mascara she's piled on, I'm not surprised.

Looks at herself in the mirror.

Thinks: God, I look a slag.

She picks up a Kleenex. Shall I wipe it off? Nah ... Stuff it. Leave it till morning. Just flop beneath that duvet.

Oh, bliss ... Darkness. Bed.

Sleep, sweet sister, sleep.

A whole new way of death is just begun.

3

She tried a different outfit every night; and tried a different make-up; even tried a different scent – Tamara had so many.

She wore Tamara's silver rings and bangles.

She wore Tamara's wigs.

Drusilla extended her trial period to a month.

She was never home before three. Sometimes she didn't get home till six or seven on Sunday mornings. It tired her out. She slept until lunchtime every day. Had breakfast at one. Skipped lunch and dinner – didn't seem to have the time.

She lost twelve pounds in weight that first month at the Casa Negra.

She got used to wearing Tamara's things. She didn't feel so self-conscious after the first week or two, didn't feel such a freak. It was like putting on a uniform for work. She wore flat shoes and jeans and a coat to travel to and fro, in the car.

The worst thing was the smoke. Sunday mornings she drove home at daybreak and she could hardly breathe. She stank like an ashtray; had to wash her hair every morning to get rid of the smell. Crystal said, 'Now you know why I shave, chook. Saves a fortune on shampoo.'

The next-worst thing was the heat. It got so stuffy in that place. She wore less and less as the weeks went by.

People kept calling her Tamara. Sometimes she told them she was Tam's sister, sometimes she couldn't be bothered; they kept calling her Tamara, anyway.

Even the other waitresses were calling her Tamara. Crystal said it was a habit, and she couldn't spot the difference without her glasses on, and she never wore her glasses. All the other waitresses did what Crystal did, and said what Crystal said, so they all called her Tam, as well. There was Mojo, who was black; and Bibi from Poland; and Lola, who was once called Lawrence. They all called her Tam.

So Briony began to call herself Tamara, too. It seemed less complicated. She plucked her eyebrows in the high-arched way that Tamara plucked hers. She even had her hair cut and styled like Tamara's – a bob with a low fringe – and dyed it black.

Nobody asked any more where the real Tamara was.

She paid the rent on 5 November. She paid the telephone bill. She paid the electricity bill. She renewed Tam's car insurance. (Four hundred-odd ... She put that on Tam's credit card.)

The car broke down. She had to call the breakdown service. The clutch had failed. The repair man towed her to a garage. About three hundred, the garage told her. She used Tamara's credit card again.

She paid the rent once more on 5 December.

She put money into Tam's 'Midas' account. She used the cashcard, she started signing cheques.

The weather turned sharply colder. Her winter clothes were still in Cornwall, at Julie's house; she had not anticipated being here this long. She began to wear Tamara's winter clothes: her trousers, her sweaters, her thick overcoat. She had lost weight, she could wear all her sister's clothes now; fitted her perfectly.

'Are you warm enough up there, Tamara, dear?' said Gloria, when they met in the hallway, one cold December morning.

She never called her Bridey again.

HOSTESS

One night, Drusilla called her into the poky office and said, 'Do you want to stay on? Or do you want to go? Or what?'

'Have I passed?'

'They seem to like you,' said Drusilla.

Briony presumed she meant the clientele. 'That's because everyone thinks I'm Tam.'

'Do you want to earn more money?'

'Doing what?' said Briony.

'Hostessing.'

'What's that?'

'Sometimes punters want their own hostess for the evening – to sit and drink with them, make them feel they're something special, instead of the jerks that most of them are.'

'What happens if no one wants a hostess for the evening?' said Briony. 'I don't get paid?'

'Sure, you get paid,' said Drusilla. 'You go on waitressing, as normal. It's just a way of earning extra money, that's all.'

'What do I have to do?'

'Sit with the punter and make him feel Numero Uno. And get him to buy champagne – which we only do by the bottle, and you then get commission on. You can do quite well out of it. Some of the guys that come here, they're seriously loaded but lonely as hell . . . because there aren't many places they can go if this is their scene. So they like to hire a raunchy chick in all the gear to be their fantasy for the evening. They like you to pose a bit, play the part – I mean, you don't just shlump there like an old tart in The Rose and Crown.'

'What else do they get for their money?' said Briony suspiciously.

'Strictly no touch,' said Drusilla.

'No touch at all?'

'Strictly *verboten*.'

'And can I say no?' said Briony.

'Say no to what?'

'If some obnoxious old lech wants me to be his hostess, can I say no?'

'If you've got a good reason I can tell them you're not available,' said Drusilla. 'But it would have to be a pretty convincing reason. We make a good profit out of hostessing. We don't like saying no.'

'So, basically,' said Briony, 'I've got to sit with anyone who asks for me?'

'Well, for fifty quid a punter, plus forty per-cent commission on the champagne,' said Drusilla, 'I don't think that's

142

too bad a deal . . . Considering they're not even allowed to hold your hand.'

'And is that what Tamara did?' said Briony. 'Was she a hostess?'

'It's what they all do if the punters ask for them,' said Drusilla. 'Who wants to clump around all night long, serving beers, when you can sit and sip champagne? But the punters are picky. They go for Bibi . . . Because she's blonde and looks about fourteen, and she's got a sexy Polish accent. Men don't go for Crystal . . . Dykes do, but not many women come here on their own, so she misses out. Tam was always popular. Guys go for that look – the straight, black hair, the fringe, the pale face, the dark lips. Whatever it is turns them on, Tam's got it in aces.'

'And what do I say if someone asks for me, and it's one of Tam's regulars, and he thinks I'm really her?'

'That's for you to figure out,' said Drusilla. 'But if you're going to try and bluff it out, you'd better get pierced.'

'What do you mean?' said Briony. 'Pierced where?'

'Everywhere,' said Drusilla, and smiled without any warmth. 'That would be a dead giveaway.'

Thinking about it, Briony said, 'But how could they tell?'

'You'd better figure that out as well,' said Drusilla.

It was getting near Christmas. It was a busy time for hostesses, the time of year that people didn't like to feel alone. She was busy almost every night.

Drusilla was right: they were all creeps. Some were sick and nasty, she suspected, and some were just rich and shy, but they were all creeps; sad, lonely creeps.

Some of them wore masks, so she had no idea how old they were or what they really looked like. Some of them wore masks because they were well-known and didn't want to be recognized, said Crystal. And most of them used false names.

There was Roman, who sat encased from top to toe in rubber, and didn't say a word all evening. There was Axel, who was a control freak and wanted to bring back forced labour, work camps and birching. There was Frankie who was fat, anaemic and hairy, and scarcely took his eyes off her all evening, and began to cry when she said she didn't want to come to his Christmas party. He walked away in tears, without any explanation, and didn't come back.

Most of them wanted to take her out for a drink when she finished for the night. She told them she had to go home to her husband. They didn't push it. Some of them tipped her before they left – the foreign ones; the English never did.

Drusilla was right, it was money for old rope. All she had to do was look cool and composed and in control (when she was actually thinking: what the hell am I doing here? This creep could be a serial rapist) and speak when she was spoken to, and keep topping up his glass with champagne.

Then, one night, a customer asked for Tamara by name – a man in his mid-thirties, in motorcycle leathers. Drusilla took Briony to one side and said, 'There's something I don't like about him . . . He doesn't look like he belongs. I've seen him in here before. He might be a copper.'

'Well, what if he is?' said Briony.

'We get the vice squad in from time to time, checking us out, seeing whether we're up to any naughties. If he starts asking questions, make sure you give him all the right answers. I know the punters like their fantasies pandered to, but don't let him lead you on.'

He was sitting, waiting near the bar. It was quite crowded. He didn't see Briony approaching. He looked familiar, even in this gloomy light. She concealed herself among the throng and took a good look at him. She knew him.

Drusilla was right, he didn't belong. But he was not from the vice squad. He was Charlie Stillman.

She went off to find Drusilla.

Drusilla said, 'Who is he?'

'He's a shrink,' said Briony. 'His name's Charlie Stillman. He had a fling with Tam at one time. I met him when I came up in September. He's trying to find out where she's disappeared to. Now, I suppose, he thinks I'm her.'

'So what do you want to do?' said Drusilla. 'I can tell him you're not available, but that's not going to solve anything. He'll just hang around till we close.'

'Just tell him it's not Tamara, it's me,' said Briony. 'Tell him I don't want to see him. Ask him to leave.'

'But he's done nothing wrong,' said Drusilla.

'This is very embarrassing,' said Briony. 'I don't know how he found out about this place. *I* didn't tell him.'

'She was coming here as a member long before she started working here. He's probably known for a long time. I've seen him in here before, but not for the last month or two.'

'Well, I don't want to see him,' said Briony. 'I've got nothing to say to him. He's a patronizing bastard and he wasn't very honest with me.'

She was never sure what Drusilla was thinking because her face was partly obscured by those large sunglasses and curtained on either side by her long frizzy wig.

'That's your problem, not mine,' said Drusilla. 'I manage a business here. I'll explain to him that you're Tam's sister and you're not available tonight. But I'm not going to throw him out. He's paid his money, he fits the dress code – just. I've got no quarrel with him.'

Briony watched as Drusilla approached Charlie and leaned towards him, putting both hands on the table and speaking close to his ear. It was not a very long conversation. Charlie nodded his head a few times.

'What did you say?' Briony asked when Drusilla came back.

'I said what we agreed,' Drusilla replied. 'That you're not Tam and she doesn't work here any more, and you don't want to sit with him.'

'What did he say?' said Briony.

'I don't think he believed me,' said Drusilla. 'But he said okay.'

Briony went downstairs to the dungeon to look after the

people down there. When she had to come back up to the main room, she avoided looking in Charlie's direction, and kept herself in the shadows as far as it was possible. She saw him leaving at about ten o'clock.

FORBIDDEN ZONE

It was after three o'clock by the time she got home from the Casa Negra. It was pouring with rain and the only parking space she could find was about eighty yards up the street. She was wearing jeans and an anorak, and trainers on her feet. Everything else she was carrying in Tamara's gym bag. She climbed out of the car, locked it, put up the hood of her anorak and jogged down the road through the rain. As she ran up the garden path to the front porch, she heard another car door slam shut and someone call out: 'Tam!'

It was Charlie Stillman.

As she struggled to get the key into the lock he came running along the garden path towards her.

'Tam . . .?' he called again, but more quietly.

There was no light in the porch.

'It's not Tam, for Christ's sake,' she said. 'It's Briony.'

She opened the front door and pressed the lightswitch.

He could see now that it was. He was panting – as if he had been running all the way from Stepney instead of sitting out there in the car, waiting. He stood staring at her, his face drooping with defeat and despondency.

'I'm sorry,' he said. 'But you do look so like her. I could've sworn . . . And seeing you get out of her car just now.'

'Yeah. Thanks for telling me about the car,' she said sarcastically.

'You didn't know?' He seemed surprised.

'No, I didn't know,' said Briony. 'Like I didn't know you were her shrink ... You didn't tell me that either. Like I didn't know she cracked up eighteen months ago, when she left the Hackney Hospital. You didn't mention that either. And you didn't mention anything about her working at the Casa Negra.'

'I'm not her shrink. It's not like that.' He looked anxious to explain. 'I'm a therapist, not an analyst.' And when Briony didn't reply, just stared at him, willing him to clear off: 'Can't we even discuss it?'

'I'm listening.'

'Like ... out of the rain?'

There was a strong wind gusting, driving the rain into the porch, but he was making a bit of a melodrama out of it; he was not very wet.

'It's three o'clock in the morning,' she said. 'I'm tired and I'm going to bed. So good night.'

'What do you mean, she cracked up?' he said. 'Who told you that?'

She tried to shut the door on him but he pushed his body across the threshold. She could have tried to push him back but it had been a long night and she didn't have the energy. She started up the stairs to the flat. He followed.

'Who told you?' he persisted, his voice becoming hushed.

She didn't reply but kept on walking upstairs. He followed her all the way up to the attic and into Tam's room.

'Just answer that one simple question, that's all,' said Charlie. 'Who told you she'd had a breakdown?'

'Who told you she worked at the Casa Negra?' Briony countered.

'She did.'

'Well, thanks for telling me.'

'Has she been back here?' he asked.

'Will you get out of here?' said Briony. 'This isn't your flat—'

'Or yours,' Charlie pointed out. 'And does she know you're driving her car?'

Briony tossed the gym bag on to the bed. 'How could she know if I haven't talked to her for the past six months?'

'Are you insured?'

'What the hell business is it of yours?' She unzipped the rain-damp anorak and draped it over the back of a chair.

'Why are you being so hostile?' Charlie asked.

'Real shrink-speak. Why am I so *hostile*? Jesus.' She opened the gym bag.

'Well, why *are* you?' he persisted.

'You lied to me. Why didn't you tell me you were her shrink? Why didn't you tell me about her car? Why didn't you tell me about the Casa Negra?'

'I didn't lie to you—'

'All right, you deceived me. I asked you if you knew where she was working and you said no.'

'I didn't know she was working there,' he said. 'I knew she went there, weekends, but she didn't tell me she had a job there.'

'And you made out you were her lover.'

'I was.'

'You mean you loved her. But she didn't give a stuff about you.'

'It wasn't like that—'

'You didn't tell me she was sent to you as a patient.'

'Patient's too strong a word . . . Think of it as counselling. But more importantly, think of me as her friend. I'm concerned about her. That's why I'm trying to find her.'

'Why did she need counselling?' Briony demanded. 'And why didn't you tell me?'

'You know why,' said Charlie. 'She was unhappy at work. It's a highly stressful profession and it's very underpaid.'

'I know all that, every nurse knows that, anyone who reads a newspaper knows that . . . But what did she need a *shrink* for?'

'I wish you'd stop using the word shrink,' said Charlie, 'it's got all the wrong connotations. I'm a psychotherapist. She felt that she was a failure. She was questioning her own sense of self-worth. They referred her for counselling. I was just someone to talk her problems through with, that's all.'

'What problems specifically?'

'Briony, please . . . I know she's your sister but a lot of what she told me was in confidence.'

'She's missing, for Christ's sake! She's disappeared. We both want to find her, don't we? We're on the same side. If she's got mental problems, I need to know.'

'I didn't say she had mental problems,' said Charlie, with exasperation. 'She was depressed and confused at the time, certainly, but that's not unusual in stress-related conditions. I certainly wouldn't say she cracked up.'

'Well, whatever you want to call it,' said Briony, 'how come she never said anything about it to me? I never got so much as a hint of it.'

'How would I know? No one's proud of being a failure, are they?'

'You think she is a failure?'

'All right, I'll rephrase that,' said Charlie. 'No one's proud of *feeling* a failure, put it that way. If we're going through a bad patch we brazen it out, put the best gloss on things. It's human nature.'

'And how long have you known about this?' Briony asked, taking the thigh boots out of the gym bag and tipping the rest of the items on to the bed.

'Known about what?' said Charlie.

'This, for Christ's sake,' said Briony, tossing a leather waspie into the air. 'This . . . this . . . this . . .' (throwing it all into the air). 'She told you about all this?'

'Yes, she told me she had a . . .' Charlie sighed and took a breath. 'A bit of a problem.'

'How long ago did she tell you?'

'Oh . . .' Charlie sighed again. 'I don't know. About the time our affair broke up. That's when it all came out.'

'And you know about this as well?' said Briony, walking across to the hidden closet, to put away the things she'd been wearing that night. She pulled open the door, reached inside and switched on the light. Charlie peered inside. He looked up at everything hanging from the rail and then down at the boots and shoes on the floor beneath.

'She talked about her feelings,' he said, stepping back out of the closet. 'She didn't tell me in any detail, no. She never showed me anything like this.'

He seemed rather coy about it – which surprised her, considering the nature of his work, listening to other people's problems all day long.

'She opened up to you about all this?' said Briony. She switched off the light and closed the door of the closet. She felt peeved that Tam had shared these secrets with someone else, rather than with her. 'I had no idea, you see. This came as a shock to me. This was a whole secret side of her.'

'Well, it's not the kind of thing that people talk about, is it?' Charlie reasoned. 'Least of all to their own family.'

'Is this why she needed counselling?'

'This was pretty much the nub of it, yeah.' Charlie sat down on the end of the bed. 'This was behind a lot of her problems, her sense of failure and low self-esteem.'

Briony sat down at the dressing table and began to remove her make-up. 'It seems such a trivial thing,' she said. 'Most people think of the fetish scene as a bit of a joke, surely? The kind of thing you read about in the Sunday papers, snigger-snigger.'

'Sure,' Charlie agreed. 'But it's not such a joke if you have a whole string of failed relationships behind you because of it. It's not a joke if you see your whole life blighted by it.'

'But why is it such a big problem for her?'

'She feels addicted to it,' said Charlie. 'It's compulsive. She doesn't seem to be able to get sexual pleasure without it. She finds it impossible to have a normal relationship . . . whatever the hell that means. And she's afraid she never will. She tries to break out of it every so often, to kick the habit, like a junkie trying to kick the needle, but, of course, she always fails.'

'Why?' said Briony. 'Why do you say "of course"?'

'Because it's not a habit. It's compulsive, it's obsessive, it's something that's rooted very much deeper in her psyche.'

'But she's so attractive,' said Briony. 'There must be millions of men out there who'd put up with such a trivial thing.'

'I know, I know,' Charlie agreed. 'You'd think it was all so simple, wouldn't you? But it's not a trivial thing with her. It's not simply fetish. It goes much deeper than that. She's not attracted to "most" guys, she's only attracted to men who are into this scene. There's a schism in her sexual psyche. One side of her wants to be "normal" – though she can't define what she means by that. While the other side of her hankers for this secret "other world" where she can live out her fantasies. Because she's torn between the two, she feels guilt. And therefore she has a low sense of self-esteem, of self-worth. And so she hides away from all her old friends. And, not surprisingly, feels lonely and isolated.'

Briony wiped cold cream from her eyes with a tissue. 'But we all have fantasies,' she said.

'Sure,' Charlie agreed. 'But most of us are clear in our own minds where our fantasies end and reality begins. Tamara doesn't seem able to draw that line . . . Or, if she does perceive the line, she feels impelled to cross it. That Casa Negra club—'

'They're just playing games,' Briony cut in. 'It's role-playing . . . like kids dressing up, doctors and nurses – except it's slaves and masters.'

'But Tamara is afraid that playing games is not enough for her,' said Charlie, 'that's the point. That's how she explained it to me.'

'So what does she want? What are you saying? She's a masochist?'

'No, she's not into physical pain at all, not as I understand it,' said Charlie. 'Quite the contrary. It's the state of being powerless that excites her. It induces extreme sexual arousal. At its best, a kind of ecstasy. It has nothing to do with pain. The pleasure is of a much more subtle kind. It involves bondage in various forms but there is no pain involved. It requires total submission on her part and it has to be entirely voluntary. She has this need, for want of a better word, to submit to what her "other self" would perceive as something perverted and degrading. It's a need to defile herself, to abase herself. This is the turn-on, if you like. It's like a self-destruct button inside her. She's drawn towards what she calls her "forbidden zone". That's what excites her: subverting her own concept of decency and morality. To that extent it *is* masochistic . . . but masochistic in a spiritual context.'

'But why?' said Briony. 'What does she want to destroy herself for? She's so bright, she's so nice to be with, she's so attractive. She's just about everything that any normal woman would want to be. I've spent most of my life wishing I *was* Tam.'

'Well, that's ironical,' said Charlie, 'because she wishes she was *you*. She envies you, if you want the truth.'

'Envies *me*? Tamara?' Briony almost laughed, but not quite, it was so preposterous. 'If that's what she said, then she was winding you up. It was always the other way round.'

Charlie shook his head. 'She doesn't like herself, you see. She doesn't want to be herself. She hates her self-image. In so many ways, she'd much rather be you.'

'A failed art student and seasonal barmaid,' said Briony, 'babysitting to pay her rent?'

'But you enjoy life,' said Charlie. 'That's what she envies: your contentment. You're uncomplicated, she says. She'd give anything for that.'

'Dumb but content,' said Briony.

'That's not quite how she put it.'

'But that's what she meant.' Briony smiled. 'One egg, two halves, we used to say. But she got all the good bits in her half . . . Or almost all: she can't cook and she can't draw, but that's about all she can't do.'

'And she can't be happy,' said Charlie. 'Which would you rather be?'

Briony recalled something her mother had said on the day of Nan's funeral. Sitting on the bed, discussing Tam, Kathleen had said, 'She's like the moon, I've always thought: there's a dark side and a light side, but we only ever see the light.'

'I don't understand it,' said Briony. 'Why is she this way?'

Charlie opened his hands, a non-committal gesture. 'Some people with psychosexual problems go through a lifetime of analysis and never find out the reason why. Analysis doesn't always explain things, anyway. Often, it just makes them seem all the more unfathomable.'

Briony sat silently for a while, thinking about what he'd just been saying. It felt as if he was talking about someone she had never met. In a sense, he was.

'You should have told me all this before,' she said. 'It was wrong of you to conceal it from me.'

'I'm in a difficult position,' said Charlie. 'She told me things in confidence. Besides, I'm not exactly proud of myself, the way I handled things.'

'How do you mean?'

'I let her down. I fell in love with her. Head-over-heels in love. You don't behave like that with a patient. But I . . .' He shrugged, 'just couldn't help myself.' He smiled feebly. 'It must sound pretty pathetic.'

Briony shrugged. 'It takes two. Tam's old enough to know her own mind.'

'But she was very confused and depressed at the time. That made her vulnerable. She wasn't ready for a relationship. I shouldn't have loaded all that on to her. It didn't last very long. And when the relationship began to fall apart, she felt even more desperate. Yet another failure to add to her list. And that was when she began to open up about the dark side to her personality.'

'Well, she obviously doesn't blame you for anything,' said Briony. 'You're still friends. She still contacts you.'

'About once a year.' He smiled ruefully. And then another thought struck him: 'If you didn't know about all this,' (indicating the hidden closet) 'how did you know about the Casa Negra?'

'She wrote me a letter,' said Briony. 'It was waiting for me when I got back to Cornwall for my grandmother's funeral.'

'And what did she tell you? That she'd been working at the Casa Negra?'

'No. She told me she'd met someone at the club. And through them she'd become involved with something she called the Foundation. Does that mean anything to you? Did she ever talk about that?'

'The Foundation?' said Charlie. 'What kind of foundation?'

'The letter didn't say. But I've just discovered that she gave a lot of money to something called The Pastoral Foundation, about three months ago.'

'How do you know, if you haven't seen her?'

'I had to talk to her building society because they stopped paying a standing order for her rent.'

'When you say a lot of money,' said Charlie, 'what do you mean?'

'Most of her savings.'

'Like . . . hundreds? Thousands?'

'That's neither here nor there,' said Briony. She was not going to say anything about the small fortune that Tam had stashed away this past year. 'The point is, she's given them a lot of money. It sounds like some sort of religious charity but I can't find out anything about them.'

'I've never heard of anything like that,' said Charlie. 'But I can ask around.'

'Did she ever mention someone that she calls the Pastor?'

He took a moment to consider that.

'No,' he said eventually. 'No, I don't remember her mentioning him. What is he, an evangelist? One of these free church ministers?'

'I don't know who he is,' Briony confessed. 'I don't know anything about him. But Tam has got herself involved with his Foundation in some way. That might be where she is . . . Wherever their headquarters are.'

'What are you saying?' asked Charlie. 'She's actually working for this religious charity?'

'If she's as vulnerable as you say,' said Briony, 'then she sounds just like the kind of person these loony sects tend to pick on: someone who's full of guilt, confused, depressed, lonely, lost her sense of self-worth . . .'

'Well, I suppose . . .' Charlie conceded. 'But is that what she said in her letter? Did she sound as if she'd run off with some loony sect?'

'No, she didn't say that,' said Briony. 'She didn't mention religion. She just mentioned this Foundation. She said they'd got her hooked on something . . . something that made her feel fantastic, out of this world. Something to do with being with this person she calls the Pastor. She'd been *with* him, she said, but she'd never seen him. She compared it to a drug. But I don't think she meant it *was* a drug, literally. I think it was more of a spiritual thing.'

Charlie looked puzzled. 'Have you tried contacting them?'

'I don't know how to,' said Briony. 'I tried BT but they don't have a phone number for them. I've looked them up in all the religious directories at the library, but they're not listed. I've searched this room but Tam doesn't have any literature about them. She doesn't even have their phone number in her book.'

'Do you still have the letter?' said Charlie.

'Not here,' she lied. She didn't want to show it to him. She couldn't see what good it would do . . . Tamara had not said anything to him about the Pastor or the Foundation. And she didn't want him stirring up trouble with Drusilla at the Casa Negra.

'What else did it say?' he asked.

'She asked me to come up and stay with her,' Briony replied. 'This was just a few days before she made that phone call. She said there was no one she could talk to, there was no one here she could trust.'

'Did she mention *me*?' said Charlie.

'No, she didn't. She hasn't mentioned you for a long time.'

'Why didn't you bring the letter with you?' he asked. 'I'd very much like to see it.'

'I don't trust you,' said Briony. 'There's too much you concealed from me in the first place.'

'But with good reason,' said Charlie.

'Then how do I know what else you might not be telling me, for "good reason"?'

'There's nothing else I can think of that could possibly help,' said Charlie.

'In that case,' said Briony, 'I'd like to go to bed, if you don't mind.'

'Briony . . .' Charlie sighed, 'be reasonable. It doesn't have to be this way. If you've got some idea where she is, then tell me. Maybe I can help. But I can't help if you wall me out.'

'Charlie,' said Briony patiently, 'I think my sister is involved with this Pastoral Foundation. I don't know what it is. I don't know where it is. And I don't know how or why she's involved – except that she's given them money. I'm trying to find out how and why she's involved. I'm doing it in my own way . . . because I can't see any *other* way. And since it seems to involve only women, I don't actually want any help from you. In fact, the last thing I need is to have you stirring up trouble among the people I'm trying to create a feeling of confidence with.'

'Those twisted freaks down at the Casa Negra, you mean?' said Charlie, clearly stung by this rejection.

'My sister's one of those "twisted freaks",' said Briony.

'I'm sorry,' said Charlie, 'I didn't mean it like that.'

'Oh, yes, you did. That's exactly how you meant it. That's why she didn't have anyone left who she could turn to or trust.'

'Briony, I'm tired,' Charlie pleaded, 'it was just a slip—'

'So am I, tired,' she cut in. 'Very tired. And I want to get undressed and go to bed. So will you please leave?'

He got up from where he was sitting at the end of the bed, seemed to be about to say something else, but then gave up, made a gesture of bewildered resignation, and walked slowly out of the flat.

TAMARA (7)

Poor Charlie.

He loves me, Sis, he truly does, in his own kind, caring, cackhanded sort of way.

I wish it had worked out. I do wish. Only Charlie cared. The only one who ever really did.

Poor Charlie, he doesn't understand how I feel. 'It's not a mental illness,' he was always telling me, 'it's quite harmless, just a sort of foible, really. Nothing to get neurotic about.' As if I was trying to stop biting my nails.

Dear Charlie, he meant it for the best. I don't know what they teach these guys at therapy school but he hasn't got the faintest idea.

It's not a foible, it's an emotional and spiritual sickness. A whole part of my psyche, of my emotional being, can't function without it. It's a crippling and terrible addiction, a need to self-destruct.

Don't ask why, Bri . . . I don't understand it either.

Damaged goods.

I have this cruel streak. You didn't know that either, did you? So much you've never known. I did some horrid things when I was a child.

I told Charlie about them.

He thinks Dad was too dominating and I was afraid of him. So I kept all my emotions in check and my own little space in perfect control. And all my fear and anger got bottled up and hidden away, like the stuff in my closet.

You remember when you were in hospital and had pneumonia and couldn't breathe and they thought you were going to die? Did you know that part of me . . . (I don't know how to say this, but you can't hear me so . . .) part of me wanted you to die. Part of me hoped you wouldn't make it through the night.

Isn't that just the worst thing you ever heard? Your own twin actually felt a kind of exhilaration at the thought that you might not be coming back.

Why? I don't know why. I resented you, I suppose. In fact I think part of me – only a part of me – hated you. I didn't want a twin. It meant I got half of everything. (That's how I thought of it, anyway.) I only got half as nice a birthday present, half as good a Christmas present. My clothes would have been twice as nice without you around. And you always let me down. You always looked so scruffy, you said such stupid things, and people thought I was you and you were me. And I hated that.

But I couldn't sleep that night, with you in hospital. I felt so guilty. I was so afraid that God would punish me terribly for what I was thinking that I concentrated my mind on this picture of you lying in your hospital bed . . . And I pumped all the energy out of my body into your body, like I was blowing up a Lilo . . . (but you know all that).

And you got better. Miraculous, they said. The symbiotic power of twins.

Did I really want you to die? Did I really, truly?

I don't know. Strange thing, a child's mind. Kids can't quite get a handle on the notion of death, can they? Death is Granny not being there any more. I always thought death was a kind of disappearance. The absence of presence, as it were. The body vanished.

Vanishing: that has always captivated me, the whole idea. To be invisible, but here.

Maybe Charlie was right: it's all Dad's fault.

Or maybe I was born this way; defective genes perhaps.

How can we ever know? It's buried too deep inside. I don't know why it's there and I don't look for reasons any more. It's just the way I am.

But I do remember . . .

I'm maybe four, five, six years old (it doesn't matter) and I think we're on the quay at Newlyn. There're boats and ropes and derricks and fish. And I'm pressing up against Dad. And he's holding my wrists very tightly. He's wearing slicks, his storm coat, that PVC oilskin kind of stuff, remember? And I'm pressing my face into him and he's holding my wrists so tightly he's lifting me off the ground. And we're kind of wrestling in a fun sort of kids-and-dads way.

I didn't know then what I was feeling, I only knew it felt good. But the truth is, horny was how I was feeling. Yeah, yeah, even at five or six years old. But I didn't know what that meant, of course.

I loved Dad's oilskin coat. Any time I could press myself against him when he was wearing his slicks, I did. I loved the smell of them, the touch of them. Remember when we used to play . . . I always tried to find some excuse to wear those slicks? I even sneaked downstairs one night, took off my nightie and rolled myself up in that storm coat, shiny side in. Mum came down and caught me.

Poor Mum. I don't know what she made of that.

I don't think Charlie knows what to make of me at all.

I don't think he quite believed me, some of the things I told him.

And yet I think he could have saved me, if I'd let him. But I chose not to. Choice, you see, Sis. We always have a choice. We always choose evil. We can always say no. But I chose to say yes.

Poor sausage . . . You looked so puzzled, sitting there, listening to Charlie droning on. You just can't get your head round this, can you? Well, I do envy you. You're such an ordinary, normal kind of woman. You keep looking for Mr Right, and you keep finding Mr Wrong, but some day soon you're going to settle for Mr Somewhere-in-Between and make some babies and live in a cottage near Mousehole with a border collie-cross with a white patch over its eye . . .

Because such ordinary things make you content. That's what I envy. I wish I could be satisfied with what satisfies you. So very little.

How could you possibly understand why I was drawn to something so monstrous as the Pastor? The Pastor needs women who are receptive to his brand of evil. Women who surrender themselves entirely to obsession, to desire. Women who can't stop themselves, who don't even wish to try to stop themselves. Women who are drawn to self-destruction; the moth to the candle.

But that isn't you, my darling, dear, beloved sister. That is totally beyond the realms of your experience . . . Beyond your capacity even to imagine the sublime rapture of anything so cruel, so terrible . . . The exhilaration of submitting to a passion so consuming that it dissolves your physical existence, wipes you away, slowly rubs your image off the glass – like a window cleaner with a chamois leather.

Even when I realized what it was doing to me, I could not control the desire. I just had to keep on going back, I could not let go.

WALDO

One evening, Drusilla said, 'There's someone here tonight we haven't seen for a while. He's asking for you.'

'Do I know him?' said Briony.

'No. But Tamara was his favourite.'

'Did you explain that I'm not Tam?'

'No,' said Drusilla. 'I'll let you do that.'

His name was Waldo. He was waiting for her in the sub-basement cellar, the place they called 'the dungeon'. He was sitting in an alcove. There was a lighted candle on the table.

'Hullo, Waldo.' She flashed him a smile and sat down.

'Hullo, Tamara.' He smiled as well. His teeth were small, crooked and yellow-brown. One at the front was made of gold. 'What happened to you?'

She wondered what he meant.

'Oh . . . this and that,' she improvised.

He had a craggy face, clean-shaven but pockmarked. In his sixties, she guessed. He was wearing a hat – a black leather trilby; a belted leather trench coat, with broad lapels, fully open; trousers and boots of black leather also. And a black shirt, buttoned up, without a tie.

He was smoking a French cigarette.

He looked like a Gestapo officer in a movie. She pictured in her mind an old Citroën Light-15 parked outside on the cobblestones.

'You disappeared,' he said.

'I did,' she agreed, still not sure whether to bluff this one out or come clean.

'I missed you.' He took a noisy draw on his Gitane and let the smoke drift and curl out of his open mouth. 'Did you miss me?'

'I'm sorry, Waldo, but I didn't miss anyone.'

The craggy face splintered into a bleak grin. 'You haven't changed.'

'Oh, but I have,' said Briony, who was beginning to take pleasure in these ambiguous conversations. 'I'm someone entirely different now.'

Waldo didn't query that; he seemed to think it was a joke.

He bought champagne and knocked it back like lager.

'You like my new hat?' he asked.

'Suits you,' she said. 'Makes you look like the secret police.'

'I am the secret police,' he said.

'What do you want from me?' she said.

'Your secrets,' said Waldo.

He had a slight accent – somewhere in Europe, but she couldn't place it.

He was the first customer she'd met who had any charm or wit. He said he was Austrian. He told her about his family in pre-war Vienna. He was a pilot with the *Luftwaffe* in the war, he said. Shot down over the Midlands and spent two years in a POW camp in Scotland. He teased her. He flirted with her. He asked her to marry him. She got the impression he had asked Tamara that question many times before.

He left around midnight and tipped her twenty pounds.

He came again the following week. They sat in the dungeon, exactly as before.

He asked her what she was doing for Christmas.

'I'm staying in London,' she said. And, to pre-empt an invitation, added: 'With family.'

He was giving her a strange look. There was a lot of humour in it. And curiosity. Perhaps Tamara had already told him that she had no family outside Cornwall. If she had, it didn't seem to worry him, this little discrepancy with the truth.

'Tell me,' he said – he prefaced nearly everything with 'tell me' – 'do you hang up your stockings still on Christmas Eve?'

'Only one of them,' she said. 'But Santa doesn't put much in it any more.'

He said he would have words with Santa, in that case.

'Does he listen?'

'I have friends in high places,' said Waldo, and winked.

'Do you hang up your stocking?' she enquired.

'I don't have a stocking,' he replied. 'Only my socks.'

'Ahh,' she sighed, but not sarcastically. 'Poor Waldo.'

'Perhaps you would give me one of yours,' he said.

'What would you want Santa to bring you, if I did?' she said.

'Only you,' said Waldo.

'I don't think Santa would ever get me down the chimney.'

'Then I'll hang my stocking out the window.'

'I don't think it'll take my weight.'

'Why don't you give me a stocking and let me be the judge?'

'You get my company,' said Briony, coyly, 'but you don't get my stockings. That's extra.'

'Everything's extra,' said Waldo.

He offered her fifty pounds.

She said her stockings weren't worth fifty pounds.

He insisted, and took a bank note from his wallet.

So she undid her suspenders, rolled down her stockings and gave them to him as a Christmas present. She pushed the bank note back towards him across the table with one extended finger. He left it there.

He asked her, if she could have anything in the world for Christmas, what it would be.

She thought about it and replied: 'My sister.'

'You didn't tell me you had a sister.'

'We're twins.'

'You never said.'

'I'm full of secrets.'

'You look alike?'

'Sometimes.'

'What is her name, your sister?'

'Briony.'

'And where is Briony now?'

'I don't know,' she said. And, at this moment, she really did feel she had no idea where Briony was, or what she was doing, or why.

Waldo stayed until after one. When he got up to leave, she stood up too. He was not a tall man – not a lot taller than she was. He asked if he could kiss her Merry Christmas.

Briony laughed. It sounded absurd, talking about Merry Christmas in this dingy cellar – a woman in a rubber basque, without her stockings, and a man old enough to be her grandfather, dressed like a Gestapo inquisitor.

She said, 'I'm sorry, Waldo, you know the rules.'

'Pretend there's mistletoe.'

'I can't. No touch. It's the rules. If I'm seen I'll get the sack.'

'Then don't be seen,' said Waldo and blew out the candle.

The second they were in darkness, she felt his mouth on hers; one hand behind her back and the other moving down across her bosom, as if he was polishing it with the flat of his hand, down across her belly. Then, just as quickly, he was gone.

She relit the candle.

Waldo had left the fifty-pound note on the table . . . And had added another to it.

A hundred pounds for a pair of stockings and a ten-second grope.

She picked up the glasses they'd been using and two champagne bottles – one empty, one half full. As she walked towards the stairs that led up to the main club room above, she noticed that someone was watching her from the shadows of another alcove . . .

It was the tall woman with the short blonde hair and the Scandinavian features, the woman she had seen climbing into the back of the stretch limousine outside . . . The woman she had seen in the woods behind Leysholme walking with her dogs.

She was alone, smoking a cigarette and holding a drink – a tall, thin tumbler of something.

BIBI

The following night, she asked Drusilla if she knew who the tall, blonde woman was.

Drusilla grinned. Her teeth were almost too white to be real. 'Why?' she replied. 'You want to be her hostess?' She arched an eyebrow – just visible above her sunglasses.

'She keeps watching me,' said Briony. 'Staring at me.'

'Perhaps she thinks you're Tam.'

'I think she does. Who is she? What's her name?'

'Does it matter?' said Drusilla. 'No one uses her own name here. Whoever she says she is, she's someone else.'

'Was she friendly with Tam?'

'She's not friendly with anyone.'

'So why does she stare?' said Briony. 'Was Tam her hostess?'

'She never has a hostess,' Drusilla replied. 'She doesn't like being with people. She doesn't like people very much. Dogs, that's all she really wants to be with. She'd like to live in a world of dogs.'

'Do you know her?' said Briony.

'I don't think anybody knows her,' Drusilla replied, as if that had deeper meaning.

She was in the club again the following evening. Briony caught sight of her talking to Bibi, the frail-looking waitress from Poland.

Later, when the club had closed for the night and Briony

was leaving, she climbed the iron stairs into Coal Street and saw Bibi about twenty yards ahead of her, walking away.

Briony called after her but Bibi didn't hear ... or else ignored her. Bibi hurried on, rounding the corner into Shadwell Road.

By the time Briony was rounding the same corner Bibi was on the other side of the road, climbing into the back seat of the long black limousine that Briony had seen here before.

She watched as the limo pulled away, heading south towards the river.

The following night, a Friday, was the last night before the Casa Negra closed its doors for the Christmas break. They were so busy that Briony scarcely caught a glimpse of Bibi all evening until they almost collided as Briony was walking into the women's room and Bibi was walking out.

'Hi, Beeb,' said Briony.

'Hi, Tam,' said Bibi, with a dreamy, soft-focus smile.

Two overweight, middle-aged women were changing by the lockers on the other side of the room. Briony drew Bibi to one side so they would not be overheard.

'I saw you going home last night,' she said. 'I called after you, I was going to offer you a lift, but you got into that fancy stretch limo on Shadwell Road.'

'*Mmm*,' agreed Bibi ... Which was about as much conversation as you ever got out of her, some nights.

She came from Lodz and didn't have much English, although she seemed to understand more than she could actually speak. She looked pale and frail. She had straw blonde hair which hung in natural ringlets – unlike Drusilla's, which cascaded down to her waist but were merely a wig. She looked about fifteen years old.

'So who's the lucky guy?' said Briony.

'*Mmm*,' said Bibi, frowning with the effort of understanding and translating her reply. 'Is, ah, priwat house. Is friend.'

'I saw you talking to that tall woman – about forty-ish? – blonde hair . . . Is she Polish?'

'*Mmm*, no, is, ah, sometimes here. Is no Polish. Is, ah, maybe Finlandia, someplace, I don't know.'

'So where did you go in the swanky limo?'

'*Mmm* . . . We go for party. We make nice party.'

'Oh, yeah? So how do I get an invite?'

Bibi frowning with effort again. 'What is, ah, inwite?'

'How do I get to come to the party? How do I get asked?'

'Ahh . . .' Bibi's face lit up suddenly and she giggled. 'You have to make, ah, good connection.'

'Get in with the right people, you mean?'

Bibi giggled again. 'Yes, is true . . . You got to make, ah . . .' She took hold of some of her hair and rubbed the ringlets lightly between her fingers. 'Blonde.'

'I've got to have blonde hair?'

'Ya, ya, *tak* . . .' Bibi burst out giggling again. 'Is true. Gentlemen prefer blonde. I give you nice, *mmm*, zhampoo . . . Change your life, hah?'

It struck Briony that the girl was bombed out of her mind on something.

'Maybe some other time,' said Briony.

'*Mmm*, yes,' Bibi agreed, turning and almost losing her balance as she reached for a door handle that was a good three feet further away from where she had anticipated. '*Oops* . . .' She recovered herself and giggled some more. 'I make you nice blonde. I make you nice for Misha's party.'

'Misha's party?'

'You don't coming to big house for New Year's?'

'What big house?'

'You don't get inwite to Leysholme?'

'A New Year's Eve party? At Leysholme?'

'Make you change nice blonde,' Bibi burbled, and was now halfway out of the door. 'Then Misha give you inwite.'

'Who is Misha?' asked Briony.

The only Misha she could think of was Dee's Misha. She

wondered if there was a connection. She tried to grab Bibi's arm but Bibi stepped back out of reach, giggling, as if this were a game.

'Who is he?' Briony persisted. 'Who is Misha?'

But that only provoked more giggles, as Bibi tottered away down the corridor, unsteady on her high heels.

THE COAT

She had ten days off.

Her mother telephoned, the day before Christmas Eve, wondering if she was coming home for Christmas and to ask about Tamara.

Briony wondered whether it would be less distressing to say nothing about the Casa Negra. But to have no news at all would surely be worse.

'I've found out where she's been working,' said Briony. 'She did give up nursing for a while. She's been waitressing at a club.'

'Waitressing?' said Kathleen, and sounded as if she didn't believe it.

'She couldn't earn a living doing agency work,' said Briony. 'She ran out of money. And full-time nursing jobs aren't easy to come by. So I think it was just a sort of stop-gap thing.'

'Well, why doesn't she call us?' said Kathleen, growing agitated. 'Is she there now?'

'No, Mum, I don't know where she is,' Briony confessed. 'She gave up the waitressing job in the summer. And she seems to have got involved with some sort of religious group. I think they're based down in Kent somewhere. I'm trying to find out. But they're a bit secretive.'

'What do you mean, a religious group?' said Kathleen. 'You mean like Jehovah's Witnesses or something?'

'It's called The Pastoral Foundation,' said Briony. 'I don't know anything about it.'

'Well, is she all right?' said Kathleen. 'Do you know?'

'I haven't spoken to her,' said Briony, 'but I've got no reason to think there's anything wrong.' Which was such a lie that she couldn't even say it with any conviction.

Her mother remained silent for a few moments. God only knew what was going through her mind.

When she did finally speak, she said, 'What about you? Are you coming home for Christmas?'

She felt sorry for her mother, being stuck at home with Dennis. Every year they were invited to one or other of his brothers' homes for Christmas Day. But Dennis resented their modest prosperity and always refused their offers. Briony could picture what Christmas Day would be like. They would go to chapel. Dennis would return home in misanthropic mood. Dinner would be a short, silent affair. Kathleen would retire to the company of her babbling television. Dennis would take Jack for a walk and then sit in his armchair, reading Thursday's *Cornishman*, tutting and scowling every time the audience laughed on television. And they would be in bed by ten o'clock.

Recalling so many Christmases past, like a flash memory, Briony said, 'I'm sorry, Mum, I can't get down. I've got a job here – waitressing at the club where Tam was working. We only get a few days off. Isn't worth coming down just for that.'

'Oh, I see,' said Kathleen. 'No, well, fair enough, my love, I understand.' Briony could hear the disappointment in her voice.

'There was one other thing,' she said. 'Julie phoned, wanting to know when you were coming back. I gave her Tamara's number . . . Did she call you?'

'No, she hasn't called,' said Briony. 'I'd better give her a ring. Thanks for letting me know.'

She called Julie a little later. She explained that she still hadn't found Tamara and she would have to stay in London for a little while longer. Julie didn't seem to mind. She said her niece had moved in for the time being and was quite happy, taking care of Beatrice.

It didn't feel like Christmas. It was the first she had ever spent away from Newlyn. Cards had been arriving through the post for Tamara these past weeks. Briony had opened them all and displayed them around the room. She had received a few herself – most of them readdressed by Julie. There was even talk of snow on the weather forecast. But it still didn't feel like Christmas.

The house was quieter than ever. Francesca and Amanda, the students who lived in the room above Gloria's, had gone home for their holidays. Diane, the slender, green-eyed woman of France who have not seen her sister since some months had flown home to her family in Tours. And Briony had seen nothing of dotty Lotte on the second floor, or any of the other peculiar middle-aged women who hid themselves away in these rooms.

The evening before Christmas Eve, Dee came knocking on her door. Briony had not seen her for more than a month.

'Someone downstairs got a package for you,' she said.

'A package?' said Briony. 'For me?'

'Rasta man. Rang my bell by mistake. Miss Carkeat, he said.'

There was no Entryphone system at The Hermitage. Briony had to traipse all the way down to the ground floor to see what it was about.

'Could be for Tam, I guess,' said Dee, leading Briony from the attic.

Briony hurried down the remainder of the stairs to the

ground floor. A black guy with a stubbly beard and a woollen hat of rainbow colours was waiting in the porch, holding a large box.

'Are you looking for me?' she said.

'Your name Carkeat?'

'Who are you?'

'Andy,' he said. 'Kay-Kay Cabs.'

'What is it?'

'Father Christmas come early.'

He handed her the box. It was wrapped in Harrods' paper and secured with some fancy Christmas gift-tie. A plain white envelope had been taped to the box. On the envelope was written: *Ms Carkeat, Top/88 Styles Lane, E5.*

She shook it. It felt like clothing of some kind. It was quite heavy.

'I don't think this is for me,' she said. 'Must be for my sister.'

'I don't care who it's for,' said Andy. 'I just need an autograph.' He gave her a receipt book to sign.

'Who's this from?' she said.

'Some guy over Highgate.'

'Didn't he give a name?'

'Something foreign,' said Andy.

'No message?'

'Just said to wait and take you back.'

'Take me back?' she said. 'Back where?'

'Highgate. Heathfield Lane.'

'Can you wait a few minutes?' said Briony.

'That's what the man said,' Andy replied. 'That's what the man paying for. I'll be in the car.'

Briony went back up to the flat. Dee was sitting on the stairs at the second floor landing, her eyes widening with curiosity.

'Prezzy?'

'Must be for Tam.'

Dee followed her up the attic stairs and into the flat.

'Maybe she's got a secret sugar daddy,' said Briony, and put the box on the bed.

'Hey, . . . Horrids,' said Dee, impressed. 'He be *my* sugar daddy too?'

Briony fetched a knife from the kitchen, put the envelope to one side and sliced through the gift-tie. Dee watched, fascinated, as Briony folded back the wrapping paper, took the lid off the box and drew apart several sheets of soft tissue paper.

'Jee-zus . . .' whispered Dee.

Briony lifted it out of the box and laid it out on the bed. It was a coat, a long winter coat, made of soft black leather, with a black fur collar.

'Who is he?' said Dee.

'I don't know. He told the driver to wait and take me back.'

'Where to?'

'Highgate.'

'Who do you know in Highgate?' said Dee.

'I don't.'

'Who does Tam know in Highgate?'

'Search me.'

Briony opened the envelope. Inside was a Christmas card. Inside the card was written: *Wear this and nothing else.* It was unsigned.

Dee was reading it over her shoulder. '*Mmm*, I like.'

Briony tried on the coat. It was mid-calf length. Belted at the waist.

'Feel that leather,' said Dee in wonderment. 'So soft. Must have cost a fortune.'

'I don't know what to do,' said Briony, admiring it in the full-length mirror. 'I can't send it back if it's for Tamara.' It looked a bit silly over jeans and a ragged jersey, but it fitted perfectly. He must have known Tam's size, must have bought her things before.

'Of course you can't send it back,' Dee scoffed. 'Keep it here for Tam. If you get cold, wear it yourself.'

Briony took off the coat and went back downstairs. The front door was still open but Andy was no longer standing in the porch. She walked down the garden path and found him sitting in the car.

He wound down the window as she approached. Rap music came thumping out into the cold night air.

'I think the package is for my sister, not for me,' she said.

'Uh-huh,' said Andy, without much interest.

'Would you please tell Mr whoever-he-is that she's not here right now? But I'll keep the package safe and give it to her when I see her.'

'You're not coming back with me?'

'I don't think it's me he's expecting.'

'No skin off my nose,' said Andy, and restarted the car. 'See yer later.'

'Happy Christmas,' said Briony.

'Sure. Have a good one.'

When she got back upstairs to the flat, Dee had gone.

She looked up Heathfield Lane in the street atlas. It was on the edge of Hampstead Heath, close to Highgate Ponds.

She looked through Tamara's address book to see if she could find an entry for anyone in Heathfield Lane. But she looked in vain.

Dee came back upstairs. She was wearing a big quilted jacket now, zipped up as if she was off to the ski slopes, and carrying a canvas bag slung from her shoulder.

'Listen, I'm off now, Bri ... Won't see you till after Christmas. You going home, see the folks?'

'I don't think so,' said Briony. 'They'll never stop questioning me about Tam. I'm okay here. I feel a bit knackered, tell you the truth. I'm waitressing, evenings. I feel like a good rest.'

'Sure.' Dee smiled. 'Button yourself up in that nice new coat and hibernate till next year.'

'Not such a bad idea,' said Briony.

'And remember,' said Dee, 'wear nothing else.'

'On my own?'

'What a waste,' said Dee. 'Gotta dash.' She blew Briony a couple of kisses, turned and was gone, her trainers squeaking faintly on the attic boards.

Christmas came and went.

The day before New Year's Eve, a Saturday, the telephone rang at about ten past seven in the evening. It rang so seldom that, every time it did, she experienced the same flurry of emotions – a mixture of hope and fear and expectation: hoping it might be Tamara but fearing that it might be the police with bad news.

She picked it up and said hello.

'I hope you had a pleasant Christmas,' a voice enquired. It was a man – not English – speaking with the telephone pushed halfway down his throat, by the sound of it.

She didn't answer. She thought it was a wrong number at first. But then he said, 'I hope you like the coat.'

Now she recognized the gravelly voice. 'Waldo . . .?

'I hope it fits,' he said.

'I can't take it, Waldo,' she replied.

'Of course you can. What are you talking about?'

'It's hard to explain. I'm not who you think I am.'

'I want you to have it. I want you to wear it. The way I asked.'

'I'm sorry, Waldo, I don't want it.'

'It's such a small request. Such a tiny thing to ask. And such a lovely coat.'

'You don't understand, Waldo. I can't take it. It's not right.'

A silence. And then:

'Very well,' he said reluctantly. 'Bring it back to me.'

'I'll send it.'

'No, bring it,' he said. 'I have someone I'd like to show you. I know you'd be very interested to see her. She looks like you've never seen her before.'

'Who's that?' she asked.

'Your sister,' said Waldo.

And put down the telephone.

A little later, a cab arrived.

THE HEATH

The driver pulled up outside a large detached house that overlooked the gaping blackness of Hampstead Heath.

The fare was on account. He wrote out a ticket and handed the pad to her for signature.

'I've never been here before,' she said, as she signed the ticket. 'Which is his place?'

The driver pointed to a wrought-iron gate in the brick wall. 'Side entrance. Basement flat.'

She handed the pad back to him and got out of the car, carrying the Harrods box with the coat inside.

The wrought-iron gate was locked. There was an Entry-phone. She pressed the button. After a few moments, she heard Waldo's voice: 'Through the gate and down the steps,' he said.

He released the gate. She pushed it and entered a small, paved yard. Some steep steps led down to the basement flat. Waldo was waiting for her at the front door.

She stepped into a small hallway.

Waldo looked older without his trilby hat on. His hair was white and cut very short. He wore the same leather trousers she always saw him in, and a matching shirt.

'I asked you to wear it,' he said, referring to the box she was carrying.

'I'm not at work now, Waldo,' she replied. 'I wear what I want.' She offered the box to him: 'Thanks, but no thanks.'

He turned his back to her and moved across the hallway. She followed him into the sitting room: a large room with a Burgundy carpet, heavy, velvet curtains, and a sofa and armchairs upholstered in grey tweed.

It was very warm in here. She could smell the remains of a meal that was an hour or two old. And the smoke of his Gitanes.

'Put the coat on,' he said. 'Do as I asked.'

'I told you, I can't accept it. I came here to see my sister, that's the only reason.'

Some bottles of liquor stood on a silver tray in a corner, beside a stereo system that looked as if it might have been high-tech in the early 1960s. Waldo poured whisky into a tumbler and added a splash of soda.

'You want a drink?' he asked.

'I want to see my sister,' she said. 'That's all I want.'

'Help yourself,' he said, referring to the tray of bottles.

'I came to see Tamara. I don't want a drink, I don't want anything. I just want to see my sister.'

'Then do as you're told. And put on the coat.'

She put the box down on the sofa.

'I don't want to put on the coat, thank you. You said I could see my sister. I don't think I believe you.'

'You don't trust me?' said Waldo.

'I don't think she's here. But prove me wrong.'

'First,' said Waldo, 'you must do as you're told and put on the nice coat that I gave you for Christmas.'

'No,' said Briony.

'Then you may leave,' said Waldo. 'I have more interesting things to do.'

She said nothing. He was different now. At the Casa Negra he had been charming and amusing. Perhaps he was being his true self tonight, or perhaps he wanted to woo her into role-playing games. Or perhaps it was even simpler: he just wanted sex.

'Do as I told you,' said Waldo. 'Or feel free to leave.'

If only to call his bluff, she removed the lid from the box and took out the coat. She unzipped the quilted jacket she was wearing, draped it over the back of the sofa and put on the coat he had bought for her. She waited for him to say something.

'That's not what I told you to do,' he said. 'What did I tell you to do?'

'To put on the coat.'

'What did I write in the card?'

'Oh, for Christ's sake,' she sighed, 'what is the point of all this?'

'Why so coy?' he enquired.

'I'm not coy,' she said, 'and I'm not Tamara either. I don't know what stupid games she played with you, but I don't play. You've got the wrong sister.'

'I know you're not Tamara,' said Waldo. 'I knew you weren't Tamara the very first time I saw you. *I* don't mind . . . But it's not me who started the game. You're the one who wants to play a game, little sister. Why do you want to dress like Tamara? Why do you want to look like Tamara? Why do you let people call you Tamara? What's *your* game, little sister?'

She said nothing.

'Men rent you for an evening at their table,' he continued. 'You put yourself out for hire. You're happy to take the fat commission that Drusilla pays you. You're happy to let them buy champagne at thirty pounds a bottle and pocket your share of the profit. You're happy to take my hundred pounds for your stockings. But it's your sister they think they're renting. It's your sister they're attracted to. You're just an imposter. "I'm not Tamara," you say – very morally superior. "I don't take off my clothes for anyone." But you're happy to take the money that you sweet-smile out of suckers at the Casa Negra . . . Suckers like me. You pretend to be someone you're not, and you milk our wallets dry. But you tell me now that you don't play stupid games. So, what then? You want

177

to *become* Tamara? You want to be the real thing? Or are you sick in the mind, are you really Tamara but can't face the truth, so you're pretending you're a make-believe sister?'

'I'm not pretending anything,' said Briony. 'You think I enjoy the work? I want to find my sister, that's all. I don't know where she is. She worked at the Casa Negra because she needed money. Now she's moved on but I don't know where she's gone. But I think people at the Casa Negra *do* know. I've got no other way of finding her.'

'You want to find your sister?' Waldo enquired. 'You don't know your sister very well, do you?'

'I thought I did,' said Briony. 'But maybe I don't.'

'Well, I'm going to introduce you to your sister,' said Waldo. 'The real Tamara ... Like you've never seen her before. The sister you never knew you had. She's in the other room.'

'I don't believe you.'

'That is your privilege.'

He sat down, lit a cigarette, made himself comfortable and looked at her, as if he was waiting for a floor show to begin.

'Then let me see her,' said Briony.

'First, do as you're told.'

'If she's in the other room, ask her to come out.'

'That's not possible.'

'Then ask her to say something. Prove to me she's in there.'

'She can't speak. She can't move and she can't make a sound.'

Briony felt so powerless, it made her angry.

'What do you *want* from me?' she said, and could feel herself beginning to weaken, could hear it in her voice.

He could sense it too. 'Do as you're told,' he said, 'and you may see your sister.'

She stood there, refusing to move, but knowing that she either had to walk out and go home, or do as he said. She unbuckled the belt of her jeans and let them drop to the floor.

She kicked off her shoes and stepped out of her jeans. She had to take off the coat to remove the rest of her clothes.

He watched with casual interest, his head cocked a little to one side, as if he were assessing an artist's painting or a sculpture.

When she was completely naked she put the coat on once again.

She stood there in taut silence.

'There now,' he said, and looked satisfied. 'Was that so very arduous? Does that feel so very unpleasant? Do you feel more like your sister now? Does that feel good?'

She refused to answer.

'You know why I want you to do this?'

'If you touch me,' she said, 'I'll take your fucking eyes out.'

'Ooh . . .' He jerked his head back in mock surprise. 'Little sister has fire.'

'Better believe it,' she muttered. 'I want to see my sister. I don't believe she's here. I think you're a liar. But I've done what you said, now you do what you promised.'

Waldo smiled, a rather sour, twisted smile.

'Sure,' he said. 'I will show you. But I want you to really *know* your sister, how it feels to be her.' He rose up from the chair. 'Put your shoes back on.'

'What for?' said Briony.

'Because I tell you to.'

They stared at each other for a minute or so, neither moving.

If only to get this over with, Briony knelt down and put on her shoes. Waldo went out of the room and came back a moment or two later, putting on a leather trench coat.

'Where are we going?' she asked.

'A short walk. Not very far.'

She picked her clothes up off the floor to get dressed but he said:

'No, no . . . Leave them.' He snapped his fingers: 'Come.'

'Not like this,' she protested.

179

'Oh yes,' he said, 'exactly like this. The coat will keep you warm.'

'That's not the point.'

'Come, come,' he said impatiently, and snapped his fingers again.

She followed him out into the hallway, buttoning up the coat as she did so. He opened the front door and stood aside to let her go first, as if he were a gentleman. She stepped out into the cold December night.

He closed the door behind him and said, 'Your right hand.'

'My what?' she said.

'Your right hand. Give it to me.'

She raised her hand. He took her forearm and snapped a handcuff round her wrist. He snapped the other cuff around his own, like a police officer with a prisoner.

'This is what you like to do with my sister?' Briony enquired with quiet contempt.

'Not quite,' Waldo replied. 'It's more the other way around.'

'This is what my sister likes to do,' Briony concluded.

'Very nearly. One modest refinement . . .'

He began to unbutton the coat.

'I don't believe this,' she said. 'This is what you get off on? This gives you pleasure?'

'Not especially,' said Waldo. 'It gives your sister pleasure. My pleasures come later.'

When the coat was fully unbuttoned, he led her up the steps, through the gate and down to a path that led around the side of the heath.

She put her free hand into the coat pocket and covered as much of herself as she could, but the other half of the coat hung open and there was nothing she could do about it. There was no frost but the temperature felt close to zero. At least there was no one about, it was so cold and dark.

They walked along the footpath at strolling pace. This

stretch of the path was lamp-lit, with an iron railing that fenced off the dark and rolling acres of the heath.

'She likes this walk,' said Waldo. 'But only after dark.'

Briony said nothing.

They came to a point where the footpath entered the confines of the heath proper, the street lamps ended, and they strolled on into darkness.

'All kinds of people wander up here in the night,' said Waldo. 'In summer, or on moonlit nights, you see shadows shifting in and out among the bushes. They wait, they watch, they move around.'

He was leading her off on to a different path now, through trees and bushes, into a large field.

'They sunbathe naked here in summer,' said Waldo. 'Have done for many years. As far back as I can remember. Tamara likes to hang around here ... Especially on warm nights, warm enough to take off her coat. This is where she likes to ... moon-bathe, shall we call it.'

He unlocked the cuff from his own wrist and attached it to the horizontal branch of a tree that was just above her head, so that she was left standing with one arm up.

'And because she prefers balance in her life,' said Waldo, 'she likes the other wrist locked as well. And there I leave her and enjoy a stroll, a peaceful cigarette. While I'm gone, all kinds of things come creepy-crawling out of the darkness, all kinds of lowlife.'

Briony was so cold now she could barely speak. He removed the handcuff from the tree branch and unlocked the other cuff as well, removing it from her wrist.

'I think I've made the point,' he said.

She buttoned up the coat and followed him back to the main footpath.

'I don't believe you,' she said. 'I don't believe this happens.'

'What she does at the Casa Negra,' said Waldo, 'she does for money. But she walks the heath for free. This she does because she likes it. It turns her on.'

181

'I don't believe you,' she said again. 'I believe it's how you get *your* kicks, but not my sister.'

'You don't have to believe me,' Waldo replied. 'You can see for yourself.'

When they got back to the flat, he took off his coat and entered a room that was next to his sitting room. He remained standing there in the dark.

'Come in,' he said. 'Come and see your sister.'

Briony came as far as the doorway but was afraid to go in.

'Don't be scared,' said Waldo. 'There's nothing to be afraid of, except the truth.'

She stepped inside. He switched on the light: a dim, red glow, like the light in a photographer's developing room.

One wall was plastered with photographs. Hundreds, maybe thousands . . . Photographs of Tamara . . . Tied, chained, strapped, masked, gagged, bound in every conceivable way, in every conceivable position. Every single picture was of Tamara.

There were mirrors on the other walls.

There was no furniture in the room. Several large iron hooks protruded from the walls. She looked up at the ceiling where four more iron hooks protruded. The ceiling was covered with mirror glass as well.

'Everywhere she looked,' said Waldo, 'she could see herself.'

'Was she . . . Is she your mistress?' said Briony.

'My mistress?' Waldo laughed. 'I wish. But I'm not a rich man. I could only afford her once a month. She's not cheap.'

'What are you saying?' asked Briony. 'She charged you money for this?'

'Of course. Five hundred pounds a night.'

Briony winced.

'You didn't know?'

'Just you? Or she had other lovers?'

'Clients, perhaps, would be a better word,' said Waldo.

'She did this with other men as well? For money?'

'I could take you to streets not very far from here, some of the most expensive property in London: Hampstead, Highgate . . . Homes of princes, ambassadors, taipans . . . Tamara knows those houses well.'

'She's a call girl?' said Briony. 'A prostitute. Is that what you're telling me?'

'But no ordinary call girl,' said Waldo. 'It's a very specialized field. She has a very particular and demanding clientele. The top girls on the S-and-M scene make a lot of money.'

She was not really shocked – he was only confirming what she'd secretly feared all along, but could not quite believe, had not wanted to face up to. Where else could all that money have come from? Over a thousand a week, and in cash . . .

'You didn't wonder?' said Waldo, surprised.

'Oh, yes,' she said. 'I wondered.'

She walked out of the room, back into the sitting room.

He followed her and poured her a glass of brandy.

'Sit down a moment,' he said.

She shook her head. 'I don't want a drink.'

'It's medicinal. It'll settle you.'

She sat down, she felt too miserable to argue.

'Are they all call girls?' she asked. 'The hostesses? Bibi, Lola, Mojo . . .?'

'You didn't realize?'

'I guess I must seem very naïve.'

'Yes.'

'So every time someone asks me if I want to go for a drink after the club closes, what they mean is: am I in business?'

'Probably.'

It was not a shock, it was just somehow depressing. She felt rather stupid for not having cottoned on sooner.

'If it makes it any easier,' said Waldo, 'I felt a deep affection for your sister. I still do.'

She looked at him with contempt. 'No man could feel

respect or affection for a woman and put her through all that,' she said.

'You don't understand,' said Waldo. 'It's not a matter of putting your sister through it . . . It's what Tamara wants. It's what she needs.'

'She wanted money, maybe,' said Briony, 'but that's all.'

'I can see it's hard for you to understand,' said Waldo. 'But it's like I tried to tell you earlier on . . . This is not a game to Tamara. She's not playing. It's for real. What I've shown you tonight, none of it has anything to do with the physical. There is no pain or violence. It's in the mind. It requires a balance of domination and submission – like a balance of positive and negative. If it doesn't have that balance, it won't work. I love your sister. I asked her to stay with me. I asked her to marry me.'

'You can't be serious?' said Briony.

'Quite serious,' Waldo replied. 'Even an old grizzly bear like me. But she feels no love for anyone. She's afraid that she has no capacity for loving anyone. She has a complicated psychology.'

Briony sipped the brandy. She didn't want to discuss it with him. She didn't want to discuss anything with him.

'How long is it,' he asked, 'since you last saw her?'

'About eighteen months.'

He was surprised. 'So long?'

'When did *you* last see her?' said Briony.

'July, I think,' said Waldo. 'When she stopped working at the club, she came to see me once more, but then she refused to come. I phoned her but she was never in, never returned my calls. I don't go to the club so often any more. I lost interest.' He smiled, but it was a tired smile, touched with sadness or regrets or both. 'But you revived it for a little while.' He looked much older outside the dark confines of the Casa Negra. He must have been well into his seventies, Briony guessed.

He left her alone and closed the door so that she could get dressed.

He called a cab for her and put it on his account.

As she was leaving, she said, 'There's a woman who goes to the club sometimes. She travels in a black stretch limo, chauffeur-driven. She's always alone. I don't know what she's doing there. She looks too elegant. She's very tall – six foot maybe – in her forties, I'd guess. She looks like a model: a very sculpted face, quite beautiful – sort of Scandinavian features. Short blonde hair, very stylishly cut . . .'

Waldo was nodding his head.

'You know her?'

'I know who you mean.'

'Do you know who she is?'

'She's the boss,' said Waldo.

'She owns the Casa Negra?' said Briony.

'I don't know that she *owns* it,' said Waldo, 'but she controls everything that goes on there. She's Russian, they say. They call her Misha.'

LOTTE

It could only be Dee's Misha . . .

That night, in bed, thinking about it, she remembered Gloria saying that Misha was Russian. Tall, icy-blue eyes, Rudolf Nureyev cheekbones . . . Wasn't that what Gloria said?

But if Dee's Misha was the Misha who controlled the Casa Negra, it seemed strange that Dee was never there. And if Dee had had heart-to-heart talks with Tamara, then surely she would have known that Tam worked at the Casa Negra?

She was trying to remember what Dee had said she did for

a living. She worked for a company, their entertainment department, some sort of management job, hanging around, keeping clients happy.

She was trying to remember Dee's face, remember it clearly, hold it like a freeze-frame in her mind.

All she could recall was her beautiful teeth. Perfect white teeth.

Someone else she knew had perfect white teeth like that:

Drusilla.

Briony pictured Drusilla in her mind and imagined taking off those large sunglasses . . . and that long wig of cascading curls . . .

The next day was New Year's Eve. She had decided to gatecrash Misha's party at Leysholme so that she could look around the house. She would wear a hood or a mask, like they did at the Casa Negra, then no one would recognize her.

That evening, she picked up a towel and some shampoo, took some small change from her purse and went down to the bathroom on the floor below. She fed three twenty-p coins into the slot-meter and turned on the Ascot.

It was an ancient-looking model; the water was hot all right – almost hot enough to make tea with – but trickled out in a thin, desultory stream. The bath took an age to fill. She left her towel and shampoo on the seat of the only piece of furniture in the room – a painted kitchen chair that had lost its back – and returned upstairs to the flat to undress.

She took off her clothes, put on Tam's towelling robe and beach flip-flops and sat watching the end of a comedy programme on the television. She had only been gone about ten minutes, but by the time she got back to the bathroom someone else was in there. The door was still ajar. She could hear music as she approached along the passage – classical music, a string quartet perhaps. She eased open the door and peered into the steam. The water was still running.

A woman was standing with her back to the door, untying

the belt of a floral-print robe – a slender woman with blonde-grey hair, short and permed. It looked like dotty Lotte. She had not heard Briony enter – there was too much noise: the music, the echo, the hissing, scalding sound of the Ascot, and the cold water gushing from the tap.

Briony was lost for words. It must have been strikingly obvious that someone else was about to use the bath.

Lotte took off her robe and draped it over Briony's towel and shampoo on the backless kitchen chair.

Perhaps it was not Lotte, after all . . . This was a young woman's body, pale-skinned but firm, well-shaped, no flab.

But as she turned and leaned over the bath to agitate the water with her hand, Briony could see that it *was* Lotte. She was an extraordinary sight: she had the body of a woman in her twenties, but the wrinkled, pouchy face of a woman in her fifties.

Lotte reached across to the taps and turned them off; the hot first and then the cold. The Ascot died with a noisy shudder.

Lotte pushed herself upright, as if it was a big effort, raised one foot gingerly over the side of the bath and stepped into the water.

She moved like an old woman.

It was bizarre: a young body, a middle-aged face, and the posture of an eighty-year-old.

Briony wondered if she'd had some serious illness, or a problem affecting her joints.

Lotte lowered herself into a kneeling position, wincing as she did so, emitting little groans – effort perhaps, or pain. She leaned forwards, taking her weight on her hands, in a dog-like position, and, as she did so, Briony noticed what looked like a large tattoo on her buttock . . .

It was that same Gothic-style letter P, or whatever it was supposed to be, that she had noticed in the mural. It was a livid-blue colour against the pallor of Lotte's flesh, and as large as the flat of her hand.

It was identical to the P which Petra Pascali had used when she put her name on the tombstone in the mural, identical to the top of the crook in the old parson's hand.

Briony had just drawn breath to speak but the sight of that tattoo froze her completely. She remained in the doorway, shocked by the sight of it. Lotte gradually eased herself into a sitting position and then lay back in the water.

Almost at once, Lotte sensed that someone was there – the draught through the open door, perhaps. She craned her head around, as if her neck was very stiff, and saw Briony in the doorway.

'Yes?' she said.

'Excuse me,' said Briony, coming a little further into the room, 'but I was about to have a bath. That's my towel and my shampoo.' She pointed to the backless chair.

'Yes,' said Lotte, turning to face the taps again, 'you may take them.'

'I was running this bath for myself,' Briony protested.

'Yes,' Lotte said again, as if it was a matter of no concern to her, 'later, this is possible. You may have your things.' She had a peculiar, toneless way of speaking, like a machine.

At that moment the string quartet ground its way up to a small crescendo and Lotte relaxed deeper into the water, closing her eyes, savouring either the music or the hot water or both.

Briony could see there was no point in arguing. The woman was *in* the bath and, short of pulling her out by the hair, there was not much she could do about it.

She tossed Lotte's floral-print robe aside, letting it fall to the floor, grabbed her towel and shampoo and flounced out of the room, leaving the door wide open so that Lotte could enjoy the icy draughts that whistled up and down the unheated landings of this fridge of a house.

She went into the loo next door. While she was sitting there it occurred to her she didn't have any more change to feed the gas meter to run a second bath.

She went back into the bathroom to complain more rigorously . . . but Lotte had gone.

Strange . . . The lavatory was next door to the bathroom and, apart from the music, Briony had not heard a sound. And she had only been in there a minute or two.

Had Lotte had an abrupt change of heart or twinge of conscience and given up the bath? Had she crept back to her room in a sulk?

In that case, why hadn't she taken her little cassette player? And why was her towel still here, and her floral-print robe? Had she gone back to her room wet and naked?

Briony looked at the filthy linoleum-covered floor beside the bath. It was completely dry. Not a splash of water, not one wet footprint.

Briony stepped back on to the landing, looked up and down the passage. She walked up to the door of Lotte's room and knocked on it.

Silence.

She pushed at the door. It was locked.

She went back into the bathroom and picked up Lotte's robe from the floor. Something slipped out of the pocket as she did so and fell on to the floor . . . Keys: Lotte's door keys.

Extraordinary. Where had she gone? It was a cold winter's night and she had no robe, no towel, and no door keys.

Briony gathered up Lotte's things, switching off the cassette player as she did so, carried them along the landing and deposited them on the floor outside Lotte's door. She had half a mind to use the keys to open the door and dump everything on the floor *inside* the room, just to add insult to injury, but she resisted the temptation.

She went back to the bathroom, closed and bolted the door, and climbed into the bath.

She wallowed in it for a good half hour.

She wondered what Julie would be doing for New Year's Eve. She thought of the log fire that would be blazing in the sitting room, and felt a wave of longing wash over her, a longing to be back there, walking the lanes, hearing the surf breaking on the rocks, feeling the moist sand beneath her toes at the cove, smelling the bread baking in Julie's kitchen.

Newlyn seemed so incredibly far away; another world.

She pictured Leysholme. Maybe Bibi had got it wrong, perhaps there was no party there tonight and this would be a wasted journey.

Or perhaps her nerve would fail at the last minute.

Perhaps it was a stupid idea to gatecrash the party anyway. It might be better if she went to the police and asked them to look into Tam's disappearance, and the cheque for forty thousand pounds she had supposedly given to the Pastoral Foundation.

But the police would want to know how Tamara had come by so much money. They would have to be told everything. And that would land Tamara in all kinds of trouble when she returned. They would want to talk to her parents and to the women at the Casa Negra. It would break her mother's heart, destroy her, if she knew what Tamara had been doing. And if there were any criminal proceedings against anyone it might get into the newspapers. It would be the gossip of Newlyn for the next hundred years.

Perhaps it was too soon to go to the police.

She climbed out of the bath and towelled down. She put on Tam's robe, picked up her shampoo and wet towel and unbolted the bathroom door. As she emerged on to the landing she looked back at the door of Lotte's room. They were still lying there, exactly where she had left them: the floral-print robe, the towel, the slippers with the trodden-down backs . . .

This was absurd. It was a very cold night. Briony was feeling the chill already, standing on this draughty landing. Lotte couldn't have got back into her room – she didn't have her keys.

So where was she?

Briony turned and went back upstairs to the flat.

LEYSHOLME

All the way there she kept telling herself this was crazy, she didn't want to do this, didn't want to go to that awful, shuttered-up house by the woods . . . And there was probably no party anyway, it was only Bibi's say-so, after all, and Bibi was zonked out of her tiny brain at the time. But she kept driving on.

She came to the genteel village of Woodhurst, with its half-timbered houses, its historic coaching inn strung with fairy lights, and its near-deserted streets. She turned left at the crossroads and was quickly back in the dark countryside. Right and left and right again, through four miles of twisting lanes to the unmarked field entrance that led down to Leysholme.

She parked where she had parked before, about fifty yards along the lane. She turned off the engine and the lights and sat in the car in the dark. She couldn't go through with it; didn't have the stomach for it. What was she going to do when she got there? And yet she had come this far: it seemed crazy to turn round and go straight back. Tam might be there, at this very moment, just a few hundred yards away.

To go on or go back? Her mind felt like a battlefield. It was all crossfire and mayhem and neither side was getting anywhere.

It was growing cold inside the car. She restarted the engine and switched on the heater fan. She would drive up to the house, she decided. If there was a party going on, there would be cars outside. If there were no cars and the house was in darkness she would drive back to London.

She drove along the lane and turned in through the wide gap in the hedgerow and bumped down the track . . . through the ford . . . and up the other side, past the trees . . . between the gateposts and along the gravel driveway, past the front of the house.

There was something happening here tonight, that was for sure: there were cars and vans and motorbikes parked all along the edge of the wide open expanse of grass that extended for acres and acres away to her left.

She reversed into an open space between two cars and sat looking directly at the front of the house. She had forgotten how big it was. A faint glow of light was visible, on the first and second floors, but everywhere else appeared to be in darkness. Perhaps they had closed the shutters or drawn drapes across the windows.

She wound down the window and listened: she could hear nothing.

It was bitterly cold outside; she closed the window again.

She was wearing Tam's leather catsuit, which was warm, at least; and she had brought a leather hood that she found in Tam's underwear drawer. It covered her head completely, as tight as a glove, with holes for the eyes and mouth and nostrils.

A pair of headlights approached along the driveway and passed the spot where Briony was parked. It was a small van. It turned on to the grass and parked, not far away. Briony watched. The engine died, the lights went out. It was too dark to see now. She heard doors bang shut and made out two shadowy shapes moving towards the side of the house. She wound the window down again and listened. She could hear feet on the gravel and heavy boot steps on the flagstones at the side of the house.

Then silence.

She took off her driving shoes and pulled on the boots she had brought. She switched on the interior lamp, pulled the hood on and aligned it comfortably over her face in the reflection of the rearview mirror, then zipped it up, from the crown of her head to the nape of her neck.

She got out of the car, leaving it unlocked, fearing she might need to make a quick getaway.

The rear of the house was closed off by a high wall inset with wrought-iron gates that were wide open. She walked through to a courtyard and across flagstones towards the side of the house. The courtyard was feebly illuminated by a single lamp, sprouting from the wall of the house like an inverted hook above the side door.

She tried the door: it was not locked. She opened it, stepped inside and pushed the door shut behind her.

She was in a rear hallway. She could hear music coming from somewhere – the upper floors perhaps; it sounded far off and indistinct.

There was no light in here but there was light in the room beyond. She walked through into a scullery; apart from the broad, glazed sinks and the wooden drainers the room was bare. Beyond it were two smaller rooms and then the kitchen. That, too, was almost empty: an enormous range, cold and rusty; bare shelves; not a stick of furniture; no pots or pans, no dishes, no crockery, no cutlery. Just an open expanse of tiled floor. And so cold.

She pushed open a door and walked through a narrow, empty room and through a pair of doors into what must once have been a dining room. It was dark but there was sufficient light from the windows for her to make out a long dining table and a large fireplace. But no chairs or any other furniture.

She opened a further pair of doors on the other side and entered a much larger room. A drawing room? Impossible to tell ... There was furniture in here but it was draped with shrouds, as if the decorators were due. There was no carpet on the floor. Two chandeliers hung from the high ceiling. There were no curtains at the windows. There were shutters but they were not closed.

She opened another pair of doors and stepped out into a main hallway, panelled with dark wood. There were lights on here but they were few and burned dimly. The staircase was broad and carpeted with some kind of coir matting. The music was louder now. It was coming from upstairs. She looked up to the first-floor landing. She glimpsed people up there, dressed in the usual Casa Negra fashion. That gave her a little confidence. She walked slowly up the staircase.

When she reached the first floor she found herself at the mid-way point of a long central passageway that ran the full length of the building. Such light as there was came from dim red or blue lamps, much like the lighting at the Casa Negra. People were everywhere. Briony began to walk along the central passage, mingling with the crowd. Wherever she went the music seemed to change. There was jazz and grunge and heavy metal, with cacophanous fusions in the no-man's-land between. And from somewhere she could hear what sounded like a church organ.

She came to a long panelled room – possibly eighty feet or more – the type of long gallery that was a feature of grander houses. A fire blazed in a cavernous hearth. Trestle tables were set out in a square formation, draped with black sheets and laden with food: tureens of soup and wedges of baguette, baked potatoes and some kind of casserole or stew, large bowls of cream-topped trifle, and demijohn-size jugs of punch and mulled wine.

She helped herself to a glass of punch and began to drift from room to room. All the bedroom doors were open and people were moving in and out, as if they were at some kind of exhibition and moving from display to display: mostly couples, playing out their master-slave routines. Nobody spoke to her; nobody appeared to speak to anybody. The music was so loud, perhaps no one could hear. It seemed to be a party without words, a party of exhibitionism, of watching, lurking, creeping, touching. Strangers approached one another, stopped and touched, stroked and caressed, and moved on . . . Or maybe they weren't strangers.

People touched Briony, males and females and in-betweens.

She said nothing; kept moving from room to room. She was looking for Tamara but sensed she was not going to find her here. Even if Tam were here she might not recognize her. A lot of these people were wearing hoods, like Briony. Some had their mouths zipped shut and their eye-holes covered. Some were partially masked. And some were so helmeted, strapped and gagged that it was impossible to see their faces at all.

Coming here was like lifting a stone in a quiet corner of a forest and discovering an underworld of black beetles, creeping among the nooks and crannies.

Lone figures of indeterminable sex sat trussed like parcels and abandoned in dark corners. Some were almost naked – she was amazed that they could stand the cold – and some were so completely sheathed in rubber or in leather that no flesh was visible at all. Some were being led like animals, tethered to chains attached to rings inserted through lips, noses, nipples, genitals ... even tongues. Some were chained or shackled, legs and arms akimbo. Some were being shaved; astringent balm was being massaged into their raw, tender flesh.

Briony was wondering if there was any 'centre' to this party, or if this was all it was, a wandering freak show. She was thinking she could look over the entire house tonight, from the top floor to the bottom, and no one would stop to ask her what she was doing.

She found a flight of narrow stairs at one end of the first floor – the sort of staircase that servants would have used in bygone days. She walked up to the floor above and along the central corridor. It was dark up here and no one was about. The only noise was the music – sometimes rumbling, sometimes thumping – from below. She peered into all the rooms as she passed by. Some were empty, some were furnished. Some looked like bedrooms, others looked like junk rooms. Shadowy figures shifted in the dark interiors. Heaven only knew what was going on; Briony didn't wait to find out.

She went up to the floor above but almost all those rooms were locked.

There was a fourth floor above that, but it was so dark up there she ventured no further than the first few steps above the third-floor landing.

She went back down to the long gallery on the first floor where the food was laid out. She helped herself to soup and French bread and more punch. She found a small sofa that was unoccupied and in a part of the room that lay in deep shadow.

She watched a couple make their way across the room, from one end to the other. The man was crawling on all fours, like a dog, harnessed in a complicated network of straps that went round his head, kept his jaws clamped shut, and around his body and arms, which were linked by lengths of chain to straps around his thighs and couplings around his ankles. His mistress wore a rubber cape over a diaphanous body stocking and high boots. She was towing him along by a chain attached to the bridle.

A voice murmured in Briony's ear: 'You're thinking to yourself: poor twisted geek, aren't you?'

Briony turned her head and found a woman walking around the back of the sofa. She sat down in the empty space beside Briony.

'Naughty, naughty,' she said. 'I don't think you were on the guest list.'

She was smoking an evil-smelling joint.

It was Dee, wearing large, round sunglasses . . . Or Drusilla without her long curly wig.

SKUNK

She was dressed for the cold: black boots over leather leggings, fishnet body stocking under a hide trench coat that must have reached almost to her ankles. Her hair was coal black and had been cut even shorter since Briony had last seen her.

Briony watched the man crawling painfully on all fours after his partner. Every so often, she tugged hard at the chain to bring him to heel.

'Are they serious?' asked Briony.

'Misha only asks the serious ones,' said Dee. 'They're more fun.'

She passed the spliff to Briony.

'What are you doing here?' Dee enquired.

'Looking for my sister.'

'You're a gatecrasher,' said Dee. She didn't sound as if she minded very much.

'So what are you going to do? Throw me out?'

'We don't throw gatecrashers out, silly,' Dee retorted whimsically. 'We have fun with gatecrashers. We make sport with them.'

Briony took a toke on the joint.

'Why Dee?' she asked.

'Why not? What else can you do with a name like Drusilla except shorten it?'

'Is Dee short for Drusilla?' said Briony.

'Well, how much shorter can you make it?'

'What I meant was,' said Briony, 'why do you want to lead two lives?'

'Don't we all?'

Briony shook her head. 'I don't, no.'

'Oh, please . . .' Dee scoffed gently. 'Tell that to the folks back home in Mackerelville.'

'If you didn't try to be two people you wouldn't have to wear a wig at the club. They get so hot, these things.'

'You don't like my wigs?'

'I only ever see the one.'

'Oh, I have lots of wigs,' said Dee. 'I like wigs. They suit my moods.'

'You moody?'

'I guess. I'm fire. My fire can burn hot, my fire can burn cold, my fire can glow, my fire can go ashy cool.'

Briony took another toke on the joint and offered it back to Dee, but Dee waved it aside.

'Has Misha seen you?'

'I don't know. I don't think so.'

'You'll be out of a job when she does.'

'I'm not coming back, anyway.'

'Had enough already?' Dee didn't seem very surprised. 'Stashed away a grand or so and going home to blow your wad on the mean streets of Mackerelville?'

'Something like that.'

Dee took a tin box from one of the deep hip pockets of her trench coat and removed a second pre-rolled joint.

'Something I said?'

'Well, don't tell me you're short of waitresses,' said Briony.

'I'm always short of waitresses,' said Dee. 'They keep disappearing.' She laughed at that and lit the second spliff. It struck Briony that Dee was already pretty stoned. 'It's all right,' she said, noticing Briony's uncomprehending look, 'in-joke.'

Briony drained her glass of punch. It was quite potent. And so was the spliff.

'I'm leaving,' said Briony, 'because I've discovered what goes on at that place and I don't want to be involved.'

'What do you mean, "what goes on"?' said Dee.

'I took back the coat that Waldo sent me.'

'Why? You don't think you're worth it?'

'I didn't do anything for him to *make* it worth it,' said Briony.

'He must've thought you were out of your mind,' said Dee.

'No, he thought I was a prostitute.'

'What does it matter what he thinks? If he wants to show his appreciation, let him.'

'Appreciation for what?' said Briony. 'He pays through the nose at the Casa Negra for what little he gets.'

'And so he bloody well should,' Dee retorted. 'Why do you think tossers like him are willing to pay good money for a hostess to sit with them all evening? Because they've got nobody else in the world, that's why. They're screamingly lonely. They want someone to talk to, someone to be their fantasy for the night. They're isolated, screwed-up creeps. They're never going to find the true-life partner of their messy little wet-dreams. But for a few hours a night we give them make-believe. We are Frankenstein. We bring their monster fantasy to life. Turn it into flesh and blood. She may be blonde, she may be brunette. She may be almost naked, she may be in latex from head to toe . . . But she is real, she is responsive, and she listens.'

Briony was beginning to feel muzzy-headed.

She looked around for an ashtray but there was none. She dropped what was left of her joint on the bare floorboards and worked it over with the sole of her boot.

'Is that all it is to you?' she asked, curious. 'Just one big rip-off?'

'Is that all *what* is?' said Dee.

'The hostess thing, the club, the whole scene.'

'What do you mean, rip-off?' Dee looked indignant. 'Where's the rip-off? They're jerks. They're tossers. They're wankers. Once they've got their little fantasy sitting in front of them, all they want to do is pour out their own pathetic, boring, little tragedies, and whine about their empty, loveless, passionless, messed-up lives. Where's the rip-off? The hostess soothes and comforts him. She listens to all his self-indulgent crap and turns him on at the same time. He comes to the club feeling sick in the pit of his grubby soul and we send him home feeling halfway human again. We cost about the same as an hour with a shrink, but the difference is we actually make him feel better.'

She put a hand in her hip pocket, took out her little tin and picked out another pre-rolled joint. She offered it to Briony.

'So what are you telling me?' said Briony, accepting the spliff. 'Your hostesses are really therapists?'

'Among other things.' Dee flicked her cigarette lighter and held the flame out towards Briony. 'You think your sister stopped nursing when she started at the Casa Negra? It's just a different *kind* of nursing, that's all. We should be available on the National Health.'

'And would that include the home visits?' said Briony.

'Excuse me?'

'How much do they charge, my fellow hostesses – the Bibis, the Lolas, the Mojos?'

'Charge for what?'

'Oh, please . . .' said Briony. 'Tam was stashing away over a thousand a week. She was saving to buy a flat at Frye's Wharf. She put away about forty grand in nine months. How many Waldos do you have to screw to make that kind of money?'

'You haven't got a clue, have you?' said Dee. 'You don't understand the first thing about fetish. Fetish is about the senses. It's about touch, feel, smell, sight. It's about plugging into some sensory network that's been wired up in a way that most people don't relate to. With women it seems to engage our inner feelings . . . We *feel* good this way. Whereas with guys it seems to engage their fantasies.'

'What are you saying? That men take Tam home just to look at her?'

'One of her regulars,' said Dee, 'liked her to come to his house in skin-tight latex. It drove him crazy. But he wasn't allowed to touch her. The deal was that she would always ignore him. She spends the night in his house. She changes her outfits several times. He may watch, that is permitted. She may take a bath, she may not, as she chooses . . . And he's allowed to watch her. He can go anywhere she goes and watch anything she does. Like he's a ghost. She's allowed no privacy at all. She can do anything she wants all night long – watch TV, drink his booze, phone her friends – maybe she even called you one time. And he can be with her. But he's not allowed to speak – in fact he's gagged. And he's not allowed to touch her – in fact, he can't – his hands are locked behind his back. If he ever touches her – any part of him, touching any part of her – she'll walk out and never have anything to do with him again.'

'And he pays *money* for this?'

'Five hundred a night.'

Briony smiled incredulously. 'So what's the turn-on?'

'He's turned her into an idol, in his own mind. All his sexual desires are focused on her. He wants her so desperately it's torture for him to see her in his own home, watching her do the most intimate things that normally she would only ever do alone. Wanting so much to touch her, to stroke her, to put his lips to that shiny, black latex . . . Tight, so tight, over every tiny curve and crease in her body. Wanting to smell that rubber, wanting to taste it on his tongue, wanting this fantasy idol of his own creation to show him some token of regard or affection. But she ignores him, as if he doesn't exist. And he knows that if he so much as touches her, she'll disappear for ever. That's the turn-on: the craving, the agony of knowing there can never be any gratification, no end to his torment, the spiritual torture of unfulfilment. It's emotional masochism.'

'Just out of curiosity,' said Briony, 'were you ever going to tell me?'

'Tell you what?'

'About Tamara . . . being a call girl.'

'Being a what?' Dee looked amused.

'You didn't think it was worth mentioning?'

'A *call* girl?' Dee laughed. 'Wow, wow . . . I haven't heard that in donkey's years. That's 1950s newspaper talk. Tam said you were a bumpkin, but you really did just jump off the milk train, didn't you?'

'Call it what you want,' said Briony. 'But were you ever going to tell me?'

'Should I have?' said Dee. 'What's it to you how Tam earns her money? She was barely surviving on a nurse's pay, slaving every hour that God made, just to pay her rent and make ends meet. Were you interested then in how she scraped a living? If she wants to buy a flat, if she wants to buy a car, if she wants to go abroad sometimes . . . Is that such a big deal? You came to me, you were desperate for money, and I gave you a job. Did I force you to be a waitress? Did I force you to be a hostess? Did I say you've got to go home with these creeps after hours? No. It was your choice. You chose to do it. Just as you choose to drink the champagne they buy, and pocket the tips they leave, the tenner here, the twenty there. The same for Tam. She wanted money. She found a way of making it. What's it to you how she did it?'

Briony said nothing.

Dee took a swig of punch and rinsed it around her teeth like mouthwash before swallowing.

'Why did you come here?' she asked.

'I told you,' said Briony. 'I want to find my sister.' She took a short sharp toke on the spliff. She was beginning to feel very stoned, or drunk, or both.

Dee was sitting back in the corner of the sofa at a sideways angle, with one leg hooked over the other, staring at her inscrutably.

'What made you think she might be here?'

'I found petrol receipts from Woodhurst,' said Briony. 'And the phone number's in her diary . . . She phoned this house twice in July.'

'But how did you know there was going to be a party tonight?'

'Bibi told me,' said Briony.

She was thinking it had been a mistake, starting on this second spliff. She offered it back to Dee. Dee took it.

'If Tam was going to be here, don't you think I'd have invited you?'

'I don't know.' Briony struggled to focus her thoughts. 'I don't know what to think.' She was beginning to feel very peculiar . . . She wasn't sure whether it was what she had been drinking or what she'd been smoking, or a combination of the two.

'You okay?' Dee enquired.

'What *is* that stuff?' said Briony.

'A kind of Thai stick. Opium and skunk.'

'What the hell is skunk?'

'It's like ganja with attitude,' said Dee.

Briony was beginning to sweat. She felt as if she might throw up at any moment.

'I think I need a loo,' she said, and tried to get up. She fell back into the sofa again.

'Help yourself,' said Dee. 'There's about a hundred to choose from.'

She managed to get up at the second attempt and walked slowly across the room. It felt as if she was on the deck of a ship that was pitching in a heavy swell. She reached the nearest of the two doorways that led out into the central corridor. She went up the back stairs to the floor above and made her way along the central passage, opening each door in succession. She found one that opened into a bathroom, went inside, closed the door and locked it. She tried the light-switch but it didn't work. There was one small window in the room and, although there was no moon visible outside, she could make out the whiteness of the bath and washbasin. She fumbled her way towards them and found the lavatory.

She knelt on the floor, propped against the wall. She felt

terrible. Felt like someone had let a mad dog loose inside her head. Felt so sick. And sweating. Felt short of breath. Felt so weak.

She lay down on the floor . . .

THE SUPPLICANT

She must have dozed off. She tried to get up off the floor, but too quickly . . . She felt giddy and slumped back down. She held on to the bath to steady herself and clambered to her feet.

She still felt sick and giddy.

She fumbled her way to the door, opened it and peered along the central passage. It was dark, deserted and strangely silent.

She had no idea what time it was, she had left her watch behind at Styles Lane.

She began to walk along the landing towards the main stairwell.

Not a sound anywhere. Why was it so silent? She wondered if she had slept for hours and it was the middle of the night and everyone had gone.

And then she heard organ music.

She wondered if she was imagining it, a sort of aural illusion, the effect of that awful skunk-mix that Drusilla gave her to smoke. But the closer she came to the central stairwell, the clearer it became. Baroque in style – Bach perhaps, something of that kind.

When she reached the main staircase there was no mistaking it. It was coming from above: the third or fourth floor, she couldn't tell which. She stood at the foot of the stairs, looking up. From where she was standing she could not see the third-floor landing without climbing several stairs. It was in total darkness up there.

Why could she hear an organ when it was so deathly silent everywhere else? There was something about the music that was aggressive, intimidating.

Or was it that mad dog, still running loose inside her head?

And then she saw candlelight . . . A moving candlelight.

Someone was coming down the stairs.

She could see only the light at first, but gradually a woman's body came into view: her legs first, bare legs, moving slowly, with the stealth of a burglar moving through a sleeping house. And then her torso. Naked. And now her head. A slight figure of a woman – so slight, she might have been a girl. Completely naked. Holding a large candle in one hand, gripping it by the stem as if it were a flag, and shielding the flame with her other hand. She reached the halfway landing and approached the second flight of stairs.

Briony could see her more clearly now. She had long, loose blonde hair. She was so pale her flesh looked almost translucent in the candlelight. As she turned at the mid-way landing and began to descend the next flight, she came fully face-on to Briony.

It was Bibi.

She looked as if she had been hypnotized or was sleepwalking, her blue eyes staring fixedly at the ground a few yards in front of her. She walked as if in slow-motion down the centre of the staircase, and the organ music – elaborate, complex, rising and falling, twisting and curling – seemed to grow a little louder all the time.

As Bibi came to within a few steps of the second-floor landing she noticed Briony for the first time. Their eyes met. Bibi stopped moving. It was no more than a hesitation. Briony stared into her eyes. Bibi's eyes looked wide with terror. And yet the rest of her features were so inexpressive she looked like a zombie.

She was so slight, so frail, and shaking with cold . . . Or was it fear – or both?

But in that hesitation Briony noticed a flicker of something dance across Bibi's face, a ghost of a smile. At almost that same moment, she shook her head, as if to say: Don't speak, don't come near, just leave me.

And then the moment was gone, the glimmer of recognition melted from her face and the eyes resumed their fixed and frightened gaze. She walked on, past Briony, across the third-floor landing, and began her descent towards the floor below.

Briony moved towards her, saying, 'Bibi . . .?'

Bibi took no notice.

Briony came to the top of the stairs and was about to follow her, when she noticed a crowd of people assembled on the first-floor landing, observing silently as Bibi approached, standing back to keep a clear path for her.

All the lights had been switched off. There was only the light of Bibi's candle. Only the sound of the organ. Bibi began her descent towards the ground floor. The candle flickered. When she reached the bottom of the staircase and entered that vast draughty hall, everyone began to make their way silently down the staircase, following her at a distance, a procession, moving at Bibi's somnambulant pace.

Briony was at the very back of them all. She still felt peculiar in her head. She wondered if she was hallucinating, if none of this was really happening.

They moved slowly across the main hall and along a panelled passage, like passengers shuffling their way to board an aircraft, or spectators passing through a turnstile at a football ground.

Briony could see nothing now except the people immediately in front of her. The organ music had become quieter and quieter as they descended to the hall, but now it was growing louder again. Briony could not understand why. It seemed to be coming from the room ahead and not from the upper floors.

Where the narrow passage ended, she found herself entering

a chapel. A private chapel. The music was louder than ever now, and coming from above . . .

She looked up and caught her breath: the chapel ceiling was about fifty feet up. And way up there, at the very top, was the organ. It must have been at fourth-floor level; that was probably the only access to it.

The chapel was packed. There were no seats. Briony was at the very back. There was a raised ledge, like a step, along the rear wall where she was jammed by the press of people. She managed to step up on to the ledge. Now she had room to breathe and could see over the heads of everyone.

It could hardly be called a chapel any more: not only were there no seats, there was no altar, no cross, no lectern, nothing of a religious nature whatsoever, except the stained glass in the windows, which portrayed the Holy Shepherd with his flock of lambs.

It made her think of Petra's mural.

At the front of the chapel was a raised dais, about a foot above the chapel floor. Where the altar would have been was a brick structure, no more than four feet high, open at the top and at the centre, about two feet above the ground. Through the opening in the centre Briony could see glowing coals. And from the heart of the coals protruded something that looked like a poker. Briony could smell the coals.

Bibi was standing almost in the middle of the dais – the only part of the chapel that was brightly lit – like an actress centre-stage, holding the candle with both hands now. Molten wax was dribbling down the side and across her fingers. Bibi didn't even flinch. She looked mesmerized, gazing at a fixed point on the floor about six feet in front of her.

The organist never seemed to pause, even for a moment.

A woman stepped out from the front of the gathering. She was sheathed in black from head to toe, but she was so tall and slender that Briony assumed it was Misha.

She approached Bibi, who sank on to her knees and bowed her head.

Misha stood beside her, half-facing her and half-turned towards the assembled congregation. She stood comfortably erect, statuesque, with her hands in front of her, toying with something she was holding – something like a rosary, but it was *not* a rosary – that much Briony could see.

Misha began to speak. The organ was playing softly now but Briony could barely hear her. And then Bibi began to speak. Then Misha again. It had a liturgical quality, like a catechism, with Misha, the priestess, questioning Bibi, the supplicant, and Bibi reciting the responses.

This went on for about ten minutes: Bibi on her knees, holding the candle, with Misha beside her, towering like the Grand Inquisitor.

When it came to an end, Misha took the candle, snuffed out the flame between her gloved fingers and put it down on the dais, so that it leaned against the brick structure where the coals were burning.

She came back to where Bibi was kneeling. She took whatever it was that she had been holding in her hands all this while and began to wrap it around Bibi's head.

Now Briony could see what it was: a harness with a small rubber ball-gag attached, which Bibi took into her mouth.

Misha tightened the harness. Bibi showed no emotion. She must have been so cold, Briony was thinking, and kneeling all this time on that hard wooden dais. Perhaps she was drugged stupid.

The organ was growing louder again.

Bibi got up off her knees, turned around, so that her back was to the congregation, and walked up to the front wall of the chapel, beneath the stained-glass windows.

She stood with her legs apart, pressed her body against the wall, and raised her arms.

Two women stepped out from the front of the congregation, attired like Misha.

One stood on either side of Bibi. They shackled her wrists

and ankles to the wall. The organ stopped. It took a few moments for the echo to fade away.

The congregation was rock still. Briony could feel the tension, like an electrical charge in the atmosphere, everyone waiting for something to happen. There was total silence.

Briony sensed that something dreadful was about to ensue but she felt so dizzy and confused, it was like a dream.

The organ music began again, quietly at first but gradually growing louder towards a crescendo. Misha moved towards the fire and with her gloved hand pulled a length of iron from the glowing coals. She held it up towards the congregation for everyone to see. It was glowing, a vivid orange. The iron had been fashioned into a curly symbol of some kind. Briony was too far away to make out precisely what the symbol was, but she could guess: the shepherd's crook, the Gothic P.

Holding it low and pointed in front of her, as if it were some kind of divining rod, Misha moved towards Bibi. As the organ reached a crescendo, she aimed the branding iron at Bibi's right buttock and rammed it hard into the flesh. Bibi's tightly-shackled body tensed and shuddered as if she had been electrocuted. The organ drowned out whatever screams the gag permitted her to make.

Briony felt as if she was going to throw up, as if her legs were liquefying, as if her mind was tumbling, spinning, into a deep black pit . . .

NEW YEAR'S DAY

When she woke up she was in a large bed, naked and alone. It was daylight outside, but dreary and grey.

A television was on somewhere in the room and there was a cigarette burning somewhere; she could smell the smoke.

She tried to remember something – anything – about the previous night. She felt as if someone had stoved in her skull.

She pushed herself up on to her elbows and looked around.

There was a wardrobe, a table and two upright chairs on the other side of the room.

A portable television sat on the table. An old film was playing. Black and white. Two Americans were quarrelling; some old Hollywood comedy. She could tell it was comedy, the way they were arguing.

A fire was burning in a corner fireplace. A bucket of coal and wood stood at the side of the hearth.

On the right of the bed, a sash window. There were curtains but they were not drawn.

The door opened.

A woman came into the room with a white towel piled up on her head and an oversize white robe open around her body. She looked like a camel-drover.

'How are you feeling?' she said.

It was Dee.

'Bloody terrible.' Briony let her head fall slowly back on to the pillow.

Dee sat on the side of the bed. She had just had a bath, Briony could smell the fragrance.

'Time is it?'

'About three o'clock.'

'Jesus . . .' Briony closed her eyes. 'Such a headache.'

'Misha's punch,' said Dee. 'Hundred-proof vodka, Greek brandy and Algerian red.'

'That a bathroom?' mumbled Briony, her eyes still closed but referring to the door that Drusilla had just come through.

'Mm-hm,' Dee murmured.

Briony slid clumsily out of bed and almost fell on to the floor. She pressed one hand to her forehead, shuffled into the bathroom and pulled a tassled cord to switch on the light. She sat there for ages; hadn't felt so ill for years.

When she returned, she found the bedroom empty. Dee had gone again.

She felt so lousy she couldn't face the thought of driving home. She slipped back into bed and closed her eyes.

When she awoke, Dee was lying on the bed, her head propped up by one hand, watching Briony impassively. She was still wearing the white robe. She had a mug of something nestling in her free hand, clutched to her chest.

'That coffee?'

Dee nodded and drew Briony's gaze to an identical mug that was sitting on the bedside table. Briony manoeuvred herself into an upright position and put one of the pillows behind her back. She picked up the mug of coffee.

'How'd I get here?'

'Misha's magic carpet,' said Dee.

There were two white tablets on the table. Briony looked at them, wondering what they were.

'Just painkillers,' said Dee.

Briony swallowed each one with a sip of coffee.

'Do you live here?' she asked. 'You and Misha?'

'Sometimes I'm here,' said Dee, 'sometimes I'm not.'

Briony looked at the coal fire in the grate.

'Who does all the work in this place?'

'We have minions,' said Dee, and smiled at her choice of word.

Briony wondered if she was being serious.

'What happened to me?'

'What do you think?'

'I remember us talking. Me in the loo. Crashing out. I don't know what happened then. I don't know what I dreamt and what was real.'

'Skunk's a bitch,' said Dee.

'I had a nightmare. About Bibi.'

Dee said nothing.

'Or did it really happen?' said Briony.

An ambiguous grin appeared on Dee's face. 'Shouldn't crash parties you're not invited to,' she said.

After a silence, Briony said, 'What is this place?'

'It used to be a school. A very posh school. But there was a scandal about masters and boys. It had to close. Then it became an orphanage.'

'And now?'

'And now,' said Dee, 'it's a house of dreams. And pleasure. And darkness.'

'Is it owned by the Foundation?'

That took Dee by surprise. She seemed unsettled. But her tone was casual enough when she enquired: 'And what do you know about the Foundation?'

'Tam mentioned it to me. In a letter.'

'What letter?'

'This was ages ago. Last summer.'

'What did she tell you about the Foundation?'

'Nothing much. Said it was called the Pastoral Foundation. And I know she gave some money to it. But that's about all.'

Dee sipped her coffee.

'Is this where he lives,' said Briony, 'the Pastor? Is this his home?'

'In a manner of speaking,' Dee replied.

'And is Tamara here?'

'No. Tamara's not here.'

'But she has been here?'

'Not since last year . . . last summer.'

'Do you know where she is now?'

A long silence. And then Dee replied, 'Yes, I do.'

'But she asked me to come to London. So why hasn't she got in touch with me?'

'It's not easy for her.'

'Is she hiding from someone?'

'Why would she want to hide from anyone?'

'It's got something to do with the Pastor, hasn't it?' said Briony.

'Is that what she told you? In her letter?'

'I think,' said Briony, evading the question, 'that the Pastor is – or was – one of her clients.'

Dee was staring at her. Large, dark brown eyes.

'And I think,' Briony continued, 'that they got too involved. And she thought she could control it.'

Dee looked bemused. 'Control what?'

'But it got out of hand,' Briony continued, 'so she had to run away . . . because she's afraid. And now she's hiding from him.'

'She's not hiding from anyone,' said Dee. 'And she hasn't run away.'

'Is she being held against her will?'

Dee smiled at the notion. 'No,' she said. 'No one's holding her against her will.'

'Then what's happened to her? Where is she?'

After another long silence, Dee said, 'Briony, I haven't been completely honest with you. Perhaps I should have been at the very start. But it's hard to explain . . .'

A lengthy pause. Then:

'You see, your sister is a woman who has some very extreme needs and desires. It would be difficult for anyone like you to understand the hunger, the craving, the lengths that a woman like Tam will go to to gratify those needs.'

'Then help me,' said Briony. 'Explain. Help me understand.'

'It can't be explained,' Dee replied. 'It's something that can only be felt. Experienced. It's about the senses. It's about sensuality. About other dimensions of existence. Tamara has explored some very dark regions of the senses. She's always looking for a more intense, a more extreme experience.'

'You make it sound as if something terrible's happened to her.'

'She's perfectly safe where she is,' Dee assured her. 'And perfectly well.'

'Then . . . Can I see her?'

Dee shifted her position. She was still lying on her side, her head at the bottom end of the bed, propped up by one arm.

'It's possible,' she said. 'But it won't be easy.'

'Why not?'

Dee didn't answer.

'It's got something to do with the Foundation, hasn't it?' said Briony. 'It's some kind of weird cult, isn't it? That's what this place is all about.'

'If it helps you to think of it that way,' Dee replied, but in a rather negative tone of voice.

'From what she said in her letter,' said Briony, 'it sounded like a spiritual experience.'

'What did?'

'I don't know. It was a strange letter. It didn't make any sense. She said it was like a drug, the way it hooked her . . . this thing, whatever it was. She thought she was controlling it for a while, but in reality it was controlling her.'

Dee gazed back in enigmatic silence.

'Well, am I wrong?' said Briony. 'What's so difficult to explain?'

'No, you're not wrong exactly,' said Dee. 'It is to do with a spiritual experience. Try to think of it this way . . . Tamara took a journey – not a literal journey, a spiritual journey. A journey into some very dark, distant regions of the senses. And the only way you can reach her – the only way you can be with her again, physically – is to make that same journey yourself.'

Briony didn't follow any of this. She wondered if she had to undergo some sort of indoctrination or 'religious' preparation to be admitted into this cult.

'What are you saying?' she said. 'That I have to join the Foundation myself before you'll let me see Tamara? Is that what you're saying?'

'It's not a question of what I'll let you do,' said Dee. 'It's not up to me. It's a question of what's physically possible.'

'Just tell me what I have to do to be with my sister,' said Briony. 'Either tell me where she is or take me to her.'

'I can't take you there,' said Dee. 'No one can take you there. Only you can take yourself. You must make your own journey . . . If that's what you truly want to do. Only you can cross those frontiers into the unexplored regions of your senses, of your sexuality. That's the only way to reach Tamara. Your own journey of personal discovery. I can arrange it for you, but it's a long, long journey, through a very dark night. You must be absolutely sure that it's what you really want.'

'You're not telling me anything,' said Briony, 'you're just talking in riddles. I want to see my sister, that's all I want. I don't care about the rest.'

'Then you have to break free,' said Dee. 'You have to throw off all your inhibitions. They're like chains that hold you back. You have to let go . . . Free your mind and free your senses, to explore new realms, enter new dimensions, a whole different consciousness. That's how you'll find Tamara.' Dee smiled that charmless smile of hers. 'But can you hack it, baby sister? That's the question. Can you really let go?'

She pushed herself up on to her knees and slipped off her bathrobe. She tossed it aside and knelt in front of Briony, her body upright, her knees wide apart straddling Briony's legs. Briony's gaze was drawn to the chunky steel loops inserted through Dee's nipples . . . Bell-shaped couplings that were closed off by a locking bolt across the bottom. She had seen pierced women before . . . But those were small, fine nipple rings. These things were gross.

Dee smoothed her hands across her thighs, away from her crotch, drawing the flesh taut. Briony's gaze drifted lower. She had no pubic hair, the skin was smooth, like a child's, and there was another one of those bell-shaped couplings inserted through the labia.

And between her navel and her pubic bone was . . .

Not easy to make out what it was at first, in this gloomy light of gathering dusk. It looked as if someone had painted it on her skin with nail lacquer, a very pale, pearly colour.

But it had not been painted on: it was a scar – pearly pink on her naturally coffee-dark skin. A complicated scar. She had been branded, like Bibi, but on her belly and long since. A huge brand, the size of a man's hand. That same Gothic P symbol.

'I didn't dream it, then?' said Briony, reaching towards it, as if she needed to touch it to believe that it was real. 'It was no nightmare.'

Dee shook her head.

'And what is the P for?' said Briony, running her finger tip along the course of the scar, feeling its silky smoothness.

'P is for pussycats,' said Dee.

'P is for Pastor,' said Briony.

'And P is for pleasure,' said Dee, taking Briony's hand.

THE FOURTH FLOOR

When she awoke it was night and she was alone.

She had no idea what time it was.

There was a lamp beside the bed. She switched it on and looked around the room.

The fire had burned itself out. Dee had gone.

So had her headache. She felt strangely light-headed now; as if she had slept too much. Perhaps she had.

She got out of bed and walked into the bathroom.

There was a door on the opposite side of the bathroom; it was shared by another bedroom, presumably.

It felt warm in there. She touched the pipes. One of them was hot. Was there central heating, she wondered? She turned on the hot tap and sat on the loo while the tap gurgled and coughed and splashed and finally began to run hot.

She had a bath.

It was like a dream, the whole thing: lying in this deep Victorian-style bath, all alone in this vast house . . .

She wondered how alone she really was.

When she got out of the bath she realized, too late, that she had no towel. She went back into the bedroom, dripping water. Looking around, she realized she had no clothes either. Not even shoes. Nothing. She hadn't noticed until now; but then, she hadn't looked until now.

What had they done with her clothes?

She looked under the bed. She looked in the wardrobe: all there was, hanging from the rail, was a long black leather coat.

It looked very familiar, this coat.

She took it off the hanger.

It came from Harrods. It looked identical to the coat that Waldo had given her. No coincidence, perhaps. Quite a complicated little joke, this . . . Assuming it was a joke.

She was beginning to shiver.

She took the top sheet from the bed and dried herself on that. She put on the coat and buttoned it up. At least it would keep her warm while she went looking for her own things.

She opened the bedroom door and stepped out into the central landing passage. The only light she could see was by the main staircase.

She couldn't hear a sound.

She walked barefoot along the passage and tried the door of the next room. It was locked. She tried each door in succession, as far as the stairwell. They were all locked.

She stopped by the stairwell and looked down. She was on the third floor. She walked downstairs to the first floor and along the central passage to the long gallery where the food had been laid out the previous night, where she and Dee had sat and talked.

The room was in darkness now. She found some antiquated toggle switches on the wall. Only one of them worked.

The tables had gone. It looked like a different room now – as if there had never been a party in here at all.

Shutters were closed across all the windows. She opened one and looked out. A solitary vehicle remained parked on the edge of the grassy acres on the other side of the gravel drive: Tam's white Mini.

Her bare feet were beginning to ache with cold.

She switched off the lights and walked along the passage, looking inside all the other rooms. The doors were not locked on this floor. There was not a single item of clothing anywhere.

She went up to the second floor and glanced in every room. There was hardly any furniture, and what there was looked as if it had been here since the days when it was an orphanage.

She went down to the ground floor. Lights burned in the hall itself but everywhere else was dark.

She went into the dining room, the drawing room . . .

So much furniture shrouded in dust covers. It was like a stately home whose owners had gone abroad a long, long time ago, and had never returned.

If Misha lived here, with her dogs, where were her rooms?

Briony went back upstairs and climbed to the very top, to the fourth floor. The layout was different up here. At the top of the stairs, the central passageway to the right was walled off, to form what looked like a self-contained apartment. There was a flattened-arch doorway in the middle, with a panelled door, which was closed. She turned the iron handle and pushed, but the door was locked.

She listened, pressing her ear to the wood, but could hear nothing.

The other half of the fourth floor – to the left of the staircase – was just like the other three floors below.

There were no lights on in the central passage, but she could see a faint glow at the far end. She walked down the passage. There was a wing at the end of the house, no more than fifty feet long. Halfway along the wing a door was standing open. The flickering light was coming from the room. Briony approached the door and peered in.

It was a bedroom. There was no one there. It felt warm and inviting. Two chunky logs were blazing in the fireplace. A third log sat at the side of the hearth.

She stepped inside.

The flickering light was coming from a three-branch candle-stick standing on a table beside a four-poster bed. It was a very bare-looking four-poster. There was no canopy, no drapes. The mattress was covered by a black sheet. There were no blankets, no quilt, no pillows. The walls of the room were panelled. There was very little furniture: a bentwood chair beside the bed; a walnut credenza on which sat a tray, upon which rested a glass of something dark and steaming hot.

Whose room was this?

One of Dee's 'minions'?

Misha couldn't be living here alone – such a huge house and so empty. Perhaps she lived in that apartment on the other side of the stairwell.

And the Pastor . . .?

Briony looked at the bed. She looked at the fire. She looked at the glass of dark, steaming liquid. She touched it. It was very hot; could not have long since been poured. She stooped a little and sniffed. It smelt spicy, like mulled wine.

Whose room was it? And where had they gone?

She turned and looked at the door.

The door was shut.

But she hadn't closed it . . .

And she hadn't heard it close.

She moved across to the door and tried to open it. But there was no handle, nothing to grab hold of. She pushed it, but that was pointless, for it opened inwards.

She banged on the door. It sounded fairly solid.

She shouted, 'Hullo!'

And, when no one answered: 'Hullo! Anyone hear me!'

She felt rather stupid in the ensuing silence.

Perhaps it had closed itself, maybe the draught had blown it shut. But then she would have heard it. And, anyway, who would be sleeping in a room with a door that had no handle? And on a bed with no covers?

She kicked the door in a flash of anger but that merely hurt her foot.

She couldn't hear a sound anywhere; couldn't hear anything at all, just the crackling of the fire.

She sat on the bed, frightened, wondering what she should do, wondering if this was some kind of unfunny joke on Dee's part ... A sort of punishment for gatecrashing the party. Perhaps they were next door, listening, or watching through peepholes.

She waited for something to happen.

But nothing did. No one came. And not a sound; just the occasional pop and crackle of the wood burning on the fire.

She looked around the room again. There was no window.

With its dark panelling, the four-poster bed and the three-branch candlestick, it felt like something out of the Tudor age.

It was getting stuffy in here – not hot but airless. The fire was consuming the oxygen.

She waited.

She got up and kicked the door again. Several times. But it was a solid piece of work; didn't even shudder in its frame. And she had no shoes on.

She sat down on the bed. Still no one came and nothing happened.

The candles were burning low now. The fire was down to glowing embers. She threw on the other log.

She got up and tried charging the door with her shoulder, but it was as hard as a wall.

One of the candles died.

She was hungry and thirsty. She picked up the glass of mulled wine and sipped it. Aromatic. It was no more than tepid now but it had a pleasant taste: spicy . . . Cloves and cinnamon.

She sat down on the bed again. This was all part of their game, part of her punishment. What was it Dee said? . . . We have fun with gatecrashers, make sport with them.

Okay, well, let them have their fun. She could wait. What the hell? She was warm. She was comfortable enough.

She sipped more wine.

Another candle died. One remained, and that was just a stub.

At least it was warm in here. She sat down on the floor, close to the fire, and drank the mulled wine.

It was quite strong. It made her feel drowsy – that and the airlessness and the heat of the fire.

The remaining candle died. There was only the light of the fire now.

She wondered what the time was; she had no idea. She began to resign herself to the thought that they would keep her here like this until morning. Her punishment. Can you hack it, baby sister?

She stretched out on the floor by the hearth and clasped her fingers beneath her head. But that was uncomfortable. She turned on her side. But the floor was hard. She got up and lay down on the bed. At least she had the leather coat to keep her warm.

She felt more and more drowsy. She closed her eyes . . .

The next thing she knew, she was either waking from sleep or entering a dream, she was not sure which.

The room was not completely dark. The remains of the dying fire still gave off a glow – not enough light to see by but enough to take the depth out of the darkness. Against the softer darkness she could make out the harder darkness of a silhouette above her – like a human figure suspended in mid-air.

She couldn't speak; couldn't even open her mouth. There was something strapped tight around her head, her jaws wouldn't move. Thrown instantly into panic, she tried to reach out but she couldn't: her arms were stretched taut on either side of her and held fast. So were her legs . . . Her arms and legs akimbo, tied or shackled, like Bibi in the chapel. And her head in a harness, her jaws tight shut.

All she could do was tense her body against the restraints. But then she felt the slightest, softest touch on her belly . . . She couldn't make out what it was. But it was not frightening, it was not unpleasant in the least. Quite the contrary: it was soft as velvet and yet light as a warm breeze and smooth as satin . . . Caressing, barely touching her belly, her midriff, her breasts . . . Moving in small circles, so, so lightly, as if polishing something of exquisite delicacy. The strangest feeling: so calm and relaxed. So soothing . . . But subtle . . . So gently arousing . . . Such a feeling of serenity seeping through her body . . . Tranquillity . . . Too serene to resist . . . Her body like a small boat, cast off from the shore, floating gently out . . .

But only a dream, a dream . . .

MORNING

It was daylight when she awoke.

She was in bed. She sat up and looked around. It was the room in which she had slept with Dee the previous afternoon.

She looked at the fireplace. The hearth was full of ashes.

There was something lying in a tidy pile on the seat of the ladderback chair beside the table: her clothes. She got out of bed and examined them. Everything was there: the catsuit, the boots, the hood, the gloves, her bra and tights and briefs, and the small bag she had worn, slung across her chest, with her keys and cash and Tam's credit card safe inside.

She remembered walking into the windowless room upstairs, with the candles, the four-poster bed and the mulled wine.

Or had she dreamt it all?

Had none of it happened? Had she never gone upstairs? Had she slept the whole night through right here in this bed? Had her clothes been lying there all the time?

She looked in the wardrobe: it was empty.

Had she dreamt of Waldo's coat as well?

She began to get dressed.

She sat on the edge of the bed and as she raised her foot to put on her tights she noticed red marks around her ankle . . . Like the elastic marks from socks that were too tight.

She thought about her dream: unable to move her arms and legs.

She lifted the other foot and examined it. There were red marks around that ankle too.

And around her wrists.

She finished dressing and walked out of the room, along the landing, towards the staircase and stood looking up at the fourth floor.

Had she really dreamed of that windowless chamber?

She walked up the stairs to the top-floor landing. Exactly as she remembered it: walled off, like a separate apartment, the whole right-hand side of the fourth floor, with a flattened-arch entrance door.

She ventured along the central corridor in the other direction, to the wing at the end of the building. The candle-lit chamber had been about halfway along the wing, on the left-hand side.

She looked: there was no door. There was a door at each

end of the wing but nothing in between; merely the panelled wall.

So she *had* dreamt of the chamber.

She looked again at the red marks on her wrists: but *they* were real.

Perhaps she had got it wrong, perhaps the door was not halfway along, perhaps it was further than she remembered . . .

She walked along to the door at the very end of the wing, turned the handle and peered in cautiously. It was an empty room: bare floorboards, bare walls.

To the right, there was a recess in the middle of the end wall, about four feet wide and four feet deep. On a plinth in the recess sat the bust of a man, sculpted in stone. It was in poor condition: cracked and thick with dust.

The man had an old, shrivelled face and hollow cheeks. His mouth was turned down at the edges and he had almost no lips at all.

There was no name along the base, no indication as to how old it was or where it came from, but Briony had seen this face before: in Petra's mural at Styles Lane.

Was this, then, the origin of her Pastor?

In the section of wall on the further side of the recess, almost in the corner of the room, was another door. Briony wondered where it could possibly lead, for she had come to the very end of the wing, there was nothing, surely, beyond this wall?

The door opened on to a narrow spiral staircase made of stone and brick. The air felt icy cold and smelt of mould. There was daylight coming from somewhere.

Oddly – for this was the fourth floor – the staircase went upwards only. Curious, Briony began to climb the steps. She came to a tiny window through which she could glimpse the woodlands to the rear of the house. She continued on a little further. She passed another tiny window.

At the top of the staircase she came to another door – into

the attic rooms, she assumed. She turned the handle, pushed open the door and peered along a passageway with rooms on either side. The doors were open, lending a little daylight to the central passageway. She felt a sudden draught – almost a gust – of freezing air. And with it came the stench of something indescribably foul. Briony could not imagine what it might be. It was a sickening, fetid smell, the stink of something putrefying . . . Like the decomposing remains of a dead animal.

She pulled the door shut. And at that very moment she heard the other door bang shut below, at the foot of the spiral staircase. It was so sudden and so loud – like a gun going off in that confined and stony space – that she gave a little gasp of shock and stood with one hand on her heart in the ensuing silence.

And then she heard footsteps . . . Footsteps climbing the stairs towards her. Heavy steps, a man's footfall, echoing, sounding like hard leather on gravelly stone. Slow and uneven, as if every step was a special effort. Coming closer and closer.

Briony stood motionless, terrified.

When it sounded as if the man was just a few treads below and about to come into view, the footsteps stopped.

Briony held her breath.

Silence.

Was he resting? Or had he sensed that there was someone there?

It was such a dreadful, threatening silence. So oppressive with menace she could almost feel it, like an electric charge in the atmosphere. Her scalp felt prickly. She began to tremble in the cold.

There was no end to the silence. It went on and on and on. It seemed to last for ever.

When she was too cold to stand there any longer, she began to creep down the steps towards him.

What *was* she going to say?

As she rounded each turn of the staircase she expected to

see his shadow or the cloth of his coat at any moment. She passed one of the two small windows, grateful for the sliver of grey light that it offered . . . Round and round, down and down . . . Past the second window . . . Step by step . . . Until she reached the very bottom. She had arrived back at the door.

Where had he gone, whoever he was?

She felt for the handle on the door, hoping and praying that it wasn't one of those that could only be opened from the other side. It was not. The handle turned, the door opened and she stepped back into the empty room.

But where in the hell had he gone?

She was about to close the door again when she heard something from above, from the spiral staircase . . . An indistinct sound. Was it the door opening at the top? And then she caught the faintest whiff of that putrid stench she had smelt upstairs. She quickly closed the door, scurried out of the room and along the corridor to the main staircase. At the central stair landing she stopped and glanced back, half afraid that someone might be following her. But she was quite alone.

How could he have disappeared like that? There was nowhere he could have gone . . . She had heard him, every step of the way . . . He was so close.

She hurried down the stairs to the ground floor. She was breathless and felt slightly sick . . . Partly the fright and partly that stink.

She left the house the way she had come in, by the side door. Outside, the January air was crisp and clean and bracing. She pulled the door shut and walked across the courtyard and the gravel drive beyond, to where the Mini stood, on the grass, the only vehicle in sight.

As she pulled away and the Mini lurched off the frosty grass on to the gravel driveway, she glanced up at the windows at the very top of the house. The first time she had seen this house, she'd taken the fourth floor to be the top floor. But above that there was an ornamental stone balustrade. And almost hidden from view behind the balustrade were windows that protruded from the near-vertical slope of a gambrel roof. It was a fifth floor, but both the central staircase and the narrow flight of back stairs ended at the floor below. There appeared to be no way up to the fifth . . . other than by that spiral staircase hidden away in the far corner of the end wing.

Briony drove back to London.

She saw no one and heard from no one all week.

She was not sure what to do for the best. She was no nearer finding Tam, she had got absolutely nowhere. All she had achieved was to put herself out of a job – and that job had been her only contact with the women of the Foundation, with the people who knew what had happened to Tamara.

Then, one night, the following week, her door bell rang. She went downstairs to the ground floor and opened the door.

There was no one there.

She looked out on to the street.

A car stood double-parked, in the middle of the road, the engine running, a soft, rhythmic sound. The rear door was wide open.

There was no one in sight. Just the car. Waiting.

She had seen it before: outside the Casa Negra and on Trinidad Way . . . It was Misha's long black limousine.

LIMOUSINE

She did what she had promised herself she would never do again: she telephoned Dee at the Casa Negra.

When Dee came on, Briony said, 'There's a car outside. Waiting for me.'

Dee said, 'Well, you know where it's going.'

And when Briony said nothing in reply:

'It'll go away, if that's what you want.'

Briony didn't know what she did want.

'Look at the painting on the wall,' said Dee.

Briony looked at the mural.

'A woman stands at a fork in the road,' said Dee. 'One path leads to a pretty little village across the hills, where the rainbow ends. The other path leads to a dark church. The woman's head is turned towards the rainbow and the nice, dinky village. But her feet – her body – are turned towards the place of darkness. She can go either way. She can follow her heart or follow her head. No one's forcing her. She's free to choose. Tamara followed her desires. You have to choose for yourself which way you want to go.'

'I want to see Tamara,' said Briony. 'That's all. You know that.'

'But how badly do you want to see her?' said Dee. 'What are you prepared to give up to be with her? That's what you have to decide.'

'I don't understand what I've got to do,' said Briony, 'and I'm afraid.'

'I told you,' said Dee, 'there's nothing to understand. It's a journey of discovery. Fear is the only barrier. Beyond it lies freedom. Beyond it lies release. Beyond it lies the dark world of the senses – like outer space, new galaxies, new realms of awareness. But you have to overcome the fear, you have to learn to let go.'

'I don't know that I can,' said Briony. 'I don't know that I've got it in me.' She felt so pathetic, but all she wanted to do was *understand*. She couldn't let go if she didn't know what was happening. It was like diving off a cliff in the night.

'You weren't afraid the time before.'

'I don't know what happened the time before. I didn't know what was a dream and what was real.'

'Why make the distinction?' said Dee. 'They're both perceptions within your own mind. They're different dimensions of consciousness, that's all.'

'But I don't think I can stomach going to that awful place on my own,' said Briony.

'Then stay at home,' said Dee. 'Do nothing and the limo will go away. It'll never come back. Go home to Mackerelville, back to the sandy beaches and the rain and the fog and the funny little pubs and your guitar and your folk clubs. Back to what you know. Back to what feels safe. No one will ever contact you. No one will bother you any more. This will all seem like a dream to you.'

'But how will I find Tamara?' said Briony.

'You won't,' said Dee. 'You'll never see her again.'

Briony bit into her lower lip as tears began to spill down her face.

'You're at the fork in the road,' said Dee. 'Where does your head want to go? And where does your heart want to go?'

TAMARA (8)

She stands staring at the woman in the mural.

That won't help you much, Sis. There's only one way to find me: the Pastor. He is the way, the truth and the darkness.

I've stood looking at that mural, too. But I knew which path I had to take. I didn't really have a choice, I'm drawn to evil.

What did Dee say? You have a choice? I bet she said you have a choice. Very democratic, Dee. She condemns women to this eternal purgatory of twilight, but she likes to feel that it was of their own choosing, and none of her responsibility.

Do you like Dee?

I first met her at the Casa Negra. I could only afford to go there once a week in those days. Friday or Saturday. The highlight of my week. I used to go there with a friend but she didn't like it, the atmosphere was too heavy for her, so I had to go there on my own for a while.

One night, Dee came to me and introduced herself. Said, 'Hi. I'm Drusilla.' We stood there looking at each other. I got that familiar kick in the heart I've come to know so well. I was picking up on something, something tuning in on my wavelength, giving me that scary, raunchy feeling.

Dee is a bad person. But hard to resist. And she knows so many secrets.

I sensed a kindred spirit.

She sussed me too.

Dee came up to me the next time I was in the Casa Negra and said, 'Are you looking for a flat?'

I wasn't, as it happened, but Dee has a way of corrupting people. She seduces them with a mix of charm and evil. I find it magnetically attractive. So I said, maybe. She said, why don't I go along and take a look, I could always say no. She gave me the address.

And that's how I first came here to Styles Lane, one dreary November Sunday. The front door was open. I looked inside. Somewhere in the gloom I heard Gloria's voice. 'We've been expecting you,' she said. She brought me up here. I stood looking at the mural, just like you. I sensed the evil in it. And – like the woman in the picture, perhaps – my head was screaming: Get out of here and never come back. But my body was drawn to that sinister, black church and that evil-looking creature with the shepherd's crook.

I was at a fork in the path, like you are now. My head said, Go, go, go ... Something kinda nasty happening here. But my heart was jumping like a fish out of water.

After I'd been here about six months, and the agency nursing wasn't working out, Dee said to me one day, 'I can use a part-time waitress, couple of nights a week. Cash in hand. Just temporary. Help you through this bad patch.'

That's how I started working there. Just a few weeks, I told myself. Till the nursing picked up.

By autumn I was working full-time.

And then Dee said to me one night, 'You know how you can make twice as much?'

She was leading me on but oh, so slowly, oh, so subtly. Didn't want to scare me off.

That's how I made the shift from waitress to hostess.

After I'd been a hostess for a month or so, and was getting a taste for all this dosh that I was pulling in, Dee said, 'This is peanuts. Do you know where the serious *money is?'*

Well, I could guess, of course . . . I'd been getting offers already, in a subtle kind of way.

I said, 'It depends what you call serious.'

'With your looks and your tastes,' she said, 'you could demand five hundred a night.'

I sort of resisted. There was a barrier there. But crossing that barrier wasn't very hard. In fact, the whole concept of it turned me on, the whole feeling of 'badness' about it. I'm driven by this urge to keep travelling out into the blackest of black worlds, a kind of outer-space of sensation and experience. I see my soul like a rogue rocket, soaring deeper and deeper into a cold, lightless nowhere-world, the Forbidden Zone.

I kidded myself it was a means to an end. I kidded myself I'd do it till I'd saved enough to buy myself a flat; I fancied something by the river. I was amazed what I could charge. Foreign businessmen and diplomats – Americans, Arabs, Japanese, Nigerians, they're all into it, they just put it on expenses.

Then, one night, Dee said, 'I know someone who'll pay a thousand a night.' She wasn't kidding.

'And what does he want for that?' I enquired, and you could hear the ironic laughter in my voice, because even I have limitations. There's a whole sub-world of sadomasochistic

231

horrors that I've peered into on occasion, but I know it ain't for me.

'No pain,' said Dee.

But they all say that.

'But what does he want?' I said again. 'What's the bottom line?'

'You can't see him or touch him,' Dee replied, 'or speak to him. You'll never know who he is and you're never to ask.'

This wasn't telling me anything much.

'But what does he get for his thousand a night?' I persisted.

'Trust,' said Dee. 'You have to trust him. You have to give yourself completely. No conditions.'

So I did laugh, this time. I mean trust, for Christ's sake... Trust is a blind tinker, travelling the world with his bagful of all-sorts. Yer pays your money, yer takes yer chances.

'What do you mean, I have to trust him?' I said. 'I give myself like a blank cheque to a man I can't see, I can't speak to, I don't know and never will. With no conditions. And all I get is a grand?'

And then Dee said the weirdest thing. She said, 'And immortality.'

Immortality. That was the word she used.

And she wasn't kidding, either.

My sister sits and paints her face. Black-cherry lips. Her grey-blue eyes buried deep in bowls of dark shadow.

She doesn't hurry... Because part of her is telling herself that, when the moment comes, she will bottle out, and stay home tonight, and will just have to wipe all that muck off her face, and so it's all a waste of time, no sense in hurrying.

I know because I went through that the first time – the first time I did it for money.

She feels sick as hell, scared shitless, but she's driven on by something... Some irrational impulse, like an electrical charge from this genetic dynamo we share as twins.

She dithers, uncertain what to wear.

232

She's lost a lot of weight. She does look so much like me now.

She tries on this, she tries on that. But it doesn't matter what she wears. The Pastor takes his victims naked and in the dark. It's her energy, her life he wants, that's all.

She dresses for the cold: leggings and a skinny-rib jumper. And then zips herself into that leather catsuit she seems to have taken a liking to. She takes one last look around the room . . . Kidding herself she's looking to see if she's left anything behind, when really she's looking to see if she can spot an excuse for not walking down those stairs and out into the street to the waiting limousine.

I know because I've been there, Sis. I know just what you're feeling.

She goes.

I imagine her walking down the stairs now . . .

And along the hallway . . .

I picture her stepping out into the night and pulling shut the door. She walks down the garden path, fear dragging at her feet like a child, crying for her to stay.

The door of the limousine is open wide.

She can't see the driver; he's hidden behind black glass.

He doesn't play the gentleman, he doesn't get out to close the door for her; lets her do that for herself.

Now is the moment. She can still walk away.

I expect she hesitates and peers into the interior of the car. But there is no one there to give her confidence. No Dee to reassure her.

Does she think about the woman in the mural?

Her head wants to take her back upstairs, while her heart is pulling her towards me.

I wait, wondering . . . Hoping she'll walk back into the room, hoping she will let the limo drive away.

But Briony does not come back.

SISTERHOOD

THE CHAMBER

The limousine pulled up in the courtyard where she had entered before. The light was on above the side door, just as it had been on the night of the party. The door was unlocked.

She hesitated. She turned and looked back at the limousine. It was already creeping away, back into the night.

Briony pushed open the door and stepped inside the house. There was enough light for her to see through to the main hall. She stood still and listened. She wondered if anyone would come.

No one did.

She wondered what she was supposed to do.

There was not a sound anywhere.

She looked along the dark passage that led to the chapel.

Or was the chapel part of her dream as well?

She walked slowly along the passage. She came to a closed door. She opened it . . .

This was the chapel.

She felt the wall beside her and found a row of light-switches. Only one dim light came on.

She walked through the shadows, across the empty floor, to the dais. It was all here: the brick kiln-like structure, filled with cold ashes, the iron rings cemented into the wall behind. She had not dreamt it.

She looked up . . . almost to the roof of the chapel, right up to the organ loft. It was so dark up there it was difficult to make out anything at all apart from the clusters of organ pipes, pointing heavenwards like shadowy rockets.

Was it her imagination? Or was somebody peering over the side of the loft, looking down at her?

So gloomy up there . . . Impossible to tell.

She quickly switched off the lights and returned to the main hall.

She walked up the staircase to the first-floor landing. To left and right the central passage was in darkness. She carried on up to the next floor. That was in darkness, too.

What was she supposed to do? Where was she supposed to go?

She continued up to the third floor.

There was no light on in the central passage but a soft yellow glow was spilling through an open doorway.

She walked towards it and looked inside. It was the room in which she had woken up on New Year's Day.

A coal fire was burning in the grate, exactly as before.

A small jug of mulled wine stood on the small table, with a glass beside it.

The bathroom door was open. The light was on, the room was full of steam. A hot bath was waiting for her; the water hidden beneath a snowscape of fragrant foam.

She turned and looked around the bedroom. A white towel lay on the bed, neatly folded.

It was not warm in here, even with the fire.

(Who laid these fires? Who kept them going? Where did they hide themselves, those minions Dee had spoken of?)

She poured herself a glass of the mulled wine, moved the ladderback chair to the hearth and sat by the fire.

Maybe Misha would come and tell her what to do.

She waited. She drank the glass of hot, spicy wine. But no one came.

The scent of that waiting bath was alluring. She imagined lowering herself into all that steaming foam and lying back, up to her chin.

She undressed, poured herself a second glass of the mulled wine and took it into the bathroom.

She lay in the bath until the water began to grow cool. She felt better now. The hot wine had been soothing, had helped to calm her down. She climbed out of the bath, dried herself off and went back into the bedroom.

Someone had been in here while she was in the bath: her clothes had gone . . . Everything, even her shoes.

And the long leather coat was back. It was lying on the bed. It had not been lying on the bed when she first walked in.

The tray had been removed, with the jug and the dregs of the mulled wine.

But she hadn't heard a sound.

Who was doing all this? They could not have been far way. If they were not actually watching her, they must have been listening. She put on the coat, opened the door and looked up and down the corridor. Apart from the main stairwell, the whole place was in darkness. All the doors were closed and no light was visible from beneath any of them.

She walked up the narrow back stairs to the top floor. To her right, the entire passageway, as far as the main stairwell and the walled-off apartment, was in darkness.

To her left, there was a glow of light emanating from the wing at the end of the building. She walked along to where the passage turned a right angle. Just as before, there was a door wide open, halfway along on the left-hand side. Candlelight was flickering, reflected, on the walls of the passage.

And yet there had been no door there at all when she had a gone up there in daylight to see.

She looked inside the windowless chamber.

Just as before, three candles burned beside the four-poster bed. The mattress was covered by a black sheet, nothing else. Two logs burned in the grate.

She entered the chamber, walked over to the bentwood chair by the credenza, moved it closer to the fire and sat down.

The mulled wine had steadied her nerves. She wondered what they put in it. Some kind of tranquillizer. Valium perhaps.

She waited. Nobody came.

239

One of the candles expired. And then another. The fire burned low.

It was cold with the door open and an icy stream gusting in from the passageway. She got up and moved around to get her circulation going, but there was no carpet on the floor, nothing but the wooden boards, and she was barefoot. She came back to sit by the fire, put her feet on the edge of the seat and hugged her knees.

The remaining candle flickered feebly. The flame revived a little, burned brightly for a few moments longer and then that, too, wilted and died.

The remains of the logs sat in a bed of glowing ashes.

The room seemed terribly dark now. But not so draughty. She looked around: the door was closed. She hadn't heard a sound.

She was beginning to feel drowsy.

She could smell something pleasant, fragrant . . . Like joss or incense. Smelt as if it was coming from the fireplace, as if there was something burning in the hearth . . . But she couldn't see. It was growing stronger. And she was feeling sleepier. Her eyelids were so heavy now. She felt totally worn out. So sleepy . . . Suddenly so sleepy . . .

TAMARA (9)

The Pastor approaches.

She has no warning, she never will. He comes like a figment of the imagination, like a fantasy born on the edge of sleep, a character created in a dream.

They say you can hear his footsteps sometimes on the rotten timbers of the floor above, but I never heard a sound.

Few people ever talk about the Pastor. A woman can

disappear for ever just for asking questions – even for speculating what he looks like. But they do talk, they do wonder, we all do, of course we do.

They say nobody knows. But *who* knows *nobody knows?* That's the beauty of a conspiracy of silence: no one can be sure if it really exists. How can they, when no one talks about it?

Some say he has the mind and vigour of a man of forty, trapped inside the grizzly outer shell of something descended from prehistoric times.

Others say quite the opposite: that his outer body is beautifully preserved, that he is handsome as well as strong and vigorous, a creature of phenomenal sexual prowess, but even he is powerless to prevent the deterioration of the brain ... That his mind has decayed down the centuries, just as Misha's mind is decaying now. He has retained his youth and striking beauty (they say) but has lost all capacity for thought and reason. His mind has rotted away and is now little more than a ball of dead organic matter. He cannot perform any natural function unaided (they say) and he roams the attic rooms like some dull, demented animal and has to be led to the chamber, where sex is nothing more than a compulsive act of instinct now.

They say the only reason the women keep him alive is to contaminate more victims, so they can draw more women into the Foundation.

Some say he never sees daylight and is only permitted to see other human beings when Misha has a party and he is dragged around on a lead, strapped up and masked and incognito, like a performing bear.

There are those who think he is all-powerful by night – like Dracula – but inert and helpless by day.

And there are even some who believe that he is half-man and half-woman ... That Misha is the Pastor, and the Pastor is Misha; that every one of his lovers is carefully chosen, hand-

picked at the Casa Negra and brought to Leysholme in the limousine to satisfy his priapic and remorseless lust.

Who knows?

Whoever he is, whatever he looks like, he is approaching now . . .

She will be asleep, ready, waiting, trussed and prepared, much as one trusses and bastes a turkey for the oven. The minions will have done everything and fled back to their underworld. All he will have to do is . . . enjoy, as Dee would say.

At some time in the night she will slip out of her drugged and semi-conscious state for a few moments and become aware of the exquisite sensations beginning to trickle through her body. And soon after orgasm – the most powerful and all-consuming she will ever experience – she will drift back into a subconscious state and be aware of nothing until morning.

MERMAID

She could open her eyes but she was in the pitch dark.

Could curl her fingers but her wrists were pinned.

Her limbs were staked out like semaphore signals, taut as bow strings.

Couldn't move her head or open her mouth . . . Something strapped tight across her lips, sealing them shut . . . Could hear nothing, see nothing, smell nothing.

Couldn't sense her own body . . . Couldn't sense her own flesh, her bones, her muscles . . . Felt as though she was anaesthetized, paralysed . . . But no pain.

Now something smooth and caressing, soft and flowing, warm and subtle, moving in whirls and swirls all over her flesh . . . Her belly, her breasts, the soft parts of her neck, inside her thighs . . . Something arousing, stimulating, but then soothing, relaxing, something that lapped through her, ebbing and flowing . . . Something that seemed to charge the nerve endings all over her flesh . . . Gorgeous, luxurious feelings radiating through her body . . . Intoxicating, ravishing . . .

Now gliding, smooth and sleek . . .

Imagining herself as a mermaid, rising, dipping . . . Through a perfumed lagoon . . . Water soft and warm . . . Lapping into every nook and cranny of her body . . . Licking every tiny part of her . . . A tide of exhilaration, flowing, ebbing, washing over her, into her, through her . . . A little stronger all the time . . . Buoying her away on little waves of rapture . . . Now drawing her back, teasing her, tantalizing . . . Now lifting her high and over a crest, her body arched, trapped, stretched tighter, tighter, then relaxing, dropping back down . . . Plunging then rising, dipping and climbing, like a switchback, surging higher, and faster, slower, lower, sliding back down . . . Now thrusting her up again, higher, still higher . . . Poised, balanced, quivering on open air for a moment . . . And now tumbling again, wheeling, spinning . . . A mermaid freefalling through sunlight, crashing through surf and rising, soaring . . . And gliding high now, like some beautiful white Arctic sea bird motionless on a current of air, born away across this ocean of ecstasy . . .

She woke up gradually, drifting in and out of strange dreams. She thought she was in a boat. It was dark and she was slumped across some kind of bed. And they were moving.

It was not a boat. She was in the car. The limousine. She pushed herself upright and peered through the darkened glass. They were driving through streets. London streets. She was almost home.

The car pulled up. She opened the door. She was in Styles Lane, outside The Hermitage. She climbed out and shut the door. The limousine reversed up the street, backed into a side turning, and drove forwards into Styles Lane again and up to the main road.

Briony watched its tail lights disappear, left, towards Hackney.

She walked slowly along the garden path. She felt light-headed, as if she was coming out of an anaesthetic. She wondered what time it was. It felt like about half past nine in the evening. She switched on the hall light and looked at her watch. She was amazed: it was twenty to five in the morning.

She noticed red marks around her wrist, beneath the watch strap.

She looked at the other wrist. It was grazed and bruised.

When she got back up to the flat she took off her shoes, her leggings and tights, and examined her ankles: they were marked as well, with scratches and contusions.

It was cold in the room, so cold that she undressed and got straight into bed. But she wasn't tired. She lay there thinking about the mermaid, wondering what she'd dreamt and what she hadn't, trying to work out what had happened in the night. The strange thing was, she didn't really care what had happened. She couldn't focus on anything but it didn't seem to matter. She felt so tranquil inside, so content.

The day wandered past her like a cloud. She sat and daydreamed: nothing in particular. And when evening came around, she wondered where the day had gone.

She had a beautiful sleep that night ... No dreams – no mermaid, no sea bird – just a long, deep, refreshing sleep.

She felt good the next day, too, but more focused, more down-to-earth.

The feeling had worn off entirely by the third day. She awoke with a slight headache and was tired and irritable. She felt slightly down for the next couple of days, not exactly depressed, but listless.

That passed. Within a few days she felt normal again, except that she had a slight sense of ... Desire was too strong a word ... A slight hankering, perhaps, to go back to the house, to that windowless chamber, to experience those delicious sensations one more time.

The following night, exactly a week after that night of the mermaid, there was a ring on her doorbell. She went downstairs and opened the door. There was no one there. She looked out to the street. The limousine was waiting, as before: double parked, the rear door open, ghostly puffs of exhaust rising in the frosty sodium-yellow air.

TAMARA (10)

She goes again. More anxious this time. But a different kind of anxiety . . . She's afraid the car might leave without her.

I know that feeling. Dee warned me I'd feel strung out once the high wore off. But she didn't mention how addictive this thing was. Just like a drug.

It steals up on you, Sis, takes control and you don't even know it's happening. Grabs your soul, whips it away, stealthy as a pickpocket.

It didn't take a drug to get me there – money was enough, and the sexual excitement, the allure of wickedness . . . something as dreadful as the Pastor, I just couldn't resist. But I guess they had to give you something to overcome your inhibitions. Maybe heavy downers. Maybe Palfium . . . You'll see the needle marks if they're putting Palfium into you.

But they won't have to give you drugs for very long. Pleasure will be the hook. It feels so fantastically good, Sis, and it goes on getting better. You'll keep going back, you'll crave to go back, you'll ache like a strung-out junkie, you'll be longing for those nights the limo shows, desperate for that ring on the doorbell.

Right now you're wondering: who is the Pastor? What does

he want? What is he doing to me? But you won't care at all after a little while. What your body craves, that's the only thing you'll care about. A crackhead or a mainliner, she'll do anything for her fix ... She'll rob an old granny, she'll whore up back alleys, she'll stab her own sister, she'll kill if she has to. Anything for her fix. That's how you'll be. You're on the path now, Sis, and you won't get off.

And – as if the nights weren't heaven enough – you feel so beautiful inside, the next few days. Isn't it just the best? I've never done smack or even crack but they tell me that's how it is ... A whole other plane of existence. But the Pastor gives and the Pastor takes, and, oh, the downers ... And they get worse, Sis, that's the killer.

And then you start to get the dark spells. And that gets really scary. They call it 'phasing out'.

I had to trust him, Dee told me. I had to give myself completely, she said, with no conditions.

I laughed. 'And all I get is a grand?' I scoffed.

'And immortality,' said Dee. (And orgasms, like, out of this world, she might have added. But I guess that pales alongside immortality.)

I sort of sniffy-laughed again and said, 'What do you call immortal?'

'You've got a face that breaks men's hearts,' she said, 'and a body they'll pay a thousand pounds a night for. How would you like to look that way for another hundred years?'

'Just another hundred?' I think I said, sarcastically.

'Then how about eternity?' said Dee.

She showed me an old passport that expired in 1950, when she was the age she looks today.

She was born Drusilla Elizabeth Jabal, in Mombasa, Kenya, on the day the First World War broke out, August 1914.

Not bad-looking, is she? ... For eighty-two years old.

TWILIGHT

Everything was exactly the way it had been on the previous occasion: the bedroom on the third floor, the mulled wine, the hot bath ready and waiting; on the floor above a door open where there was no door; candles burning in the windowless chamber, the plain black sheet on the four-poster bed; the candles expiring, one by one, the fire burning low; the sweet smell of joss, the sudden sleepiness descending over her, the irresistible desire to close those heavy eyelids . . .

A period of blankness.

And then those gorgeous sensations beginning to creep through her . . . Her body pegged out and taut, like hide left to dry in the sun . . . The softest touch all over her . . . Delicate as lace . . . Light as a breath . . .

And when she woke up she was in the limousine and almost home again.

And again those feelings of tranquillity and dreamy contentment, followed by a day or two of general weariness.

She wondered how long this would go on for before they would let her see Tamara. Was it some kind of induction ritual, her rite of passage into the cult? It no longer worried her; it had been scary at first, and it was so *cold* in that bleak monster of a house, one vast warren of draughts. But the rest had been like one long, rapturous dream.

Each week – at the same time, always the same evening – the limousine came to pick her up. And the same thing happened on each and every occasion, the same sequence of events, the same small details. Nothing ever changed, except the bodily sensations. Every time she went it left her wanting just a little more. And every time she came back, she felt so calm, so at peace with the world; a harmony of mind and spirit. Each time she returned from Leysholme these sensations seemed to get a little stronger, until nothing mattered any more. She had no worries, she felt placid and serene. She had no desire to be anywhere or do anything. The days slipped by without her noticing. She felt no hunger. She felt almost nothing. She couldn't even feel her body. The bruises and the grazes around her wrists and ankles, they were not even sore. She pricked her flesh with a pin: couldn't feel a thing. She pricked herself all over – hard, until she drew tiny beads of blood – but she couldn't feel it. During these days of serenity her body was becoming numb; losing all its sensitivity.

Just as the good feelings intensified with every passing visit, so too did the languor and fatigue that followed. After two days, that serenity would evaporate overnight, and she would wake up feeling worn out, as if she hadn't slept all week. It was like a long, drawn-out hangover. She awoke with head-aches; she took tablets but they did no good. She lacked energy; even a walk to the shops left her exhausted. Sometimes she felt so drained, she slept all morning long.

It affected her at night as well. The days of serenity were coupled with nights of perfect sleep; if she dreamed at all she had no memory of it, and if she woke at all she was not aware of it. Whereas the low days that followed, the days of languor and depression, of dull headaches and fatigue, were made worse by nights of wakefulness, of tossing and turning, and by bad dreams which melted from the memory upon waking but which left an abiding impression of gloom hanging over her, of something indefinable but sinister in the air.

She stayed at home on these low days, drank coffee to try and stimulate her system, ate almost nothing, sat in front of the television for hours on end, could remember nothing of what she had just watched, and cared even less. For much of the time she just sat with her eyes closed and dozed. They were not even catnaps. It was a sort of in-between state, neither fully awake nor quite asleep, and she felt no better when she woke up. A growing sense of unease – not quite depression – would descend and hang around her for several days, though she had nothing in particular on her mind.

As the high days got better and the low days got worse she began to long for her weekly visit to Leysholme, to her night in the chamber. It took away all her pains, blew away these clouds of unease, sent her spirits soaring like a kite into the sky. She began to ache for those nights, for the rapture, and the days of serenity that followed. It took her over completely, it became an end in itself. She had not forgotten Tamara, but Tamara had become unimportant. The only purpose in what she was doing was to satisfy her craving. She no longer wondered who the Pastor was or whether he existed at all. She no longer cared if he was just a figurehead or a myth. It was the pleasure that mattered, the rapture, the days of serenity.

She never saw another living soul at Leysholme. She heard noises sometimes – a door closing somewhere or the distant sound of the organ – but the passages, the stairways, the rooms, they were always deserted. Occasionally, she thought she heard footsteps moving across the ceiling above the panelled chamber and the creak of floorboards. It brought back the memory of being trapped on the spiral staircase and the footsteps climbing towards her, and the gut-churning stench that had wafted out of the attic gloom.

She could never quite pluck up the courage to look inside that end room – the empty chamber, with the bust of the shrivelled old man – a second time.

One morning, after a night in the chamber, she awoke and she was not in the car going home. She was woken by an unfamiliar drubbing noise. Intermittent. She opened her eyes. It was day. She was in bed – a warm, comfortable bed – but not Tam's bed at Styles Lane. She raised herself on to one elbow and squinted against the light. She was still at Leysholme. She was in the bedroom on the third floor; her usual room. Rain was being driven against the windows by flurries of blustery wind. That was the noise that had woken her.

She got out of bed and almost collapsed. She felt very strange indeed: so light-headed she thought she was going to faint. She made it to the bathroom. She tried to work out what had happened, why she was still here. But she could not put her thoughts together; they were like the pieces of a torn-up photograph that she couldn't reassemble.

She went back into the bedroom and looked around. The fire had gone out; the ashes were still in the grate. The table was bare, the jug of mulled wine and the glass had been taken away.

No clothes.

She always left them just here, on the ladderback chair. But someone had taken them. She looked in the wardrobe: the leather coat was hanging there. She put it on, opened the bedroom door and looked along the corridor. There was no one to be seen and not a sound anywhere.

What time was it? She looked around the room again. They had not only taken her clothes, they had taken her watch.

She walked slowly towards the main staircase. She felt wobbly on her feet, as if she'd been drunk the night before. When she reached the stairwell, she looked down into the darkness of the hallway, three floors below. She was going to call out, to attract someone's attention. It seemed the obvious thing to do: there had to be someone around, somewhere. But as she drew breath to speak she felt all the breath go out of her body and her legs giving way beneath her . . .

She reached out to the mahogany balustrade that ran along the edge of the landing, above the open stairwell, but she had no strength . . . Suddenly so weak . . . As if someone had pulled a plug out of her body and all the energy was flooding out of her.

It began to grow dark, very quickly, as if the same hand that had pulled the plug from her body was now turning a switch and dimming the daylight. Everything around her was growing darker, darker. It was like twilight now. And she was sinking to the floor . . . Couldn't hold herself up.

There were people sitting on the stairs, watching her.

Women. Gazing at her with fixed, expressionless faces.

'Somebody help me,' Briony said weakly. 'Can't somebody . . .? I can't get my breath.'

They all stared back in blank silence. No one moved to help her.

Briony tried to get up but she had no strength at all. She couldn't even pull herself on to her knees.

'Somebody . . .?' she pleaded. But even her voice lacked strength. The words came out as a breathy whimper.

She looked along the central passage. There were even more women watching her now . . . Dozens of them. All the way along the passage, as far as she could see on each side of the staircase. All motionless, sitting or lying, gazing at her with bored, impassive faces.

All of them were naked.

'Can't anybody . . .?' she begged.

They observed her as if they were watching an animal in a cage. There was not even curiosity on their faces.

Summoning all her strength, Briony pushed herself up on to her knees, clasped the balustrade with both hands and hauled herself to her feet. Using the balustrade to prop herself up, she stood, eyes closed, trying to recover her breath.

Her strength began to return. She felt it seeping back into her, as if someone had restored the flow of blood to her veins. When she opened her eyes again it was fully light once more and there was no one there: the stairs and the central passageway were deserted. All the women had gone.

She was completely alone. And she was naked.

PRISONER

The coat was lying on the floor beside her.

She leaned heavily on the balustrade, trying to get her breath back. She was aware of someone behind her. She turned to look.

It was Misha.

She hadn't heard anyone approaching.

Misha's face had a sculptured, iceberg kind of beauty. It expressed neither warmth nor the slightest emotion.

'I don't know what happened,' said Briony. 'I think I fainted.'

'And you saw something,' said Misha.

'I think I sort of ... had a little dream. It went dark suddenly.'

'Did you see people?'

'People, yes. There were people here but they wouldn't help me.'

'What sort of people?'

'Women. Here. Everywhere. Watching me.'

'Go back to your room,' said Misha. 'You need rest.'

'I don't understand what happened.'

'You don't need to understand,' Misha replied. 'Go back and rest.'

Briony was confused. There was something she had been meaning to ask, something about her clothes ... But she couldn't piece her thoughts together, everything was such a muddle in her mind.

She picked up the coat and put it on again.

Those good feelings – the tranquillity, the contentment – were trying to assert themselves, but they were like the sun obscured by a mist and struggling to burn through. She walked slowly back along the passage. She still felt wobbly.

She thought that Misha was following her but, when she reached the bedroom, she found she was alone.

She entered the room. Someone had been in here to clean up. The bed had been remade and the ashes had been swept from the hearth, but a new fire had not been laid. She wondered how long that strange 'twilight' spell had really lasted. It had felt like seconds. But how could anyone have tidied up the room so quickly?

It was cold in the room without the fire; she got back into bed.

She fell asleep.

She was awoken by the sound of the door closing. She sat up and looked around. Someone had left a tray on the table. She got out of bed and put on the leather coat. They had brought her a sort of lunch: a bowl of vegetable soup and some black rye bread, and a cup of milky coffee. She sat down at the table. She was not hungry but she picked up the spoon and tasted the soup. It was hot and spicy; she tasted ginger. She broke off a piece of the rye bread: thick-textured, dark and slightly sour-tasting but not unpleasant. She ate it all.

When she had finished eating, she picked up the cup of coffee and got back into bed, to keep warm.

She must have dozed off again. The next thing she knew, Misha was beside the bed, looking down at her.

'Sit up,' she said. She held out a glass of what looked like lemon squash.

'What is it?' asked Briony.

'Drink it,' said Misha. 'You need it. To restore electrolytes.'

'Restore *what*?' said Briony.

Misha said: 'Just drink.' And, opening the palm of her hand, offered her a large white tablet.

'What is it?' asked Briony.

'Glucose,' said Misha. 'You need energy.'

'Why? What's wrong with me?' said Briony.

'You need energy,' Misha said again.

253

The tablet was too large to swallow.

'You can chew it,' said Misha. 'Won't matter.'

Briony drank the fluid and handed the glass back to Misha.

'What's happened to my clothes?' she asked.

'You don't need clothes,' Misha replied. 'You're not well enough to travel.'

She walked out of the room and closed the door.

Briony lay back down in bed. She sucked the tablet. It dissolved like glucose but it had a bitter aftertaste. She wondered if it had been laced with something.

She felt worse as the day wore on. Her body ached, as if she was sickening with flu. She felt as though she might faint again at any moment; as if she was not taking in enough oxygen when she breathed.

She slept for a little while.

When she awoke it was almost night outside.

She switched on the bedside lamp.

Someone had been in and had left more food on the table. She got out of bed to see what it was. Soup again – a thick chicken-coloured broth, with a piquant, spicy smell, like the vegetable soup she had had before.

She was cold, standing there with nothing on. She looked for the coat. It was not on the ladderback chair where she had left it. She looked in the wardrobe. It was empty. They had taken the coat away.

She tried to open the door that led out into the central passageway.

It was locked.

She pulled and pushed, but it was a solid door and tight in its frame; there was no movement at all. The exertion left her panting for breath. She sat on the side of the bed.

She went into the bathroom and tried the door on the other side of the room. It was not locked. She entered a room that was identical in size to the one she was sleeping in.

The only piece of furniture in the room was an iron bed

frame. The springs were intact but nothing else: no mattress, no headboard, no tailboard.

From each corner of the iron frame dangled a length of iron chain attached to metal sleeves, wide as shirt cuffs.

On the floor, beneath the bed, lay an enamel basin, about two feet in diameter and six inches deep.

She turned and crossed to the door that led out into the central passage. She tried the handle. This door was locked as well.

She walked back across the room and trod on something that dug into her bare foot like a sharp stone. She picked it up. It looked like a chip of white marble but there was not enough light to see properly. She took it back into the other room and examined it beneath the lamp.

It was a tooth; a human tooth.

Fear began to concentrate her mind.

Were they trying to poison her? Or drug her into some kind of useless mental state? What other explanation was there? That was why they wouldn't let her go home, that was why they'd locked her in, had taken away her clothes, and were bringing her this spicy food. That was why she was feeling so peculiar and why she had passed out by the staircase.

Was this what they had done to Tamara? Was this how they had got the money out of her?

She dipped the spoon into the broth, blew on it to cool it down and tasted a little. It had something very hot in it, like Cayenne pepper ... so hot they could have dissolved a cocktail of almost anything in it – benzos, barbiturates, speed, acid – and no one would have tasted the difference.

She took it into the bathroom, tipped it down the lavatory and put the empty bowl back on the tray.

She was beginning to shake with cold. She slipped back beneath the bedcovers.

Only one thought preoccupied her now: how to get out of this place.

But where could she go without clothes? Where would

255

Misha have put her things? They could be anywhere. It would take an age to search this huge house. And so many rooms were locked.

She waited in bed with the light off and pretended she was asleep when someone came to her room to collect the tray.

Was it Misha?

She didn't dare open her eyes to peep.

She heard the door closing again and the key being turned in the lock. She waited a few minutes before getting out of bed. She pulled a blanket off the bed, wrapped it around herself and walked through the bathroom, into the other bedroom.

She tried to open the door that led out into the central passageway but it was locked tight.

She knelt down and squinted into the keyhole. It looked as if the key had been left in the lock.

An icy draught was gusting through the gap beneath the door. She looked down and felt the gap. She could almost slip the tips of her fingers between the floorboards and the bottom of the door. If she could just find something that would dislodge the key . . .

She got up and looked at the bed frame. The base was a latticework of small spiral springs, interlinked with short lengths of thick, strong wire. She fumbled in the semi-darkness, afraid that if she switched on the light it might be seen. Several of the springs had broken. Where they had snapped away from the iron frame, the wire lattice sagged. And where it sagged she managed to prise loose one of the interconnecting lengths of wire and unhitch it completely.

Removing the blanket she was wearing, she slid a corner of it beneath the door and pushed it as far as she could into the passageway. Inserting the wire into the keyhole, she managed to turn the key back a little, into a position where she could simply push it clean out of the lock. It fell with a muffled clunk on to the blanket. She drew the blanket back inside the room, but there was not enough clearance beneath the door for both the blanket and the key. As she pulled the blanket through, the key collided with the bottom edge of the door and was knocked off the blanket, on to the floorboards outside.

She lay belly-down on the floor to see where it was. It was tantalizingly close. She pushed the length of wire beneath the door and managed to tease the key towards her with the length of wire. Gradually, inch by inch, she eased it through.

She got up off the floor, wrapped the blanket round herself once more and unlocked the door. She opened it cautiously and peered along the corridor towards the staircase.

She closed the door behind her and crept along the passage, trying the handle of every door. Some were locked, some were not. She looked inside every room that she could gain access to. Most of them were empty. Some were furnished but looked as if no one had been in them for ages.

She could find no clothes, of any kind, anywhere.

And then she heard the organ.

THE APARTMENT

The sound came creeping like a waking monster out of the cavernous silence of the house: that lofty organ, high above the chapel.

She stood still and listened.

It was like stereo . . . the music was coming from above and below. And the sound that was coming from above – from the top floor – seemed louder than the sound that was drifting up from the hallway.

She walked a little further along the passage. She was immediately under the walled-off apartment now. She came to a narrow flight of stairs that corresponded to the back stairs at the other end of the building. The staircase was in total darkness.

She felt for the banister rail and walked up to the floor above. At the top she came to a closed door. She put her ear to it and listened. All she could hear was the organ. She felt for the door handle, opened the door a few inches, peeped through the gap and listened again.

She edged cautiously into the apartment beyond and glanced up and down the well-lit passage. To her right: the end of the building and the short wing, the mirror of the wing at the other end of the building, where the windowless chamber was located. To her left, the passage led straight along to the flat-arched entrance door.

It looked identical to the central corridor on all the other floors, except that it was thickly carpeted and well decorated. It was warmer up here, too; much warmer.

A bedroom was what she needed . . . A coat and a pair of shoes would be enough. Most of the doors were partially open. She glanced into the nearest room. It was in darkness but it looked like a dining room. She moved along to the next room. This too was in darkness but she could see it was a kitchen. She turned the corner at the end of the building, into the wing and glanced around the door of a spacious sitting room. The lights were on – several table lamps. There were floor-to-ceiling bookcases; a grand piano; two armchairs on either side of a fireplace; long, heavy drapes drawn across the windows. A fire was burning in the grate.

The dogs were lying in front of the fire – the dogs she had seen in the woods with Misha. Big, ugly creatures, the size of mastiffs. One of them looked up. And then the other. Both stared at her for a moment, as if they were trying to recollect the face. Then they started barking.

Briony scuttled across to the other side of passage, into a darkened room, and shut the door.

The barking went on and on . . . She wondered if it would ever stop. Then she heard Misha calling to them – she didn't catch the words, the organ music was louder in here. The dogs fell silent.

Briony looked around. She was in a bathroom. There was a second door, at right angles to the first. It was ajar. She eased it open and tiptoed into a large bedroom. Some light was spilling into it through a doorway off the main passage. This was a room that was in daily use. It was fully furnished – elegantly furnished, by the look of it, antiques, perhaps – and there were clothes and personal bits and pieces scattered around.

Misha's bedroom?

There were two large chests of drawers and a tallboy, but no wardrobe. Briony opened drawers at random, pulled out a sweater and put it on. It was too large, but it was thick and warm. She found a woolly bonnet, like a fisherman's hat, and took that as well.

The dogs had started barking again. There was a third door at the far end of the room. Briony scurried across to it, clutching the blanket round her like a skirt. She stepped into darkness and eased the door shut behind her.

Those bloody dogs . . . How was she going to get *back*?

She looked around. She was in a small, square room with wardrobes along two walls, a window on the third side, and another door, which was shut. She looked in the wardrobes. They were packed tight with clothes. She pulled out a thick coat and tried on some shoes, but everything was at least a size too large. She found some long, thick sea-boot socks, put them on and zipped her numb feet into a pair of suede, fur-lined boots.

She opened the other door. It led into a cold, draughty passage. The organ music was much louder now. She closed the door of the dressing room. The passage went both ways – to her left and to her right. Left, she could see, would take her back into the apartment. She fumbled her way through the darkness in the opposite direction and came to some steps – not very many – that descended in a spiral into pitch blackness. She collided with a door. Pushing it open, she stepped down into . . .

What was this place?

It was like entering a private box at the theatre. She was standing on a balcony. She peered over a waist-high wall and looked down into the empty hollow of the chapel. There was light but she could not see where it was coming from.

She was in the organ loft: a forest of tall pipes all around her in eerie shadows. The organ was loud but not deafening; it was the same kind of baroque music that she had heard the night that Bibi was branded. She could not quite see the console from where she was standing. There was a narrow approach that curved through a quarter-circle.

She wanted to see his face . . . Just a glimpse, just to see him once. It was more than Tam had ever done.

She edged her way around towards the console until she could see the entire bench . . .

There was no one there. The bench was empty.

She drew closer. She stood in front of the console. Even in this shadowy half-light she could see that it was covered with cobwebs. She reached down to touch the keyboard. Both manuals were covered with thick, furry dust. She pulled her hands away as if she had just touched a live electric wire . . . And the music stopped.

It seemed to stop in the middle of a bar. The sound reverberated around the four-storey hollow of the chapel, faded to silence.

Briony shuffled backwards, away from the console, in cold terror, turned, and stumbled towards the door. She had to go back the way she had come, blindly feeling her way up the spiralling steps. But in her panic, and in the darkness, she missed the door that led back into Misha's dressing room. She continued to climb up and up the narrow stone steps. She realized now: she was walking up a spiral staircase identical to the one that led up to the attic floor at the other end of the building.

She stopped and was about to turn and feel her way back down, when she heard footsteps emerge from the organ loft below and begin to climb the stairs towards her . . . Just like the steps she had heard climbing the other spiral staircase . . . Slow and halting . . . Drawing steadily closer.

But this time they didn't stop. And this time she was in total darkness.

She stumbled on until the stairs ended and she collided with a door that she knew could only lead into the attic rooms. She fumbled feverishly for the handle, turned it and blundered into the black void beyond. She could feel a bitterly cold draught coursing through the place, like an Arctic breeze. A sudden gust snatched the door from her fingertips and it slammed shut.

Her hands groped the wall on either side of the door, hunting for a lightswitch. They found nothing. She walked forwards, her hands feeling the way. She touched the wall to her right and kept one hand on that in the hope that the layout up here was much like that on all the other floors. She passed a closed door, and then another a little further on, and arrived at the point where the wing met the main body of the house.

She felt that icy breeze gust through the place again. She stopped and looked back. She heard the door closing behind her in the blackness and the footsteps coming towards her along the bare floorboards. She stood frozen to the spot, petrified. Those same unhurried, halting footsteps, coming slowly closer . . .

She forced herself to move on and tried to turn into the main part of the building but instead walked headlong into a solid wall. She groped her way to the right and then groped her way to the left. There was no long central passage up here. It was not like the floors below. It was walled off. She was trapped: it was a dead end.

Moving to her left, her fingers touched the edges of a door frame. Her heart was racing. The palms of her hands skidded across the panels of the narrow door . . . found a handle . . . turned it . . . Please let it be open, please God . . .

She entered a large square room with windows along one wall which took the intensity out of the darkness, though it was a foul night outside. She could make out some bulky silhouettes – furniture perhaps, draped with shrouds. The air was damp and musty in here, like an old church hall. She half-ran, half-shuffled across the room in the oversized boots she had taken from Misha's dressing room. She found a door on the far side and hurried through to another room that was almost identical, through a door on the other side of that and into a wide empty space that ran from the back to the front of the house.

She ran across to a door in the opposite wall, but that was locked. There was another door, further along, closer to the front of the house. She tried that. It began to open but something was jamming it on the inside, there was something in the way – a piece of furniture perhaps. She pushed as hard as she could. Whatever it was, it began to move. She managed to create a gap that was wide enough to squeeze through.

She found herself in another pitch-dark room. The windows were covered by shutters. She tried to cross to the other side in as straight a line as possible but kept colliding with large boxes and crates, and tripping over what felt like books on the floor.

When she reached the wall on the opposite side she found an open doorway. The shutters were closed in the room beyond but it seemed to be empty in there, and she groped her way through it, unimpeded, and found a pair of doors on the opposite side.

She walked into an empty gallery – very like the long gallery on the first floor where Misha had laid out all the food and drink at her New Year's Eve party. She stopped for a moment to listen, wondering if the footsteps were still coming after her . . .

She couldn't hear a sound.

She felt safer in here. It was such a long, wide, empty space, and so much lighter after what had gone before. There were windows at frequent intervals all along the exterior wall and all the shutters were open. She walked along the gallery towards the double doors on the far side. One of the doors was partly open. There was no light at all in there.

When she had walked almost the whole length of the gallery, she heard something. She froze in mid-step and listened . . .

Those footsteps . . . Coming now from the opposite direction. Coming towards her. Approaching the partly open door just ahead of her, coming slowly through the blackness . . .

She turned in panic and gazed down the full length of the gallery. There were three doors along the interior wall. She tip-toed towards the nearest of them, opened it, crept into a wide passageway and scuttled across to a door on the opposite side. She entered a large empty room that looked out on the woods at the back of the house. She ran through the adjacent room, and the one beyond that – stumbling, slipping, tripping in her desperation to get away – and blundering into a room where a sash window had fallen wide open and the wind was bustling in. Startled pigeons rose up around her and fluttered about with a frenzied clatter of wings.

Briony ran blindly on into the next room, awakening yet another covey of startled birds and skating over a shallow heap of slippery objects that skidded away beneath her feet like thin sheets of ice. Her legs went skating away in two different directions and she came down hard on her backside with a thump. They were not thin sheets of ice, they were slates . . . from the roof. A whole section of it had fallen in and she was suddenly looking up at the stormy night sky and rain was pattering down on her. She picked herself up but the floorboards were saturated and rotten. They began to sag and break up beneath her feet . . . It was like running on sponge. At one point her foot went right through the crumbling timber, became momentarily wedged, and she fell over yet again. This time she went sprawling, face down. Her hands slithered in a mess of pigeons' droppings as she struggled to pick herself up. As she tried to regain her feet these floor-boards too began to sag and break up beneath her weight. She crawled frantically on hands and knees to the rear interior wall, where the boards were dry. There was a door here that opened on to a passage which brought her to the wing at the far end of the building.

This wing, too, was walled off. She remembered the dread-ful, fetid stench she had smelt on the previous occasion. She was almost too afraid to open the door – not afraid of the smell itself, but afraid of discovering decomposing remains or whatever it was that was causing it. But there was no other way down. She turned the handle and threw open the door . . .

She caught one whiff of that repulsive stink and was very nearly sick on the spot. Holding one hand across her mouth and pinching her nose, she reached behind the door with her free hand, feeling for a lightswitch. To her surprise she found one. And to her even greater surprise it worked. Two low-wattage bulbs, without shades, dangled from a ceiling that had partially collapsed, revealing the beams and rafters above.

There were two rooms on either side of a wide central passage. The doors were open. She peered into the first room, on her left. It was empty. It had almost rotted away. The floorboards had virtually crumbled out of existence. The ceiling had fallen in completely and she could see gaping holes in the slates above. But the most bizarre thing was the wall – the wall that backed on to the room she had just come from. It was covered in huge fungal growths . . . some the size of giant toadstools, others like deformed ears growing through the wall, as big as cabbages . . . Speckled browns, patches of vermilion, dirty cream and dull orange . . . And clusters of hideous-looking rose-like things whose flesh was almost black. She had never seen or smelt so much putrid fungus and decay in her life.

She had to breathe: she snatched a quick breath through her mouth, masking it with the flat of her hand.

She glanced in the other rooms: the two small chambers on the right side of the passage seemed unaffected, but the other room, on the left, was even worse than the first. Three walls had been taken over by these hideous growths. Some of them protruded through the wooden laths beneath the crumbling plaster like human hands reaching out to grab passers-by, like the hands of prisoners or madmen trapped behind bars.

Almost overcome by the noxious atmosphere up here, Briony ran to the door at the end of the passage, stepped gratefully out on to the spiral staircase and banged the door shut behind her before she dared take in a deep lungful of air. She began to feel her way carefully down the steep stone steps. She was back in the pitch dark again.

She was almost at the bottom when she sensed that she was not alone. It was nothing that she'd heard – the place was as silent as a grave. It was pure intuition. She had that prickly feeling that she'd felt once before – a feeling of something trapped in the air, like a static electrical charge, a feeling of hidden menace. When she reached the very bottom of the stairs she found that the door into the fourth-floor chamber was standing wide open.

She stood still in the doorway and peered nervously into the empty room beyond.

There was nothing in there.

But then she felt something right behind her . . . Like fingers moving through her hair. She screamed with shock. She would never discover what it was . . . She fled from the chamber and ran along the passage to the nearest flight of stairs and scampered all the way down to the ground floor. She went first to the side door – the courtyard entrance – but that was locked. She went back into the main hall and tried to open the front door but that was locked as well. *Dear God, after all this* . . . And now she was beginning to feel faint again.

She went into the large drawing room and struggled to

open the sash windows, but it was a waste of time: there were iron bars across every one. It was like a prison.

She had that dizzy feeling again. She reached out to support herself on something as all the strength ebbed from her body. She collapsed into a sofa that was draped with a dust-sheet. Her lungs wouldn't work, she could hardly catch her breath. She could feel herself falling into a black pit . . .

And then it began to grow lighter . . . Not completely light, but somewhere between day and night.

And it was not so cold now . . . but not warm either; not really anything.

There were other women in the room. They were sitting or lying down. They were all naked. Some appeared to be asleep or lost in meditation. Some were gazing vacantly into nowhere and some were staring at her with expressionless faces.

Then Briony heard someone call, 'Tam . . .?' She tried to look around to see who was speaking but her neck was painfully stiff. It would hardly move.

'Tam?' the voice called again, a little louder this time.

With great effort, Briony craned her neck around and saw a familiar face: it was Sheila – Sheila Matthews.

'Sheila?' said Briony, but her voice came out as little more than a whisper. She tried to get up off the sofa but she had no strength in her legs. And she couldn't catch her breath . . . Like being on a high mountain without oxygen. Sheila was smiling, but it was the strangest smile: it seemed such an effort, as if her face was paralysed and she was learning how to make it move again.

'It's not Tamara,' Briony tried to say, but it was barely audible. 'Her sister . . . Briony. Remember?'

All the pleasure drained from Sheila's face. A look of anguish came into her eyes. 'Sweet Mother of God,' she whispered. 'Not you too?'

'They promised me I could see Tam.'

'You have to get away,' said Sheila earnestly. 'In God's name, get out of this place.'

'I don't understand what's happening to me,' said Briony. 'The light . . . so many people . . .'

'There's no time to explain,' said Sheila, growing agitated. You'll think it's been a dream. But it'll happen again. He's draining the life out of you . . . You need a lover, Briony, you need your man.'

But already Briony was beginning to feel better again. She was breathing normally once more . . . The strength was returning to her body. She tried to get up. It was easier now.

'You're leaving me, Briony,' said Sheila. 'Try to remember what I told you . . .'

The half-light was already fading. It was growing very dark again. And cold. Suddenly so much colder.

'You need a lover,' Sheila gasped, straining to make herself audible. 'You need—'

But her voice was cut off, abruptly, as if someone had flicked a switch. And now everything was plunged into darkness again as . . .

Briony awoke.

She was on a sofa in the drawing room. She seemed to have collapsed, passed out.

She was cold. So very cold. She looked down at her body. She was naked. The sweater she had taken from the apartment, the woollen bonnet and the coat were lying on the sofa. She was *sitting* on the coat. The thick socks and the fur-lined boots were on the floor.

When had she undressed?

She had had such a vivid dream . . .

Sheila.

ESCAPE

She could hear something knocking, somewhere. It sounded as though it was coming from the kitchen area – a door or shutter banging in the wind, perhaps. She got up off the sofa and walked out of the drawing room, into the hallway. She heard footsteps: the sound of hobnailed boots on a tiled floor. She hung back in deep shadow and watched.

A skinny woman with a shaven head appeared from the scullery area, struggling lopsidedly with a large bucket of coal. She crossed the hallway and started up the central staircase.

As soon as she was out of sight Briony hurried towards the scullery. Between that and the old kitchen was a narrow passage that led to a rear door. It was unlocked. Briony stepped outside and pulled the door shut.

She was at the back of the house, near a row of lean-to coal bunkers.

It was raining ... More than rain: sleet. She pulled the woollen hat down so that it covered her ears, raised her coat collar, and hurried around the side of the house, across the courtyard and through the open gates. She walked quickly past the front of the house, keeping to the grass in case Misha heard her footsteps on the gravel driveway. The turf was mushy underfoot. The soles of the boots were smooth. She slipped and slithered in her haste.

She was wondering about that skinny woman with the coal bucket. Was she one of the 'minions' Dee had spoken of? How many more were there? Was that what had become of Tamara? Was she there in the house? Had she been there all the time, one of Misha's minions?

She reached the dark, woody area beyond the brick boundary wall as car lights appeared, turning in off the country road. She stepped back off the path and waded through tangles of wet bracken, into the cover of the trees. The lights came slowly down the slope towards the ford, lurched through the water and began to climb up through the woods.

It was the limousine. It passed by.

She clambered back through the bracken, on to the driveway and walked quickly down to the ford. She couldn't remember if there was a footbridge. It was too dark to see. She just had to splash through the water and hope the stream was not too swollen by a week of heavy rain.

She felt icy water trickling into the boots but it was probably not much more than ankle-deep.

She climbed the muddy slope to where the driveway met the road and walked in the direction she would have driven, towards Woodhurst.

The sleet had stopped, thank God, but her feet were now drenched.

She had walked about half a mile when headlights came towards her. There was nowhere to run, nowhere to hide, the hedgerow was too high and there wasn't a field gate in sight.

But it was not the limousine, she could tell; it was something with a noisy exhaust. She turned and stuck out her thumb. It was a pickup truck. It stopped. She opened the passenger-side door.

'Only going as far as Woodhurst,' said the driver.

'That'll be fine,' she said, and climbed in.

He tried to make conversation. She could've chosen a better night for hitching, he said. He had a rural accent. She said she was trying to get to London. Take a bus to Crawley, he recommended, then pick up the train – fast to Victoria. Best way.

She asked him what the time was. About ten past eight, he said. She was surprised: she had thought it was much later.

He dropped her off at the bus shelter in Woodhurst, on the Crawley road. But she had no money so she started walking and hitching. She had been on the road about twenty minutes when an Escort van stopped. The driver said he was going to

Gatwick Airport. She climbed in. He was a maintenance engineer, working nights.

When they reached the airport he left the van in the staff car park, walked with her to the terminal building, where she followed the signs down to the railway platform. There was a Victoria train waiting. She climbed aboard.

The carriage was half full: people with red, peeling faces and large suitcases and plastic bags of duty-free, coming back from their seven days at Alicante, or wherever, going back to their ordinary homes, having ordinary conversations. She was so relieved to have got away from that dreadful place and to be safe among strangers that she began to cry. She turned her face to the carriage window, sat in a huddle and wept soundlessly.

A little later a ticket collector came along. She said she'd been robbed but was not trying to dodge paying. He could see she'd been crying. He asked her for some identification but she had none. He said there would be a ten-pound excess plus the single fare. She said she would send a cheque as soon as she got home and that was the best she could do. He took her name and address and wrote out a penalty ticket. Everyone was staring at her. They were still stealing glances at her as the train pulled into Victoria. She wondered why . . . until she noticed how muddy and exposed her legs were, and remembered she had nothing on beneath the coat except the sweater.

She walked through Victoria station and took a black cab all the way to Styles Lane. When they pulled up outside The Hermitage she explained she would have to get some money from upstairs. The driver gave her an old-fashioned look and said he would come to the front door with her, to save her the bother of all that walking up and down the garden path.

When they got to the porch she had the embarrassment of having to ring Gloria's bell to ask if she could use the spare keys to get into Tam's flat.

'Gracious me, dear,' said Gloria, 'the state of you. What *have* you been up to?'

She gave Briony the spare key. Briony went upstairs. The driver waited at the front door.

Briony never took anything to Leysholme, except her doorkeys, so her handbag – with her wallet and everything intact – was sitting on the table, waiting for her. She took her bag downstairs to pay the cab driver.

Gloria came out of her room again as she was starting back upstairs.

'Are you sure you're all right, dear?' she said with concern.

'Fine,' said Briony, although she was getting that giddy feeling again.

'Only, you do look a trifle ... eccentric,' said Gloria, 'if you don't mind my saying so.'

'I got caught in the rain,' said Briony. 'I had to borrow some clothes.'

'I see,' said Gloria, and did not sound very convinced. 'Got long arms, your friend, hasn't she?'

Briony continued on upstairs to the flat.

PETRA'S BOOK

Someone had been in here – had slipped the lock with a credit card or something – and had not even tried to cover their traces. All the drawers were partly open – the dressing table, the bedside cabinet, the 'toy cupboard' – and it looked as if all the clothes had been tossed out of the chest of drawers and carelessly tossed back in again.

But none of the obvious things had been stolen – her handbag, wallet, cash, Tam's television, video recorder, sound system, CDs ...

She suddenly remembered Tam's letter and felt a flutter of panic . . . It was about the only evidence she had to back up her story. Without that, everyone would think she was demented.

She'd hidden it beneath the bedside cabinet; had slipped it into the narrow gap between the bottom shelf and the floorboards. She tilted the cabinet back a little and slipped one hand underneath . . . They hadn't found it, thank God; the letter was still there. She would mail it to Charlie Stillman, that was the very first thing she would do. She left the letter lying on the bed, picked up the telephone and tapped out his number. It rang four times and then his answering machine kicked in. She left a message, asking him to call her as soon as possible.

She was shaking with cold. She had to get out of these wet things. She switched on the fan heater, pulled off the wet socks and boots, the coat and sweater, and put on two layers of the warmest things she could find.

She looked around the room, wondering if anything *had* been taken, and noticed that the door to the hidden closet was not quite flush with the wall. She looked inside the closet and switched on the light. Nothing appeared to be missing: the rail was still packed with Tam's fetish outfits, the boots and shoes were still lying on the floor beneath.

But that was not all that was lying on the floor: she picked up a tissue, slightly crumpled and pastel green in colour. *She* hadn't dropped it there – she didn't use coloured tissues and there were none in the flat. Someone else had been in here. And very recently.

As she picked up the tissue she noticed something else that she hadn't seen before: the end wall of the closet – the one that was directly opposite the door – did not quite touch the floor. There was a gap beneath part of it. She pushed the wall and it swung open, away from her. It was a door, exactly like the door on Tam's side of the closet.

She stepped through into the darkness beyond: she was in

the attic store room that was next to Tam's flat. She wondered whether there was a light in there. She went back into the flat and lit the stub of candle that was standing on the dropleaf table. She carried the candle through the closet, into the store room and looked for a lightswitch. She moved down the room, towards the door that opened from the landing.

The water tanks were in here and a collection of broken or forgotten furniture.

Beside the landing door she found a switch. Two lights came on: a bare bulb at each end of the room.

She blew out the candle and walked back to the other end, threading a path through broken chairs, tables, lamps, mirrors, pots, pans, rugs, linoleum, a tubular-framed bed and a wardrobe without doors.

The far end of the room, by the door that led into Tam's closet, was cluttered with baggage – suitcases of all shapes and sizes, overnight bags, even cabin trunks. It looked like a left-luggage office at a central railway station.

An Aer Lingus label caught her eye. It was tied to the handle of a gripbag. She took a closer look. It was a tag for cabin baggage. *S. Matthews. 88 Styles Lane, London E5.*

She picked it up. It was not empty. She unzipped it and looked inside. There were a few small items of clothing, a hair drier, brush, cosmetics, toiletries, writing paper, a radio, a travelling alarm clock, a telescopic umbrella, several books and a passport: Republic of Ireland.

Briony opened it: *Matthews. Sheila Mary Bridget.*

Next to the gripbag was a suitcase of pale blue vinyl. A plastic-covered address label was strapped to the handle. Briony glanced at it. The ink had faded. All she could make out was the end of the address: *Rathfarnum, Co. Dublin.*

She felt the weight of the suitcase. It was heavy; felt full.

Gloria had told her that Sheila had moved out without giving notice. Why would she have left all this behind? And her *passport*, of all things?

She opened Sheila's grip again and looked at the books: six of them, including a Bible. The rest were paperbacks.

Sheila had said that Tam had brought something to her for translation. From Italian. Petra's book, that was all she'd said.

But none of these books was in Italian.

Briony laid the pale blue suitcase down on the floor and snapped open the catches. The case was full of clothes and shoes, and a few cosmetics. She foraged down to the bottom. The only books of any kind in here were school exercise books ... Or that was what they looked like. Two of them. Briony glanced through them.

There was a name on the inside cover of one of the books: Petra Pascali.

One book was a home-made diary. The first entry was dated 22 *giugno* 90. The entries had been made sporadically, sometimes as much as a month apart. The last entry – about three-quarters of the way through the book – was dated 9 *dicembre* 91. Everything was written in Italian. Briony didn't understand a word of it.

Only about ten pages of the second notebook had been used. Again, everything was in Italian.

Where the text ended were half a dozen loose pages of what appeared to be Sheila's translation. The handwriting was small and neat. There were a lot of words and phrases crossed out – sometimes whole lines – and passages with question marks beside them. Briony read:

House of the Good Shepherd, Amsterdam, for orphaned
girls. Closed 1760s. (Ref. 'Sex, the Church and the Devil',
Carol Neames, Pressmark/US, 1976.) 'Lewd, cruel and
improper activities'. Mysterious disappearance of girls.
'Der Pastor', short story (German/folk tale), 19th century.
Orphan girls become maids to Pastor figure – half-living,
half-dead – and fade away into dark other-world.
House of the Good Shepherd, 'humanitarian refuge for fallen
women' (East London Gazette), Dukes Mill Lane, Stratford,

East London. Docklands. For beggar girls and prostitutes. Closed 1868. Twelve women reported disappeared/missing. Inmates referred to a 'Pastor' (never seen) and an unnamed 'Good Shepherd'.

Leysholme. Estate of Admiral Lord Bayle, endowed to college for sons of army and naval officers. Closed 1860s. Orphanage until 1929. (Matron, Mrs Packerman!) Scandal of missing children. (Ref. 'Kentish Times', 1927.)

Packerman . . . Mrs Packerman . . . Why was the name so familiar? Briony just couldn't place it at that moment.

She turned instead to the third page of the English translation. This looked more like an essay. Ignoring the many crossings-out and corrections, Briony read:

THE PASTOR

No one knows who he is. No one knows how old he is. He is ageless. No one has seen his face. No one knows where he comes from or how he began. He comes from a realm where there is no time and no feeling; where the living-dead are suspended in time, visible to each other but not to mortals on earth. He cannot exist on earth and live among us without absorbing the energy of the living. He draws life from women, sucks the vitality from their bodies and drains the life out of them. As he does so, he 'infects' his victims with his own condition, like a virus that he is passing on. For their part, his victims experience heightened sexual pleasure – in many cases peaks of ecstasy that few have ever known. This becomes addictive, dulling the woman's natural fear of these bizarre experiences, and blinding her to the damage that is slowly being done to her metabolism.

Once 'infected' the woman begins to suffer dizzy spells and mild attacks of fainting. These seem to take place mostly when she is resting or on the edge of sleep, when her heart rate is low. For that reason, they may also happen when she is asleep, but go unnoticed. During these periods she seems to (dematerialize??) and is briefly invisible to others – but not to other souls among the living-dead, whom she will now be able to see, if only briefly. When she recovers – it can be a matter of seconds in the early stages – she has almost no memory of what happened, or, if she does, she tends to think of it as a dream.

By this stage, she is already slipping into the dimension of the living-dead from which he comes. He continues to use her until she has so little vitality or (life force??) left in her body that she is of no further use to him. When he has virtually drained the life out of her, he abandons her.

By now, she is spending most of her time resting or sleeping – during which she experiences longer and longer dream-like periods in the half-world into which she will soon pass for ever. When she does so, her (dematerialization??) is complete and irreversible. She is trapped there – alive, but with no metabolism, no bodily strength, no sense of feeling – for ever after. She will perceive the mortal world through her darkness. But the mortal world will not perceive her.

There is no return, but it seems that total dematerialization is not inevitable, the process can be controlled. He passes on his (condition??) through body fluids, like a virus, and some women are more susceptible to 'infection' than others. Once 'infected' the woman's metabolism begins to change. The vital energy, the 'life source' which is being drained from her can be replenished to some degree by a sexual partner who is uncontaminated. Since the female does not seem to pass on this acquired condition to her male partners, it would appear that almost any healthy male partner can revitalize her. This suggests that whatever it is that is wreaking this havoc on her metabolism is connected with insemination and the womb.

Time does not seem to have any healing effects. Once 'infected' the victim's metabolism seems to undergo irreversible change. She remains this way for life and will always need energy drawn from the male if she is to avoid a gradual slide into (dematerialization??). The metabolic changes in the woman radically affect her normal hormonal activity. She ceases to menstruate. She needs little food to sustain healthy life. She appears to acquire immunity to infection and disease. Nature is retarded to a point where she barely ages at all. In effect, her body is locked in time.

But where the 'infected' woman fails to get the vital energy she needs from sexual partners the natural ageing process appears to speed up dramatically. When this happens and the process of (dematerialization??) begins to take hold again, she will age at a much faster rate than normal women. Within a year she may look as much as five years older. A woman who has looked thirty for whole decades can look sixty within the space of a few years.

Once she has allowed this process to begin, it becomes harder and harder for her to attract the sexual partners she needs to maintain her energy levels. And so the (dematerializing??) process accelerates, and she ages even more. And so she becomes locked in a vicious downward spiral from which she cannot escape. Women who looked so young for so long suddenly look old, develop arthritis, osteoporosis and other afflictions of age. Frequently, they become suicidal or reclusive, suffering their rapid physical decline in fear and despair, with only a year or two of mortal life, at most, before their final disappearance into the dark and silent universe that awaits them.

Where is he from, this diabolical creation, where did it all begin? Is he man or myth or magic? Do they conjure him from the darkness? Is he an invention of the female mind, a spectre born of drug-induced fantasy? Or does he live and breathe like mortal men in some secret chambers in his own bleak and hostile mansion? We have no answers.

Perhaps we do not really want to know. We fear him but we desire him . . . We crave his gifts of ecstasy and immortal, unfading youth. He is our shepherd, and we his willing, obedient flock. There appears to be no end, no way of ridding ourselves of this self-perpetuating horror. Without us he would slip back into (un-existence??), melt away into the realm of living-dead for ever more. But there are always women enough – young and beautiful, vain and stupid – unable to resist the lure.

That was where Sheila's translation ended. Petra's own text went on, for several more pages, but Briony could not understand a word of it.

GLIMPSE

She read it through again.

Was Petra mad?

There were echoes in her notes that Briony could relate to: the ecstasy, for one thing, and the fainting spells.

And then there was dotty Lotte who looked about fifty and moved like a woman of eighty . . . She disappeared from the bathroom on New Year's Eve. And Sheila vanished suddenly in the woods behind Leysholme, leaving her clothes in a heap on the ground. And there were all these other zombie-like women in this house who hid themselves away.

Briony pulled out another suitcase. There was no label on it. She laid it down, flipped the catches and opened the lid. This was full as well – outer wear, underwear, shoes, raincoat, books, cosmetics . . .

And a letter . . .

Riverside Crescent, Halifax. Dated 2 October 1986.

My dear Becky . . .

Briony skipped to the end: *All our love, Mum and Dad.*

She found a diary at the bottom of the case: it belonged to Rebecca Foreman.

There was no one of that name living here now.

Briony looked inside another suitcase . . . That was full too.

And another.

And another.

She looked through Rebecca Foreman's diary. It gave a home address in Yorkshire and a telephone number. She went back into Tam's room, picked up the phone and tapped out the number. She was connected immediately to a recorded message from BT: wrong code. She tried again, putting in an extra figure one.

It began to ring.

A woman answered. Briony asked if that was Mrs Foreman.

'Speaking,' the woman replied.

Briony said she was a friend of Rebecca's from London; had lost touch, hadn't seen her for donkey's years; wondered if she was back home in Halifax.

No one had seen or heard from Rebecca in almost ten years, Mrs Foreman replied. They didn't know whether she was dead or alive. They had no idea what had happened to her.

Briony expressed her regrets, made her excuses and rang off.

She wondered how many more tenants like Rebecca had gone missing. She went back into the store room and began to look through all the other baggage. Every bag and suitcase was full – packed with clothes and personal belongings: letters, photographs, passports, driving licences, cheque books . . . The possessions of at least twelve women were hidden away at the back of this attic.

At the very back she found an old cabin trunk. It was spotted with the torn remains of travel labels – P & O; Ellerman Lines; White Star. One label in particular stood out:

London, Brighton and South Coast Railway. Passenger Luggage in Advance. There was a price on it: one shilling. And a name: Mrs G. M. Packerman.

Briony moved some of the suitcases that had been stowed tightly around it, pulled the trunk out into an open space, unfastened the catches with some difficulty, and opened the lid.

There was almost nothing in it: a pair of wooden shoe trees, the belt of a dress in floral fabric, some loose hair grips, an embroidered handkerchief, a child's teddy bear with one leg missing and a used envelope, bearing a penny-halfpenny stamp. There was nothing inside the envelope. The postmark was illegible but the date was 1925. It was addressed in elegant handwriting to: Mrs Gloria Packerman, Matron's Office, The Pastoral Home for Orphaned Children, Leysholme, Nr Woodhurst, Kent.

Gloria. 1925.

Seventy years ago.

Briony felt sick with fear ... Was there anyone in this house who wasn't part of it?

She switched out the light, went back into Tam's room and shut the closet door, struggling to think straight. Above all else, she had to get out of this house. It would not be long before Misha noticed that she was gone ... Perhaps she had noticed already. She was in no fit state to drive very far. She would find a cheap hotel room for the night ... At the very worst she could sleep in the car.

Or perhaps she should go to the police right now? One missing person would be of no interest to them, but with all that baggage hidden away in the attic – and Rebecca Foreman not seen or heard of in ten years – surely they would have to investigate?

She wished desperately that Charlie Stillman would call back.

She quickly made a pile of clothes and personal things to take with her and began to stuff them into her backpack.

That feeling of faintness was drifting through her again. She sat down on the bed. She felt so very, very weak. She could hardly keep her eyes open. All the strength was draining from her body. The light in the room – the very table lamps themselves – seemed to be fading.

She heard a voice: 'Hey, Sis . . .'

She looked up, startled by the sound.

Tamara was sitting on a chair at the dropleaf table, smiling at her.

'Tam . . .?' Briony wondered if what she was seeing was real or a hallucination – an effect of the drugs they'd been giving her at Leysholme. Or was this another dream? 'Where have you been? It's been so *long* . . . You've worried us half to death.'

'I've not been anywhere,' Tamara replied. 'I've been here all the time.'

'I don't understand,' said Briony. 'You called me . . . You left a message. You really scared me.'

'I know,' said Tamara. 'I can't explain now – we won't have very long this time. But there'll be other times. And soon. I promise.'

'What do you mean, we don't have long?' said Briony. 'Where are you going?' She tried to get up off the bed but she could hardly move. It felt as if she were up to her neck in some treacly liquid.

'Don't try to move,' said Tamara. 'You can – it is possible. But not far. And it takes so much effort. You'll get used to it in time. It does get a little easier.'

'What's wrong with me?' said Briony. She was hunting for breath after that attempt to stand up. 'What's happening?'

'It's scary, I know,' said Tamara, 'but don't panic. You'll feel no pain here. Nothing can happen to you, you feel almost nothing at all.'

Even as Tamara spoke, her voice was beginning to sound faint. Briony could feel her lungs expanding as her breathing returned to normal, and the strength came trickling back into her body . . .

And she came to, on the bed. Must have dozed off.

Had such a vivid dream: Tamara seated at the table.

It had all seemed so real . . .

Briony felt so desperately sad at that moment. Such a painful sense of loss flooded through her – as if some divine being had brought Tamara back to her for one glimpse, one fleeting glimpse, before snatching her away again.

It suddenly occurred to her how cold it was in here. God, she was so cold. She shivered and hugged herself for warmth . . . And only then realized: she was naked. Completely naked.

TAMARA (11)

Gone already? So soon?

But I can still see you, Bri, even though you can't see me . . . or hear me. You sit there shivering. You look so agonizingly lost, poor thing, in such utter despair. You wonder in your misery why you've got no clothes on.

Don't cry, Sis. I know what you're going through. It's like you're trapped in a partial eclipse of the sun, isn't it? And you're paralysed . . . Like someone throws a mains switch and all the juice goes out of you at a stroke. No warning. It feels like the gateway to Hell, doesn't it?

Perhaps that's what it is.

But we'll be together soon. There'll be more times. And I'll try to explain, try to help you understand. The next time it'll last a little longer. And each time after that, a little longer still. And each time it will happen again just that tiny bit more frequently . . . Until eventually you're spending more time in my world than you are in your own.

I'm so new I think I'm still visible sometimes – just momentarily – in your world. I've been doing everything to try and make you see me. The firemen saw me. Just a glimpse. Then I was gone again. It's something to do with low-frequency light waves. In this dimension we're not visible to you, the living. Your eyes can't see at this low frequency. Your ears can't hear.

Do you remember once, we were going to a fancy-dress party at Alison Treneer's? And I took off all my clothes and you wrapped me up in cling film and sprayed me with silver glitter, and you put me in the back of Nick Pengelly's van, and I went to the party as a mermaid? Well, that's kind of how it feels being here: like a beached mermaid, washed up on a sandbank. You just sit on your lonely stretch of sand, watching, waiting.

Setting out on your journey to this lonely realm is like crossing a wide stretch of water: there's a point when you're so far away from the shore that you're almost out of sight. Almost. But not entirely. People watching think you're beyond their range of vision, but then they catch sight of you again for just a moment. Then you disappear. They think you're gone, but a wave buoys you up and they catch another glimpse. Eventually you're gone, completely gone ... But only from their point of view. You've moved out too far across the horizon, and from that moment on you're only visible from the other shore.

I wanted you to get here before I was too far out across the horizon, Bri ... So that I could tell you, so I could explain what was happening. I hoped there was something you could do to help me.

But I don't think there would have been. I left it far too late.

Think of me as that stranded mermaid. And think of yourself as setting out to search the seas for me. Think of yourself at home, walking along the quay. Walk down the granite steps of the harbour wall and step into this little rowing boat. You put the oars into the water and row across the harbour and out into Mount's Bay . . .

It's a beautiful day, a clear blue, sunny sky, and a calm sea. You keep on rowing, and rowing, and scanning the horizon, searching for your poor lost mermaid. But now the daylight starts to fade. The sky turns the colour of gunmetal and seems to be sinking slowly, ever so slowly, towards the sea. It comes lower and lower, till you feel as if those threatening clouds are going to envelope you. There's a chill in the wind now and the sea grows choppier. You look up and the sun has gone completely. You look around but you can no longer see the shore. It grows still darker, even colder. You want to turn back, you are beginning to feel afraid, but you've lost your sense of direction – you don't know which is onwards and which is homewards. A hostile twilight descends around you like a shroud.

Oh, yes, it's darker on this shore, Sis, much, much darker, in this silent world of living-dead: always on the edge of night.

I feared all kinds of things when I first started phasing out . . . Scared me half to death. I thought there was something wrong with my central nervous system, affecting my vision and my brain. I panicked, I thought about all kinds of things I didn't know anything about – like Motor Neurone Disease. I knew it could strike anybody, any time, without logic, without reason. I looked it up in medical textbooks, I went to see my GP . . . But I couldn't tell him everything, of course.

But it's not MND, it's not a stroke, it's not viral, it's not anything pathological they can diagnose or understand.

The truth is, the Pastor plants something in the womb that grows inside us and changes our whole metabolism. It's as if he's impregnated us with something and we've conceived, but there's no foetus. It's a kind of reverse-energy thing: he draws the life out of us, like the marrow from our bones, or the very essence of our DNA. Without it, you see, he can't survive.

Right now your metabolism is giving out for brief periods, stuttering like a car engine that's running out of fuel. You're slipping into a different dimension, Sis, where the frequency of light and sound defies the laws of Earth physics. There are no laws of science here. All the medical specialists in the world won't find an illness ... Because you're not ill: you're vanishing.

By the time you grasp that truth, it'll be too late ... You'll be too far gone: there's a point when it becomes unstoppable, like a retro-virus that's raging out of all control, replicating inside you, destroying you, cell by cell.

When I discovered that, I panicked. That was my mistake.

No ... No, that wasn't my mistake. My mistake was: I panicked but I thought I could control it. I thought I could have all that ecstasy, all that money, and still walk away. But you can't simply walk away from the Pastor ...

As you will very soon discover, my poor darling sister.

MRS PACKERMAN

She had no memory of doing this, and yet this very same thing had happened in the drawing room at Leysholme: she had taken off all her clothes. Why? And when? She was sitting on them – her underwear, sweatshirt, the thick sweater she'd put on over the top of that. Her jeans and the leggings she was wearing had almost slipped off the side of the bed on to the floor, where her socks and trainers lay.

She felt a draught from the doorway. She looked around. The door was wide open. Gloria was standing there, watching her.

'Ah, you're getting into bed, dear,' she said, entering the room, 'that's a good girl. You look terrible, if you don't mind me saying so. Look as if you haven't slept for a month.'

She was carrying a broad-rimmed breakfast cup and saucer.

'Don't sit there without your nightie on, you'll catch your death. Under the covers, come on, chop-chop. Look as if you're going down with a chill or something. Here you go: I've brought you a nice hot drink, help you sleep.'

She came around the front of the bed to where Briony was sitting in a state of paralysed confusion.

'Oh, no, I wasn't going to bed,' said Briony, and got up so suddenly that Gloria drew back in mid-step and spilt some of the hot drink into the saucer. Briony snatched up the leggings and began to get dressed again. 'I was just . . . just, you know . . . changing, that's all. Because I've got to . . . got to . . .' She pulled on her jeans, desperate to focus her mind on one thought and one thought alone: she had to get out. Say anything, do anything, but just *get out*. 'I have to go home, back to Cornwall,' she burbled on. 'Just for a few days . . . Not long . . . I'll be back by the weekend.'

'Not going out again at this time of night?' Gloria protested, placing the cup and saucer on the bedside table. 'You look all in, sweetheart.'

'Oh, I'll sleep on the train, I'll be fine,' said Briony, trying to bluff it out and appear self-assured, in control.

'Will there *be* a train this late?' asked Gloria doubtfully.

'Oh, yes, the night sleeper from Paddington.' Briony struggled into the sweatshirt – it was back to front, but to hell with it. It's very comfortable, I've done it before, I'll be fine, I'll sleep really well—'

'And you're not taking this great big thing on your back?' Gloria interrupted, lifting the backpack to see how heavy it was. 'My giddy aunt, that's a weight. You've got plenty in here to last you a couple of days . . .' And then with a sudden change of tone: 'Oh, I say, isn't that Tamara's writing? You've had a letter from her, dear . . . You didn't tell me.' Gloria picked it up off the bed.

'Didn't I?' said Briony. She pulled on her trainers – didn't even bother with socks. 'I thought I did, I'm sure I did. She's

– she's – she's absolutely fine, Tam, and so . . . You know . . . That's a really big relief—'

'And goodness gracious me,' Gloria cut in, lowering her weight on to the front edge of the bed now and picking up Petra Pascali's notebooks, 'your old schoolbooks, are they? Italian . . .?' (Flipping slowly through them.) 'Now that's interesting . . .' (And, flipping back to the inside cover:) 'Oh, Petra . . . Where did you find these, dear? Fascinating girl, Petra. Very creative mind.'

'Oh, just lying around,' said Briony vaguely, hurriedly doing up her shoe laces, 'in that red cupboard over there, actually. But I don't speak Italian so—'

'And my word, Rebecca Foreman,' Gloria interrupted a third time, now looking at the pocket diary. 'She left donkey's years ago. Well, did you ever? The stuff you find buried away if you poke around hard enough.'

'Anyway,' said Briony, grabbing her door keys and her wallet and not caring about the rest, 'I really do have to go now, Gloria, I'm sorry. It was sweet of you to bring me something to drink but the cab'll be waiting for me outside now, so I'd better get off or I'll miss the train and everyone's expecting me so . . .' She could hear herself gabbling but she couldn't control it.

'Bridey, Bridey,' Gloria interrupted gently, 'slow down, dear, slow down . . . No need to rush off, darling, we'll get you to the station all right—'

Briony grabbed Tamara's letter and Petra's notebooks. 'See you in a few days,' she said, walking quickly to the door, knowing that, exhausted or not, she could easily outpace Gloria down the stairs – she would be out of the front door even before Gloria had made it down the first flight of stairs. 'Sorry, I've got to dash off like this but . . .' She hurried out of the room and along the passage.

She could hear Gloria calling, 'Bridey, dear, don't be so silly . . . You haven't even got your bag, sweetheart . . .'

The stairways and landings were in total darkness but she

didn't waste time pausing to press lightswitches. She ran pell-mell down the stairs, all the way to the ground floor and along the front hallway to the door. She turned the latch and pulled . . .

But the door wouldn't budge.

Had Gloria bolted it? Briony felt for the top right corner of the door . . . But the bolt was not in place. She bent down and reached to the bottom of the door, but that bolt was not in place either. Gloria had locked it. There was a mortice lock – though no one ever used it – and Gloria must have had a key . . . It was locked fast, the door wouldn't move.

Briony turned back towards the staircase . . . There was a small side window opposite the stairwell, and the much larger window alongside the landing midway between the ground and first floors. Maybe one of those would open. But, as she turned, she realized she was no longer alone. There were shadowy figures gathered around the stairwell . . . Several . . . Moving very slowly towards her . . . More than several . . . A dozen, maybe more . . . Briony stopped where she was, in the front hall, about halfway between the front door and the staircase. They were in what looked like a huddle, like sheep. There was something about the way they moved that made them all seem very old – stooped and lame and shuffling.

Someone was coming down the stairs, in no hurry at all. From the shape of the silhouette as it passed the landing window, Briony could see that it was Gloria. She reached the foot of the stairs and stood looking at Briony.

'You didn't have any of this delicious nightcap, Bridey, dear,' she said, as pleasantly as always. 'Never mind, it's still hot. Come along. Come into my room, darling. We'll soon have you right as rain.'

The shadowy huddle shuffled backwards to make room for Gloria to pass through their midst.

As if she knew that Briony wasn't following, Gloria stopped and turned and said, 'Come along, sweetheart. You're all in. I think you'd better sleep down here tonight. Come along. Don't be shy. You're among friends.'

Briony didn't move.

'Come along, dear,' Gloria coaxed her. 'You know it's for the best.'

Briony was thinking she ought to follow her: it would be easier to escape from Gloria's room. There were French windows with tall, wide panes; she could smash the glass with a chair or something.

She walked towards the rear hallway, passing among the sheepish huddle in the deep shadows. She recognized dotty Lotte and some of the other old women – the creepy, silent ones, the hermits, Gloria's 'zombies', who very rarely emerged into the light of day.

She followed Gloria into her room and closed the door.

They were not alone in here either. Some familiar faces were waiting to greet her: Crystal and Mojo from the Casa Negra; fat Tracey from the room across the hall; and Doreen, the Geordie with the bony, witch-like face.

Gloria moved across the room to a divan bed in the corner. It was draped with a coverlet of faded green velvet.

'You look about ready to drop, dear,' she said sympathetically. 'Why don't you lie down and get some rest?'

Briony began to edge back towards the door.

'Bridey, please . . .' said Gloria. 'Don't make this any more difficult for yourself.'

She moved some scatter cushions aside and drew back the faded green coverlet. The bed was fully made up.

Briony was thinking about Gloria's kitchen: the door was wide open. She had never been in there but there had to be a window.

She nodded passively and began to approach the divan. At the very last second, just before she reached it, she turned and bolted through the kitchen door, slamming it shut behind her.

There *was* a window but it was above and behind the sink unit. She managed to scramble over the draining board and flip open the catch that sealed the window, but it was a futile effort ... They were there within seconds. Crystal grabbed her ankles and hauled her backwards.

'You won't be told, dear, will you?' said Gloria, as they bundled her back into the sitting room. 'You really are a silly girl,' she added, a dash of spite giving an edge to her exasperation.

Mojo and Crystal pushed Briony on to the bed, face down, and held her there, while Fat Tracey tugged off the thick sweater that Briony was wearing, and the sweatshirt beneath that.

Briony struggled but Crystal and Mojo were too strong for her and all her energy was spent.

She could hear Gloria saying, 'Don't fret, darling, it's just something to help you rest ... make your journey a little more pleasant.'

Briony managed to turn her head to one side so that she could see what was happening. Doreen was holding a hypodermic syringe towards the light and squirting a few droplets of liquid through the needle to push out all the air.

Briony felt a rush of panic ... And then a twist of pain as her arm was wrenched around ... And then the prick of the needle entering her flesh.

'Don't upset yourself,' she heard Gloria saying in a soothing voice. 'It's for the best, sweetie. It really is. Trust me.'

SLAVE AND MASTER

It was daylight when she came to.

She was in bed, in that familiar room at Leysholme.

She had no idea how she'd got there. Nor did she care. She drifted back to sleep. She came to again, a little later. Someone was standing beside the bed, looking down at her. Briony felt too groggy to make out who it was. She closed her eyes and slept some more.

Someone brought her some lunch. She didn't see who it was, but she awoke and was so sure that someone had just spoken that she sat up and looked around the room. There was no one there, but a tray was sitting on the table.

Briony got out of bed.

She looked at the food: some sort of risotto. But she had no appetite.

She looked for her clothes. They had been taken away.

She got back into bed.

A little later, Dee came in to see her. Briony turned her gaze towards the window. She heard Dee move the ladderback chair closer to the bed and sit down.

'I'm disappointed,' Dee said. 'You let me down. I thought you wanted to see Tamara?'

Briony could not be bothered replying. It wasn't going to get her anywhere.

'Why did you run away?' said Dee. 'What was all the panic about?'

'I came here of my own choosing,' said Briony, 'and I'll leave of my own choosing.'

'I'm afraid it doesn't work that way,' said Dee. 'We're a sisterhood. There are disciplines.'

'You said I could see my sister, you didn't say anything about being locked up like a prisoner.'

'It's for your own good.'

'I'll decide what's good for me and what isn't, thank you,' said Briony.

'You're not in a position to decide what's best for you,' said Dee. 'You chose to make a journey – the journey that Tamara made. A journey of sensory exploration. You've begun to experience unusual sensations – both physical and psychological. They may frighten you. They'll certainly confuse you.

You need friends around you who understand, who can take care of you.'

'And I'll decide who my friends are,' said Briony.

'Like it or not, we're the only people who can bring you and Tamara together again.'

'Because she's a prisoner too?' said Briony. 'Or is she dead?'

'I told you before,' said Dee, 'she's perfectly safe and well. But without us you'll never be able to see her again.'

'And will anyone ever see *me* again?'

'Of course they will. Why shouldn't they? What do you think is going to happen?'

'I found a lot of luggage in the attic at Styles Lane,' said Briony. 'It's full of clothes and personal belongings. Sheila Matthews' things are there … A woman called Rebecca Foreman, who hasn't been seen for ten years …'

'Yes, Gloria told me you'd been exploring,' said Dee.

'They were drugged or poisoned, weren't they?' said Briony. 'They were lured to this place – like Tamara, like me – and used for … God knows what you use them for.'

Dee looked amused, as though Briony was a child who still believed in goblins and elves. 'They're not dead, you silly thing – Rebecca, Sheila, none of them. There is no death where they are. There is no pain, no suffering, no dying. You've read Petra's notes. She seems to have understood it pretty well.'

'Yes, I read them,' said Briony. 'And Petra sounds barking bloody mad.'

'Your rational mind tells you she was crazy,' Dee sympathized. 'But your instinctive mind tells you something else. Deep down you're afraid it could be true, aren't you? You don't want to believe it but you have that niggling doubt … Because you've started phasing out, haven't you?'

'What do you mean, "phasing out"?'

'You have blackouts. And when you come round, you think you had a strange but realistic dream, don't you?'

Briony didn't answer ... Because it was true, and that frightened her.

'And in those dreams you've seen Tamara, haven't you?' said Dee.

'I don't know,' said Briony. 'You spike my food here, you give me drugs and ... I don't know what. I can't tell what I'm dreaming and what's real any more.'

'Suppose I told you it was *all* real,' said Dee. 'That there are different dimensions of reality, that's all.'

Briony was not in the right frame of mind for more riddles and gobbledegook.

'Jesus said: In my Father's house are many mansions,' Dee continued. 'What do you think that means?'

Briony didn't answer.

'Do you have a faith?' said Dee. 'Do you believe in God?'

'I was brought up to go to chapel,' Briony replied. 'But I don't know what I believe.'

'You believe in reincarnation? You believe in the transmigration of the soul?'

'It's not something I ever think about. I really don't care.'

'How can you not care about your spirit?' said Dee. 'You care about your body ... But your body won't even last a hundred years – a speck of time in the infinity of the cosmos. You are a chemical reaction. You are carbon and hydrogen and oxygen. No more than that. That's all you are, DNA with big ideas. You're here and gone.' She snapped her fingers. 'Whereas your spirit moves on to other realms. Death is just a migration of the soul, a continuation of existence in another dimension.'

'Right now I'm alive,' said Briony, 'and one day I'll be dead, that's all I know. That's all any of us knows.'

'Western culture,' said Dee, 'is very primitive. An either/or culture. It accepts only two states of being: alive and dead. Even when you're dead, Christianity persists with this either/or notion. The spirit either goes to heaven or it goes to hell. And yet Jesus said: In my Father's house are many mansions.'

'I don't think that's quite what he meant,' said Briony. 'Not the way I learnt it, anyway.'

'Africans have an older and richer culture,' said Dee. 'They believe that when a man dies his spirit stays close to the family for as long as those who knew him remain alive and hold him in their memory. This is his *Sasa* time, when his spirit is still among them, as a kind of living-dead. It is not until all those who knew him have died and he disappears from living memory that his spirit leaves the earth for ever. It then passes into a remoter dimension, the *Zamani*.'

'If you say,' Briony conceded with a shrug. 'I don't know anything about it.'

'Hindu culture, which is older and richer still,' said Dee, 'embraces the notion of souls migrating from one body to another after death.'

'What are you trying to tell me?' said Briony. 'You want me to believe that my sister is alive and well in another dimension?'

'I don't mind what you believe,' said Dee. 'I'm not your guru. I'm simply trying to help you reach her – if that's what you truly want.'

'You keep saying that,' said Briony. 'You know it's what I want. But I don't trust you, or anybody here, and I don't believe anything you tell me.'

'You realize what would happen to you,' said Dee, 'without our help?'

'You expect me to believe what Petra wrote?'

'I thought she grasped the concept very well,' said Dee. 'But you, you have the Western disease: what you can't under-stand, you deride. We all need energy to survive. You couldn't survive without the energy you get from food and drink. But suppose your bodily system couldn't generate energy in that way? Suppose your metabolism had undergone a mutation?'

'Like your master,' said Briony cynically.

'The Pastor needs energy like any other living creature,' said Dee. 'But he has to draw his life-source in other ways.'

'From the bodies of women,' said Briony. 'How very convenient for him.'

'Why do you find that concept hard to grasp?' said Dee. 'Women are the primary source of all life-giving energy in mankind. All human beings begin life inside the womb. It was the primary source that gave *you* life ... and me, and everyone on earth. Why should it be any different for our Pastor?'

'And what would happen to him,' Briony enquired, 'if there were no women left to supply him with this "life-source" that his body needs?'

'The same thing that has already begun to happen to you,' Dee replied. 'He would start to phase out, to slip back into the other world. He would experience exactly what *you* are starting to experience as your metabolism changes and you begin to lose energy: periods of dematerialization ... Brief periods at first but gradually, longer and longer periods, as your capacity to sustain life drains away.'

'And is that what you want me to think happened to my sister?' said Briony.

'That is exactly what happened,' Dee replied.

'In that case,' said Briony, 'how were you going to arrange for me to see her again, to be with her?'

'We can control this thing,' said Dee, 'so that you share your life with her, whilst doing almost anything you want – within reason – and leading a normal existence.'

'Control what?' said Briony, remembering something that Sheila had said when they were in the woods ... She had done a deal, she said, and they would help her control it. 'What exactly do you mean?'

'Your energy loss,' said Dee. 'We have ways of replenishing it. It's like recharging a battery. But it needs a controlled environment. That's why we have this house. And you would have to commit yourself to the Foundation, and pledge yourself to the service of our Pastor. That goes without saying.'

'Who is he?' said Briony. 'Who is this Pastor? Where does he come from?'

'What do you imagine?' Dee replied. 'How do you see him?'

'I imagine him like any other of these crazy cult leaders,' said Briony. 'Into drugs. Into sex. And into money. He owns the Casa Negra. He makes a lot of money out of it. He's got lots of slum properties like the house at Styles Lane, and probably a string of seedy businesses to do with clubs and the S-and-M scene and pornography. He gets off on women who wear this way-out fetish gear. He has bizarre parties here and gets all the sex he wants. Lures women into his S-and-M cult, drugs them silly, makes them whore for him or simply takes all their worldly wealth off them, like he did with Tamara.'

Dee smiled. 'That's what you think?'

'More or less,' said Briony. 'And nobody sees him, so nobody can identify him, so no one knows who he is.'

Dee was still smiling.

'How am I doing?' said Briony.

'Not very well,' said Dee. 'You read Petra's notes.'

'Only what Sheila translated. There was more I didn't understand.'

'It seems,' said Dee, 'you don't understand any of it.'

'Then explain,' said Briony.

'Is there any point?' said Dee. 'You can't even get your head around the concept of parallel existence. Our Pastor is ageless. He is timeless. He has come down to us through generations, across dimensions. He is indefinable. He is recorded in literature, all through the ages. You should read your Bible more often.'

'You mean he doesn't really exist?' said Briony.

'Of course he exists,' said Dee. 'He's been taking the nourishment from your body and giving you the gift of immortality in return . . . How can he not exist?'

'Then he is a man,' said Briony, 'like any other man?'

'He is man,' said Dee. 'And he is spirit. He is beyond imagining. And his power is awesome.'

'And what are the people who come here?' said Briony. 'His devoted followers? His slaves?'

'He is our master and our Pastor,' said Dee. 'We are a sisterhood. The Foundation is a business, much like any other. It invests in property, clubs, restaurants, fashion, publishing, the leisure industry. The Foundation is run entirely by women – by ourselves, by our sisterhood. We control everything.'

'Ironical then,' said Briony, 'that it's all for the benefit of a man.'

'A man,' said Dee, 'who can't survive in this world without us. Without the sisterhood, he can't procure the women he needs to sustain life. Without us he would fade back into his own dimension, into the world of half-life. But without him, women would lose his precious gift of immortality. The Pastor takes, but the Pastor gives.'

'In that case,' said Briony, 'is he really your master? Or is he really your slave?'

Dee grinned. But didn't answer.

THE DRAWING ROOM

She was left alone to think. It was growing dark outside. Someone came to her room – a ragged-looking girl with a shaven head, carrying yet another tray. Briony had glimpsed her once before, the night that she escaped: the skinny young woman she'd seen struggling with a bucket of coal.

She put the tray on the table, turned and walked out without so much as a glance at Briony. Seeing her again now, close to, there was something very familiar about that face

. . . Briony struggled to place it. It took a minute or so to come back to her:

It was Bibi.

Briony was shocked by the sight of her: all that curly blonde hair had been shaved off. She was dressed in oversized black coveralls – far too large for her emaciated frame – and what looked like old army boots.

Briony got out of bed, wrapped the blankets around her body, opened the door and looked down the passageway. Bibi was already out of sight. Briony closed the door and hurried after her. When she reached the stairwell she looked down. She could hear footsteps fading away, several floors below. Briony scurried down the stairs after her. By the time she got to the ground floor Bibi had vanished.

Briony listened: not a sound anywhere. She crept from room to room along the whole length and breadth of the ground floor. But the place was deserted as always.

When she came back to the main staircase a little later, she saw a light burning in the main drawing room. The door was half open. She crept towards it and glanced into the room. Bibi was mopping the floor beside a bay window.

'Bibi?' Briony called to her softly, as she crossed the room.

Bibi turned, startled, and then saw who it was and looked worried. 'Why are you in here?' she said sternly. 'Is very bad . . . You get cold, no energy, you get sick.'

'There are questions I want to ask you,' said Briony. 'Things I need to know about this place. Why are you doing this, Bibi? What's happened to you?'

'Is, *mmm*, rain come in, from window,' said Bibi, pointing to a broken pane. 'Is kaput, the glass.'

'I mean why are you here?' said Briony. 'Why are you carrying coal, why are you mopping floors? What have they done to you?'

'Shh . . .' Bibi came closer, placing a finger over her lips. 'I can't talk,' she whispered. 'Is, *mmm*, not permit. I get bad punish.'

'But what have they turned you into? Misha's skivvy? Why have you let them do this to you?'

'Is important,' said Bibi, frowning because of the difficulty she had with English. 'Is, *mmm*, necessary. I work hard and do fine, Misha happy, I get better job, I go modelling, I leave here. But is necessary first to be servant.'

'They're asking me to do what you've done,' said Briony. 'Join the Foundation.'

'Good, is good,' said Bibi. 'Foundation is power. Is money. Is you stay beautiful for ever.' Bibi grinned. 'I like very much I stay beautiful.'

She had been beautiful before. She didn't look beautiful now. She looked like an inmate from a prison camp.

'Have you seen yourself in a mirror lately?' Briony asked.

'Is no mirrors here,' said Bibi. 'Is no permit. No clothes, no anything is mine . . . No comb, no hair. You must start from very low. You must serve. Is necessary.'

'They said I could be together with Tamara again. But I have to pledge myself to the Pastor.'

'Then you pledge. Is good. Is power. Obey Misha is good. You see Tamara.'

'But there's things I want to know. I've got so many questions. Dee won't give me a straight answer. I want to understand what's going on.'

Bibi shook her head. 'Is no permit, is no possible. Not now.'

'Bibi,' Briony pleaded, 'You've got to help me, there's no one else here I can talk to.'

'No can talk now,' Bibi hissed, and began to look agitated. 'Is not permit. No possible. I get bad punish.' She turned away. 'You must go back your room. You get cold, get sick. Maybe tonight you come. Maybe in here, later, I can see you. Not now. Go, go . . .'

She shooed Briony away, pursuing her across the room and closing the door behind her.

Briony went back upstairs. She was shaking with cold.

She looked down at the tray that Bibi had left. A bowl

of lukewarm broth sat waiting for her, and some crusty bread flavoured with caraway seeds. She ate the bread but tipped the broth down the lavatory, fearing it was drugged.

Dee did not come back to see her that evening.

Briony had a bath. It was odd: this was such a numbingly cold house, but there was so much hot water.

She was wondering if Bibi would show up. They should have fixed a time. She waited until ten o'clock, in case Dee returned for another talk, and then wrapped herself in the blankets and went downstairs again. The drawing-room door was closed. There were no lights on. She sat down on the sofa, on top of the dust-sheet, where she had blacked out on the previous occasion. She waited for about twenty minutes but Bibi did not appear. When she was too cold to wait any longer, she went back up to her room and got into bed to warm herself up.

She came down yet again, an hour later, and sat waiting. She waited for so long that she lost track of time. She was just beginning to feel sleepy, just thinking that it was about time she returned to bed, when that sensation of faintness came over her all of a sudden: that feeling of her muscles weakening and her bones turning to rubber. The room had begun to grow lighter . . . As if dawn was breaking.

She heard a soft voice say: 'Briony . . .?'

She tried to sit up, but couldn't.

'Briony?' The voice again.

She looked: there were women all round the room. Most of them appeared to be asleep or lost in meditation, but some of them were watching her.

'Briony!'

She managed to turn her head a little. It was Sheila, sitting on the floor, not very far away.

'What are you *doing* here?' Sheila scolded her. 'Why didn't you go? I told you to get away from here!'

'I tried,' said Briony, 'but they brought me back. They say

that Tam and I can be together . . . But I have to pledge myself to the Foundation.'

'You can't be with Tamara,' said Sheila.

'I have to,' said Briony. 'I can't abandon her.'

'You can't be with her,' Sheila said again. 'Not in this world. It's not possible.'

'They tell me it is,' said Briony. 'Dee promised me. If I give myself to the Pastor they'll bring Tam back. And we can live wherever we want and be together.'

'They're lying,' Sheila replied. 'If Dee promised you that, she's trying to cheat you. Trust me, Briony, believe me . . . It's a trap. There is no coming back. There is no way out. Where Tamara is, she's there for ever.'

'That can't be,' said Briony. 'Dee told me I could share my life with Tamara and do anything I wanted.'

'She's lying, she's lying,' Sheila insisted. 'The only way you and Tamara can be together is for you to be in *her* world, this world where we are now. At the moment, you're slipping in and out of it from time to time. But it'll get worse and worse if you don't do something to stop it. And once you've slipped too deeply into this state, you're here for ever, there's no return.'

'But why would Dee lie to me?' said Briony. 'What's in it for her?'

'They need skivvies to run this place. You've seen them . . . You were talking to one this afternoon. Once you submit, pledge your life to the Foundation, they'll lock you up here, shave off your hair, strip you of every dignity, of everything you possess. You'll have to do all the menial work for as long as they want. Misha tells the skivvies if they work hard they'll be promoted to better things. Some of them are . . . But only Misha's favourites. Some of them have been here for years – decades, they say – the ones that Misha doesn't like.'

'But why me?' said Briony. 'All I want to do is find Tamara. I don't want to be involved in *any* of it.'

'They want you because it's hard to find women who'll give

themselves to the Foundation,' said Sheila. 'They have to be forced – tricked or coerced or brainwashed into it. Many of the women who get lured into it are runaways or into drugs, or illegal immigrants. They're seduced by what they can earn. But any woman who's got her wits about her – even at the Casa Negra – is too scared to get too involved with the Foundation.'

'But Dee said they can control this thing,' said Briony. 'And *you* told me, that day in the woods, they were going to help you control it.'

'They tricked me, too,' said Sheila. 'They got me here to shut me up. I had Petra's books, I'd been helping Tamara understand this thing, I was talking with people in the Catholic Church about it. They knew I was talking to you. They told me if I moved in here at Leysholme and stopped making trouble, stopped talking to people, they would help me control this thing, so that I wouldn't slip away completely like Tamara did.'

'What do they do?' said Briony.

'We are in the condition we're in,' said Sheila, 'because our metabolism has ceased to function as it should. We need what they call a life-source – a kind of energy – to sustain us. This can only come from the male. What they promise to do is to keep you here, in one of these rooms, and bring a man here every so often to re-energize you.'

'Is this who they mean by the Pastor?' said Briony.

'No, no, no,' Sheila protested. 'He is the very last thing you need. He is the source of what's destroying you. God knows what he is . . . Part man, part spirit, some creature of the half-life, the living-dead. Any mortal man can re-energize you, as long as he's producing healthy sperm. That seems to be what carries the life-source that sustains us . . . Just as it seems to be the way the Pastor infects us in the first place. Misha finds men to serve the purpose from the Casa Negra. There's no shortage. They pay, of course – they've no idea what their true function is.'

'And that's all it takes to cure it?' said Briony. 'That gets rid of this thing for ever?'

'I wish,' sighed Sheila. 'Oh sweet Lord, I wish. No. There is no cure. That will merely restore your energy for a while ... Enough to keep you from phasing out too often. You'll need that every month or so, to stop you phasing out completely. Once you've lost too much energy – which is what happened to Tamara – you go into what they call terminal phase-out. And then it's too late to bring you back.'

'But then what happened to *you*?' said Briony.

'They tricked me, they cheated me,' said Sheila. 'I was losing energy too fast. I couldn't control it. I was frightened of what was going to happen. They told me they could save me from a terminal phase-out ... But I would have to come and live here for a while, I would have to break off all contact with the Church and with you. I would have to accept the disciplines of the sisterhood. But as soon as I got here they abandoned me, left me in isolation. That's all they had to do. They did nothing to control it, they just kept me in a room on my own. I tried to run away but it was hopeless. I didn't have the strength and I was phasing out too frequently. It was past the point of control. And now ...' She didn't finish. She looked in utter despair.

'But why?' said Briony. 'Why did they do this? Just because you talked to a Catholic priest? Because you were going to talk to me?'

'Any threat to the sisterhood is a threat to the Foundation,' said Sheila. 'And the Foundation is business, big business. Any threat to the sisterhood, any breach of discipline, they stamp on it. And locking people up here until they run out of energy is a kind of bloodless execution. It requires no effort. Costs nothing. It instils terror. The threat of eternity in this dimension, the half-life. It's all they need to maintain discipline and loyalty to the sisterhood. If you're a difficult skivvy and don't work hard enough, or if you upset Misha – cross her in any way at all – you'll be locked up here. Women are terrified of that ... Of ending up like I have, trapped here for ever. That's how the sisterhood survives and thrives: on terror.'

'If the Pastor can't survive without mortal women,' said Briony, 'why don't the women rebel? If people like Misha and Dee were to stop bringing women here, he'd waste away. They could starve him of his life-source. He would slip back into half-life for ever. They could take over the Foundation themselves ... It could be a proper sisterhood ... The slave become the master.'

'Only that will never happen,' said Sheila.

'Why not?'

Sheila smiled. 'Greed. Self-interest. Like an empire that's founded on evil, it can only survive by evil. When you pledge yourself to the Pastor you become a slave in this house. It's in your own interest to try to be the *best* slave ... so then you get promoted out of here to better things. And it's like that all the way to the top of the organization. There's intense competition for the top jobs inside the Foundation. It's dog eat dog ... or bitch eat bitch. And any woman who steps out of line – even a whisper of disloyalty – is locked up here, in this place, and kept in isolation, chained up if necessary, if she's an escape risk. She's given no access to men. So she doesn't get the life-source she needs. So, after a time, she goes into rapid ageing and begins to phase out. She might then be released – looking twenty years older – if they think she's been punished enough. Or they let her go into terminal phase-out and get rid of her completely.'

'Is there nothing I can do for Tamara?' said Briony. 'Nothing at all?'

'Nothing,' said Sheila.

'But I can't just abandon her.'

'She's past helping. She's trapped for ever where she is, just as I'm trapped here where I am.'

'I can't accept that,' said Briony, 'I can't believe that.'

'Whether you accept it or not,' said Sheila, 'do not trust

Misha. Do not trust Dee, or any of the women who work with them. You mustn't believe their promises. You don't need them to help you control your condition. You can control it yourself well enough. All you need are men . . . And God knows there are plenty enough to choose from. Any normal man can regenerate your system, in just the same way the Pastor contaminated it. Insemination was the poison, and insemination will be the antidote.'

'But what happens to the man?' said Briony. 'Don't we just pass it on, perpetuate this nightmare?'

'No, that can't happen,' Sheila replied. 'We can't pass on the condition, because we can't inseminate. You can take a lover, a husband, without any fear of that. You don't need the Foundation, Briony. That's what I'm trying to tell you. You don't need any sisterhood to save you. You can control it all yourself.'

Briony began to feel a trickling sensation through her veins. She could feel the energy flowing back into her body. The twilight was darkening.

'I think I'm losing you,' she said to Sheila. 'I'm feeling stronger now. It's coming back.'

'Then go, Briony,' said Sheila. 'Run from this place. Forget your sister. Save yourself now.'

'But how can I go?' said Briony. 'Go where? They've taken my clothes, I've got nothing.'

'Go to the cellars,' said Sheila. 'That's where they keep the skivvies' coveralls. Grab something and run. Leave by the woods. Stay on the path that leads from the back of the house. Don't stray off it and you'll be all right, even in pitch dark. It comes out on a road that goes to Woodhurst and—'

Sheila's voice gave out abruptly at that moment, and Briony jerked awake, as if she had just been startled from a deep sleep.

She was back in the dark once more. And cold, so very cold . . . The blankets had fallen off her body.

It *did* feel like a dream. But, unlike a dream that fades on waking, this was all so clear in her memory. She could recall precisely what Sheila had just told her.

THE WOODS

She walked out of the drawing room, across the hallway and into the kitchen area. She opened every door until she found the entrance to the cellars ... It looked like the door to a pantry or a broom closet.

She walked down a flight of stone stairs. There was a light on down here but it was not very bright. It was warm and smelled of heating oil, but the smooth stone was like ice on her bare feet. At the bottom of the stairs she found two separate cellar areas. One housed the furnace to heat the domestic hot water. The other was a very much larger area – an interlinking series of chambers, one leading on into the other.

The skivvies' coveralls and boots were laid out in a part of the boiler room, on slatted wooden shelves. They all looked much the same.

She could hardly breathe in here for oil fumes but at least it was warm; it was like a sauna after the chilly rooms above.

She tossed aside the blankets she was wrapped in. There were no shirts or vests of any kind. She grabbed a pair of coveralls from the pile and scrambled into them. They were heavy, quite thick – ex-airforce jumpsuits perhaps, dyed black, and much too big, but she had no time to waste. She turned up the bottoms and zipped up the front.

The boots were like old army boots, with hobnailed soles and leather laces. There were no socks of any kind and not enough light to read the size of the boots. She chose the smallest pair she could see – about four sizes too large, and laced them up tightly.

It was only when she tried to walk that she realized how noisy this was going to be: the boots made such a clatter. She took them off again and walked back through the cellar and up the steps in her bare feet. When she reached the back door she put the boots on again and retied the laces. The back door was unlocked. She opened it and was about to step outside when she noticed someone behind her, watching her from the shadows. It was Bibi.

Briony thought she was going to try to stop her leaving. But Bibi said nothing at all. She simply smiled as Briony stepped outside and closed the door.

Briony tried to walk quietly into the woods. The darkness was almost impenetrable once she was in among the trees, but Sheila was right: the footpath was straight and broad.

She was troubled by that smile on Bibi's face. There was something unsettling about it. She had only been on the path a few minutes when she understood. She heard barking from the direction of the house. The dogs were out. So that was why Bibi had been so pleased to see her sneaking away ... It had given her a chance to go telling tales to Misha.

Briony tried to run, but it was impossible in those big boots and on the rough, woodland path in the pitch black. The path was muddy after all the sleet and rain. She lost her way completely at one point and blundered headlong into a tree. She flailed her way through bushes until she found the path again and hurried on, slithering and sliding.

It was difficult to tell from the barking alone if the dogs were getting any closer, or even whether they were following her at all.

It was coming on to rain again. She could hear it before she felt it. If it rained hard enough, she was thinking, perhaps it would deter the dogs or confuse their hearing, or even wash away the scent. She tried to walk a little faster but immediately tripped on something – a protruding tree root perhaps – and fell flat on her face in the mud. She picked herself up, wiped the muck from around her mouth and eyes and kept walking.

The barking was getting closer. They could probably hear the thump of her boots on the ground by now. Or perhaps they were just following the path they knew so well. There was no way she was going to outpace them. She kept pushing on. The rain came down harder. She lost the path again and walked into a thick, spiky bush. She stepped back a few paces to try to pick up the path and discovered that it forked left and right at that point. She chose the path to the right, because that was the side of the woods where the bridle track ran.

The barking was not getting any closer. Perhaps the dogs had taken the left fork. She had reached the top of the ridge and the path was going gently downhill now. The ground felt firmer beneath her feet. She quickened her step, she even managed to break into a slow jog but she didn't have the energy to keep that going for very long and one of her boots had come loose. The lace was undone. She slowed to a walk, but the barking was closer now – the ground was firmer here so they might have heard her running – and she didn't want to risk stopping to retie the lace. But now the other boot was coming loose as well . . .

She stopped and knelt down. The leather laces were sodden with rain and mud and were slippery between her fingers. She tied them but they were difficult to pull tight and they came undone again a little further along the path. The dogs sounded much closer now. She kept shuffling onwards rather than lose time retying the laces yet again.

She glanced back . . . She saw a light some distance behind her . . . A torch, a flashlamp, something of the kind. She tried to break into a jog again but the firmness underfoot suddenly softened and turned to thick mud. She slithered sideways and one of her boots came off. By the time she had regained her balance she was several steps further along the path. She splashed back through the gooey mud, dropped down on to her knees and groped around for the lost boot.

It was a futile search. She had to give up: there was no time and she was not far from the road now – she could see moving car lights flickering through the trees ahead. She got up off her knees and struggled on with one bare foot. Glancing back a second time, she saw the torch light again. She tried to quicken her pace, but she was still slithering.

And then she trod on something with her bare foot. It felt like a spike protruding from the ground, hard as iron but sharply pointed. It pierced her instep. She yelped out loud, hopped a couple of steps in pain, skidded as she did so and fell again . . . but harder this time, on to her side, and felt an even sharper pain in her upper arm. It knocked all the breath out of her.

She sat in the mud for a minute or so, cradling the arm she had just fallen on. She tried to move it . . . The pain was high up, in her shoulder. She tried to lift it but it was agony. She managed to shift herself on to her knees and – still clutching her injured arm – attempted to stand up. But she slipped again and fell back down.

She glanced back up the path. The torch light and the dogs were so close now . . . Twenty, thirty yards away, at most.

She was cold and wet and exhausted. The pain from her injured arm sapped what was left of her spirit. The will to resist drained out of her. She just sat there in the tumbling rain and waited.

THE OPTION

They took away her other boot and made her walk back in bare feet. They put her in the usual room, stripped her – indifferent to the pain she was in – took away her wet, muddy clothes and locked her in.

She lay in a hot bath; they permitted her that, at least. It eased the pain a little but drying herself was agony.

She got little sleep that night.

Dee came to see her in the morning. She brought nothing with her, not even a cup of coffee or an aspirin.

Briony said, 'I need to go to hospital. I've dislocated my shoulder or something.'

'What you need and what you'll get,' said Dee, 'are two totally different things.'

Briony bit her lip. She was not going to plead; was not going to give Dee that much satisfaction.

'That was a very silly thing to do,' said Dee. 'Running away once, I can understand – the first time you phase out can be very spooky. But to run away *twice* . . .'

'I didn't have much option, did I?' said Briony. 'You lied to me. You won't bring my sister back . . . You *can't*.'

'I don't remember saying that we would,' Dee replied in a tart, pedantic tone.

'You said I could share my life with Tam, as long as I dedicated my life to the Pastor. But I can't share my life with Tam . . . because you can't bring her back.'

'You read what Petra wrote,' said Dee. 'It's not possible to get the necessary life-source in that dimension. There's nothing I can do to help Tamara . . . even if I wanted to.'

'So she'll be there for ever?' Briony concluded.

'I told you you could share your life with her,' said Dee.

'Yes, that's exactly what you said.'

'And so you can,' said Dee. 'But I didn't say we could bring her back.'

'Share my life with her and stay in *this* world,' said Briony, 'that's what you promised.'

'And so you can,' Dee repeated. 'If you give yourself to us, we can help you to control the situation, so that you remain in this world for most of the time, but phase out for short periods, at regular intervals, when you can be with Tamara in *her* world.'

'But Tam's trapped where she is,' said Briony. 'She can't move anywhere.'

'Then you'll have to live in that flat at Styles Lane, won't you?' said Dee.

'But you said I could go wherever I want and lead a normal life,' Briony protested.

'Within reason,' said Dee, 'you can. You'll have to do what the sisterhood tells you, of course, but we're not vindictive or difficult. If you want to go on living at Styles Lane so that you can be with Tamara whenever you phase out, then we can permit that. You'd have to work for the Foundation, of course – wherever they tell you to work – but we could base you in London. I don't see any problem ... As long as you behave sensibly.'

'You mean I'd have to spend the rest of my life at that house,' said Briony, 'or never see Tamara again?'

Dee gave her a hard look. 'You chose to make this journey to find your sister. I never said it was going to be easy. On the contrary, I seem to remember trying to put you off.'

She had not tried very hard, as Briony remembered. She must have known that it would take an awful lot to keep twin sisters apart.

'What will happen to Tamara as she gets older?' Briony asked. 'Will she die there – in that world, where she is, and trapped in that attic room?'

'She won't die,' said Dee. 'In the half-life, the metabolism stops completely. There is no need to eat, so she never feels hunger. There's no need to drink, so she never feels thirst. Viruses and bacteria cannot survive in that dimension, so there is no disease. She will never grow older because there is no such thing as time where she is. It's not possible to die, for there's nothing to cause death. She will live for ever.'

'If you call it living,' said Briony.

'And do you call it living,' Dee countered, 'the way that three-quarters of the people on this planet spend their lives?'

'At least they have some kind of freedom.'

'They have no freedom,' Dee retorted. 'They're slaves to poverty and exploitation.'

'Tam had freedom, but you took that away from her.'

'Tam was a slave,' said Dee scornfully. 'We're all slaves in the free world – slaves to big business, to the bankers, the oil companies, the arms manufacturers, the chemical conglomerates, the currency speculators ... But there are no slaves where Tamara is. There is no pain in that world, no suffering of any kind.'

'And no happiness either.'

Dee looked as if she pitied Briony. Or perhaps it was just contempt.

'And *you*,' said Briony, 'will you grow old and die?'

Dee laughed. 'You speak as if I'm some alien species. But you're one of us now, baby sister. Your metabolism is already changing. The process has begun. It can be controlled but not reversed.'

'Bibi told me she can be beautiful for ever,' said Briony.

'Maybe she can,' said Dee. 'Maybe she can't. Time will tell.'

'If nobody in this condition ages,' said Briony, 'why does a woman like Gloria look as if she's in her sixties? She must have been young and pretty when she gave herself to the Pastor.'

'It's not true that nobody in this condition ages,' said Dee. 'We age if our energy level falls too much and we start phasing out again. When that happens we begin to age very quickly – much faster than a normal woman.'

'And what about the women at Styles Lane?' said Briony. 'Some of them live like hermits. Lotte, for example: she shuffles around like she's ninety, but her face looks fifty. And her body's almost youthful.'

'A few years ago Lotte looked about thirty,' said Dee. 'But this condition affects the mind sometimes. Women find they just can't go on like this any longer. They turn away from men and from sex. The whole thing becomes repulsive to them. This is a common problem; why so many women give up. Lotte became reclusive. So she stopped getting the energy she needs . . . So she started ageing very rapidly. She's almost into terminal phasing now. She's given up, resigned herself to what's coming. I think she almost looks forward to it.'

'And what happens eventually to someone like you?' said Briony.

'Eventually is a long time away,' Dee replied.

'In my Father's house are many mansions, you said,' Briony reminded her. 'Do you really want to be stuck in this one, looking thirty for the rest of eternity? And then you get forgetful one time and don't have sex for a month and – whoops! – you wake up looking sixty.'

'I don't think about the downside,' said Dee. 'I'm too busy enjoying life.'

'But if you can't die—' Briony began.

'Of course we can die,' said Dee. 'Cut us and we bleed. Strangle us and we choke. We can be murdered, have a car smash, fall under a bus, like anybody else. But as long as we get the life-source we need, nobody knows how long it's possible to go on. Maybe we'll lose heart after a while, like Lotte. There's evidence that the brain decays in strange ways in women with our condition . . . which could be a problem. You might end up a body without a mind.' Dee smiled humourlessly. 'Some people say that Bibi already is.'

Briony's shoulder was hurting so much that she was not

concentrating on what Dee was saying any more. She closed her eyes and winced.

'I'll get you something,' Dee murmured, and walked out of the room.

She came back about five minutes later with two tablets and a glass of water.

'It's Ibuprofen,' said Dee, 'two hundred mills. Misha takes them for her migraines.' She helped Briony to sit up.

'She gets headaches?' said Briony with a sardonic note. 'I thought she was above all earthly pains and ills?'

'I think it's that other thing I mentioned,' said Dee. 'Something affecting the brain.'

'You don't sound very worried.'

'What's the use in worrying? She's been around a very long time. No one could possibly say she's had short measures.'

Briony swallowed each tablet with a sip of water.

'If you can help people in this condition,' she said, 'if you can control it like you say, then why wouldn't you help my sister?'

'She got greedy,' said Dee. 'She had only herself to blame.'

'How do you mean, greedy?'

'Some women see it as just a quick way to get rich. They want to grab the money and run. And they love all that feel-good stuff that comes with the physical sensations. It can be very addictive. So they're not content with sleeping with the Pastor one night a month. They get hooked and they start to want him every week. But the body can't handle that . . . If a woman loses too much energy too quickly, their metabolism crashes, they start phasing out very suddenly for long periods . . . And they panic. I warned Tamara she couldn't handle this on her own. I told her we could control it for her. But she wouldn't listen, wouldn't trust us. She wouldn't take our help. She went to her doctor instead. She had examinations and blood tests. But it was all pointless: she was looking for medical explanations for non-medical phenomena.' Dee

314

shrugged. 'I tried to help. But she walled me out. In the end there was nothing I could do.'

After a pause, she added: 'I hope you're not going to be as stupid as your sister.'

'Didn't she realize,' said Briony, 'that all she needed to control this thing was a normal healthy male?'

'It's not as easy as that.'

'I think it is. I think you use this as a means to frighten women into joining the sisterhood.'

'You actually think you can get through this without our help?' said Dee.

'I do, yes.'

'Then you're stupider than I thought.'

'Give me one good reason why I should pledge my life to the Foundation,' said Briony.

'No one can force you,' said Dee. 'But you do realize that if you refuse to join us you'll never see your sister again?'

'So you say,' Briony replied.

'And for one very simple reason,' said Dee. 'You'll be evicted from that flat at Styles Lane. And since Tamara is trapped there for all time, you'll never be able to see her again.'

'Who says she *is* trapped there?' said Briony. 'I don't trust a word you say.'

'Of course you don't,' said Dee. 'Why should you? But what if I'm telling you the truth? Can you afford to ignore the possibility? This could be the only hope you've got of ever seeing her again. Are you prepared to take the risk and walk away from that flat for ever?'

'If I were,' said Briony, 'would I be allowed to leave? Would you let me walk away?'

Dee declined to answer. Perhaps that was for Misha to decide.

'You told me I was making this journey of my own free will,' Briony reminded her.

'You are,' said Dee. 'You have free will. You always have a choice.'

'Then, if I choose to walk away?' said Briony.

'I'm afraid that won't be possible,' said Dee. 'You've been among us too long. You know too much about us. You've been privy to our secrets. If you won't accept our hand of friendship, I'm afraid you'll have to take the other option.'

A silence.

'And that is?' said Briony.

'Oh . . .' Dee sighed. 'Nothing too grisly. We'll find you somewhere to sleep, here in the house, and give you something useful to do. But without our control programme you'll have no access to men. So you'll go on losing energy. And you'll phase out more and more . . . Until we lose you completely. But that could be as much as a year away.'

'In other words,' said Briony, 'I can either stay here . . . Or I can stay here.'

'I suppose that's what it amounts to,' Dee conceded.

'Some choice,' said Briony.

'You have the option of joining us,' Dee reminded her.

Briony smiled bleakly. 'And some option.'

THE PORTRAIT

Winter turned to spring. The months crawled by at Leysholme. Her routine seldom changed. She swept and scrubbed floors, she washed windows, she washed clothes, she carried coal and laid fires, she cleaned baths and sinks. And once her dislocated shoulder had fully healed the work grew harder, not easier, and the hours grew longer.

Some of the women skivvying with her had been here for years. Some were here as a punishment, some had simply

316

fallen from grace, had upset the sisterhood for some petty reason. Some of them had been here so long they were like old lags in prison: they had lost the urge to be free, had grown to fear it, had become accustomed to the safety of servitude. Whereas Misha's favourites skivvied for a few months and were then quickly on the ladder of promotion.

Briony had seen almost nothing of Bibi. Bibi was one of Misha's favourites. Bibi was on the fast track. She was a member of the sisterhood now, had taken the pledge, had given her life to the Pastor. She was living in London by the spring, embarked on her new career, modelling fetish outfits for mail-order catalogues ... The Foundation owned the mail-order company; it also owned the company who manufactured the fetish wear; and it even owned the modelling agency.

These were the whispers that reached Briony's ears, at any rate, passed on down the skivvies' hush-hush grapevine. But there was no way of knowing what was true and what was not. Bibi could be dead or locked up on the third floor and no one would ever know.

Not a day went by when Briony did not contemplate escaping. But it was not easy. She was not allowed to leave the house, except to shovel coal. She had not been outside in four months – not since the night she tried to run away and dislocated her shoulder in the woods.

She slept in a dormitory on the first floor with four other skivvies. She had an old bed with a frame of tubular steel, and a horse-hair mattress. She was permitted two blankets and a pillow, but no personal possessions of any kind, no toiletries, no clothes of her own, just the heavy cotton coveralls. She developed skin rashes all over her body. She was not allowed to bath. She had to use the old shower room, dating from orphanage times – cold water only.

The food was sufficient but it was laced with tranquillizers (so the whispers went) – diazepam and temazapam, to dull the skivvies' minds and keep them docile. And Briony believed the whispers, noting how the skivvies wandered about their duties, day after day, placid and accepting, spying on each other, telling tales of petty misdemeanour to their mistress, Misha, hoping to curry a little favour. They would even betray and lie about each other for something so small as the privilege of being allowed to work outside, sweeping the yard or tidying the garden.

Briony ate as little as possible, to keep her mind clear, but that left her short of calories, of protein and carbohydrates, and made her daily work all the more tiring. Her blackouts were getting worse. She was phasing out more and more frequently, and for longer and longer periods . . . always when she was tired and resting.

The thought of escape was the only thing that kept her going, but she had very little means and very little opportunity. She was locked in at night and kept under watch all day. The other skivvies were spying on her constantly; the smallest misdemeanour was reported back to Misha in the hope of earning some small reward.

Dee came to see her once. Briony was in the laundry room, washing Misha's bedlinen by hand in an enormous sink.

'You like it this way?' said Dee. 'You've played at slaves, now you really are a slave, you like it?'

Briony turned to face the wall.

'Because this is where it's going to end,' said Dee. 'You really want that?'

Briony refused to answer.

'It doesn't have to be this way,' said Dee. 'There's still time. We can control it for you. All you have to do is join us.'

Briony said nothing.

'Show a little humility,' said Dee. 'That's all you've got to do. Give yourself up. Kneel to the sisterhood. Take the pledge.'

Briony was tempted, sorely tempted . . . Not because she was ready to join them but because a little humility and contrition might make for easier conditions and a better opportunity for escape.

'It's not so painful,' said Dee, 'if that's what you're frightened of. We give you a shot.'

Briony smiled to herself . . . Not so painful. They give you a shot. Some shot . . . She had seen Bibi, her whole body rigid and quivering, like they were putting twenty thousand volts through her, and screaming in silence.

She would never trust Dee's word. And the thought of saying yes to this bunch stuck in her craw.

'Tell the Pastor,' she said, 'he can kiss my arse.'

Dee smiled contemptuously. 'Just like your sister,' she said, and walked away.

Briony expected things to get worse from then on . . . though it was difficult to imagine how much worse it could get. But nothing changed. Her daily workload got no easier but no harder either.

Another month or so went by – it was difficult to keep track of time.

One day, when she was nosing through a grocery box that had been left out by the refuse bins, Briony found a pencil and a large pad of plain white paper that had been stained by spilt coffee. She kept them, but secretly. ('Stole' them, Misha would have said.) And to occupy her mind at nights she tried to sketch faces from memory: Tamara, for one, and her father, for another. And Dee and Misha and Bibi. They were not very good likenesses. Disappointed with them, she began to doodle some designs for fantasy clothes. It filled in the hours of boredom in the evenings.

One of the other skivvies saw her drawing one evening and reported it to Misha. It was an offence to photograph or record anything about Leysholme or the sisterhood. Misha summoned Briony to her apartment on the fourth floor. She was in her sitting room with the dogs. It was a warm summer night. The windows were wide open. Briony handed her the sketches.

Misha sat near an open window, her long legs crossed, looking at the drawings by the light of a reading lamp, with the fingers of her free hand dangling and idly combing the head of her beloved dog, Rika.

She was silent for what felt like an age. Briony wondered what her punishment would be. Misha was a sadist. It was whispered that some of these locked rooms housed women who had been there for years.

Then Misha said, 'This I like.' And pointed with a spear of scarlet fingernail at one of Briony's fantasy creations. 'You are artist?'

Misha's Russian accent had a soft, languorous quality.

'I did art and design at college,' said Briony.

'I want you paint picture of me,' said Misha, 'in this.' And tapped the sketch again. 'You can paint pictures?'

Briony didn't know what to say. She could sketch a bit but she could no more paint a portrait than sing opera.

'It's just a rough doodle really,' she said.

Misha got up very suddenly. The dogs came alert. Briony wondered what she was going to do . . . One never knew with Misha, she was so unpredictable. She could fly into psychotic rages at the slightest provocation. And it was whispered that she was losing her sanity completely.

Misha crossed to an antique secretaire, switched on another reading lamp and pulled out a chair for Briony to sit down.

'Is paper, is pen,' she said. 'You write what is you need. You get everything you need. I want you paint this picture.'

Briony sat down at the secretaire, picked up the pen and stared at the blank sheet of paper. 'There are so many things I'd need,' she said, 'it's hard to make a list. I need a good art shop, for a start. I need to browse around, pick things out.'

Another silence ensued. Briony didn't dare look round. She kept the pen poised over the blank sheet of paper.

And then Misha said, 'Okay. Tomorrow.'

Briony went back to her dormitory.

The following morning she was summoned to Misha's

apartment again. She was given back her own clothes – the winter clothes she was wearing on the night they first brought her here from Gloria's room.

Misha came with her. They were chauffeured to Tunbridge Wells in the black limousine. They walked through the centre of town. Briony had to ask passers-by if there was an art shop. Misha didn't say a word; it was a warm day but the sun did nothing to melt that glacial soul.

Briony bought tubes of acrylic and oil paints, water colours, brushes, drawing inks, steel-nibbed pens, a rainbow range of felt-tips, 2HB pencils and cartridge paper.

On the way back, in the car, Misha asked, 'You don't buy canvas? For painting?'

'I'll do some mock-ups on paper first,' said Briony. (She had never painted on canvas.) 'We'll get the outfit right. You can change bits if you don't like it. Then we can talk about the size of the picture and whether you want it on board or canvas.' She was waffling because she was completely out of her depth.

But Misha seemed satisfied.

When they got back to Leysholme Briony said she needed somewhere to work, with a large table and good light.

Misha gave her one of the spare rooms in the apartment and had a table moved in there for her. Briony began work that same afternoon. Misha came in every so often to view the progress. There was nothing really worth seeing by the evening – only some larger pencil drawings on cartridge paper – but Misha was so enthused that she told Briony she could have a bedroom, there, in the apartment, until the work was completed. She was given the bedroom next to her work room. She even had her own bathroom.

That first night in her own room, she stripped off her clothes and looked at herself in the mirror. She had not seen her own reflection for four months. She looked dreadful: she had lost so much weight, she was skin and bone, and she had not seen sunlight for so long that her flesh was the colour of tripe.

She ran her hand over her bald head. Skivvies had to shave their heads each month. It was regarded as a privilege to shave a new skivvy. Misha had given Bibi the privilege of shaving Briony. Bibi had used dressmaker's shears to crop the hair down to the scalp and then an old-style straight razor to finish it off. She had brought a fresh white towel to dab away the blood and had taken her time, had enjoyed her task. She had even shaved Briony's eyebrows. Had loved every second of it. Painstaking, Bibi. Had not left a single hair on Briony's body. Knew how to please Misha. She would go far, Bibi.

But at least she hadn't given in, Briony told herself, looking at that reflection. She could stare at her own body and it was *her* body, there was no one's brand on her, no fancy Gothic symbols; it was her body, all her own, it belonged to no one else. She was no one's chattel, no one's slave. And nor was Tam.

The following afternoon, a pile of clothes appeared. They were left on her bed, as if by magic. They were summer clothes – mostly Tamara's, but they fitted perfectly. They had been brought from Styles Lane. The room had not been re-let as yet ... They were so sure that they could break her, that she would give up in despair before long and submit to the sisterhood.

She took her meals in Misha's kitchen ... Always on her own, for Misha ate alone in a grand dining room that looked like something from a hunting lodge of the Tsars.

Briony finished the coloured mock-ups. Misha liked them. She wanted Briony to get on with the painting now. She was impatient. She wanted this picture on canvas, she informed Briony; about one and a half metres wide. She wanted to be seated. And she wanted her two dogs to be in the picture too. One on each side of her. She asked how long she would have to pose for. Briony said she preferred to work from photographs. But, when Misha looked disappointed, added hurriedly: 'To begin with, at any rate.'

The truth was, she didn't know what she was doing. She could design fantasy outfits, that was no problem. She could even paint them. And she had done some drawing in life classes. But she had never painted human flesh; had never had to paint a face.

Misha had a camera. She posed in the chair that she wanted to be painted in. She was very photogenic. Briony shot two rolls of film and took pictures of the dogs as well. Misha had had the film developed by the following afternoon.

Back they went to Tunbridge Wells. Misha insisted that they bought an easel: the very best.

Briony began to paint, using only the photographs.

She left the face and hands till last and practised painting them, secretly, at night, on a spare canvas which she kept hidden beneath the bed by day. Her efforts improved slowly. She had finished painting the dogs, Rika and Sasha, before she even started on Misha's face.

Misha kept coming in to review the progress. She decided now she wanted the dogs the other way round – with Rika, her favourite, on her right hand, head raised. She wanted Sasha's head turned and looking up at her.

Briony painted them out and started again. She didn't mind; it gave her more time to practise Misha's face in secret.

She was letting her hair grow. Either Misha had not noticed or was according her the privilege; she said nothing. Briony was eating better food now and it was not drugged. She was putting on weight. Misha told her that she had a bad complexion, she should go out in the sun more. So she began to go for short walks during the day. She thought of escaping – it would be so easy now, almost nothing to stop her . . . But then she could never go back to that flat in Styles Lane and she might never see Tamara again.

She finished painting the dogs and began work on Misha's hands and face. Misha had stopped coming in to pry. She seemed nervous now, as if the completed work might threaten her self-image in some way.

One evening, she crept into the room while Briony was in the kitchen, washing up some dishes. Briony came back and found her staring at the picture, her arms folded across her chest, her body held very erect, a severe expression on her face.

Briony was thinking, *Uh-uh, here we go . . . She hates it.*

Misha said, 'How much more you have to do?'

The picture was as near to being finished as it was ever likely to be, but Briony said, 'Oh . . . This and that,' with deliberate vagueness. 'Bits here and there, things I'm not happy with.'

It didn't look much like Misha, she had to admit – although she reckoned she had caught the psychotic coldness of those pale blue eyes, and the meagre cruelty of those wide, thin lips. The truth was, the dogs came out of it very much better than their mistress.

But that was all that Misha seemed to care about. She nodded slowly and a glow of satisfaction settled on her face. It was not a smile but a look of deep affection.

'My Rika,' she said, reaching out and touching the paint with the tips of her fingers – as if she was touching the animal itself. 'And my boy, Sasha . . .' She didn't seem remotely interested in how *she* looked: it was solely the dogs that captivated her.

She left the room without another word.

The following morning, Briony was sitting in the kitchen, having breakfast, when Misha appeared in the doorway.

'I don't want you touch my picture any more,' she said.

Briony couldn't tell whether she was angry or not. She *sounded* angry. But you could never tell with Misha.

'Why not?' said Briony.

'Is perfect,' said Misha. 'You touch more, you spoil.'

Briony wasn't going to argue. As long as Misha was happy.

'What it is,' Misha asked, 'you want to do now?' She was frowning at Briony as if she was suddenly displeased.

'What do I want to do?' said Briony, not quite sure whether she was still talking about improvements to the picture or whether she was referring to Briony's personal hopes and wishes. 'I want to go back to Styles Lane,' she replied cautiously. 'So I can be with my sister.'

Misha's expression changed a little. It took on a dangerous, accusing look. Just as she had the previous night, when she saw Misha glaring at the painting, Briony thought, *Uh-uh, here we go* ... And assumed she'd misunderstood the question.

But then Misha began to screw her eyes shut. Her face twisted into a grimace of pain and she pressed her hands over her skull, as if it was about to split open and she was trying to hold it all together.

Migraine. Briony had seen this before. It was like someone pushing white-hot iron through her head; that was how Misha had described it to her. She moved very slowly towards the table where Briony was sitting, and sank down on to a chair.

When the moment had passed and the pain had eased – as much as it ever did – Misha said, 'I want you paint my Rika. Also my Sasha. But separate. I want three, four paintings maybe, each: my baby girl and my big, handsome boy.'

Thinking this was really not the time to push her luck, but pushing it anyway, Briony said. 'May I do the work in London? At my sister's flat?'

Misha looked at her with a maudlin sort of gaze. Perhaps it was the constant pain she was in. 'You don't like here, this place?' she asked.

'I'm very comfortable,' said Briony. 'I like your apartment. But I love my sister.'

Misha was silent. After a moment she nodded sympathetically. 'I understand,' she said. 'I loved her too.'

And then an extraordinary thing happened: Misha smiled. It was the first time Briony had ever seen her smile. It was said that she never did; it was said that there was something wrong with the muscles of her face, that she was physically incapable of smiling. But maybe that was just the bitchiness among the other women.

'But she could not love me,' Misha added. 'Is not her nature.'

Even more extraordinary: Briony felt a twinge of sympathy for her at that moment. Something about her forlorn tone . . . It hinted at the desolate loneliness she must have felt deep down inside. It was the first time that Briony had caught even a glimpse of humanity in her.

'You may go see your sister,' Misha agreed reluctantly. 'When you have finish some more paintings of my dogs, you bring them back to me. Then I decide what it is we do with you. Maybe you design some nice clothes for us, I don't know.'

'I can go now?' said Briony. 'Today?'

'Yes, yes,' Misha snapped irritably. 'Go now.' She flipped her hand as if she was dismissing a servant from the room. 'Go back to your sister.'

NO SECRETS

The limousine took her back to Styles Lane. Nothing very much had changed. The garden was no more or less a jungle than it had been the previous summer. Tall weeds and sunflowers were in bloom.

She had so much to carry, with her summer clothes and her art materials, that she had to make two trips up and down the stairs.

The house was as quiet as ever.

There were letters waiting for her in the flat, in an untidy little heap on the dropleaf table. She opened the mail and played back the messages that had accumulated on Tam's answering machine. Her mother had called, several times. And Charlie Stillman too.

She woke up early, the following morning. Just before dawn, was how it felt; that quality of light.

Tam was lying on the bed beside her.

'Hey, Sis,' she said.

She looked so beautiful to Briony at that moment. Briony reached out with her fingers and touched Tam's cheek.

'Jesus,' she whispered. 'At last . . .'

'Has it been long?' said Tamara.

'Nearly five months.'

'That much? Doesn't seem it. But it doesn't seem anything in this place. Time doesn't really exist.'

Briony pushed her head closer across the pillow and kissed Tamara's face.

'Where've you been?' Tamara said.

'Painting dogs,' said Briony.

'For five months?'

'They're big dogs.'

That night, Briony said, 'Dee told me she wanted to help you, but you didn't trust her.'

'You blame me?'

'No.'

'Dee didn't want to help me,' said Tamara, 'she wanted to get rid of me.'

'Because of Misha?'

'Because of Misha,' echoed Tamara. 'She was jealous as hell. I don't know why. I never gave her cause. Not my scene.'

One morning, Tamara said, 'Why don't you just take off?'

'Take off where?' said Briony.

'Anywhere. What's stopping you?'

'I've got Misha's paintings to do.'

'Screw Misha,' said Tamara. 'What could she do? Come after you?'

'She could stop me coming back here.'

'So what? You could live anywhere. You don't need to be here.'

'Without my sister?' said Briony.

'Screw your sister,' said Tamara.

'Not my scene,' said Briony.

It was a hot summer.

They saw each other almost every day – usually late at night or early mornings, when Briony was lying down and close to sleep.

She began work on Misha's pictures. She would paint four of Sasha, and four of Rika, using the photographs that she had brought from Leysholme. She painted in the mornings. And in the afternoons, on fine days, she would lie out in the sun, in the long grass down by the river.

She telephoned Charlie and said she was sorry that she hadn't been in touch. She told him she had been away, working – which was true. He asked about Tamara. She told him she had seen Tam and that she was safe and well. He was like a small boy who had just been told the circus was in town. He kept asking how she looked and what she was doing. Tam had been involved with someone, Briony explained, and that was what all the trouble had been about. She had been through a bad time and might not be coming back to live in London.

Charlie said, 'We must have a drink some time – very soon. Catch up on the news.'

Briony said, 'Let's do that.' And only later wondered if his idea of 'we' was intended to include Tamara too.

He dropped by a few days later. Just passing, he said. Thought he'd look in, see if anyone was at home. He had brought a bottle of white wine, already chilled. She brought a couple of glasses and a corkscrew and left it for him to open.

She had a tan by now and her hair had grown – though it was still quite short: the ragamuffin look. He told her he liked it like that, it suited her. She said she had shaved it all off for Lent. He thought she was kidding. She said she was perfectly serious. He laughed, did not believe her for a second. Suited her, he said again, the ragamuffin look.

It was a warm night. He was wearing shorts and a polo shirt. He was very tanned. She asked him where he'd been. She could picture him on an Aegean island, clambering the ruins of a vanished civilization.

He said he'd been in Holloway.

Not the prison, she said.

No, he said, just his back garden. And asked her where *she* had been.

Working, she said, skivvying at a big house on the Kent–Sussex borders. But that was finished now.

He looked at two paintings of Sasha and Rika that were waiting for delivery to Misha. 'Unusual dogs,' he said.

'They're huge,' said Briony. 'As big as mastiffs, but bits of everything in them, by the look of them.'

'Where did you see them?'

'In the country.' She showed him the photographs. 'They belong to an old flame of Tam's.' She turned to the bed and grinned, wondering if Tam was watching . . . probably poking out her tongue at that remark.

'They look like Siberian wolfhounds,' Charlie said. 'But they can't be.'

'Why not?'

'They were royal hunting dogs,' said Charlie. 'Bred only for the Tsars. Said to have been the largest dogs in the world. The Bolsheviks shot most of them in 1917, or set them loose. They've been extinct for fifty years or more.'

He poured some wine and asked her about Tamara, about why she had disappeared like that, and what all the trouble was about. Briony prevaricated, improvised, told half-truths about the Foundation, about Misha and Dee. Charlie pressed her further: wanted to know who she'd been mixed up with and what had gone wrong. But Briony said she'd rather not discuss it; it was not the sort of thing that sisters gossiped about. Tamara would explain, one day, perhaps.

That night, when Briony phased out on the very edge of sleep, Tamara said, 'I think you should have an affair with him.'

'With Charlie?' said Briony. 'Why? What ever for?'

'Well, who else is there?'

'What do you mean who else?' Briony laughed. 'What do I want an affair with *any*one for? Aren't we okay the way we are?'

'You're not okay,' said Tamara. 'You're not at all okay. You're phasing out too much. You phase out every night now. And often in the mornings too.'

'But that's what's so wonderful,' said Briony. 'We're together so much more.'

'But you're phasing out too frequently. And it's going on for too long. It's too much.'

'How can it be too much?' said Briony. 'How can we see too much of each other?'

'But your metabolism's changing,' said Tamara. 'It's a creeping thing, like a slow virus. If you let it go too long you lose too much energy. And then it's too late. Your whole body system flips out of control, like a plane going into a crash-dive. That's what happened to me . . . Because Dee didn't tell me how I could re-energize. You need a man, Sis, believe me. You've got to get energy into your body before this gets out of control.'

'But why bother?' said Briony. 'Why fight it? Why don't I just let it happen? It wouldn't be so terrible, you and me, here. We've got each other. What more do we need?'

'You mustn't think like that,' said Tam. 'It's like saying, because one of us has fallen off a cliff, the other one's got to jump off as well. That's a crazy way to think.'

'But I don't fancy Charlie.'

'You don't need to fancy him, you need the energy, that's all.'

'But I've got to *like* the guy,' Briony protested.

'How can you not like Charlie?' said Tamara. 'He's very good-natured. He doesn't deserve to be alone. And he looked so miserable, the other weekend, when you said about me getting involved with another man.'

'How do you know he looked miserable?' said Briony. 'Could you see him?'

'Of course I could see him,' said Tamara.

'All the time?'

'Of course all the time. We can see everything in *both* dimensions, even though we're only visible in this one.'

That had never occurred to Briony. 'You mean . . . You've been watching me ever since I first got here, last September?'

'You can't be serious?' said Tamara. 'You didn't know that?'

'How am I supposed to know?' said Briony. 'There's no one else around when I phase out. Except, maybe, down by the river. But then I'm looking at the sky, anyway.'

'And you never see a plane go overhead?' said Tamara. 'You never see a bird flying?'

'I've never really looked,' Briony confessed. 'I've never thought about it.'

'It's something to do with the frequency of light.'

'So you've seen me . . .?' Briony didn't finish. She was mortified by the thought of what Tamara might have seen.

'Seen everything,' said Tamara. And grinned.

'Jesus,' said Briony, and squirmed. 'How embarrassing.'

'Yeah, but it cuts both ways. Think how I felt when you found my secret cupboard . . . All my clothes.'

'You were watching that too?'

'Everything.'

'Oh, that's the pits . . . And you saw me try them all on?'

'You see, in the end,' said Tamara, 'we have no secrets.'

Briony thought about that. She liked the irony of the situation, the way it had turned about.

'No secrets,' she agreed.

PHASING BACK

Charlie took her out for a meal, the following week. He came back to the flat for coffee but he didn't stay very long.

The following morning, in bed, Tamara said, 'He definitely fancies you.'

'Who does?' said Briony, knowing perfectly well who she meant, but fed up with discussing it.

'Charlie.'

'I'm quite sure he doesn't,' said Briony.

'I can see he does,' said Tamara. 'The way he looks at you.'

'But when he looks at me, he's seeing *you*.'

'So what? If he wants you because you look like me, does it matter?'

'Thanks a whole heap. Of course, it matters. Would you go to bed with a guy because he only fancies *me*?'

'That's not the point,' said Tamara.

'Then what is?'

'He's a sweet guy at heart—'

'So's Father Christmas.'

'He needs you, and you need him.'

'I don't need your hand-me-downs, thank you.'

'You need the energy.'

'I could never go to bed with Charlie, it's out of the question.'

'Why, what's wrong with him?'

'There's nothing specially wrong with him, it's just . . .'

'Just what?'

'He was your fellow.'

'Oh, not really,' said Tamara. 'Not for very long, he wasn't. He doesn't qualify as a steady or anything. He qualifies as an also-ran, maybe.'

'It still *feels* wrong,' said Briony. 'We agreed we'd never do that. We made a pact.'

'We never made a pact about also-rans.'

'We made a pact we'd never go with each other's—'

'We made loads of pacts,' Tamara interrupted. 'We were always making pacts. We made a pact we'd be virgins till we were twenty-one.'

'Yeah, but we were about six at the time,' said Briony.

'Precisely,' said Tamara. 'We've broken every single pact we ever made. What's different about this one?'

The next time she saw Charlie it was another warm summer evening and they went out for a drink at a pub by the Thames, near the old East India Docks.

When he drove her home she asked him upstairs for coffee, as she had the last time. While she was waiting for the water to boil, in that tiny kitchen, he came up behind her and put his hands on her hips and said, Oh, by the way, could he have his without milk.

Without milk, she repeated, and put her hands on top of his hands. And they stood like that, like statues, until the kettle came to the boil and switched itself off and she took her hands away from his and poured water into the two mugs and stirred them.

Then she turned round, so he had to take his hands off her hips. And she looked at him, wondering if he was going to kiss her. But he made a sort of tutting noise and said he was sorry, he hadn't really meant that to happen. She said it was okay, she hadn't meant it to happen either, but it was okay, anyway.

So then he did kiss her. And they went down into the big studio room and kissed a whole lot more.

About midnight, he said, God, was that the time. And he supposed he ought to go. She said he didn't have to . . . unless he had to.

So he stayed.

And when they made love, all she could think about was Tam.

He went home at some ungodly hour of the night.

'It was awful,' said Briony, the next morning, when she phased out before breakfast.

'Why was it awful?' said Tamara.

'Knowing you were watching.'

'I wasn't really watching . . . I mean, I didn't *stare*.'

'I kept imagining you there beside us. I couldn't concentrate. I couldn't relax, let go. I was tense. He could sense I was tense.'

'You made noises.'

'Did I?'

'You made a lot of noises.'

'I'm sure I didn't.' And then: 'Well . . . maybe some. Baby ones.'

'Panting and groaning and moaning,' said Tamara. 'You hardly shut up.'

'But I was faking.'

'Didn't sound like you were faking.'

'Well, I was. I didn't feel a thing.'

'But *I* did,' said Tamara.

'How do you mean?'

'I don't know. I just felt something.'

'You mean, like . . . turned on?'

'No, no. Like . . . little jolts. Little electric shocks going through me. My whole body. A sort of throbbing. Kind of pins and needles.'

'I thought we don't feel anything in this dimension?' said Briony.

334

'That's what I thought. We don't usually. I've never felt anything before. But something even stranger happened.'

'What's that?'

'I was able to move,' said Tamara. 'Quite easily. My hands, my legs. It was like being in the normal world again.'

'Can you move now?'

Tamara tried. 'Not really. It's started to wear off.'

'What is it?' said Briony. 'You're not going sick on me, are you?'

'I don't know,' said Tamara. 'I've never experienced it before.'

Charlie telephoned. He said he'd found something about Siberian wolfhounds in one of his old photography magazines. Just an article. She might be interested.

It was his way of asking for another date.

They went out. He'd brought the magazine to show her. He was right: Rika and Sasha did look very like Siberian wolfhounds. And the article did say they were extinct, like the Tsars who'd bred them.

Charlie came up for coffee, as before. And slipped away at another ungodly hour of the night.

'Is he married?' said Briony.

'Not any more,' said Tamara. 'His wife did the dirty on him. But that was years ago. She got the house and children, as well.'

'So why does he keep sloping off in the middle of the night, do you think?'

'How should I know? Ask him.'

'I don't think this is going to work. He's kind of strange. He's not very relaxed. But I'm not, either.'

'What do you think of?' said Tamara.

'When?'

'When you're making love.'

'I don't think anything much. I'm not enjoying it. I think

it's a mistake. The truth is, I'm picturing you watching us and I feel guilty . . . Like I'm in your place. I'm in *your* bed, being screwed by *your* fellow. It feels all wrong.'

'You're thinking about me?' said Tamara. 'While he's doing his stuff, you're just lying there imagining me? That's all that's in your head?'

'Well . . . pretty much. I can't help it.'

'This is amazing,' said Tamara, growing quite agitated. 'See, the reason I'm asking is, I felt it again . . . The same thing, but even more so.'

'What, the little jolts, the electricity thing?' said Briony. 'The pins and needles?'

'I got up off the bed,' said Tamara. 'I moved around. I could move, I mean really move.' She had begun to grow excited. 'I had strength in my body. I didn't feel the way we feel in this dimension – like you're up to your neck in quicksand – that all faded away. And the light changed for just a few seconds. It went darker. I felt the temperature change . . . for just a few seconds. And I smelt the room. I smelt things for the first time in ages.'

'What are you saying?' said Briony, bewildered. 'You phased *back*? Back into the other world?'

Tamara's face now creased with doubts. 'It doesn't seem possible, does it?'

STICKY FINGERS

'Suppose,' said Tamara, 'just suppose . . .'

And lapsed into thought again.

'Suppose what?' said Briony.

'Remember when you were in hospital, that time? I sneaked downstairs and heard Mum crying and Dad talking on the phone ... Something about you couldn't breathe, you couldn't get air in your lungs. He said you were sinking, you weren't going to make it. I sort of understood what he meant but I crept back to bed, imagining your body like a punctured Lilo on the sea with all the air gone out of it, and it was going to sink. I just had that image. I remember lying in bed, with this picture of you in my mind ... Imagining myself pumping the air out of my body into yours and pumping you up again. And I kept on and on until I could picture that Lilo floating in the water again.'

Briony knew the story well enough. But she didn't interrupt.

'You were out of danger by the next morning,' said Tamara. 'You were so much better. The doctors said it was a miracle. Your temperature was falling, your heartbeat was stronger, blood pressure was down. That same morning they found me unconscious in the bedroom. My blood pressure was incredibly low. My temperature was about two below normal. My heart rate was down to about thirty beats a minute. They never did discover what was wrong with me. The doctors said twins could do strange things like that, they couldn't explain how or why. It was a telepathic phenomenon.'

'What are you saying?' said Briony. 'That's what's happening now? I'm using the energy that Charlie's putting into me to transfer energy to you?'

'Well, how else is it happening?' said Tamara.

'But that was different when we were kids,' said Briony. 'That was a disease, a medical condition.'

'It was a transfer of energy,' said Tamara, 'that's what it was. Of power, of life, by this ... I don't know what it is ... This symbiotic thing we have.'

'But there's no coming back from half-life,' said Briony. 'They say it can't be done. They say there's nothing anyone can do for you.'

'That's what they said about *you* once,' said Tamara.

*

337

The next time Briony saw Charlie he was in a strange mood all evening; as if he was secretly anxious to be somewhere else, or was avoiding telling her something.

When he took her home at the end of the evening, they sat outside in the car and he said, 'I don't think we should carry on with this. I think I made a mistake. I'm sorry.'

It didn't bother Briony especially but she knew that it was going to worry Tamara. Tam had a theory about Charlie being an essential element in this symbiotic lifeline.

'Any particular reason?' said Briony.

'You'll hate me for it.'

'I don't think I'll hate you, Charlie,' she said, smiling. 'You're not the sort of man who seems very hatable.'

'I'm still in love with Tamara.'

'You think I don't know that?'

'I'm just using you,' he said. 'I don't mean to, I don't do it deliberately. It's just that you look so like her, and I find myself pretending you are her.' He looked at her despondently. 'I feel terrible about it.'

'Don't you like making love to me?' said Briony.

'But it's not you I'm making love to.'

'Charlie,' she said, 'can I shock you?'

'I don't think so,' he said. 'Shrinks have heard most things.'

'I don't feel anything special for you.'

'I sensed that.'

'I like you. But that's all.'

'Then we ought to call it quits,' said Charlie.

'But I need some sex at this particular time in my life,' said Briony. 'That's enough for me. Nothing more. No ties, no emotional complications. I need that and you can give me that. In return, you need something I can give you. We lie down in the dark and you pretend it's Tam in your arms. And that's okay by me. Don't feel guilty about it. Why should we deprive ourselves just because we're both getting what we need – even if it's not exactly what we want? That's so . . . English, isn't it?'

338

Charlie smiled and nodded. 'I suppose it is, yes.'

'So let's just enjoy it for a while,' said Briony. 'No strings, no complications.'

She opened the drawer of the chest where Tamara kept her two wigs. She took out the one that was styled in a bob, with the thick fringe, cut just above the eyebrows.

She sat, almost naked, at the dressing table and pulled the wig down over her own ragamuffin hair and adjusted it.

She took a bottle of Tam's favourite perfume and dabbed a spot on her neck, beneath each ear.

She put Tam's silver chain around her neck. And some of Tam's rings on her fingers.

She went into the secret closet and strapped herself into a studded harness, put on leather briefs and a fishnet crop-top, stockings and suspenders.

She came out and moved towards him. His eyes were wide with wonder and expectation, like a little boy seeing his first Christmas tree.

She came right up to where he was sitting. To her surprise he shifted to the edge of the chair, sank to his knees and buried his face against her belly. She could feel the passion in his hands as he gripped her flesh. And she knew then that this was how Tamara was in his imagination, the part he had always wanted her to play but had always been too afraid to ask; his guilty fantasy. The very thing he had been so busy trying to cure her of, he most wanted her to be.

She heard him whisper Tam's name and felt his teeth on the inside of her thigh.

He cried her name again, much later, his body jerking in spasms in the darkness, their limbs tangled, their flesh glossy with sweat. Ferociously she clung to that mental image of Tamara.

And the moment that she felt the energy go out of him, his muscles slacken and his body sag and fall away on to the other side of the bed, she let go of the image, opened her eyes . . . And saw only the empty darkness.

Charlie sloped away, as usual, in the middle of the night.

The following morning, she was sitting at the dropleaf table, eating toast and honey, drinking coffee, when she heard Tamara say, 'Briony?'

She turned to look behind her. Tamara was sitting upright in bed.

'Sweet Jesus . . .' Briony whispered.

Tamara looked startled. 'Have you come to me,' she said, 'or have I come to you?'

Briony got up and crept towards the bed, as if any sudden movement might shatter the image.

'You've come to me,' she said. 'You're back in the real world.'

She held out her hand. Tamara reached out. Their fingers touched.

'Sticky fingers . . .' said Tamara, and started to laugh.

Briony sat on the side of the bed. 'Taste the honey.'

Tamara held Briony's fingers and licked the honey and butter off them. 'I can taste,' she said. 'Oh, dear God, I can taste!'

'My hair,' said Briony, 'smell my hair . . . my shampoo.'

She moved closer. Tamara put her nose to Briony's wet hair.

'I can smell,' she said. And her eyes began to water. 'Don't say I can cry as well,' she said, and began to laugh again. 'Coffee . . . get me coffee! I could kill for coffee.'

Briony got up and crossed to the table. She picked up her mug of coffee and turned . . .

Tamara had vanished again.

Briony sat on the bed in the hope that she'd come back. She left the mug of coffee on the bedside cabinet, just in case.

*

Charlie telephoned that evening.

'I hope you don't feel bad about last night,' he said.

'I don't feel bad,' said Briony, 'I feel great.'

'Did you mean what you said about . . .' He tailed off awkwardly.

'Each other's needs, yeah,' said Briony. 'Yeah, I did.'

A brief silence. And then he said, 'So . . . Perhaps we could get together again sometime?'

'Soon,' said Briony.

'Soon's good,' said Charlie.

PILLOW TALK

She was seeing Charlie so regularly now that she had stopped phasing out completely by the autumn and no longer slipped into Tamara's twilight world at all. And Tamara was phasing back so frequently that they were together now, in the mortal world, for several hours each day.

Each time Tam rematerialized, it lasted a little longer than the time before. And the appearances recurred more and more frequently as the weeks went by. She was afraid at first that it might be a freak occurrence and wouldn't last. But her confidence began to grow. She went outside on to the street one evening and walked up Styles Lane with Briony. She was scared . . . What if she phased out *here*? she said to Briony. She'd be trapped outside on the street, instead of in the flat.

But it didn't happen.

Even if it were to, Briony reasoned, she would phase back again a little later.

But what about her clothes? said Tamara. All her clothes would be left lying on the pavement . . . And someone would

341

steal them . . . And when she phased back she would be in the middle of the street and stark naked.

Briony started laughing.

Tamara said that wasn't funny. It was not the slightest bit funny. And started laughing too.

But her confidence grew a little more each day. They went out at nights, in the car, and drove around and sat in pubs. Tamara started venturing out on her own in daylight – though never very far, only to the local shops. She met Gloria in the hallway one morning.

'Bridey, dear,' said Gloria. 'Did Dee tell you? Rika died last week.'

Tamara was so surprised to be mistaken for her sister that she forgot who Rika was at that moment.

'Misha's favourite,' said Gloria, noting the blank look on Tamara's face. 'She's devastated. Inconsolable.'

'Oh, the dog,' said Tamara. 'Of course . . . No, I hadn't heard.'

'She'd like a few more paintings,' said Gloria. 'She's frightened she'll lose Sasha now. They're very rare, those dogs. They're irreplaceable.'

'Okay,' said Tamara. 'I'll tell Bri.'

Gloria gave her a strange look. Tamara realized what she'd just said and quickly corrected herself. 'I mean Dee,' she said. 'I'll talk to Dee about it . . . if I see her.'

'This is going to get difficult soon,' said Briony, as they slipped into bed that night. 'Gloria's going to see us both together one of these days, and that'll put the cat among the pigeons.'

Thinking about that, Tamara said. 'Why don't we just go? Pack our stuff and disappear.'

'Disappear?'

'Well . . . In a manner of speaking.'

'What about Misha?' said Briony. 'What about the Foundation?'

'Screw Misha,' Tam scoffed. 'What can she do? You don't need the Foundation now, we don't need any of them. They had a hold over you because you didn't want to be kicked out of this flat . . . because I was trapped here in half-life and we'd never have seen each other again. They thought that was enough to control you because no one's ever come back from that world, as far as they know.' Tamara laughed. 'But we've stuffed 'em . . . We've done what couldn't be done!'

It suddenly occurred to Briony that she was right . . . That *was* the only hold they'd ever had over her: the fear of losing Tam for ever.

'They could come looking for us,' Tam conceded. 'But it's a big world.'

Briony began to laugh too. Of course . . . It was so simple. There was absolutely nothing to stop them.

'Where will we go?' she said. 'We can go anywhere.'

'Anywhere,' Tamara agreed. 'Anywhere there's men.'

'We should go home for a little while,' said Briony. 'For Mum's sake.'

'Oh, Jesus . . .' Tamara groaned. 'Anywhere in the whole wide world, and all you can think of is Mackerelville.'

'Just for Mum's sake, that's all,' Briony repeated. 'To put an end to the worry. She's been so miserable, not knowing.'

A little later, feeling not the least bit sleepy, Briony said, 'Suppose we end up in a place where there are no men?'

'There are always men,' said Tamara. 'Everywhere you go . . . Unless you want to live on the Galapagos Islands.'

'But suppose we don't find any we like?'

'We'll have to shut our eyes and fantasize.'

'Fantasize?' said Briony, in a mildly shocked tone. '*Us?*'

After a little while, Briony said, 'I sort of fancy living on the Galapagos.'

They couldn't get to sleep.

Briony murmured, just thinking aloud: 'What will we do about Charlie?'

'What do you mean, do about him?'

'Don't you think we owe him something?'

'Why? He's been having a whale of a time.'

'But he does love you . . . Through me. In his own funny way.'

'I suppose,' Tam agreed.

'And he has put in a lot of sweat and effort for us.'

'He's been loving every damn second of it.'

'Even so . . .'

'How many men do *you* know who get to have sex with twin sisters simultaneously?'

'Even so,' Briony repeated, 'you wouldn't be here, remember, if it wasn't for Charlie.'

'You'd have found some other guy.'

'But not one who was concentrating all his thoughts on *you* . . . while he was making love to *me*.'

'Probably not,' Tamara conceded.

'And he's got no one in the world except us. We shouldn't just disappear out of his life without saying goodbye. You should say thank you to him. You owe him that at least.'

After more thought, Tamara said, 'I suppose you're right.'

Finally, when Tamara was almost asleep:

'Tam . . .?'

'Mm?'

'Are there really no men on the Galapagos?'

'Only what's-his-name . . . Attenborough.'

'That all?'

'Mm.'

'Ah.'

And a little later:

'I guess he'll do.'

PROOF OF HEAVEN

One night in October, Charlie arrived at the flat and all the lights were out, but there was a candle burning on each side of the bed.

Briony opened a bottle of champagne and said, 'Tonight's a special night.'

Charlie said, 'What's special about tonight?'

'I'm leaving this flat,' said Briony. 'I'm moving out. I'm going back to live in Cornwall.'

Charlie had known in his heart that this wouldn't – couldn't – last for ever. He felt indescribably sad but he put a brave face on it.

'I thought you would, sooner or later,' he said. 'But I can't say I blame you. Who'd want to be *here* if they had the choice of being there?'

'But it's not goodbye,' said Briony. 'You must come and see us. You must come and stay.'

'I think I will,' said Charlie. 'I won't need asking twice.'

'And tonight,' said Briony, as it's our last night in this dump, 'I have a special surprise for you.'

'Champagne and candles,' said Charlie. 'That's nice.'

'No, no,' said Briony. 'Something much more special. Close your eyes.'

He closed his eyes.

'Keep them closed.'

He kept them closed.

'No peeping.'

'No peeping.'

'Hold my hand.'

He took hold of her hand. She led him across to the bed and told him to sit down. He sat down. She took off his shoes. And told him to sit on the bed with his feet up and his back to the wall and keep his eyes closed. He did as he was told.

He felt her weight as she lay down on the bed.

'Now you can open your eyes,' she said.

She was lying beside him. She had undressed almost impossibly quickly but that was the only surprise. She was not quite naked – a few bits and pieces, the kind of things he liked – she varied it from night to night. So that was no surprise, either.

He said, 'What's so special?'

She grinned mischievously but didn't answer.

'Briony?' he said, wondering if he had missed something very subtle, or even rather obvious. 'What's the surprise?'

'I'm not Briony,' Tamara replied.

'Dear God,' said Charlie. Even in this light he could see that it wasn't Briony. 'Tamara ... Where *did* you come from?'

She grinned mischievously. 'Another world,' she said.

She undressed him, slowly and carefully.

She began to make love to him. And at some point, when he was lying on his back, sensing Tamara's lips and tongue-tip creeping slowly down his belly, he began to feel her lips on his face as well ...

He opened his eyes and saw Briony's face, upside down, a few inches from his own. Her lips now touching his. Or was it Tamara ...? He raised his head a little from the bed and looked ... And saw Tamara, on her knees, between his legs ... Or was it Briony?

Briony gently pressed his head back on to the pillow and kissed his mouth ... or was that Tamara's tongue? While Tamara straddled his hips and lowered her weight on to his thighs ... or was that Briony?

Charlie no longer even cared. He had died, he decided. And Heaven existed, after all.

MERMAIDS

Autumn has turned to winter, winter to spring.

The twins are lying naked on the sand in the sun at Treveene Cove, near Land's End, beside that rock – their special rock – where they used to lie when they were children.

'Do you know something . . .?' Tamara murmurs.

'Mm-hm?'

'I never really liked the name Tamara.'

'But we always called you Tam.'

'I didn't want to be Tam *or* Tamara. I always wanted to be Briony. I was supposed to be Briony. But when we were baptized the minister got us the wrong way round.'

'Who told you that?'

'Mum.'

'I think that's a myth.'

'She swears it's true.'

'It's probably why I never liked being called Briony, then.'

'Never ever?'

'Tamara's more romantic. I always preferred Tamara.'

'How about we swap? From now on I'll call myself Briony and you call yourself Tamara.'

'Then no one will know who we really are.'

'No one knows who we really are, anyway.'

'Even we'll be confused.'

'What's new?' Tamara says.

The twins close their eyes and lie half-dozing in the sun.

Women nearby, bronzed and naked, lie at attention, like dead sentries, on the sand.

Middle-aged men, sag-bellied, pendulous, paddle in their flip-flops ankle-deep at the water's edge.

Young men with muscular physiques massage oil into each other's delts and traps and rhomboids.

The next time anybody looks, the two sisters are nowhere to be seen. They are not in the sea, they are not on the sand, they have vanished.

The sisters open their eyes. It has grown quite dark; like a partial eclipse of the sun. Their bodies have the strength of rag dolls. They feel no warmth from the sun. Nor do they feel cold. They feel nothing much at all . . . except exasperation.

'Bugger,' says Tamara. 'Where did that come from?'

It has hit them, like an athlete's attack of cramp, out of nowhere, no warning.

'Time we invited Charlie down to stay again,' says Briony.

'I told you we shouldn't have left it so long,' Tamara reminds her.

It is only May and the sun is losing its strength by late afternoon.

The bronzed women, the muscular jocks, the sag-bellied men, they all pack up their things and begin the long, effortful trudge up the rocky steps to the top of the cliff, where their cars are parked.

The twins' towels still lie on the sand, beside their special rock, together with their plastic bottles of sun lotion, their shorts and T-shirts and their beach bags.

No one has seen them for some hours.

'This is bloody silly,' Briony says to Tamara. 'How much longer?'

The sun sinks low across the ocean on the western horizon.

The tide is coming in.

'Suppose that something's gone wrong?' Tamara wonders. 'Suppose we left it too long?'

The tide encroaches further and further up the beach.

The sun goes down. Darkness falls.

But the light does not change in their world. They do not

348

feel the chill of night, or the coldness of the sea that now laps around their rock, their special rock.

One tidal surge, bolder than the previous, rushes at their rock and carries away a plastic bottle – two hundred mills, sun protection factor four.

Surf breaks across their rock. Briony's flip-flops float away; Tamara's espadrilles. Their towels, their clothes, their beach bags are borne back into the restless ocean.

'Suppose we don't phase back again?' says Briony. 'What if we're trapped here for ever?'

The sun rises over Treveene Cove.

The morning tide recedes, leaving a jagged wedge of firm sand.

The nudists return: the bronzed women and the muscular jocks; the sag-bellied men who are bald and alone.

They all glance at the rock, they look for the twins, but the twins are late coming down to the beach today.

The day passes. Nobody lies on the sand by the sisters' rock, for that is their special place, and there is an unspoken desire among the nudists of Treveene for the twins to be there, to occupy their usual spot, to maintain the balance of things, some sense of everyday normality. There is comfort in this.

But the twins do not appear at the cove today.

Nothing is said, but people miss them. There is unease.

The sun goes down.

They sit on their rock, in perpetual twilight.

Sometimes they call out to people walking past – to the bronzed women, the muscular jocks, the fat, bald men – but nobody hears them, nobody sees them.

Now somebody else has taken that patch of sand for their own special place.

On the mass of rocks that lie at the foot of the cliff, among the flotsam and jetsam marooned by the pushy and unfeeling tide, lies one of Tamara's espadrilles. And, not very far away, in a tangle of dried-out seaweed, a plastic bottle – two hundred mills, sun protection factor four.

Time passes.

Occasionally – without any warning – the twins rematerialize, become visible for short periods, sitting on their rock, tanned and naked. Winter or summer, rain or sun, they are tanned and naked.

Sometimes they appear in the early mornings, around dawn; but more usually after sunset – the time the French refer to as between the dog and the wolf. They are suddenly there; and, just as suddenly, they are gone again.

They are there for such short periods – sometimes several minutes, and sometimes only seconds – that they feel no urge to move, to try to climb the two hundred steps to the top of the cliff, from where Tamara's car has been stolen long since, wrecked and abandoned.

Whenever they are seen, the sisters are sitting in the same position: Briony with her knees up to her chin, her hands clasped around her shins. (Or is that Tamara?) And Tamara with her lovely slender legs stretched out, one knee just slightly bent, both arms behind her, supporting her body. (Or is that Briony?)

They don't feel the winter gales. They are unmoved by the pounding surf that, down the years, has driven so many vessels to their rocky graves along these shores.

They are not bored, they have no sense of passing time. Day and night, winter, summer, are all one to them. They are not lonely, for they have each other.

Some say the Carkeat sisters drowned here one night, and these are their ghosts come back to haunt the beach. The tale is told in any pub these days around Lamorna, Porthcurno and St Buryan. But not many folk believe the story thereabouts.

There are local fishermen who say they have glimpsed the sisters on occasion, seated on their rock, like stranded mermaids; usually around the break of day or after sunset. Mariners regard them with affection. They call them the Mermaids of Treveene and always keep an eye out for them if they pass the cove. They are regarded as a favourable omen.

But the sisters, they will tell you, never show themselves to non-believers.